BEAR HASKELL, U.S. DEPUTY MARSHAL

Bear Haskell, U.S. Deputy Marshal

A FRONTIER DUO

Peter Brandvold

FIVE STAR
A part of Gale, a Cengage Company

Farmington Hills, Mich • San Francisco • New York • Waterville, Maine
Meriden, Conn • Mason, Ohio • Chicago

GALE
A Cengage Company

LIBRARY OF CONGRESS CATALOGING-IN-PUBLICATION DATA

Names: Brandvold, Peter, author. | Brandvold, Peter. Gun trouble at Diamondback. | Brandvold, Peter. Jackals of Sundown.
Title: Bear Haskell, U.S. Deputy Marshal : a frontier duo / Peter Brandvold.
Other titles: Gun trouble at Diamondback. | Jackals of Sundown.
Description: First edition. | Waterville, Maine : Five Star, a part of Gale, Cengage Learning, [2018]
Identifiers: LCCN 2018004737| ISBN 9781432843045 (hardcover) | ISBN 9781432843076 (ebook) | ISBN 9781432843069 (ebook)
Subjects: | GSAFD: Western stories.
Classification: LCC PS3552.R3236 A6 2018d | DDC 813/.54--dc23
LC record available at https://lccn.loc.gov/2018004737

First Edition. First Printing: August 2018
Find us on Facebook—https://www.facebook.com/FiveStarCengage
Visit our website—http://www.gale.cengage.com/fivestar/
Contact Five Star Publishing at FiveStar@cengage.com

Printed in Mexico
1 2 3 4 5 6 7 22 21 20 19 18

TABLE OF CONTENTS

★ ★ ★ ★ ★

Gun Trouble at Diamondback

★ ★ ★ ★ ★

CHAPTER ONE

Emma Kramer had to be one of the prettiest young ladies Deputy U.S. Marshal Bear Haskell had ever laid eyes on. And he'd laid his eyes—and more than just his eyes—on a few. But Emma seemed dead set against advertising her beauty.

In fact, she seemed determined to conceal it.

The girl was dressed in a loose wool shirt with a grimy red neckerchief tied around her neck, and threadbare, wash-worn denim jeans with patched knees. Her old stockmen's boots were as worn as ancient moccasins. Over the man's wool shirt she wore a smelly buckskin vest probably twice as old as she was at twenty-one.

The nasty, grease-spotted, weather-stained garment was several sizes too large for the girl, and Haskell thought he remembered that her deceased father had worn it around multiple smoky cookfires way back when he and Haskell were both hunting buffalo just after the Little Misunderstanding Between the States.

Not only wearing the ancient garment, but wiping his greasy fingers on it while devouring buffalo hump or bits of a spitted sirloin.

No, the old man's lovely daughter didn't advertise the fact that she was pretty. However, no amount of her pa's stinky attire could conceal the girl's full, ripe figure, with its slender waist, rounded hips, and long, well-turned legs. From a distance, you might not be able to tell she was about as pleasing to a man's eye as any woman on God's green earth. But close up like Haskell was now, lying next to her on a sandy shelf in southern Colorado, his right hip almost touching her left one, it was hard to remain ignorant of the fact.

How could this lovely creature beside him be the fruit of the loins of the likes of the two-timing, double-crossing, butt-ugly Coyote Kramer? The old joke amongst the hunters was that Coyote was so ugly that a horse doctor had helped his mother give birth in the back forty.

Emma lay belly down beside him on the shelf, to his right. She was peering through Haskell's field glasses toward an age-silvered log trapper's cabin on the far side of a brush-sheathed dry wash. "Do you think it's really those killers, Marshal Hask—?" She stopped abruptly. She'd caught him staring at her. Her perfectly sculpted, suntanned cheeks flushed. Color also rose into her ears, behind which she'd tucked her long, wavy, tawny hair.

"Marshal Haskell, what are you doing?" she asked, crisply indignant.

Haskell blinked, turned away, turned back to her, his own ears burning. "Wha . . . huh?"

"You were staring at me. *Lasciviously!*"

Haskell blinked again. "Absolutely not, Miss Kramer! And I will forgive your conceit!"

"You were!"

Haskell chuffed, haughtily indignant. "I was merely consider-ing the situation. *Pondering* my next course of action."

"I don't believe you." Emma narrowed a pretty light-brown eye at him. "My father warned me about you."

"Your father warning anybody about anything is like a grizzly bear warning a goat about a mountain lion." Haskell gave another outraged chuff, then held out his hand. "Do you mind if I have my government-issue binoculars back?"

"Here are your government-issue binoculars, Marshal Haskell."

"Thank you, Miss Kramer."

"You're welcome."

Haskell wagged his head in disgust, then cast the girl a quick, furtive glance to see if she was buying his act. He couldn't tell. She'd returned her attention to the shack across the wash. Since she was facing away, he couldn't help taking one last quick peek at her wares, trying to blaze the image onto his brain for later recollection.

As she began to turn her head toward him again, he quickly raised the binoculars and adjusted the focus. The old trapper's cabin swam into view.

It sat in thick brush about forty yards away from the wash, in a grove of cottonwood and box elders. A falling-down lean-to stable and corral flanked the place, as did another lean-to off to the left of the stable. Probably a woodshed. The place was quiet now in the midafternoon. Five or six horses stood in the corral, facing different directions, a couple switching their tails at flies.

One man clad only in dull red longhandles and boots sat on a stump chair to the right of the cabin's door. He leaned forward, resting his elbows on his knees and brought what must have been a quirley to his lips, though Haskell couldn't see it from this distance of three hundred or so yards.

"What do you think, Marshal?" Emma asked. "Do you think it's them? Like I said when I saw you in town, there were six of them. They crossed my land yesterday afternoon, heading this way. I had a feeling they were the men who robbed that stagecoach last week. They had a look about them, and one had a pair of gunnysacks—bulging gunnysacks—draped over the back of his horse. About the only folks who hole up in that cabin these days, since the half-breed trapper, Leonard Two Eagles, died, are outlaws on the run."

Haskell lowered the field glasses. "You know what I think, Miss Kramer?"

"What's that, Marshal Haskell?"

"I think you got a good eye."

She flushed a little with pride.

"Well . . ."

"And I think it's a good thing we ran into each other in town, and that, having just finished up my last assignment, I was free to ride out here and check you out."

Emma narrowed that same pretty brown eye again. "Check *what* out?"

Haskell's ear tips warmed once more. The girl's pretty tits had his brains scrambled. "Check out your *situation* out here, is what I meant to say. Pardon my tangled tongue. A man who spends as much time on his own as I do, campin' out nights under the stars, trackin' outlaws from sunup to sundown, from as far north as Billings, Montana, to as far south as Corpus—"

"I get your meaning, Marshal Haskell. Don't you feel a sense of urgency here? If the men who held up that stage and then ran it off a cliff and killed all those people . . . including a minister's young daughter . . . are in that cabin—"

"If they're in that cabin, I doubt they'll be headin' out anytime soon. Nah, they'll sit tight for a while, then pull out when they think the posse from Socorro has played itself out and gone back home." Haskell raked a thumbnail through the three-day beard stubble on his chiseled cheek. He didn't normally shave when he was on the trail. Too many other things to think about—namely, staying alive. "Just to make a windy story only breezy, what I meant to say about what I *said* was I don't talk near often enough to be much good at it. That was likely the cause of our misunderstanding."

He grinned, trying to disarm the girl.

She was not having it, however. "Oh, I think you're better at talking than you give yourself credit for, Marshal Haskell. That being as it may . . ."

"Yes, that being as it may . . . time for me to go to work." Haskell gestured to her. They crabbed backward away from the lip of the wash. When Haskell thought they were out of sight from the cabin, he and the girl rose and walked, crouching, down to where their horses stood ground-reined in a rock-lined depression roughly thirty yards from the wash.

Haskell dropped his field glasses into his saddlebags. He shucked the big Smith & Wesson New Model No. 3 Schofield revolver from the soft holster positioned for the cross-draw on his left hip.

He broke open the top-break piece, which was nickel-finished and boasted a seven-inch barrel, and plucked a fresh cartridge from one of the two shell belts encircling his waist. (He'd hated it when, long ago, pinned down against more owlhoots than he could count, he'd run out of cartridges, so he kept a good sup-ply attached to his person.) He shoved the bullet into the chamber he normally kept empty beneath the hammer, so he didn't accidentally shoot his pecker off, and closed the heavy gun, chambered in the .44 caliber in his rifle. He didn't like to get complicated by toting around more than one caliber bullet.

Bear Haskell was appropriately named. Bear was his given one. It had been the nickname of his great-grandfather, Zekial Haskell, a heroic freedom fighter in the Revolutionary War. By all accounts, his grandson was his spitting image—a big, burly man, a striking one, an alluring one by most women's standards. Women were drawn to him irresistibly. There was a primitive pull.

Most men found him intimidating, though that was due mostly to his size, for Bear was good-natured but also quick to rile. He was tender without being timid, but when pushed, he could tear a saloon apart and leave it little more than strewn matchsticks. If Haskell's broad-shouldered, muscular, six-foot-six stature didn't turn heads when he walked into a room, the dark, ruggedly chiseled face with warm, deep-set blue-gray eyes usually did.

His thick, dark-brown hair curled down over his collar. A hide thong adorned with grizzly claws hung from his neck, down over his calico shirt—his one note of ostentation. (He'd killed the bear himself, before it could have killed him, and he saw the claws as a totem of sorts but also as an emblem of kinship with his great-grandfather, who was said to have worn a bear claw necklace of his own.) This Bear wore a bullet-crowned black hat with a braided rawhide band, and dark-green canvas trousers, the cuffs of which he always wore stuffed down into the high, mule-eared tops of his cavalry style boots.

Residing in a pocket sewn into the well of his right boot was a "Blue Jacket" .44-caliber pocket revolver manufactured by Hopkins & Allen—a beautiful piece with gutta-percha grips and a leaf motif scrolled into the nickel finish.

Haskell slid his Schofield revolver into its holster and turned to Emma Kramer, who watched him closely, a concerned frown wrinkling the skin above the bridge of her resolute nose.

"You stay here and stay down," he told her.

As he walked around to the right side of the horse he'd rented in Socorro and shucked his rimfire Henry .44 from its saddle boot, Emma followed him, saying, "You're not going to try to confront those men alone, are you? I counted six of them, Marshal Haskell. There might have been one or two more waiting for them in the cabin. That would make up to eight! I'd heard that the gang split up right after they'd robbed the coach and murdered all those poor, innocent souls!"

"No doubt," Haskell said, removing the loading tube from beneath his Henry's barrel, making sure that the sixteen-shooter, too, was fully loaded and ready to dance. "But if I waited for help to make its way down from Denver, they'd likely be back on the trail before anyone got here. Besides, most of the lawmen in Chief Marshal Dade's stable are out on the trail, just like I've been for the past month and a half. As for local help . . ." Haskell shook his head. "Jack Todd might be a service-able town marshal, but he tends to be drunk by noon, and, since"—he narrowed an eye at the sun—"it's pushing on toward one-thirty, he's likely pretty far down in his cups by now."

"Oh, my gosh, but, but . . . what if something happens to you?"

Haskell levered a live cartridge into the Henry's chamber and gave the girl a confident wink. He cocked his hip and set the rifle on his right shoulder. He feigned more confidence than he actually felt, but there was still more than a bit of the schoolboy in the six-foot-six Bear Haskell, and he couldn't help showing off for the uncommonly beautiful daughter of Coyote Kramer. "It won't. You can bet the bank on that."

He gave her another wink, then started to turn away. A second thought turned him back to face her. "But . . . just in case it does, you'd best start back to your ranch. You stay there, and when I've cut off the heads of those snakes, I'll ride over for a cup of coffee and maybe a snort of thunder juice, if you have any on hand. If you'll pardon me for bein' so bold to invite myself, that is."

He smiled and tried like hell to keep his gaze from flicking down to her shirt, because he knew she was on the scout for such a peek. She must have seen the strain in his face, for she blushed again and said, "Of course." She crossed her arms on her chest. "As long as coffee and whiskey is all you'll be calling for, Marshal. Remember, my father warned me about you."

She tapped a boot in the dirt.

"Oh, I remember." Haskell gave a wry chuckle. "I'll see you later, Miss Kramer."

er

Haskell moved down the hollow, away from the wash, intending to trace a wide course around the cabin and steal up behind it. When he'd walked only ten or so yards, Emma called behind him, "Marshal?"

Haskell stopped, turned back to her, and arched a brow.

She dropped her arms from her breasts and turned her mouth corners down with a vague chagrin. "Do be careful."

Haskell smiled, feasted his eyes once more, pinched his hat brim to her, and moved on down the slope.

CHAPTER TWO

Haskell raised his Henry high across his chest as he moved through the brush, the rear of the cabin now appearing dead ahead of him. He was glad to see a small, plank door in the center of the back wall.

He dropped to a knee in the tall grass and looked around.

The stone-colored rear of the cabin was dappled with sunlight and shade. Cottonwoods stood off both corners, fluttering their large, round leaves over the sod roof. Closer to Haskell was a leaning privy built of vertical split logs.

To the left of the privy and nearly directly behind the shack was a lean-to attached to a corral of peeled cottonwood poles. Horses milled languidly inside the corral. The corral was left of the lean-to. Noises were coming from inside the lean-to.

Haskell pricked his ears, listening. He picked up a man's voice. Someone was out there. Haskell would have to take care of whoever was in the lean-to before he approached the cabin.

He cursed silently. He'd hoped to have all of his quarry inside the cabin. But, then, he'd been hunting curly wolves for several years now and had come to know that things rarely went as planned.

He looked at the cabin's back door, then rose from his knees and, holding the Henry straight up and down in front of him, moved quickly but as silently as an Apache through the high, wind-brushed grass. He'd learned to move lightly during his time in the war, in which he'd served on the side of the Union, for he'd spent a considerable time operating behind Confederate lines, blowing up ammunition dumps and supply trains.

The hills in which he'd worked with a small team of guerrilla fighters had been eerily silent on those warm, windless summer nights, and the least sound would have alerted enemy pickets and likely gotten him and his men killed or worse—captured and sent to one of the South's infamously horrible prison camps.

As Haskell approached the corral, he kept an eye on the horses. One had winded him. It had turned its head toward him, watching him incredulously, twitching its ears. The other six mounts were staring in other directions, one nosing a tin feed bucket along the ground with dull pings.

Again, the man's voice rose from the lean-to, louder this time.

Haskell stopped and crouched behind an ancient tree stump.

"How do you like that, you nasty bitch?" the man said, his voice pitched with anger. "How do you like it? Huh?"

The man laughed.

A young woman groaned, and said, "Oh, you're a savage. Stop! Please! You're *hurting* me!"

The man grunted, saying, "That's the plan, bitch! I intend to hurt ya! I intend to hurt you real good!" He grunted especially loudly. It was almost a yell.

The girl shrieked.

Haskell remembered the preacher's daughter who'd been on the stage. The gang must have taken her. He remembered hearing that it had been nearly impossible to identify the bodies after the gang had run the stage off a cliff, because they'd also doused it with coal oil and burned it.

The outlaw laughed and grunted, and the girl sobbed.

Haskell started to move toward the lean-to once more when he heard the wooden scrape of a door opening. He dodged back behind the stump, and dropped low. He doffed his hat and peered out around the side of the stump.

A bearded man with thin, curly brown hair had come out the shack's back door. He was clad in only a wash-worn balbriggan top, canvas pants, and suspenders, which dangled down his arms to his waist. He stood in the worn spot on the ground fronting the door, grinning as he listened to the commotion in the lean-to. Unbuttoning the fly of his pants, he flexed his knees and sent a yellow stream arcing out into the weeds before him. The urine glinted in the sunshine filtering through the leaf canopy above him.

He lifted his head and yelled, "Hey, Bean—don't use her all up, now. Save some for me an' the others!" He laughed.

"Fuck you, A.J.!" shouted the man in the lean-to, grunting.

A.J.'s stream dwindled, then stopped. When he'd tucked himself back into his pants and buttoned up, he headed back inside the shack. Haskell had been hunkered none too patiently behind the stump, squeezing his Henry in both hands. He rose, strode out from behind the stump, and walked through the brush to the corral.

Now three horses were watching him.

Haskell gritted his teeth, silently beseeching the mounts not to give him away.

He stopped at the lean-to's corner and peered over the top corral rail into the shelter's murky shadows. He could see two dusky figures moving around in there amidst what appeared stacked firewood, but he could see neither figure clearly.

"How do you like it, huh?" Bean asked. "Tell me how you like it, bitch! Tell me how you like it, bitch!"

"Oh, you're awful," the girl cried, grunting. "A wicked, wicked man. Look what you're doing to me! I'm ruined!"

"I think you like it, bitch! I really think you like it!"

"You'll burn in hell for this!"

"I think you like it!"

19

"Oh, god! Oh, god—you're a *savage*!"

Bean howled.

"What will Father say when he finds out about this! Oh, my poor dear mother!"

Bean howled louder.

Haskell crouched under the corral's top slat. He glanced at the horses, all of which were looking at him now with typical horse-like incredulity. He held up a placating hand to them and then stole forward into the lean-to, which was half-filled with stacked firewood. He stepped around one stack to the stack behind it.

Bean's back was facing Haskell. The girl lay back against a saddle blanket spread out atop the firewood. Her bare legs were spread wide. Bean was pumping his hips against her. His faded denim trousers and longhandles were bunched around his boots. His gun belt and two pistols lay on a stump near the ground to his right. Close to the stump lay a white dress, petticoats, and pantaloons.

Bean had long, tangled brown hair—thick like a girl's and spotted with dust and seeds. Bean's skinny ass was pale and dimpled and peppered with thin little tufts of light brown hair.

The girl's bare legs flopped against his sides as he rammed himself savagely against her, pushing in, pulling out . . . pushing in . . . sliding out . . . He had a hand wrapped around each of the girl's slender knees.

Haskell gritted his teeth as he stepped up behind the man. He had to take him down quietly so as not to alert the men in the cabin. He glanced over the man's left shoulder. The girl spotted him. She stared at Bear, wide-eyed, mouth open, as Bean continued to rape her. Haskell placed two fingers on his lips and then rammed the butt of his Henry against the side of Bean's head.

The outlaw gave a yelp and staggered to his right, dazed.

Haskell tapped him again.

Bean twisted around to face Haskell as he fell back against the woodpile, blood from the two Henry kisses trickling down the side of his head, over his left ear. Bean's head wobbled. He slitted his lids, trying to focus his gaze on Haskell, who raised the Henry club-like behind his right shoulder, and swung it forward.

It smashed against Bean's right temple with a cracking thud.

The girl cried, "Oh, my—!"

"Shhh!" Again, Haskell pressed two fingers to his lips. The girl's eyes flicked to the deputy U.S. marshal's moon-and-star badge pinned to his calico shirt, just inside his left suspender.

Bean dropped to his knees. His busted head wobbled heavily on his broken neck. Liver-colored blood from the grisly wound in his right temple gushed heavily down his cheek. Haskell stepped back as Bean tumbled forward and hit the lean-to floor on his face.

"Get dressed!" Haskell ordered the girl, keeping his voice low.

"Oh, my god!" she said in a voice hushed with awe, staring down at her attacker.

"Get dressed and wait out here!" Haskell grabbed her arm and squeezed. "All right? Can you do that? You're gonna hear some shooting, and when the smoke clears, if it's not me you see heading back this way, you light out, okay? Just start running straight back through the brush. I'll try to get as many of them as I can, but there's no such thing as a sure bet!"

She was staring down at Bean. Her eyes glittered with shock. A pretty girl, not much over sixteen, with a slender, buxom body and heart-shaped face with a little mole on her chin, another on her neck. Haskell squeezed her arm again, shaking her gently. "Do you understand?"

The girl looked at Haskell. She nodded. "Yes," she said.

"Okay. Okay. I'll get dressed."

Haskell walked to a corner of the lean-to and cast his cautious gaze at the shack. Leaf shadows darted across the old cabin. A couple of blackbirds were perched on yellow weeds growing up from the sod roof.

Haskell heard a click behind him.

He turned to see the preacher's daughter aiming a pistol at him. She had both hands wrapped around the gun. "Bastard!" Gritting her teeth, she turned her head to one side, closed her eyes, and squeezed the trigger.

The gun thundered.

The bullet plunked into a lean-to post just over Haskell's left shoulder.

Haskell staggered backward in shock, dropping his Henry as he reached for the lean-to wall.

The girl looked at him again, saw she'd missed her mark, and tried once more. She turned her head away again as she fired, and the second bullet also sailed wild, thudding into the ground beyond Haskell, between the lean-to and the cabin.

"Hold on!" Haskell barked in confusion, sliding his big Schofield from its holster.

The girl clicked her gun's hammer back, and aimed again.

Haskell's Schofield roared. The girl's gun also roared. Her bullet thudded into the underside of the lean-to roof as she staggered backward. Haskell's bullet carved a neat round hole between her cherry-nippled breasts.

She screamed as she smacked her head against the woodpile, then dropped to the ground where she lay staring up at Haskell, her soft brown eyes quickly turning opaque as blood formed a river between her breasts.

"What the hell?" Haskell said, staring down in shock at the girl.

"What the *hell?*" echoed a man's shout behind him.

Haskell picked up his rifle and whipped around, casting a look around the corner of the lean-to. Two men in various stages of dress had just run out of the cabin, wielding rifles. The cabin door barked sharply as it slammed against the shack's rear wall. One man stuffed a hat down on his head as he and the other man looked around wildly, whipping their rifles around, looking for a target.

Shouts rose inside the cabin behind them.

Haskell aimed, then fired.

One of the outlaws screamed and flew back against the cabin wall. The other cursed and jerked his rifle toward Haskell, who dispatched the man before he could get his own shot off.

Before the second outlaw had piled up in the depression fronting the door, Haskell was running through the waving grass toward the cabin, ejecting the last spent cartridge from the Henry's breech, sending it tumbling, smoking, over his right shoulder, then jacking a fresh round into the action.

"What the fuck—who's out there?" another voice shouted from inside the shack.

A rifle cracked. Haskell could see the flash inside the shack's shadows. The shooter was standing about four feet back from the door, shooting blindly. Haskell dropped to a knee and fired three quick rounds, pumping and firing.

There was a loud wooden thud.

The shooting inside the cabin stopped but the shouts from the other men did not.

Haskell ran past the cabin door, pressing his back against the rear wall. The open door was to his right. He snaked his Henry around the doorframe, poked the barrel inside, and hurled three more rounds into the darkness, evoking more shouted curses, more stumbling around and yelling. Haskell bolted through the open doorway and dropped to a knee.

A man lay writhing on the floor before him, groaning, spitting blood. Haskell finished him with a bullet to the head, then cast his gaze into the shadows.

The shack was only one room, crudely outfitted, cobwebs and filth everywhere. A small sheet-iron stove hunkered in the middle of the room near the front door. One man was crouched behind the stove while another just now peered over the top of an overturned table around which playing cards, coins, paper money, and whiskey bottles were scattered.

Haskell dropped to a knee as a man's head and a rifle rose up from behind the overturned table. Haskell hammered several rounds at the table, the bullets plunking into the table as well as into the head of the man behind it, punching him back against the front wall, screaming and dying.

A deafening blast assaulted Haskell's ears.

He heard the screaming rip of a large caliber round hurtling over his left shoulder, feeling the warm air curling near his earlobe. There was a loud smacking sound behind him. He glanced back to see that the rear door had blown partway closed. Something had smacked it open again, then bounced it off the rear wall.

It was starting to close again, wobbling on its hinges. There was a hole the size of a man's fist in the middle of it.

Shit!

A buffalo rifle. Had to be . . .

The man behind the stove rose screaming, raising two pistols. He was shirtless and he had a tattoo on his right cheek and long, stringy blond hair. A name matching the man's likeness on a Wanted circular flashed across the lawman's brain: "Curly" Ray Buford. Before Curly could level either of his revolvers on Haskell, the deputy U.S. marshal emptied his sixteen-shooter into the man's bony torso, punching him back into the front door.

The man knocked the door off its hinges, and he and the

door landed in the front yard.

Curly triggered both his pistols wild as he screamed, dying hard.

The screams died in mid-scream. Curly moved his arms and legs like a bug on its back trying to right itself. Then the body relaxed atop the blood-washed door.

Haskell lowered the smoking Henry. He looked around.

There were two dead outlaws in front of him. He turned around to stare toward the back door. Another man lay dead just inside the rear door. Two dead outside. Another one dead in the lean-to with the girl.

He stepped through the ruined back door and counted the horses in the corral.

Seven.

Had the girl, who had apparently thrown in with the rawhiders, had her own separate horse?

Or had there been another outlaw in the cabin?

CHAPTER THREE

Haskell ran through the shack and out the front door.

He looked around. Movement ahead and to his left. One of the outlaws was running through a heavy stand of trees and brush that trailed off toward the wash. He was about fifty yards away from Haskell, running hard, leaping deadfalls and swerving around shrubs.

When the shooting had started, the seventh man must have skinned out a window or through the front door. Haskell started after him, then stopped and stared straight off toward where he'd left Emma Kramer.

His heart thudded.

Emma hadn't headed back toward her ranch headquarters. She wasn't keeping her head or anything else down, either. She was standing on the ridge on the far side of the wash, roughly three hundred yards away. Her horse stood beside her, switching its tail. Emma stared toward the cabin.

"Goddamnit," Haskell bit out, lunging forward as though to run to her, then stopping and angrily waving his arm.

She'd heard the shooting and she was wondering if he was still alive. He wanted to yell at her to get the hell away from there, but if he did, he might only be pointing her out to the outlaw. If the outlaw hadn't already spotted her. She and the horse were clearly outlined against the sky. The outlaw would want that horse. Maybe Emma, too.

Haskell remembered what she looked like.

Hell, yeah—the outlaw would want Emma, too!

Haskell waved again, leaping up in the air and throwing his arm forward, trying to indicate that she should get the hell away from the wash. She returned his wave with an uncertain one of her own. She'd didn't understand his meaning. Maybe she thought he was only trying to tell her that he was all right but that she should wait there.

"Goddamnit!" Haskell said.

He looked at the outlaw still running through the trees. Suddenly, the man dropped down out of sight. He was in the wash. By now he'd certainly seen Emma and the horse, and he was going to try to sneak up on her.

Haskell remembered the Sharps.

He swung around and ran back into the cabin. The Sharps, a 45-70, lay by the dead outlaw who'd almost blown Haskell's head off with it. It was an 1874 model with a Vernier rear sliding site. Cartridges spilled from a box lying on the floor nearby. Haskell picked up the big buffalo gun, grabbed a cartridge nearly as long as his index finger, and hurried to the small window left of the door. The window was partly concealed by a drooping branch of a cottonwood.

Haskell had fired such a buffalo gun before. But not this one. And it had been a while.

And he didn't have time to adjust for the wind . . .

He raised the rifle, peering through the sites. The outlaw was climbing the bank on the opposite side of the wash. He was a good thirty yards to Emma's right, and he was closing on her, but she couldn't see him from her position. It was the girl and the horse he was heading for, all right.

The outlaw slipped up and over the lip of the wash, crouching and looking toward the girl and the horse, and dashed out of sight into the brush beyond. Haskell drew the rifle's heavy hammer back to half cock and pulled down the trigger-guard cocking lever, opening the block.

He knew he'd see the outlaw again in a few seconds.

Haskell drew a deep, calming breath as he slid the long cartridge into the rifle's action and closed the block. He drew the hammer back to full cock, set the rear trigger with the front one, pressed his cheek up to the neck of the stock, and gazed down the barrel through the sites.

His heart thudded heavily, anxiously.

Emma continued to stare toward the cabin. She had the horse's reins in one hand. That hand rested on her hip. Her other boot was cocked forward. Her head was canted at a quizzical angle.

The horse switched its tail.

The outlaw was nowhere in sight. Nothing but sky beyond the horse and the girl.

"Come on, you son of a bitch," Haskell said, drawing another breath to calm himself.

The horse turned its head to peer behind.

Haskell's pulse quickened.

The outlaw came into view, moving slowly toward the horse and the girl, coming up behind them and to one side. He was going to steal around behind the horse and come up on Emma, surprising her. He was a hatted silhouette from Haskell's vantage.

The outlaw was within ten feet of the girl and walking slowly, lightly, on the balls of his boots, holding up one placating hand toward the horse.

Haskell lined up the sites on the man's chest. He drew a breath, then let out half. He lined up the sites just left of the girl and the horse, anticipating where the outlaw would be in two seconds. He slowly tightened the first joint of his index finger on the trigger.

The outlaw's silhouette slid into the sites.

Haskell's gloved finger took up its slack.

The Sharps thundered, punching back against his shoulder. The echo of the shot was swallowed by the huge sky. The acrid smell of burned powder blew back against Haskell's face and was swept away on the wind.

The outlaw turned toward the girl, jerking his left hand toward her right arm. Emma whipped around to face him. The outlaw lurched away from her, stumbled backward, throwing his right hand up high above his head. He twisted around to his right and fell in a heap, legs bouncing off the ground.

Emma stood frozen, staring at the outlaw lying before her.

The horse lifted its head sharply. Haskell heard the distance-muffled whinny a second later. The horse jerked its reins out of Emma's hands and ran away. Emma stood staring at the outlaw on the ground.

Then she dropped to her hands and knees.

She was throwing up.

"Now, that was some fine eatin'!" Haskell said, swabbing the last of the gravy from his plate with a baking powder biscuit and sticking the biscuit into his mouth.

He chewed, swallowed, and washed the biscuit and gravy down with the last of his coffee. He looked across the table at Emma Kramer. "Yes, ma'am—you're one heckuva cook, Miss Emma."

"Thanks."

"No—thank you." Haskell grinned at her.

Emma didn't look at him. She was finishing her own stew, fork in one hand, piece of torn biscuit in the other.

She hadn't said more than five words to him since they'd ridden to her ranch headquarters toting the loot the outlaws had stolen from the stage. Haskell had hauled the body of the girl whom he assumed was the preacher's daughter to the ranch, as well. He'd wrapped her in blankets and tied her, belly down, over a horse. He'd merely dragged the outlaws into the dry wash and left them to the predators. He didn't believe in wasting time burying bad men. Bad men didn't deserve the extra work. Life was too short and there were too many other bad men he could spend that time chasing.

The West was full of thieves and killers just like those he'd left in the wash.

Haskell wasn't looking forward to hauling the girl back to her family in Socorro and telling them he'd been the one to shoot her and why. But that was part of the job. He assumed she'd taken up with one of the outlaws somehow, and must have helped subdue the other stage passengers from inside the coach.

Funny—she hadn't looked like the type. But, then, he'd been totin' a badge long enough to know you couldn't judge anyone—man or woman—by their face.

Emma Kramer's face had been long ever since he'd found her sitting on a rock near the dead outlaw, her pallor decidedly jaundiced, but Haskell didn't know what had caused her to carry a chip on her shoulder. He'd been too busy until now to worry much about it.

He took another sip of his coffee, set down the cup, set his elbows on the table, and entwined his fingers. "Miss Emma, if you don't mind me sayin' so, you seem a might piss-burned. Have I done somethin' to offend you somehow?"

She looked up from her plate, curling a nostril. "You were showing off."

"What's that?"

"With that shot. You were showing off. Trying to shock me. That's how men are."

Haskell snorted. "Shock you? Showin' off? Hell, I was tryin' to save your life!"

"You could've done it another way. You were showing off."

"You could have done it another way by not standing right out in the open in the first place!"

"I was trying to see if you were still alive!"

"What if I hadn't been?"

"Then I would have seen that you weren't, and I would have galloped away!"

"That's not what I told you to do."

"Told me to do? Well, if that isn't just like a man—trying to tell a woman what do on *her own land!*"

"I'm a deputy U.S. marshal!"

"You're a man first and then a marshal!"

Haskell sat back in his chair, befuddled. "Look," he said, "I understand if you're embarrassed about losin' your lunch when my bullet caught up to that feller right in front of you. But if I hadn't shot him with that Sharps, you and him would likely be a long way away from here by now. In fact, he would probably have already had his way with you more than a few times, shot you in the head, and dumped you in a wash!"

"There you go again," Emma said, rising from her chair and snarling like a bobcat—she sort of looked like one, too, with her hair hanging down and uncombed—"trying to shock me again. Typical man—just showing off!"

She grabbed his plate and her own off the table and dumped them into the wreck pan simmering on the range behind her.

Haskell watched her, pensive, as she cleared the rest of the table. She didn't look at him but just went about her work angrily, keeping a nostril wrinkled and one half of her upper lip curled.

Haskell plucked one of his favored Indian Kid cheroots, which he bought by the handful, six for a quarter, in a little smoke shop on Colfax Avenue in his hometown of Denver, out of his shirt pocket, and bit off the end. "How many suitors you got?"

Standing at the wreck pan, she looked at him over her shoulder. "How many *what* do I have?"

"Suitors? You know—gentleman callers?"

She looked at him again, tossing her tangled hair. "That's none of your business."

"Humor me."

"No."

"Come on."

"You're being impertinent, Marshal."

"I bet you don't have a single one, do you?"

She glared at him. "What's that supposed to mean?"

Haskell grinned knowingly as he rolled the cheroot around between his lips, and pulled a lucifer from his shirt pocket. "You got three old men in the bunkhouse, one middle-aged half-breed with a bad leg, a dog"—he indicated the spotted mongrel sleeping in a tight, comfortable ball on the braided rug fronting the cold fireplace in the parlor to his left—"and a half a dozen cats. There's not one male around here under the age of forty."

Haskell struck a match to life on the heel of his cavalry boot and touched it to the end of his cheroot, puffing smoke. "And that's just how you planned it, ain't it?"

She blinked. "Planned what?"

"Your life. Free of men. Free of any chance of . . . love."

"You're crazy," she said. "You must have taken a blow to the head in the old trapper's cabin."

"Why are you so afraid of it?"

"Of what?"

"You know." Haskell set his cigar down on the table so that the smoldering coal hung over the edge, and rose from his chair. He walked around the table and stood beside her. "Of love."

She looked up at him towering over her. "I am not afraid of . . . love . . . Marshal Haskell."

"There—you see. You can hardly even say the word. Why?"

"Don't you think you're overstepping your jurisdiction just a little?"

"Yeah, maybe a little. But don't change the subject." With his left hand, he tucked a stray, tangled lock of her tawny hair back behind her left ear. "How come you don't brush your pretty hair? How come you don't change your clothes, wear somethin' that flatters you instead of makes you look like some undershot grubline rider?"

"I have a lot of work to do every day. I don't have time to dress in the silks and taffetas of a parlor queen."

"You're a beautiful woman, Miss Emma. Once of the prettiest I've ever seen. Yet you do nothin' to show it off or even just display it, and right now, with me standing a foot away from you, you're trembling like a newborn fawn. Why, you're getting all flushed. I do believe you're startin' to sweat."

Haskell reached up to touch her cheek but she jerked her head away and stepped back. "How dare you?" She grabbed a chair back as though to steady herself. She glared up at him. "How *dare* you! This is my house!"

"Have you ever had a good old-fashioned tumble, Miss Emma?"

Her anger turned to hang-jawed, bug-eyed astonishment. *"Wh-what?"*

"Have you ever bumped fuzzies?"

"Have I . . . ? That is not the kind of question—!"

"Your old man was a rabble-rouser. He was many things, ole Coyote Kramer was, plenty of them bad, but one thing he was not was a coward. He believed in living life with his dick out. That's how he himself put it. Now, I know your ma was a city girl . . . high-bred . . . but I gotta believe you got some of your old man in you, as well. Maybe you got so much of ole Coyote Kramer in you that you're scared. Is that it, Miss Kramer? Are you afraid of the kind of feelin's you have—is that why you sur-round yourself with men who don't kindle any of those feelings like I am now?"

"That's ridiculous!" Emma crossed her arms on her breasts.

"Answer the question."

"What question?"

"Have you ever made love, Emma? Have you ever lain with a man?"

Emma stomped her foot down hard on the puncheon floor, waking the dog, who turned toward the kitchen and gave an inquisitive moan. "That is none of your business!"

"Do you mean to tell me you've lived for twenty-one years and you've never had the pleasure of . . ." Haskell let the ques-tion trail off into the ether. She was staring up at him wide-eyed, her full blouse rising and falling heavily, sweat glistening on her forehead, a flush in her perfect cheeks.

Haskell stepped toward her, wrapped his right arm around the small of her back, crouched over her, and pressed his lips to hers.

She tried to pull away, but Haskell held her fast, kissing her hungrily. She stiffened her lips, turned her face to one side, struggling against him. But then she met his mouth head on. Her lips parted and she welcomed his tongue, pressing her own against it. She moaned, reached up to wrap her arms around his broad back, and stepped forward to press her swollen bosom against his chest.

He trailed his hands down her back, then brought them around to her sides, placing them over her breasts. They were warm and full and swollen, expanding and contracting as she breathed. He raked his hands across her nipples, which he could feel pebbling against the fabric.

She pulled back abruptly, breaking free of his embrace.

She turned away, giving him her back, and brushed the back

of her right wrist across her mouth. She was breathing hard, as though she'd run a long way. She took another step away from him, placing one hand on the table, then the other on the counter to her left as though to steady herself.

She said nothing for nearly a full minute but then, without turning to face him, she said, "There was one."

"One what?"

"One man."

"Go on."

She turned to him, frowning, incredulous, exasperated. "Why should I tell you?"

Haskell gave her a gentle smile. "Because you want to."

CHAPTER FOUR

Emma again turned away from Bear Haskell.

She studied the far wall for a time and then she said, turning toward him but unable to meet his gaze, "There was one. Before Pa died of his heart stroke. He worked here at the ranch. He was a few years older than me." Her voice hardened to bitterness. "He seemed very nice. Pleasing to look at. A hard worker. He picked me flowers. We met . . . we met a few times at the old trapper's cabin."

"Go on."

Emma lifted her eyes to Haskell's. Her cheeks were beautifully flushed, her eyes sad. "We met there three times, Jason an' me. And then he left the ranch. Just asked Pa for his time, took the money, saddled his horse, and rode toward town. I was devastated. I couldn't believe he'd just leave me like that . . . after . . . after what we did. After what I thought we'd come to mean to each other. I couldn't eat or sleep. Figuring out the cause of my heartbreak, Pa . . . he rode to town."

"Coyote rode to town and did what?" Haskell gently urged her.

Emma drew a deep, calming breath. "Pa rode to town, found Jason gambling in one of the saloons. Drunk. He had a pleasure girl on his knee. He was bragging to the other men at the table about . . . me."

Emma dipped her chin. A tear rolled down her cheek.

"Pa got so mad . . ." she said, sniffing, angrily brushing the

36

tear away and lifting her heated gaze again to Haskell, "that he took his rifle and shot Jason dead."

That surprised even Haskell, who didn't think he could be surprised by anything Coyote would do. "Whoa!"

"Yeah, well . . . he shot him, all right." Emma dipped her chin and sobbed, then brushed the tears away and cleared her throat. "Pa spent a few days in jail, but several of the other men in the saloon were friends of Pa. They lied and testified that Jason had drawn first. So the marshal let Pa go."

Emma sobbed again, no doubt in memory of the boy she'd loved and who'd betrayed her. Obviously, she still lamented his death. But she couldn't blame her father for killing him. Old Coyote had only been exacting revenge for his daughter, whom he'd loved.

Haskell walked up to her, wrapped his arms around her, and pressed her head to his chest, hugging her. "No wonder you guard your heart so. And everything else."

Emma's body jerked as she sobbed against him.

"I'm sorry, girl."

"I'm sorry. I'm just bein' plumb silly."

Haskell kissed her forehead, then pulled away from her. He walked around the table, plucked his cigar up off the edge, poked it into his mouth, and retrieved his saddlebags and bedroll from the floor by the door.

"I reckon I'll be sayin' good night." Bear winked across the table at Emma, who watched him dubiously. "Thanks for supper."

He pulled his hat off a peg and opened the door.

Emma frowned. "Where are you going?"

"Out to the bunkhouse."

"You can throw down in Pa's old room."

"Nah, the menfolk belong in the bunkhouse." Haskell drew the door wider.

Emma strode resolutely around the table and closed the door. "Old Riley snores like a mountain lion with the winter crud. Wilfred walks in his sleep. Sometimes he runs outside and fires off his old cap-and-ball pistol at Injuns that aren't there! You take Pa's old room. You'll get a better night's sleep there than out in the bunkhouse with those old reprobates."

She canted her head toward a door in the rear wall of the parlor.

Haskell shrugged. "All right, then. Obliged." He pegged his hat again and started for Coyote's old room.

"I'll heat some water so you can wash up a bit before you turn in," Emma called behind him.

Haskell stopped at the door, then half-turned back to the girl still standing by the table, watching him. "It'd feel good to wash off some of the trail dust. Thanks, Miss Emma."

"Don't mention it, Marshal."

"You think you might call me Bear?"

She gave a shy half-smile. "All right. Bear."

He went into the room and dropped his saddlebags and bedroll on the floor by the door. He lit a lamp and glanced around.

The room looked just like what he would have imagined Coyote would have slept in. Small and neat and rustic, with a four-poster bed constructed of pine, and a pine headboard Coyote himself had likely built. A couple of sewn-together cougar hides served as a spread. Several more hides decorated the pine-paneled walls.

There was a stout dresser and an armoire, and a washstand beside a curtained window that looked back into woods and a creek. The window was partly open, and Haskell could smell the creek. A braided hemp rug adorned the floor. Haskell sagged wearily onto the bed and removed his grizzly claw necklace. He unbuttoned his calico shirt, shrugged out of it, and tossed it onto a ladder-back, hide-bottom chair.

He was kicking out of his boots when Emma nudged wide the door he hadn't fully closed, and glanced tentatively into the room. "You decent?" She had a pot of steaming water in her hands, and a washcloth and a towel draped over one arm.

"That's a matter of some debate," Haskell said.

She came in and poured the hot water into the washbasin on the stand. She hung the cloth and the towel on a wooden bar beneath a small, chipped mirror. "There's a little lye soap here on the stand." Turning to Haskell, she said, "Is there anything else you need? A chamber pot should be under the bed."

Haskell kicked it with the heel of his right foot. "It is. That should do me."

She watched him from the door.

"Thanks again, Emma."

She looked somehow troubled. She moved her lips as she watched him, as though she wanted to say something but couldn't find the words.

"That's everything I need, Emma," Haskell said. "Thanks again."

Emma nodded. "All right, then. Good night, Mar . . . I mean, Bear." She glanced at him once more as, holding the empty pot in one hand, she drew the door closed with the other.

Haskell skinned down to his birthday suit, and took a sponge bath with the hot water and soap. It felt good to get clean. He hadn't had a bath in weeks. When he'd toweled dry, he sat naked on the bed, letting the cool air from the open window finish drying him, and smoked the rest of his cheroot.

While he smoked, he thought about Emma living in this big, rambling house alone, with only the dog and her cats and the memory of her father and the young man old Coyote had shot. She was awfully young to be living with such snaggle-toothed demons tearing around in her brain.

Haskell had to give a chuckle at what old Coyote had done, however. It was just like the old frontiersman to shoot a man who'd treated his daughter so shabbily. It was just like him to have friends who'd help him get away with it, too.

Haskell walked over to the washstand and poured a glass of cold water from the pitcher. He drank it down, set the glass back down on the stand, and looked at the door. There was a bolt on it. He walked over, stared at the door for a minute, deciding, and then slid the bolt across the frame, locking the door.

He turned down the lamp's wick and crawled under Coyote's sheets and cougar hides. He knew he'd start thinking about the girl he'd shot earlier—the preacher's daughter—the minute his head hit the pillow. And that's exactly what happened.

He was almost glad for the distraction when the knock he'd been half-expecting sounded on the door. He lifted his head. "Go back to bed, Emma."

She rattled the doorknob. "Let me in."

"Go back to bed."

"Let me in, Bear."

"I'm not gonna be the one, Emma. I'm sorry I got you thinkin' about it, but I'm not gonna be the one."

For nearly a minute there was silence on the other side of the door.

Then, softly: "Please."

"You go to town. Find someone who'll treat you right."

Again, silence. Footsteps retreated into the parlor.

Haskell released a held breath. He'd just closed his eyes again, when a loud *crash!* jerked his head up off the pillow. There was a secondary *bang!* as the door bounced off the wall.

He could see Emma's silhouette standing in the open doorway, holding a heavy wooden footstool, which she'd used to bust open the door. She tossed the footstool out into the parlor.

Somewhere, the dog gave an excited bark.

"Everthing's all right, Buster," Emma called to him.

Weak lamplight slithered into Haskell's room from the parlor, silhouetting the girl as she moved to the dresser. She turned up the wick on the hurricane lamp. She wore only a blue and white striped quilt about her shoulders. Her tawny hair hung down, glistening in the lamplight. She'd brushed it until it shone.

Her long, pale legs were bare beneath the blanket. Haskell could see the tangle of dark hair at her crotch.

She moved to the bed, stared down at him, holding the blanket around her shoulders. She grabbed the edge of Haskell's covers, drew them slowly down, exposing his broad, hairy chest, his flat belly, and then his cock, which was fully engorged and angling back over his belly button.

Staring at the impressive member, she drew a deep breath.

"I'm gonna be gone in the morning," Haskell told her, his voice thick.

She dropped the towel, then reached forward and wrapped her left hand around his manhood, in which a tiny heart was beating insistently. "I wouldn't have it any other way."

"All right, then." Haskell swung his legs over the side of the bed, facing her. He drew her between his knees and massaged her breasts, licking and sucking her nipples.

She groaned, moaned, squeezing his cock tightly in her left fist.

Her nipples grew hard as sewing thimbles.

She sank down to her knees, taking his jutting manhood in both her hands, looking up at him. "I want to suck it."

"Go ahead."

"It's big."

"I've been told."

41

Peter Brandvold

Emma touched the tip of her tongue to the underside of his member, beneath the swollen mushroom head, and narrowed an eye as she gazed up at him. "My pa warned me about you."

"What'd he say?"

"He said you were a charmer. That you'd probably come around one day. He just wanted me to be prepared."

"So . . . are you prepared?"

She smiled, sliding one of her hands down the length of his cock to cup his heavy balls in her hand. "I think so." She closed her mouth over the swollen mushroom head and ran her tongue around on it.

"Oh," Haskell said, grabbing the sheets in his fists and lifting his chin toward the ceiling. "Oh, yeah. Oh, Christ . . ."

Her mouth was warm and soft and wet. She sucked the head of his dong for a good long time and then slowly slid her lips down it until the end of his cock was halfway down her throat. Her mouth contracted around the swollen, thudding shaft.

Haskell's heart surged, hammering against his breastbone.

Emma gagged and pulled her mouth off of him, raking a long, ragged breath into her lungs. "Oh, god!" she cried, laughing at the same time.

Her eyes crossed as she gazed up at him, her lips slathered in saliva. His cock was lathered in spittle, as well. Haskell curled his toes. Pre-cum bubbled up out of the dimple at the end of his staff.

"Our father in Heaven," Haskell said through gritted teeth, reaching down, placing his hands on the girl's slender arms, and drawing her to her feet. "Hallowed be your name . . ."

Emma's breasts jostled as she moved. They were the size of pale melons—ripe melons ready for plucking from the vine. The light-red nipples jutted from the pink areolas that covered the tips of each splendid bosom, which angled slightly away from the other. They were swollen and hard with desire.

42

Haskell took each in his hands and squeezed it as he swirled his tongue around inside her belly button.

"Oh," Emma said, wrapping her arms around his head, mashing his face against her slightly convex belly, her breasts sloping against his forehead. "Oh . . . oh . . . oh, god, your tongue feels sooo good!"

" 'Your kingdom come, your will be done,' " Haskell resumed the prayer, pushing her back slightly and rising from the edge of the bed, "on earth as it is in heaven."

She wrapped both hands around his jutting mast again, and gave him a foxy half-smile, gazing up at him from beneath her brows. "Are you a Christian man, Marshal Haskell?"

"Sometimes," Haskell grunted, turning her around and shoving her down on the bed. "In trying times like these," he grunted again, trying hard not to blow his load. The girl's hot mouth and frisky tongue had stirred him to an inner frenzy.

He crawled onto the bed, crouched over Emma, wrapped his arms around her, and slid her farther up on the bed. Her eyes were glistening. Her mouth was swollen. Her hot breasts rose and fell heavily as she breathed. She spread her knees. She kept tugging on his cock, mewling, and grinding her heels into the cornshuck mattress.

She was a lynx in heat.

"Fuck me," she breathed. "Fuck me, Bear!"

CHAPTER FIVE

Haskell pried Emma's hands off his cock, which was so hard he thought it would split like a boiled sausage.

He lowered his head and licked his way down her body, starting at her neck. Her skin was sweaty, salty, and nearly hot enough to burn his mouth. He licked his way down through the valley between her heaving breasts, kneading them with his hands, and down her belly and into the warm, moist, tangled hair at her snatch.

"Ohhh!" she groaned, arching her back when he flicked his tongue across her clit, swollen to nearly the size of an almond. "Ohhhh, gaawd!" she cried, louder, when he stuck his tongue into her.

She dug her heels deeper into the mattress and arched her back, lifting her bottom several inches up off the bed. Haskell, his head buried in her pussy, pushed her back down on the bed and held her there fast with his head as he tongued her.

She sobbed and groaned and writhed beneath him as he lapped at her womanly core.

Haskell had tumbled with enough women to know when he had one at nearly the point of climax. He pulled his face out of her snatch.

"What are you doing?" she screeched. "Please, don't stop!"

Haskell knelt between her spread legs, then sat back against his heels. He grabbed her legs under her knees and drew her down toward him, sliding her sopping, glistening pussy toward the head of his bulging cock. She lifted her head from the pillow, widening her eyes as she stared down past her frantically expanding and contracting belly at his throbbing member.

"Oh, Lord," she laughed, "you're gonna kill me!"

"We'll see, darlin'." Haskell drew her again until he was sliding slowly, slowly . . . ever so slowly inside her.

She watched for a time, panting like a woman in labor. "Oh," she wheezed as his cock slowly disappeared, sliding deeper and deeper into her. She threw her head back on the pillow, the chords standing out in her neck. "It's like . . . it's like being fucked with an ax handle!"

"Should I stop, darlin'?"

"Don't you dare!"

Haskell chuckled.

He bottomed out inside her, then shoved her back away from his hips until she was nearly off of him, just the very head of his cock snugged inside the petal-like flesh showing pink inside her wet pubic hair. He pulled her toward him again, the folds of her pussy opening to receive him, his thick, bulging cock disappearing inside her once more.

"Oh, god," she said, and swallowed, reaching above her head to grab two willow sapling spools of the headboard. "Oh, god! Oh, god! Oh, god!"

Gradually, the hotter and wetter she got, the easier he was able to slide in and out of her. He increased his pace until he was drawing her toward him and then away in a near-violent frenzy. He bucked up hard against her, his flesh smacking hers.

The bed squawked and pitched like an angry mustang. Emma squealed and howled, holding tight to the spools above her head. Her breasts bounced in circles on her chest, the nipples hard and jutting.

"Oh, god!" she cried. "Oh, god! Oh, god!"

Haskell grunted as he hammered away at her.

They were going at it so violently now that a picture dropped from a nail to crash to the floor. The lantern on the dresser guttered and smoked, its mantle ringing. Both of the willow spools Emma was clinging to broke, and she grabbed two more.

Haskell felt as though his cock was about to explode. He forced back his desire, reciting the Lord's Prayer again in silence, but there was no way he could keep from reaching his fulfillment within another minute or two. Emma's madly jouncing breasts were colored gold by the watery lamplight, glistening with sweat. Sweat shimmered on her belly, as well. Her pussy was like a small, hot hand clenching him, releasing, then clenching again while bathing him in hot honey.

Hearing something, Haskell stopped.

Emma stopped screaming.

The bed fell still.

A man's phlegmy voice called from the front of the house, "Miss Emma—you all right in there?"

Emma's eyes snapped wide in shock and horror, and her cheeks turned red. She turned her head toward the half-open door. "I'm just fine, Riley! Thanks for checking on me, though!"

"All right, then." There was a throaty chuckle and then the front door closed.

Emma and Haskell exploded in embarrassed laughter.

The interruption had helped to damp down some of the lawman's flames. He began riding Emma again, his pace slower. He savored each measured stroke. Gradually, he increased his rhythm until they were going at it again like two lusty minks, grunting, groaning, cursing, and causing another picture to fall from the wall.

Another spool broke off in Emma's hand, and she reached for another one.

When Haskell could feel that she was close to her time, he placed his hands beneath the small of her back and held her hips up taut against his belly. She curled her toes.

Emma screamed as her pussy shivered around his cock, bathing it in wave after wave of hot cream.

When she'd stopped spasming and had begun to relax, Haskell pulled his still ramrod-hard staff out of her, leaned forward, and slid it up her belly.

"Squeeze your tits together!" he yelled.

"What?"

"Squeeze your tits together!"

"Oh!"

As he rammed his nearly bursting cock up between her splendid, swollen orbs, she squeezed them together, sandwiching them around his cock. He thrust twice with his hips. His come jetted up from the top of her cleavage to cover her chin, throat, and shoulder with his thick, milky jism.

Emma laughed and licked the come from her lips.

Then she cleaned his cock with her mouth.

They slept with their limbs entangled for the rest of the long night. Haskell slept dreamlessly.

He woke in the morning to Emma, bathed in golden morning sunshine, gently stroking him back to life. She smiled at him. She was like a naked angel crouched over his belly, her lips as red as cherries, hair like spun honey in the sunlight. She didn't say anything, just continued stroking him until he came in her hands.

Then he drifted back to sleep.

A hand nudged him. As though from far away came a man's soft voice, almost too soft to be heard: "Uh . . . excuse me, Bear."

Sleep had a hard, jealous grip on Haskell. He just wanted to lie here in Emma's bed . . . or the bed of her dead father and Haskell's old pal, Coyote Kramer . . . and savor the memory of his and the girl's recent lovemaking, and enjoy the aroma of bacon and eggs and boiling coffee that emanated through the partly open door from the ranch house kitchen. He could hear her in there, humming softly, happily, while clanging pans around and opening and closing the squawky oven door.

A hand squeezed his arm, shaking him so that his head wobbled. The man's unwelcome voice again: "Bear!"

Haskell jerked awake, scowling and angry. "What in the hell . . . ?"

He let his voice trail off when he saw the familiar, craggy, long face of conductor George April beneath the leather bill of his purple wool hat. April was leaning so close to Haskell that the deputy U.S. marshal could smell the sweet smell of plug tobacco on the older man's breath. "Sorry, there, Bear. You must have been havin' a good one—grinnin' like a boy starin' through the half-moon in the girls' privy door!"

April chuckled.

"But we done stopped in Denver," he continued. "If you don't get off soon, you're gonna be headed up to Cheyenne."

"What?" Haskell looked around. A keen disappointment touched him when he did not see Coyote Kramer's crudely but efficiently appointed bedroom surrounding him. No, what surrounded him instead were the paneled walls, brass bracket lamps and luggage racks, and the stiff-backed, plush-covered wooden bench seats of the Denver & Rio Grande Flyer he'd caught down in Socorro.

Still, the dream was stubborn. Haskell lifted his head, sniffing the air. "Where the hell is the smell of bacon and eggs comin' from?"

April straightened his whipcord lean frame, and sniffed. "I don't smell nothin' but the usual sweat, coal smoke, and farts. Besides, breakfast is long over. Hell, it's noon. You must be hungry, Bear. Why don't you go out and buy yourself a roast beef sandwich from one of the handcarts always lined up on Wyandotte Avenue this time of the day? It's pushin' noon."

Haskell sniffed again. He now smelled only what April had smelled. He wrinkled his nose against the contrast between the smell of bacon and eggs and boiled coffee and the smoke and farts lingering in the coach car. The dream was gone. Damn.

"All right, all right," Haskell grouched, plucking his hat from the seat beside him and stuffing it down on his head. "I can take a hint, George. I'll be on my way."

"You need any help with your gear, Bear?"

"Nah, I got it."

"All right, then. See ya next time, Bear."

"See ya, George."

Haskell reached up into the overhead rack and pulled his gear down into the aisle—his Henry repeater, saddlebags, canvas war bag strapped to the saddlebags, and bedroll. He traveled so much that he'd learned to pare his possibles down to what he could carry on his shoulders the average distance from a train or stagecoach station to a livery barn or hotel without snapping his back or busting a gut.

He draped the saddlebags and bedroll over his left shoulder, resting the sheathed Henry on his right shoulder so that, being right-handed, he could pull it down fast, skin it from its leather scabbard, and commence firing if the need arose.

He'd been hauling in owlhoots long enough that there was always some chip-shouldered, snake-eyed hombre wanting to feed him to the crows. Not every day or even every week, but enough times every year—and it seemed to be happening more and more often—that he'd learned to grow eyes in the back of his head, and to move quick when he heard someone yell something akin to, "There's that damn peckerwood of a U.S. marshal that hauled poor Cousin Clancy in so's the federal judge could play cat's cradle with his head!"

Haskell was glad to not hear anything like that now, however, as he stepped off the coach car's rear vestibule onto the cobbled platform, the cacophony of coupling train cars rising around him, coal smoke billowing overhead.

As he made his way through the bustling Union Station, he couldn't resist sniffing the air again. The odor of bacon and eggs and boiled coffee had been so real in the dream that he couldn't get it out of his head.

It had only been in his head, however. All he could smell now was cold sandstone and wood varnish and the potpourri of the hundred or so bodies moving around him, heading toward the platform and the tracks at one end of the cavernous building or toward Wyandotte Avenue at the other end, as well as the scent of tobacco smoke and horseshit and the cattle pens emanating through the big doors opening ahead of Haskell, where golden sunlight shone like that at the far end of a long tunnel.

As Haskell strode under his load, he was unaware of a fond smile curling his mouth as he remembered rising two mornings ago from Coyote Kramer's damaged bed, refreshed though also a little stiff and sore, his dick chafed, from his frolic with the old-timer's beautiful daughter. Haskell had dressed and followed the sound of Emma's humming into the kitchen, where the smell of bacon and eggs and boiling coffee swelled to the size of a vast, sweet rain cloud, causing Haskell's mouth to water like that of a panting dog, and the hunger pangs in his gut to kick like an angry mule.

"Good morning, Marshal!" Emma had intoned, turning potatoes in a skillet sputtering on the range. Then a rosy flush rose in her cheeks and she gave a sheepish little smile as she added, "I mean . . . Bear."

"Good mornin' yourself, darlin'," Haskell had said, his lower jaw hanging in shock as he stopped at the end of the dining table to stare at her. At least, he thought it was Emma Kramer, though she looked so different that one-quarter of his brain wondered if the creature he was staring at could be an imposter.

Gone were Emma's ratty shirt, patched denims, and unkempt hair, as well as the customary soil smudges on her cheeks and neck. In short, gone was the beautiful savage.

In her place was a sparkling young woman who could have been dropped down from some mythical finishing school in the sky. Emma had pulled her thick, tawny locks into an alluring chignon behind her head and held them in place by a tortoise-shell comb.

Her face was fresh-scrubbed, her eyes wide and sparkling. Her high-busted, long-legged figure was spryly radiant in a clean cream housedress printed with brown and yellow flowers and edged in white lace. The shoes showing beneath the dress's hem were not scuffed stockmen's boots but black patent ladies' shoes with gold side buttons. The frock was buttoned to her neck, but it fit her voluptuous figure so tightly that the girl might not have been wearing anything at all. The cambric material strained back against the two wondrous mounds of her bosoms, which had given him such pleasure the night before.

"You're not Emma," Haskell said with mock castigation. "What did you do with Emma, you charlatan?"

Emma laughed as she grabbed a plate off a shelf above her, and began filling it with scrambled eggs, bacon, and a heaping spoonful of potatoes fried with onions and butter. "I don't know what got into me," she said as she set the plate on the table. "When I got up this morning, I just felt like throwing a dress on."

She looked at Haskell, roses blooming in her cheeks, and shrugged.

Haskell went over, wrapped his arms around her, and kissed her.

"Do you like it, Bear?" Emma asked, pulling her head back

from his, entwining her fingers behind his neck.

"You're beautiful, purely a sight for sore eyes," Haskell said, and kissed her again. "And that breakfast smells so good I'm liable to faint before I can sit down and eat it!"

"Well, you'd better hurry then!"

Something bothered him. He frowned as he held her, and stared into her eyes, which gazed up at him, fondly sparkling. "Emma . . ."

"What is it, Bear?"

"Listen, Emma, I . . . I . . . I'm pullin'—"

"Oh, I know—you're pullin' out this morning. Don't worry. I didn't take last night as anything more than what it was, dear man . . ." She sandwiched his big, rugged face in her hands and pressed her lips very gently and tenderly to his. "A wonderful night with a wonderful man. In the aftermath of that good . . . *coring* you gave me"—she dipped her chin, blushing and grinning devilishly—"I just felt like dressing a little more feminine this morning than usual, and cooking you a nice breakfast. You have a long ride ahead to Socorro and an even longer one back to Denver. Believe me, as soon as you're out of here, I'll be hauling out my nasty old duds, rolling up my shirtsleeves, and heading out to dynamite some water holes!"

Haskell didn't realize he was chuckling out loud until an old woman just then entering Union Station ahead of him pulled a younger woman wide of the laughing, obviously demented, stranger, and told her to keep walking. Haskell pinched his hat brim to the pair hurrying off behind him now, and started to turn back to the large oak doors.

"Marshal Haskell!" sounded a voice behind him, barely audible above the echoing footsteps and loud conversational hum. He turned to see a man in the uniform of a ticket agent hurrying toward him, sashaying through the crowd and waving a small envelope above his head.

Haskell recognized Boyd Anderson, the ticket agent who usually handled the government pay vouchers Bear always used to purchase his train tickets. Haskell also gambled with the man on occasion, in the gambling den of the Larimer Hotel, where Bear kept a small suite, his only home, his having so little time or need for a real home.

"Almost missed you!" Anderson called, smiling with relief as he approached.

With a pang of dread, Haskell noted the small envelope in the man's pudgy hand. "Ah, shit," he said half to himself. "What now?"

Chapter Six

"A note from the head honcho," said the ticket agent.

"Henry Dade?" Chief U.S. Marshal Henry Dade, that was.

"The marshal had a messenger bring it down here yesterday. He wanted me to see that you got it. The chief marshal wanted me to know it was very important that you got it before you headed back to the Larimer."

Haskell leaned his rifle against a marble column and accepted the small envelope with his name scrawled on it in the spidery hand Haskell had come to recognize as that of his boss. "Hell."

"What's the matter?"

"This note means that ole Henry's likely gonna want me to hop, skip, and jump off to another job before I even have time to change clothes and shave and throw down a few belts of bourbon."

"No rest for the wicked," the ticket agent said, grinning.

Haskell, surly ever since he'd been so rudely awakened from his bacon-and-eggs dream in the coach car, scowled at him. Anderson cleared his throat sheepishly, pulled his broadcloth trousers up his broad hips, and trotted back toward his cage.

Haskell opened the unsealed envelope and shook out the folded lined notepaper, and gave a snort as he read his boss's typically succinct order: *"Report to office pronto!—H.A. Dade."*

"Damnit, Henry," Haskell said, crumpling the note and envelope and dropping them into the nearest trash can. He set his rifle back up on his shoulder and headed on through the station's front doors, grumbling, "What in the hell's so damned important it can't wait until I've had a bath and one night to drink and gamble and carouse a little? Shit, I fought in the War of Southern Rebellion to outlaw slavery!"

Still grumbling, he hailed a hansom cab and then sat back, grumbling some more and lighting an Indian Kid cheroot as the coach rocked and rattled up Sixteenth Street toward the federal building on Colfax Avenue near the gold-domed state capitol. When the hansom cab reached the bottom of the federal building's broad, stone steps, Haskell lumbered out of the coach with his gear, cheroot tucked into a corner of his mouth, and tossed some coins up to the waiting, top-hatted driver, a fellow named Dalton Briggs, whom Haskell also gambled with from time to time at the Larimer.

"Want me to wait for you, Bear?" the driver asked, knowing Haskell didn't like to walk much farther than, say, the distance from one saloon to another saloon on the same block.

"Yeah, why don't you," Haskell said. He'd likely be heading back to either the Union Station a mile and a half away, or, hopefully, the Larimer Hotel, a good six blocks away. While he hoped his next destination would be the latter, he had a feeling it would be the former.

Either way, they were each farther away than he wanted to walk.

He trudged up the sandstone steps into the federal building, then took the marble inside staircase to the second floor hall; on the left side of the hall, about halfway down, stood the stout oak door in which CHIEF UNITED STATES MARSHAL had been stenciled in gold-leaf lettering in the door's upper, frosted glass panel.

Haskell fumbled open the door and strode into Henry Dade's outer office, and stopped abruptly, throwing out his hand to ease the door closed behind him. A lurid smile curled his upper lip as he stared at the pretty, round backside of Henry Dade's secretary, Miss Lucy Kimble. Miss Kimble, the daughter of State Senator Luther Kimble, was bent forward to stoke the fire in the colonial-model heating stove abutting the outer office's outside wall.

Lucy Kimble was another one like Emma Kramer—a rare beauty who did everything she could to hide her charms. While Emma hid her wares inside ten pounds of soiled flannel and patched denim, Miss Kimble hid it by pulling her dark-brown hair into a knot as tight as a clenched fist, until it drew her eye corners up to resemble those of a Chinese. Miss Kimble also wore grim, shapeless old-lady dresses—the kind old ladies wore to funerals—and stumpy, black or brown side-button shoes. If she wore any jewelry, which was rare, it was usually a small gold cross hanging from a gold-washed chain or prosaic cameo pinned to her breast.

Nothing could hide the fact, however, that beneath such dowdy attire lurked the body of a succubus. Whether Lucy herself knew it or not was open to question. Haskell often wondered. While she didn't have tits the size of Emma Kramer's (though it was impossible to tell with the way she reined them in), Haskell had a feeling that behind the taut corsets she always wore under her dresses, and probably several other undergarments as well, her bosoms were firm and perky and would feel right supple in a man's hands.

Haskell, who often opined on such subjects with only a modicum of chagrin, doubted that any man had ever had the chance to judge for himself. By all accounts, Miss Kimble lived a sheltered life up at her family's stately Sherman Street digs. Outside of work, Haskell never saw her in public. While she did have a beau, who was the son of another senator, the girl's shy, dour, humorless, and altogether unfriendly demeanor told him that they'd likely never even held hands, much less swapped spit. At least he couldn't imagine it, though he had to admit he'd once thought the same thing about Emma Kramer, and she'd turned out to be damned near deadly in the old mattress sack!

Was Miss Lucy, as well?

Intriguing, Miss Lucy was. The stuff of a man's fantasy, all the more alluring by being so cussed unattainable.

Studying that very subject as the girl continued to poke around inside the stove, Haskell rolled his cheroot from one side of his mouth to the other, drew in a long drag, and blew it out his nose. Miss Lucy lifted her head, sniffing. She turned her head to one side, then, seeing the big man standing behind her, gave a startled "Oh!" and whipped around, flushing.

"Marshal Haskell, indeed!" she intoned, breathless, nudging her small, oval, steel-framed spectacles up her fine, clean nose. "I didn't know you were standing there. You might have said something!"

Haskell opened his mouth to speak but closed it when Henry Dade's office door opened and Henry Dade himself poked his lean, gray head into the outer office, frowning. "Bear, for god's sake, get your ass in here, you big galoot. My note said pronto. That doesn't mean take time to pester my secretary!"

"Indeed!" agreed Miss Lucy, who held her hands behind her as though she could still feel the burn of his eyes on her shapely backside.

"Right—sorry, Chief," Haskell said, leaning his rifle against the hat tree near the door, and setting his bedroll and saddlebags on a chair in the same location. "I do beg your pardon, Miss Kimble," he said, pinching his hat brim to the girl as he headed for Henry's office. "Cat just got my tongue there for a second, I reckon." He gave her a wink, which brought some badly needed color into her fair cheeks, then stepped into his boss's office and drew the door closed behind him.

Chief Marshal Henry Dade had walked around behind his mammoth desk, which nearly filled his small, cluttered office. Smoke from the chief marshal's ubiquitous cigars forever hung in toxic clouds the color of coal smoke ejected by a Baldwin locomotive's giant, black diamond stack. Dade cast his senior-most deputy U.S. marshal an incriminating glare, then poked the stubby stogie in his right hand at Bear, and said, "What have I told you about pestering Miss Kimble?"

"I wasn't pestering her, Chief," Haskell said. "I was *admiring* her. There's a difference."

"Not to her there isn't. Not to her father, either. If Luther Kimble ever caught you ogling that girl's ass, he'd have you strung up by your little toes, stripped buck naked, and marked with a brand to each butt cheek!"

"Ouch!"

"Yeah!"

"Just for admiring her ass?"

"Her family goes back to the Pilgrims."

"I don't doubt it a bit!" Haskell grinned. "You tryin' to tell me, Henry, you never took a peek at that girl's derriere?"

"Never have," said the chief marshal. "At my age and state of ill health, an erection would kill me." He pressed a fist to his bony chest and coughed rackingly until Haskell's own lungs felt raw.

"Christ, Henry—you really oughta stop smoking those things!" Haskell waved at the thick smoke billowing around him, causing his eyes to water. *"Jesus!"*

Dade plopped down into his high-backed leather chair. "These and coffee and bourbon are the only things keeping me alive. Myrtle can't cook for shit. Never has been able to, and now her one-hundred-year-old mother has moved in with us. These days, that old abomination takes up even more of

Myrtle's time that she could be using to learn how to boil an egg."

Dade looked like a man who subsisted on coffee, bourbon, and cigars. The chief marshal weighed maybe a hundred and twenty pounds dripping wet. His shabby, three-piece suits hung on his bony scarecrow frame. His face was gaunt and the hue and texture of old paper. He wore a thick, brushy mustache about two shades darker than the close-cropped, iron-gray hair on his head. He had a mole on his right temple. It owned a nasty dark color, and Haskell would have sworn it was growing before his very eyes.

He feared his middle-aged boss, who looked twenty years older than his actual age, which was around sixty, was hanging by a thread. Too bad, too. Haskell had nothing but respect for Henry Dade, who'd been an adjutant to General Grant in the War of Southern Rebellion, and then a hell-for-leather colonel in the Texas Rangers. Henry's own father had died at the Alamo. An ex-man-of-action himself, Dade was about the only man on God's green earth who understood the wild and woolly ways of Bear Haskell. Henry Dade always tried to act as a buffer between Haskell and the higher-ups in the marshals service, who, because of Bear's often "imaginative" law-enforcement methods, Bear often would have butted heads with otherwise.

"Anyway," the chief marshal said, pounding his chest once more and giving one more nasty-sounding cough, "let me have your report on this last manhunt." He extended a gnarled, age-spotted hand across the desk.

"Not done yet, Henry!" Haskell said in exasperation, slacking into the uncomfortable wooden Windsor chair angled before his boss's desk. (The chair was without padding for a reason—the chief marshal, not given to chitchat, didn't want anyone to linger.) "I just got into town not ten minutes ago!"

"Oh, right. Well get it to Miss Kimble as soon as you have

time to scribble something down, and try to be more detailed this time, will you?"

Haskell grumbled at that.

"I heard you ran into some extra trouble. So said the town marshal of Socorro in the telegram I guess you directed him to send."

"Yeah, I'll put it in my *detailed* report, Henry. Say, could we get down to brass tacks? Why did you haul me in here before I even had time to wash my mouth out with some cheap bourbon?"

"Bad news."

"It always is. I reckon that's what keeps vittles on our plates, Henry. When old Myrtle is up to boilin' an egg, I mean." Haskell grinned.

"Okay, Bear—enough beating around the bush." Dade took another couple thoughtful puffs off the short, fat stogie.

"Right," Haskell said, gently prodding. "Enough beating around the bush."

"Lou Cameron is dead."

Haskell stared across the cluttered desk, a confusion of words tangling themselves in his throat so that, while he parted his lips as though to speak, no sounds came out.

"I'm sorry," Dade said, meeting his deputy's gaze head-on.

"How?"

"Ambushed. His night deputy found him out behind his office up in Diamondback, two bullets in his back. Apparently, he'd just walked out of the privy. That's when the killer threw down on him."

Haskell ground his molars. "Backshot."

"That's right."

"Any suspects?"

"Not yet. That's where you come in."

"You want me to go up and investigate."

"Would you want me to send anyone else?"

"Nope." Haskell leaned forward in his chair. He felt a little queasy and disoriented. It was like he'd been hit across the back of his neck with an ax handle. "I sure wouldn't."

"I'm sorry, Bear. I know you two were close once."

"We still are . . . were . . . despite everything."

"Yeah, I heard about that. Damn women. Cameron was a damn good soldier back in the war, but, then, no one knows that any better than you do."

"We fought together in the same unit—Silas's Sonso'bitches, they called us, though in letters home, of course, we were the Zouave of the 155th Pennsylvania Volunteers. Silas Sanders was our colonel. I was a too-young first lieutenant. Cam was a wise old sergeant, five years older than me. A true-blue pain in the ass, but I'll be damned if I didn't love that stocky, hard-drinking bastard." Haskell felt a tightness in his chest. The world had just changed for him, become a little darker, in the way it always does when someone close to us dies.

He sleeved a tear from his cheek. "Who sent word?"

"County sheriff from up that way. Delbert Ford. Resides in the county seat of Casper. Ford's strung out way too thin, short on deputies and trying to prevent a shooting war between two ranching factions. Casper's a good twenty-five miles from Diamondback. Ford requested our help in bringing Cameron's killer to justice."

"Is that all you have?"

"That's all I have. You'll be starting from scratch."

"All right, then. Travel vouchers?"

"My secretary finished typing them up an hour ago. The Burlington Flyer to Cheyenne, and then . . . ah, hell . . . you know the rest."

"Yeah, I know the rest." Haskell had been over that route more than a few times over his ten years in the service.

61

The big lawman rose from his chair. It groaned as it gave up his weight. As he turned to the door, Dade said behind him, "You all right, Bear?"

Haskell shook his head. "No." He hardened his jaws as raw anger began to burn up through his grief. "But I will be just as soon as I find whoever killed Lou."

"Bear?"

Once more, Haskell turned from the door.

"What is it, Chief?"

Dade stared at him through the billowing smoke cloud encircling his head like a fallen halo. "Is she still there?"

Haskell hiked a shoulder. "I don't know. I reckon I'll know soon enough."

He went out.

CHAPTER SEVEN

Three days later, Bear Haskell rode a sleek buckskin through a remote, high-desert Wyoming valley as arid, dusty, and vast as any he'd seen in Arizona or northern Mexico.

He'd acquisitioned the horse from the quartermaster at Fort Laramie. He'd spent the previous night in the noncommissioned officers' quarters at Laramie, where he'd lightened his pockets by twelve dollars playing stud poker with three sergeants, a corporal, and a florid-faced fort sutler—all sun-seasoned men driven a trifle mad by the remoteness and barrenness of their assignment.

Haskell didn't regret the twelve-dollar loss, for it made the men who'd won it from him happy indeed, if only because they'd won it from an unfamiliar face. If only because, even now after Red Cloud's Sioux had been brought to heel, there was little to be happy about at Fort Laramie.

Not long ago, riding through the country northwest of that remote outpost would have been a death sentence. It would have been the equal of riding through Geronimo's Apacheria in southern Arizona. The Indians had been quelled, but the sun-bleached human and horse bones Haskell occasionally spied amongst rocks or littering the bottom of a dry wash, likely dug up from shallow graves and strewn by coyotes or wolves, were stark testament to the depredations that once haunted this vastness.

The area Haskell was riding through not only resembled the

southwest; it was nearly as hot, as well. Crossing a low divide abutted on both sides of the trail by chalky haystack buttes with only a few scraggly blond weeds growing out of the alkaline soil, the deputy U.S. marshal lifted his canteen and drank sparingly, trying to carve a hole through the dust caking his throat.

He was careful with his water because, while he'd visited Diamondback twice in the past, he couldn't remember its exact location. There were few obvious landmarks out here in this pale, dusty vastness capped with a sky as large as all eternity. The bluffs and mesas around him looked like all the other bluffs and mesas around him, and government survey maps were notoriously unreliable.

For all the lawman knew, he might still be a good four or five hours away from his destination. He had only a few sips of water left in his canteen, and good luck finding any water holes in this parched country. At Laramie, Haskell had learned it hadn't rained in over a month.

The buckskin must have smelled the water. It lifted its head and snorted. "Sorry, boy," Bear said. "Soon." He patted the horse's neck and regretted not carrying a third canteen.

He would have taken the stage, but it only passed this way once a week. He took a shorter route than a stage could have taken—one following an ancient Indian hunting trail. At least, he assumed it was a hunting trail, for in addition to the bones remaining from dead soldiers and Sioux warriors and their horses, many bison bones also littered the desert around him.

The sun was becoming a furnace. Sweat popped out on the lawman's forehead and rolled down his cheeks and into his shirt. He rolled his sleeves up his forearms and tipped his hat brim low as the sun continued to climb and grow brassier and hotter.

He paused to give the horse a few sips of the remaining water, then mounted up again and followed the next broad, high-desert valley for another two-and-a-half-hours. Ahead, the Wind Rivers rose—furry green and wax-tipped—against the western sky. To the north, the Bighorns jutted like craggy ramparts. To the south swelled the Laramies.

He remembered feeling as small as a bug while riding through this country before. He felt the same way now, and hoped the buckskin didn't throw a shoe. There were no Indians left to put him out of the misery of dying slow and hard and without water under a merciless sun.

It was with a slow sigh of relief that he rode into the little town of Diamondback in the midafternoon. He'd picked up the stage trail a half a mile back, and now the stage trail became the town's main drag, cleaving the town in two from east to west.

As Haskell continued slowly into the dusty little windblown, sun-seared settlement, outlying shanties and stock pens dropped back on both sides of the trail.

Looking around, Haskell noticed several faces staring at him through dusty windows and over saloon batwings. A man in an apron was splitting wood in the gap between a grocery store and the Wyoming Café When the man saw the stranger riding into town atop the lathered buckskin, he stopped splitting wood to stare. The hot, dry breeze ruffled his thick, gray-streaked brown hair and the waxed ends of his handlebar mustache.

Haskell pinched his hat brim to the man. The man just stared.

The lawman turned toward the Blind Pig Saloon on his right. A head suddenly dropped down beneath the batwings. Haskell could see the owner of the head's bent knees beneath the doors. The man was peering through the batwing's slats.

Haskell turned to his left again, and several faces pulled back from windows in Miss Yvette's Slice of Heaven Sporting Parlor, a dilapidated board-and-batten structure gaudily painted in bright red and dark blue and sunset orange. A carving of a naked woman—naked save for ostrich feathers in her hair and a man's hat across her snatch—was mounted on the face of the whorehouse's second story, near where three half-naked young women lounged on a balcony that looked ready to crash to the street below with the next stiff breeze. Haskell touched his hat brim to the girls as the buckskin clomped on past.

One of the girls smiled. The one sitting next to her, a black girl, elbowed her in the ribs.

Haskell glanced at the moon-and-star badge pinned to his calico shirt. Apparently, Diamondback wasn't all that happy to see a federal lawman ride into town. Unless everyone here was just shy, or half-loco, like the men he'd played poker with back at Fort Laramie. Or maybe for some reason they didn't want a federal lawman poking around and asking questions about their deceased town marshal . . .

Haskell followed a slight bend in the street, which ran gradually upward—for Diamondback had been built on the crest of a low mesa with a rocky ridge rising to the north—toward the town marshal's office. The local law office resembled a giant stone domino with a white-painted front porch, which stood on two-by-two foot-square stilts about six feet above ground. The building's stone basement, partly underground, served as the jail block. The jail block's three front windows, just above ground, were all barred and covered with a fine, rusted iron mesh, to keep anyone from tossing a gun or anything else through the bars.

Haskell pulled his horse up to the North Star Saloon, which stood just west of the jailhouse. Its name was curious since the rough-hewn, log-and-stone grog shop sat on the street's south side. A brush ramada fronted the saloon, and he wanted to get the buckskin out of the sun. There was a filled stock trough there, as well. Dismounting, he turned to the saloon.

Here, too, faces pulled away from windows. A heavy silence poured out over the batwings from the saloon's dark interior.

There were only the sounds of the buckskin loudly drawing water and happily switching its tail as it did.

Haskell slid his Henry repeater from his saddle boot, and draped his saddlebags over his left shoulder. He turned to the folks in the saloon and said, "I got a dollar here for anyone who wants to stable my horse for me."

Silence even thicker than before oozed out of the saloon.

"Alright—two dollars, then," Haskell said, adding, "That's a bottle of good whiskey."

A few more seconds of silence and then footsteps sounded from inside the saloon. The steps grew louder, and a craggy face beneath a cockeyed bowler hat appeared over the batwings.

The man glanced sheepishly behind him then, wiping his large, bony hands on the shabby jacket of his cheap suit, and pushed through the batwings. He was a wizened old fellow, though Haskell thought he probably looked older than his years. Longish, unkempt hair curled over his collar, and he had bags the size of half-filled tobacco sacks beneath his drink-bleary eyes.

He looked at Haskell, then at the buckskin, then back to Haskell again. "I'll take your hoss over to the Bighorn if'n you pay up front . . . uh, Marshal." He squinted at the badge on Haskell's broad chest.

The lawman reached into the pocket of his canvas trousers, and tossed a silver dollar up to the man on the saloon's front porch. The man lifted a hand a good two seconds too late. The coin bounced off his chest and dropped to the porch floor.

"I'll set the other one right here," Haskell said, setting the second coin atop a post of the hitchrack fronting the saloon.

"Much obliged," the drunkard said, stooping with a grunt to pluck the first coin off the floor.

"What's your name?" Haskell asked him.

"Louis Bernard. Who're you . . . Marshal?"

"Bear Haskell."

"You, uh . . . you here to . . . ?" Louis Bernard let his voice trail off, casting another sheepish glance behind him.

"Find the son of a bitch who killed your town marshal—you got it." Haskell dipped his chin to emphasize his determination. "And I'm not gonna leave until I do." He glanced into the shadowy saloon behind the drunkard. "I know that'll likely put the good citizens of Diamondback at ease."

Bernard gave a weak smile as he continued to fidget atop the porch.

"Take good care of my horse, Mister Bernard. I'll check on him later."

Haskell set the Henry on his shoulder, wheeled, and strode over to the jailhouse. He slowed his stride as he climbed the porch steps. A loud din was coming from inside the office—a man and a woman talking in strained voices, and a wooden thumping sound.

Haskell crossed the porch and tipped an ear to the door. A man's grunts and a woman's laughter sounded behind the door planks. Scowling, Haskell tripped the latch and threw the door wide, taking one step inside as he did.

He turned to his left, where Lou Cameron's large desk sat near the far wall but facing the room, beneath a gun rack sporting three old-model rifles and a sawed-off shotgun. A man and a woman were on the desk, fucking.

The woman lay beneath the man, her skirt pulled up to her belly, the top of her dress pulled down to just below her cherry-tipped, alabaster breasts. The man's denim trousers were pulled down to his boots. He wore a buckskin shirt. His bony ass rose and fell sharply as he hammered away between the girl's spread knees. The girl's large breasts jiggled as the young man pumped away at her.

He was grunting and chuckling and the girl was moaning

and laughing. The girl's bare legs flapped against the young man's sides. They both had their eyes squeezed shut. Now, apparently sensing a third party in the room, they both opened their eyes at the same time and jerked their heads toward the big lawman standing just inside the open doorway, the Henry resting on his shoulder.

Their eyes snapped wide in shock.

"What the *fuck*?" yelled the man, immediately pulling away from the girl, rolling off the far side of the desk. "You ever heard of knockin', you big, ugly son of a bitch?"

"Town's on fire," Haskell said. "I figured you'd want to know pronto."

"The town's—*what*?" yowled the man, pulling his pants up, but not before he took a step forward. He fell in a heap over his jeans. The girl said, "Oh!" The man—he was young, maybe twenty, if that—cursed again sharply as he heaved himself back to his feet and yanked up his pants. He shuffled to a window, shook a lock of his unruly sandy hair out of his left eye, and looked out.

"I don't see no smoke," said the kid, looking this way and that around the street. "If there's a fire, how come nobody's ringin' the bell?"

"There's no fire," Haskell said. "I was just messin' with you."

The girl looked at the lawman. She was still sitting on Lou Cameron's desk, and she still had her dress pulled up to expose her snatch and the top pulled down to show off her pretty, porcelain-white breasts. Her breasts were chafed. She was a cute, plump little blonde with a heart-shaped face and curly golden hair. When she laughed, she covered her mouth as though to hide the fact that she was missing an eyetooth.

The kid snapped a piqued look at Haskell. "You was *what*?"

"Messin' with you. Sort of like you was doin' with the girl, only from a distance."

The girl laughed again and shuttled her delighted blue eyes between Haskell and the young man who, Bear noticed, wore a five-pointed star pinned to his brown leather vest. The kid turned an angry, taut-jawed look at her. "Will you stop laughin', Marlene? He ain't funny!"

"He's kinda funny," Marlene said, running her glittering blue eyes up and down Haskell's frame, letting her gaze linger brazenly at his crotch. "He's a big son of a bitch—I'll give him that." She looked at the badge on his shirt. "You a lawman?"

"Bear Haskell, deputy U.S. marshal. I'm here to find out who killed Lou Cameron."

"Ah, shit," the kid said. "That's all we need—a federal badge-toter pokin' his ugly head around here."

"He ain't ugly," Marlene said, staring at Haskell as though mesmerized by the big lawman. "He ain't ugly at all. And he's a big son of a bitch, sure enough." She chewed her bottom lip.

"Why, thank you, Marlene," Haskell said, leaning his Henry repeater against the wall to his left. "You're right pretty."

"Thank you, Marshal."

"Goddamnit!" the kid complained to Marlene.

"Who're you?" Haskell asked him.

The kid had grabbed two holstered six-shooters and a shell belt off a shelf and was wrapping the belt and guns around his lean waist. "Me? I'm 'Big Deal' Melvin LaBoy. Big Deal to you, pal!"

As he buckled the belt, he strode slowly toward Haskell, glaring with menace, spitting out his words through his gritted, crooked teeth.

"Big Deal, huh?" Haskell chuckled and shared a conspiratorial look with the girl. "I seen what you was ticklin' Marlene with, and I've fished with bigger worms than that!"

Marlene laughed again, then again covered her mouth.

"Goddamnit!" exclaimed Big Deal LaBoy. He snapped up

his right six-shooter—a pretty Colt Lightning .44 with an ivory grip—and aimed it at Haskell from four feet away. "No one laughs at Big Deal? You got it, Mister? *No one.* Includin' federal badge-toters. As a matter of fact, *especially* not federal badge-toters!"

CHAPTER EIGHT

"Hold on, now, Big Deal," Haskell said, raising his hands. "You go shootin' me, you'll big a big deal, all right. A big deal doin' big time in the big house if you're not hangin' from a big gallows!"

"I don't like bein' laughed at, see?" Big Deal complained, his smooth, youthful cheeks as red as two ripe apples.

"I understand." Haskell whipped his left hand forward so quickly that the kid didn't see it coming. Bear jerked the pistol out of the kid's fist.

The kid yelped and grabbed his right hand. "Ow—goddamnit!"

"You okay, Big Deal?" Marlene asked, suddenly concerned. She climbed off the desk, stuffing her breasts back into her skimpy dress.

"I apologize for laughing," Haskell said, holding the kid's pistol down low by his side. "I shouldn't have teased you. I was out of line." He genuinely regretted it. The kid obviously wore a large, very heavy mantle of pride on his slender shoulders. Haskell knew how it felt. He'd been young once, too.

"You all right, Big Deal?" Marlene asked the kid again. She stood beside him now. "Let me look at your hand."

"It's all right. I'll live." Big Deal cast a glowering look up at Haskell towering over him.

"What you two need is a drink." Marlene walked over to a stout oak cabinet standing against the room's back wall, near the potbelly Sherman stove and a box half-filled with kindling and split pine logs. A rocking chair Haskell recognized as his old pal Cameron's was there, too. Marlene half-filled two water glasses with amber liquid from an unmarked bottle. She brought the glasses over and gave one to Haskell and the other one to Big Deal.

"There you go," Marlene said. "Now, you boys drink to friendship and gettin' along. I'll be going. I can tell when there's gonna be boring man-talk." She shook her hair back, ran her hands through it, and looked coquettishly up at Bear. "If you need the services of an experienced courtesan," she said, obviously enjoying pronouncing the word, "come look me up. I work over at Miss Yvette's."

"I saw it on my way into town," Haskell said, raising his glass to the girl.

"Bye, then." She winked at Haskell, pecked the still pouting Big Deal on his cheek, and left, humming.

"Down the river of no return," Haskell said to Big Deal, and raised his glass. He took the entire half-filled glass down in two long swallows. "Oh, Jesus—did that hit the spot!"

Suddenly, he felt like a new man. One without the sundry aches and pains and sunburn and windburn of a long ride through tough country. His brain was clear.

He stepped back and drew a deep breath as Big Deal tried to empty his glass in a similar fashion. The kid didn't make it. He took one swallow, then two, his eyes growing bigger and more watery. The third swallow only went halfway down before coming back up and, leaning forward, the kid spat it onto the floor in a broad spray, convulsing.

"Jesus Christ!" he said, straightening his back and running a sleeve of his cream flannel shirt across his mouth. "How in the hell did you do that? That's Marshal Cameron's who-hit-John. Hell, I can taste the snake venom in it. I think one of the stingers on the scorpion Jester Whittle throws into the vat when he's brewin' the stuff is stuck in my throat!"

The kid cleared his throat loudly, worked his jaw, and swallowed.

"What don't kill you makes you stronger," Haskell said, chuckling. He looked at the unlabeled bottle standing on the cabinet. "That ole Lou—he favored the bottom-shelf stuff, he purely did. Good thing, too, since he never made much money, and what he did make slipped through his fingers like pounding rain from a summer storm. His words, not mine."

"You friends of the marshal?"

"That's right. We fought in the war together, came west together. Saw the elephant together a few times. I went into the U.S. marshals service after working for a couple of years for the Pinkertons, and ole Lou went into the saloon and whorehouse business in mining camps up in the Rockies. All of those ventures went bust and then, somehow, Lou took to lawdogging on the local level."

"The marshal never said too much about his past," said Big Deal. "At least, he never told it to me."

"You worked for him, I assume."

"I was his deputy."

Haskell looked at the town marshal's badge on the kid's vest. "So I reckon when Lou got bushwhacked, you got promoted."

Big Deal's eyes narrowed with renewed acrimony. "What are you sayin'? You think I killed him?"

Haskell went over and set his empty glass on the liquor cabinet. "Pull your horns in, Big Deal." He held the kid's gun out, butt forward. Big Deal took it and dropped it into its holster. "You from around here?"

Big Deal shook his head. "New Mexico. I came up here four years ago to work at the Circle-Q, Mister Quimberly's spread." Big Deal palmed both of his pretty Bisleys, spun them on his fingers, and dropped them back into their oiled holsters. "I was a gun-for-hire. When the rich fellers had someone who needed killin'—rusters or nesters, say—around here everyone knew their answer was me. When Marshal Cameron needed a night deputy, he just naturally asked me first."

"Oh, so, you come by that handle honestly, then."

"What—you think I gave myself the nickname just because I like the sound of it? Listen here, Marshal Haskell, around here I am a big-fuckin'deal, and don't you forget it." Big Deal poked his chest three times hard.

"You sure are proddy for such a big deal."

Big Deal canted his head suspiciously to one side. "What's that mean?"

Haskell gave an ironic chuff. "Tell me what you know about Lou's murder."

"How would I know anything?"

Haskell stared at him.

"You think I killed him, don't ya? Just to get his badge!"

"Did you?"

"Hell, no!"

"All right, then," Haskell said, not quite knowing what to make of the younker. "I believe you . . . for now."

"Well, good, then!"

Haskell had sauntered around the office, scoping everything out. He'd made his way over to Cameron's desk upon which the kid had been diddling Marlene, and hiked a hip on the edge. "Tell me what you know about his murder."

"All I know is I found him with three bullet holes in his back. Out there. By the privy." Big Deal pointed toward a back door that didn't fit its frame snugly enough. Sunlight shone around the edges and underneath, where a knot had worn away on the very bottom.

"Show me."

75

"Huh?"

Haskell was getting irritated. "Show me where you found him, Big Deal!"

"All right—you don't have to yell. This whole thing makes me nervous enough as it is. Why, prob'ly half the town thinks I killed ole Marshal Cameron for his badge!"

The kid flicked the back door's locking nail from its hasp and shoved the door wide. Haskell followed him into the jailhouse's backyard.

An old chair sat in a bare spot beside the door. On the ground beside the chair was a dented tin coffee cup. Coffee had dried to a brown crust on the bottom. Beyond, a hard-packed trail angled toward a one-hole privy that sat about fifty feet from the jailhouse, a half-moon carved high in the door. A sun-bleached deer skull was nailed to the privy above the door.

The yard around the privy and the trail leading to it was all buckbrush and sage and stunted cedars and rocks. Split stove wood was stacked four- to six-feet high against the jailhouse's back wall, to either side of the door and the chair. A chopping block sat to Haskell's left as he faced the privy. The head of a splitting maul was embedded in the block.

A pile of split wood surrounded the block on three sides.

"I found him right there when I came to work for the night-shift at seven o'clock a week ago last Wednesday night." The kid pointed at the ground beyond the chair, near the piled wood abutting the jailhouse.

"You think he was shot comin' out of the privy?"

"Musta been. There was scuffmarks and blood right in front of the privy when I found him." The kid walked slowly toward the privy, raking his gaze along the hard-packed trail. "More blood here . . . and here . . . and there."

Haskell followed the kid toward the privy. Dried brown blood marked the clay-colored dirt of the trail and some of the rocks along both sides. There were scuffmarks, as well. Spurs had dragged across the ground, chewing into some of the slender sage branches.

Haskell stopped near the privy door. Just in front of it was a fist-sized patch of blood splashed across a blond tuft of buck-brush. There were two roughly round shapes in the soft dirt of the trail.

"You're right, Big Deal. Good detective work. He fell here first. Must've risen and stumbled his way to the jailhouse." Haskell walked slowly back toward where Big Deal had found Cameron, following the scuffmarks and blood splotches. "He fell again here. Looks like he must've . . . looks like he must've crawled to where he finally . . . collapsed."

Haskell stood staring down at the ground beside the chair and just in front of the wood piled against the jailhouse, to the right of the door now as Haskell faced the building.

"He must've been trying to get to the door."

"That's how I figured it," Big Deal said. "Just couldn't make it."

"Three bullets in him, eh?"

"Yep, three."

"With that many bullets . . ." A thought occurred to the federal lawman. "Wasn't he wearing a gun?"

"No."

"Wasn't that odd?"

"Not if he was usin' the privy."

"How so?"

"When ole Lou used the privy he always . . ."

Big Deal let his voice trail off as he looked at the stacked stove wood right of the door.

"What is it, Big Deal?"

"Sometimes when he'd come out to use the privy he'd leave his pistol and shell belt on the woodpile there."

"Right here?"

"Yeah, about there."

Haskell looked around atop the pile. He shoved his head up close against the jailhouse's stone wall, and looked into the dark, foot-wide gap between the wall and the wood. "I think I see it."

"Sure enough?"

Haskell tried to reach into the gap but it was too narrow. "I need a stick."

He and Big Deal looked around. "There's one." Big Deal walked out into the brush and found a four-foot-long cedar stick with a dogleg bend at one end. "Will this work?"

"I'll give it a try."

Haskell poked the stick down behind the pile and, grunting and chewing his lips for over a minute, finally worked a shell belt with a gun and holster attached to it to where he could grab it with his left hand. He pulled the rig out of the gap and set it atop the woodpile.

Haskell recognized Lou Cameron's shell belt and holster. It was the same one he'd won off a buffalo hunter in Texas when he and Haskell had first come west together. The pistol was the same old cap-and-ball he'd used during the war—an unwieldy, walnut-gripped, nondescript piece he'd had converted to shoot .44-caliber metal cartridges.

"How did it fall back there, I wonder?" Big Deal said. "He musta reached for it and somehow shoved it off the woodpile."

Haskell looked around, scratching his chin. Finally, he shook his head and looked at the gun on the woodpile. "He was down on all fours by the time he reached the woodpile. I have a feeling he was shot once when he first walked out of the privy. He was shot a second time as he stumbled toward the jailhouse. That shot felled him. He crawled from there to here, where you found him. He was probably shot the third time here. He was trying to get to his gun but he couldn't make it."

"Then, how . . . ?"

"The killer must've dropped the gun back behind the wood-pile."

"Why would he do that?"

Haskell felt a ball of fury ignite just beneath his heart. "He was taunting his victim. He was mocking Lou. The killer probably told Lou that he'd give him a chance to get to his gun. But he didn't let him, of course. I bet the killer was laughing all the while. Then he walked around in front of Lou, when Lou was crawling, and dropped the gun and shell belt down behind the woodpile, where Lou could never reach it."

Haskell stared at the gob of dried blood in front of the woodpile. More fury surged through him, causing his ears to ring. He could almost hear the killer's jeering laughter in his own head. "That's when the killer finished him with one more round." Bear shook his head. "Whoever killed Lou did so in a rage. Must've really hated him."

"Jesus," Big Deal said, cupping his chin in his hand and wagging his head as he stared down at where Lou Cameron had died. "That'd take a hard-tailed, bona-fide, died-in-the-wool son of a bitch to pull a dirty trick like that."

"Yep." Haskell nodded, thinking it through, imagining how it had happened. "A hard-tailed son of a bitch who had one hell of a mad on."

Big Deal grunted, then shook his head again.

"Who was that mad at him, Big Deal? Think it through. *Remember.* Ole Lou must've piss-burned somebody right smart. Now, I know Lou was good at that sort of thing, but think recent. Do you remember his getting into it real serious-like with anyone within the last couple of weeks?"

Big Deal stared at the ground in frustration, slowly shaking his head.

"Think!" Haskell urged.

"I am thinkin'," Big Deal said, getting angry again and glaring at Haskell. "You're makin' me nervous!"

"How nervous?" Haskell studied the younker shrewdly. "Nervous enough to jerk those hoglegs again and tear down on me?"

Big Deal ground his jaws. His eyes flashed with fury. "I knew that was comin'. I just knew you was gonna think it was me who killed Marshal Cameron because I wanted his badge. But it wasn't me, I tell you! Me an' the marshal—we got along! Hell, he was like a pa to me, ole Lou was. The pa I never had!"

Big Deal ripped the badge off his vest and extended it to Haskell. "Here—take it! I don't want it! I don't want nothin' to do with it!"

Haskell took the kid's badge. Big Deal wheeled and ran into the jailhouse. His footsteps echoed loudly in the cave-like building. The front door squawked open and slammed closed.

Big Deal was gone.

Haskell pondered the badge in his hand.

CHAPTER NINE

A half hour later, Haskell stared down at the words freshly chiseled into a stone plaque at the head of a mound of fresh dirt in the Diamondback cemetery, on the shoulder of the nearly bald rise just north of town.

TOWN MARSHAL LOUIS J. CAMERON
1840–1889
SHOT FROM AMBUSH
"The Lord hath given him rest from all his enemies."
11 Samuel 7:1

Uncertain of his next move after visiting the place of Lou's murder, Haskell had decided to pay his last respects. The cemetery hadn't been hard to find. There was really no other place for it on the craggy shoulder of the mesa on which the humble town sat.

Haskell had walked here. It wasn't far, but it was uphill in the heat, and he wasn't accustomed to walking. His feet were hot and sore inside his boots, which hadn't been made for walking. But he'd used the walk to do some thinking, though he'd come to no conclusions about anything. While he'd at least learned that whoever had killed his friend had probably done so in a rage, Haskell was really no closer to finding the man or men than he'd been an hour ago.

So why not say a final goodbye?

81

He held his hat in his hands as he stared down at the stone plaque. A handful of withered wildflowers had been laid at its base. Haskell felt heavy with sorrow as well as regret for the harsh words that had come between him and Lou in recent years. While they'd remained friends, because the roots of their friendship had been driven so deep, the friendship had taken a battering.

Haskell felt the need to say something about that now, though he wished like hell he'd done it before he'd had to say it to a rock monument and a pile of dirt only a few feet from which a rattlesnake had left its papery skin. The hot breeze was playing with the skin now, skidding it a few inches this way and that along the ground.

"Well, shit, pard," Haskell began after clearing his throat, feeling a mite foolish about talking to a rock, but also sensing his old friend's presence here just the same. "I sure am sorry we had to meet up again this way. With you down there and me up here. Just know you were my best pal for a lot of years, and I'll remember all the good times we had. As for the bad ones . . . well, hell, I'm sorry I . . . I'm sorry about that. Deeply sorry. That was all my fault. I still can't quite believe I let something like that come between us. I'm gonna make it up to you, pard. I'm gonna find out who did this, and I'm gonna make sure they swing. So, I reckon that's all I got to say. I hope you can forgive what I done. See you later."

"Well said," sounded a voice somewhere behind Haskell.

The lawman wheeled, one hand on his Schofield's grips. He left the gun in its holster when he saw the woman standing about ten feet away from him on the trail that wound up the cemetery hill from the heart of Diamondback.

Haskell's throat constricted at the woman's beauty. Long, dark-brown hair hung to her shoulders though some of it was pinned up beneath the small, black decorative hat trimmed with fake flowers she wore.

Cobalt-blue eyes blazed out from a cameo-perfect, heart-shaped face with smooth, olive skin. She wore a cream frock with small brown flowers printed on it—a conservative dress buttoned to her throat but revealing the swell of her firm breasts beneath it. She wore long, white gloves, and a beaded reticule hung from her right wrist.

"How is it you haven't aged, Suellen?" Haskell asked her.

"Oh, I have. In more ways than one. You can't see them all in this light."

"You're as beautiful as ever." Haskell's tone was vaguely incriminating.

"Why, thank you, kind sir." She gazed at him. "I suppose a kiss would be inappropriate." She glanced at the headstone behind Haskell.

"I suppose it would. Under the circumstances. Is this a chance meeting, Suellen? Or did you see me walking up here? Certainly you don't brave this heat and this sun to put flowers on your husband's grave every day."

"You assume wrong, Marshal Haskell." With a sneering curl of her ripe upper lip, Suellen Cameron strode forward and opened the reticule. She pulled out a spray of relatively fresh wildflowers, though no picked wildflower remained fresh long in this heat. She crouched to set the flowers beside the ones already there, and picked up the old ones. She held them by her side as she straightened and gazed up at Haskell once more.

"I didn't request you outright, but I'd hoped they send you."

"Of course, they sent me. You have any idea"—Haskell looked down at the grave—"who . . . ?"

She followed the lawman's gaze to the marker, and shook her head. "If I did, you'd already know about it."

"Are you sure it's not a jealous lover, Suellen?"

That jerked her head around, cobalt eyes snapping javelins of angry light at him. Her fine jaws hardened, though her lips parted in another sneering half-smile. "I haven't had any lovers since you, Bear. You were the only one."

Haskell's ears warmed. He tried to maintain his composure. "Is that so?"

"Indeed, it is so." The former Suellen Treadwell's southern accent was coming out now, along with her haughty anger. "And, if I remember correctly, that was as much your doing as mine. It wasn't like it took much to seduce you. In fact, I'm not sure which one of us seduced whom!"

"All right, that's enough."

"Oh, now it's enough. Now that you've got your licks in. You don't want to talk about it anymore because you want to hold onto your fantastical idea that I was the lone culprit—the spoiled southern belle, the spoiled, *restless* southern belle who was simply too much for only one man so she had to go after his best friend!"

"Yeah, that's how I remember it!"

"You remember wrong!"

"I didn't come here to argue with you, goddamnit. I came here to find Lou's killer. If anyone would know if someone had a grievance against him, it would be you!"

"Maybe," she said, backing away. "Maybe I do know something." She stopped, gazing up at him, and there was that leering little smile again. "Stop by later for a drink. Maybe, if you mind your manners, I'll fry you a steak. And we can talk."

"Not a chance."

"What's the matter—you don't trust me? Or is it yourself you don't trust?"

"Let's stay on topic."

"What does it matter what topic we discuss, Bear?" Suellen threw a dismissive arm out. "He's *dead*!"

"I thought you southern folk were better at honoring your dead."

Suellen kept her voice low as her eyes smoldered up at the tall lawman. "There got to be too damn many to honor . . . after you Yankees were finished."

"That was your own damn fault."

"There it is—my being southern rears up between us once more. That was the first thing you hated about me. And the second thing—well, we both know what the second thing was."

She chuckled jeeringly, then turned and started walking back down the path. "Stop by later, unless you're afraid, and I'll fix you that drink and that steak."

She cast another challenging smile over her shoulder.

Haskell stared after her, trying to keep his gaze off her round, swaying bottom and her slender back. Her lush, dark-brown hair blew out from her face in the wind. "You still in the same house you were in last time I rode through?"

"That's right!" she said, keeping her head facing the town as she sashayed down the hill.

Haskell whipped his head back around to Lou Cameron's grave, cursing under his breath. He felt a raw male pull in his loins. The more he tried to suppress it, the worse it became. It took some will, but he returned his attention to what had brought him to Diamondback in the first place. He reached into his shirt pocket for a cheroot, for smoking always lubricated his thinker box, but in the pocket he found only matches.

"Shit."

He hadn't had time to stock up on his Indian Kid cheroots, his favorite only because they were cheap and his lungs were tough, before leaving Denver, and he'd smoked his last one at Fort Laramie. The sutler there had been out of all kinds of tobacco, another thing that had the soldiers there looking woolly-eyed fowl and generally off their feed. Surely he'd find

Indian Kids or something similar in the mercantile here.

He needed forty-four shells, as well, and the errand would give him something to do until he could figure out a course of action for identifying and pursuing Cameron's killer. Also, he might learn something in the mercantile, such a business being a commercial hub of sorts.

Seeing that Suellen had drifted on out of sight, Haskell pinched his hat brim to his dead friend, promised him once more that he'd find his killer, and tramped down the hill. Ten minutes later he walked up to Bennett's Mercantile, which was on the north side of Diamondback's main street, not far from the Blind Pig. Haskell had passed it on his way into town.

A loading dock fronting the place stood a good five feet above the ground. Three young men of various ages were handing feed sacks down to a bearded, overall-clad gent standing in the back of a supply wagon beneath the loading dock.

"Well, if it ain't the federal," said one of the three young men—a stocky blond with a broad, sunburned face and deep-blue eyes. The sleeves of his checked flannel shirt were rolled up to his bulging biceps.

"Well, if it ain't so," said the tallest of the three obvious brothers. Appearing also to be the oldest—around twenty-two or -three—this one had sandy hair but the same blue eyes as the stocky kid.

Just finishing handing the sacks down to the man in the wagon, all three young men turned to Haskell. They were sweating and flushed from working in the harsh sun in the mid-afternoon.

The one who hadn't spoken yet, who appeared to be the middle one in age, was the only one of the three wearing a hat—a ratty brown bowler atop a cap of tight red curls. He had long sideburns and a flat, crooked nose. It had likely been broken at one time. His eyes were brown and set too close together, making him look both simple-minded and mean, but otherwise his features resembled those of the other two.

"I'll be damned if they don't pile the government shit deep nowadays!" he said, laughing. "Shit, this federal's as big as a damn mountain!"

"The bigger they are, the harder they fall!" laughed the youngest—the blond husky kid.

The man in the wagon gave the three younkers and Haskell a consternated look, then sank into the wagon's driver's seat, released the brake, shook his reins over his horse's back, and rattled quickly away.

Haskell gained the top of the loading dock and faced the husky kid, bland-faced. "You wanna make me fall?"

The husky kid looked Haskell up and down once more, flushing. "No," he muttered. "I was just sayin'."

The other two laughed. The kid in the shabby bowler said, "You was just sayin' what, Shane?"

"Shut up, Ferrell, or . . ."

"Or what?" Ferrell said, laughing.

Haskell turned toward the mercantile's front door, which was flanked by several shelves and barrels of sundry merchandise. The tallest, oldest kid crossed his arms as though to block the door. "We don't cotton to federals mixin' in Diamondback's affairs."

Haskell walked straight up to him and stopped one foot away. His shadow covered the tallest of the three, whose face blanched. Slowly, he lowered his arms.

"What's your name?"

"Why?"

Haskell just stared at him.

"Cotton," the tallest of the three kids said, looking a little intimidated. "Cotton Bennett."

"Well, Cotton Bennett, what do you know?"

"Know about what?"

"Lou Cameron."

"Lou Cameron?" said Shane Bennett, the husky kid. "He's dead. That's what *I* know about him." He laughed.

Loud muffled voices rose from inside the shop. They seemed to be coming from a back room. Haskell couldn't make out any of the shouted words, but he could tell that one of the shouters was an older man. Judging by the pitch of her voice, the other was a young woman.

"What's that all about?" Haskell asked Cotton Bennett.

"That ain't none of your fuckin' business," said Shane.

"Get out of my way," Haskell told Cotton, who stood blocking the front door, which was propped open with a barrel bristling with garden rakes, picks, and shovels.

"We don't allow federal badge-toters in the store," Cotton said.

Haskell reached up with his left hand and grabbed Cotton's right ear.

"Ow!" Cotton complained as Haskell, tugging on the kid's ear, moved him out of the doorway.

Haskell released the kid's ear and said, "Next time you get in front of me, prepare to lose that ear."

Cotton rubbed his ear and wrinkled his nose, pouting. Behind Haskell, Shane and Ferrell were laughing. Haskell stepped into the mercantile, a small, cramped store that smelled of new denim and wool and cotton and leather boots and freshly milled grain.

A crude plank counter ran along the rear of the store, fifteen feet from the door. A curtained doorway shone behind the counter. Beyond the curtain, the man and the girl continued to argue passionately, but Haskell still couldn't make out their words. There was a cowbell over the door. He reached up and gave it a good shake with his hand.

Instantly, the arguers stopped arguing.

The man said something sharply, tightly, and then footsteps rose behind the curtain flanking the counter. The curtain parted and a pretty blond girl, red-faced from crying, poked her head into the store.

"Can I help you?" she said, sniffing and wiping tears from her plump cheeks with the backs of her hands. Her voice quavered with her barely tethered emotion.

"Looks like you could use the help, Miss," Haskell said, placing his hands on the counter. "Anything I can do?"

The girl's eyes found the badge pinned to his chest. She hesitated and then, swallowing, averting her gaze, pushed through the curtain and walked into the area behind the counter. She was big-boned but pretty, with a round face, button nose, and long, slanted eyes. She wore a simple, gray muslin housedress, long-sleeved and without a single frill. Straw-yellow hair was pulled back into a severe bun pinned behind her head. Her voice was tomboy-husky. "No. I'm just being my typical, cork-headed self, that's all. I don't know up from down and never have."

"I don't get your meaning, Miss . . ."

"Bernadine. Bernie for short. Don't mind me, Mister . . ."

"Marshal Bear Haskell. Deputy U.S. Marshal Bear Haskell."

The girl's watery lilac blue eyes flicked to the badge again, and she nodded. "I see."

"See what?"

She shook her head and gave her cheeks another quick swipe with the heels of her hands this time. "Don't mind me, Marshal Haskell. I'm a silly girl. Given to flights of fancy. Always have been, always will be."

Haskell glanced at the young men milling on the porch behind him, staring into the store. "Those your brothers out there?"

"That's them, all right," she said with a sigh.

"I bet they're a handful."

Bernadine Bennett didn't say anything as she gazed up at Haskell, holding his gaze with an oblique, stubborn one of her own. Haskell sensed a rumbling volcano of emotion inside her. She could barely contain it. He had a feeling, however, that she would contain it, and his prodding her further would only cement her resolve to keep quiet about whatever her problem was.

"I'd be needing some Indian Kid cigars, if you got 'em, and two boxes of forty-four cartridges. Rimfire."

The curtain was swept aside behind her, and a big man—nearly as big as Haskell—stepped out. He'd appeared so suddenly that Bernadine gave a startled gasp as she swung her head toward him.

"Who're you?" the big man asked Haskell. Then his eyes found the badge on Haskell's shirt, and his gaze slid back to the lawman's face. He didn't look pleased.

"Come meet Deputy U.S. Marshal Bear Haskell, Father," Bernadine said, all smiles now though said smiles were stiff as two-by-fours. "Deputy U.S. Marshal Bear Haskell, meet my father, Zach Bennett."

CHAPTER TEN

Zach Bennett had a big, round head with the bulging forehead and dark, demented eyes of a dim-witted brute. His hair was coarse and dark brown, lightly sprinkled with gray. He didn't have much of it left—just a wispy dusting atop his head. The rest of his hair hadn't been trimmed in a while. He wore a long green apron over a blue flannel shirt and denim trousers.

He grabbed his daughter's arm and pulled her back behind him, turning her around as he did. "You git back to work in the storeroom. I want every one of them feed sacks counted and stacked proper before the riders from the Drumstick get here. You count 'em accurate, too, or I'll tan your bottom!"

"You just think you will!" Bernadine retorted, scrunching up her face.

Bennett drew his arm back as if to smack her with the back of his hand. She gave a clipped yowl, bolted through the curtained doorway, and was gone.

"You rule with an iron hand," Haskell said when Bennett turned back to him.

"You gonna tell me how to raise my kids?"

Haskell glanced at the man's sons all standing just outside the open door, glaring in at him, narrow-eyed, thumbs in their pockets or arms crossed on their chests. Haskell turned back to Bennett, chuckling. "You're obviously doin' such a fine job— why would I want to intrude? Bright-eyed, bushy-tailed passel you have there. Cream of the crop!"

"You bein' smart with me, Mister?"

"Pull your horns in, Bennett. You might teach your sons to do likewise before someone snaps 'em like pickup sticks. Just the smokes and the forty-four shells."

"Fresh out of both."

"Really? That's funny." Haskell leaned over the bar and grabbed two boxes of .44 shells off a shelf in the back wall. Then he plucked a cigar box off another shelf a little lower down, grabbed a handful of the Indian Kids, and set the box back on the shelf. "Your inventory must be off."

Haskell laid the cigars on the bar beside the shells, stuck one in his mouth, bit off the end, and spat it on the floor. "Tally 'er up. I got me a drink waitin' somewhere."

"A dollar and six bits for the shells, fifty cents for the cigars."

Haskell reached into his pants pocket. A shadow moved across the counter from behind him. He'd heard the floorboards squeak but he'd waited to react until, out of the corner of his right eye, he saw a long, slender shadow flick toward him.

Wheeling, he raised his left arm in time to keep the garden rake from cracking his skull. He sent his right fist into Shane Bennett's face, smashing the boy's nose sideways. Blood splashed across the kid's face and into both eyes, making him howl.

Ferrell Bennett ran at Haskell from the door, bellowing and lowering his head, intending to bull Bear over backward. Haskell stepped to his own left, grabbed Ferrell by his shirt collar, twirled him around, and threw him through the plate-glass window and onto the loading dock in a shrill screech of breaking glass.

"Ohhh!" Zach Bennett intoned. "Oh, Jesus Christ—my *window*!"

Hearing more footsteps thumping toward him, Haskell turned to see the tall, skinny Cotton Bennett hurling himself at him, swinging a brand-new hatchet.

Haskell ducked.

The hatchet whistled through the air above his head.

He straightened as Cotton was half-turned away from him because of the hatchet-swing's momentum. Haskell jabbed his left fist into Cotton's right ear twice before soundly felling the younker with a right jab to the screaming kid's right temple, splitting it open.

The kid's knees had just hit the floor when Haskell jerked him to his feet and hauled him outside and across the loading dock, tossing him into the stock trough near a hitchrack at the dock's far right corner. The kid hit the water on his back, bellowing and bobbing, the water closing over him. He heaved himself up out of the water and fell over the side of the trough and into the boggy mire the displaced water had formed around the trough in the street.

The kid grabbed his head in both hands and wailed.

Haskell turned to see Ferrell Bennett lying on a bed of broken glass on the boardwalk, waving his arms and stomping his boots, cursing loudly. His shabby bowler lay nearby, speckled with glass. Haskell walked back into the shop. Zach Bennett remained behind the counter, glaring at Haskell with such fury that the lawman thought the older man's dung-brown, close-set eyes would pop out of their sockets.

Shane Bennett was on his hands and knees, clamping both hands over his badly smashed, bloody nose. He glowered at Haskell through fast-swelling eyes.

"Forgot my purchases," Haskell told the older Bennett.

He swiped the smokes and shells up off the counter, then crouched to retrieve the cheroot he'd dropped when Shane had tried to decapitate him with the garden rake. Straightening, he turned to Zach again and said, "You an' me an' your demon spawn are going to powwow about the murder of Lou Cameron. After this little do-si-do in here, all four of you have just moved yourselves up to the top of my list of suspects. You'd best talk about it, get your stories straight."

He tossed a few coins onto the counter, winking at the glaring Bennett. "Till later . . ."

He swung around and walked out onto the loading dock. Ferrell was sitting up now, plucking glass out of his left arm.

"Fuckin' bastard," the kid muttered poutily as Haskell walked past him and descended the steps to the street.

"Careful, boy," Haskell said. "Or I'll arrest you for bad-mouthing a federal lawman while in the pursuit of his duties."

He chuckled at that and looked along the street toward the east and the heart of the ragged-looking, rough-hewn town. A hang-headed figure was slouching toward Haskell on the street's left side. The lawman recognized Big Deal as the kid turned to enter Miss Yvette's Slice of Heaven Sporting Parlor. Haskell paused to light his cheroot, then began strolling toward the whorehouse. Obviously, the townsfolk had heard the cacophony rising from Bennett's Mercantile. Just as when Haskell had first ridden into town, men on either side of the street eyed him warily. So did the only two ladies out and about now in the late afternoon—two gray-hairs in gaudy gowns and picture hats chinning in front of the grocery store.

Haskell touched his hat brim to the ladies and continued heading for Miss Yvette's. He pushed through the heavy wooden door, which was painted lime-green and had a small oil painting of a high-heeled red shoe nailed to it.

The room he found himself in was a large parlor with furniture from different eras, most of it sun-faded and shabby and peppered with burns from cigarettes or cigars. The furniture appeared to have been arranged willy-nilly, and was probably hastily rearranged according to the needs of the clientele.

A baby grand piano sat in one corner, with an American flag

draped over it and an oil painting of George Washington on the wall behind it. A woman's black corset hung from one corner of the gilt frame.

The only two people in the room—a young man and one of Miss Yvette's doves—sat in a deep, brocade-upholstered sofa on the room's far right end, facing a window in that wall. Two young boys were peeking into the dusty window at the pair on the sofa, but neither sofa-sitter seemed to notice. The young man was sobbing about some girl leaving him, and the dove was patting his back and consoling him in soothing tones. Over the young man's shoulder, the dove's gaze strayed to Haskell, and she gave a lascivious little smile and a wink.

The big lawman grinned and pinched his hat brim to her.

He walked straight ahead through a broad open doorway framed by two stout posts from which oil lamps hung, and entered what appeared an eating and/or drinking area with several small tables. Big Deal sat at a table against the wall to Haskell's left, facing the lawman. He had a soda bottle with a metal swing top on the table before him, and he was sulkily building a quirley. A crude stairway of bare pine planks ran up the wall to Haskell's left.

Beyond the eating area, through another broad open doorway, lay a kitchen with a big iron range. Two doves sat at a table near the range. They looked like they hadn't been awake very long. They still had sleep ribbons in their hair. They were dressed in drab wool housecoats over corsets and busters and men's wool socks. They were speaking in low, intimate tones while smoking small, black cigars.

A stocky Chinaman was chopping vegetables at a stout wooden table fronting the range on which two large cast-iron stew pots bubbled and steamed. A big coffee pot smoked on a warming rack. The Chinese looked at Haskell warily, one eye narrowed, muttering to himself around the loosely rolled quirley dangling from his mustached lips.

Haskell waved and grinned at the man, who kept eyeing him suspiciously while chopping vegetables.

"I'd take a cup of coffee from you, Pete," Haskell called to the Chinamen, whom he didn't know from Adam's off-ox. "Dump some whiskey into it, will you?" He tossed the man a quarter. The Chinaman caught the quarter with one hand, wrinkled a nostril at the newcomer, then turned to the range.

Haskell turned to Big Deal, whose table he was standing near. With a sour expression, the kid licked his quirley closed. Haskell gestured at the bottle on the table, near Big Deal's right elbow. "Sarsaparilla?"

Big Deal cocked a reluctant look at the big lawman, sniffed through one nostril, and said, "I try not to hit the firewater till after five o'clock. At five o'clock, though, you'd best look out. Since I'm jobless now, I can get good and drunk all night long. Might paint the town red and shoot it up."

Haskell kicked a chair out and slacked into it across from the kid. He didn't like sitting with his back to the front door, especially in the wake of the trouble he'd encountered at the mercantile, but he saw no way to avoid it save his asking the kid to exchange places with him. He'd keep an ear skinned for trouble coming up behind him.

"That's what I wanted to talk to you about," he told Big Deal.

"What—me paintin' the town red or shootin' it up?"

Haskell opened his mouth to respond but stopped when the portly Chinaman brought over a steaming, chipped stone mug and a whiskey bottle. He set both on the table without saying anything, only staring skeptically down at Haskell, squinting against the smoke rising from the quirley in his mouth. He gave a slow blink and then turned and shuffled back into the kitchen.

He said something under his breath but since it sounded like

Chinese, Haskell couldn't understand it. He didn't need to. Obviously, the Chinaman didn't cotton to him any more than anyone else in the town seemed to.

Haskell reached into his shirt pocket and withdrew the town marshal's badge. He tossed it onto the table near Big Deal's sarsaparilla bottle.

"What's that for?" Big Deal said.

"Pin it on your shirt. That outfit needs somethin'."

Big Deal looked at him dubiously.

"Go on," Haskell said. "I don't think you killed Lou Cameron."

"Well, I didn't."

"I know you didn't. I was fishing. You jerked my line but you're off the hook now, so swim down current. It's less work."

"What's that supposed to mean?"

"Pull your horns in. There's nothing worse than a lawman with a short fuse."

"Well, it's just that . . . I never would have killed ole Lou. Me an' him was pals. He was like a pa to me."

"So you said. I believe you."

"What made you change your mind?"

"There's others in town acting more suspicious than you. Hell, everybody in town looks at me like they were the ones who dropped the hammer on Lou. I'm not sure how in the hell I'm gonna smoke out the killer, but I'm going to stay here until I do. And smoke out his reason for killin' Lou, to boot!"

Big Deal pinned the badge to his shirt. Instantly, renewed confidence blazed in his eyes, and his shoulders seemed suddenly straighter. A more natural pallor plumped his cheeks. "Marshal Haskell?"

Haskell splashed whiskey into his coffee and stirred the mixture with a spoon. "Call me Bear."

"All right. Bear, I got to thinkin' about somethin' after you

97

left the jailhouse."

Haskell blew on his coffee and whiskey, and took a sip. "What's that?"

"You was askin' about the days leadin' up to the marshal's murder. If anything unusual had happened. I remembered somethin'."

Haskell took another sip of the bracing brew and set the mug down on the table. He looked at Big Deal with interest. "What did you remember?"

"About three days before he died, he came and got me over to my boarding house, Mrs. Bjornson's place. I usually pulled the nightshift, but when the marshal had to leave town for one reason or another, he fetched me to man the office. He didn't say much about where he was goin', only that he had to ride out to Weeping Squaw Springs. The marshal rode out there and came back all jittery and short-tempered. I asked him what was wrong and he said, 'Nothin'.' Just like that. No, it was more like, 'Nothin'—just you never mind, Big Deal!' Them was his exact words. So I didn't mention it again."

Haskell sat back in his chair. Finally, a clue . . .

"Well, I'll be damned," he said.

"Yeah." Big Deal touched a match to his quirley, lighting up, blowing the smoke out his nose. "You reckon his trip to Weeping Squaw Springs might have somethin' to do with why he was killed?"

"I don't know," Haskell said. "But I reckon it's worth looking into, sure enough."

He had Big Deal draw him a map out to Weeping Squaw Springs on a piece of notepaper, and tucked the paper into his pocket. He'd ride out there first thing the next morning and see what he could find. Miss Marlene came down the stairs and sat at their table, smiling because Haskell and Big Deal appeared to have made such good friends.

"Which one of you would like to take me upstairs?" Marlene asked, shuttling her gaze between the two men. "I reckon Big Deal got me feelin' all frisky and frustrated, and there ain't been much business yet today." She squirmed around in her chair like there were ants on it.

"I can't," Big Deal said, standing up. He finished off his sarsaparilla and stuck his quirley into one corner of his mouth. "I got me a full-time job, safe-guardin' Diamondback till I can find me a deputy or two."

All business, Big Deal tipped his hat brim to Marlene and then to Haskell, and strode self-importantly across the parlor and out the door.

Marlene placed a hand on Haskell's right forearm, squeezed, and gave him a lusty smile. "How 'bout you, big man? I bet you'd be like fuckin' a mountain, and my pussy just feels so alive right now!"

CHAPTER ELEVEN

Fucking Miss Marlene was like fucking a very animated, very soft pillow.

One that ran her fingernails lightly down his back while he fucked her, and entwined her ankles around his ass, and sighed very quietly but with such luxury and abandon that he could tell she was enjoying it. While Marlene's body was soft, she was deliciously sexy, with a plump belly and breasts like filled bladder flasks—firm yet pliable, the nipples responding to his touch.

In fact, every inch of the sweet, succulent whore seemed to respond to his touch, no matter where he caressed or kissed her. When he ran his hands along her thighs, which were pinned up against his sides, gooseflesh rippled across the smooth, creamy flesh. Nibbling her earlobes made her entire body quiver. When he kissed her throat, she threw her head far back on her pillow, and groaned.

Haskell didn't normally go down on whores, because you just never knew where they'd been, but this girl was so sensual and alive and respondent that he would have eaten her right down to her core, just to find out her reaction. Only, he never got around to it. As soon as they were done on the bed, his shaft was hard again in a minute (in fact, he'd never really lost his erection after he'd climaxed), so he carried her over to the dresser, set her on top of it, spread her knees, and very gently and slowly fucked her while standing. She sat before him, running her hands through his hair and occasionally leaning forward to kiss his lips, his nose, his ears.

She watched, smiling in delight, as his thick, ramrod-hard piston slid in and out of her. Occasionally she slid her fingers down there to let them slide across the top of his love wand as he fucked her.

"I've never been with a big man like you," she said, touching him again, leaning forward to whisper into his ear, "but don't tell Big Deal I said that."

"It'll be our secret," Haskell said, chuckling, pulling her hair back from her face with both hands and gazing into her eyes, six inches from his own.

He liked the way her copper irises glittered, the pupils appearing to expand and contract with the rhythm of his thrusts.

"You sure are fun to fuck, Marlene," he said, grunting softly.

"Oh, Bear," Marlene whispered, closing her eyes lightly and groaning. "Oh, Bear . . . oh, Jesus . . ."

Haskell increased his rhythm.

When he came, he gripped both her plump ass cheeks and drew her taut against him, shuddering. She leaned back on her elbows, cupping her tits and mewling loudly.

When he was finished spewing his cum, he staggered away from the whore and said, "Sorry I came in you, Marlene. I intended to pull out, but . . . I reckon I got distracted." He sagged down onto the edge of the girl's bed. "I hope you don't have a mini-Bear in your oven."

"Not to worry," Marlene said, sliding down off the dresser. Cupping her crotch with both hands, she walked bull-legged over to a washstand. "Miss Yvette has a secret French potion. It takes care of all that—even the menses, thank god!"

When Marlene was done cleaning herself, she went downstairs for a pot of hot water, and returned to the room. Haskell lay back on the bed while the girl cleaned him with the hot water she'd tempered with cool in the basin, and cleaned him with a flannel cloth.

"My, you're impressive," Marlene said, giggling as she eyed his now flaccid dong, gently running the flannel down it in a corkscrew motion. "Are you gonna be in town long, Bear?" She grinned up at him.

"Just long enough to find out who killed my friend Lou Cameron," Haskell said, propping his head on his elbow.

"Oh, that's right." Marlene frowned.

"Marlene?"

"Yes, Bear?"

"Do you have any idea who killed ole Lou?"

"None whatsoever!" She must have realized she'd given the response a little too quickly. She tried to amend it with a softer, more offhand, "None whatsoever, Bear." She tried to give him a level look but she was trying too damned hard.

Haskell sighed and laid his head back on his arm.

Marlene giggled.

Haskell lifted his head to look at her, and saw that his cock was hard again. "Now look what you did," Haskell complained.

"I think it likes me." Marlene smiled lustily, showing her missing eyetooth, which Haskell found precious as hell. She lowered her face to his cock, pressing her lips to the underside of the bulging head. "Don't worry. This one's on the house."

She smiled sexily up at him and then closed her pink mouth over the head of his cock and slid it down toward his belly.

Nearly an hour later, well-fucked and fortified with coffee and whiskey, Haskell paid Marlene for her services, kissed her on the cheek, and stepped out into the cool, dark Diamondback night.

He'd frolicked with Marlene longer than he'd intended. He'd figured that a half hour to an hour with the comely, talented dove would bleed off enough sap that he wouldn't be tempted by the wiles of Lou Cameron's infuriatingly ageless and tauntingly beautiful wife, Suellen. Marlene had been even more talented and alluring than he'd expected, however, and he'd spent nearly three hours with the girl. The late afternoon had turned to midevening, and his wallet was lighter by seven dollars and fifty cents, as Marlene's going rate was two-fifty an hour.

Well worth it, Haskell thought, taking a deep drag off the cool night air touched with the tang of pine smoke. He strolled east along the street's north side, habitually keeping to the shadows of the false-fronted business buildings. The shadows would conceal him from would-be bushwhackers. An ambush was always a threat for a man in his line of work and even more so now, what with the reception he'd so far received from the Diamondback townsfolk.

All except Marlene, that was. She'd treated him just fine. Suellen could greet him at the door of hers and Lou's house on the southeast side of Diamondback in nothing but a smile, and he wouldn't be tempted. In fact, his dick would probably crawl up into his belly at the prospect of any more hide-the-sausage this evening.

Haskell grinned at the thought as he ambled along the street, noting the burning oil pots set out in front of Diamondback's two saloons. From both places—one on either side of the street and three blocks apart from each other—came the low hum of conversation and the competing tinny patter of piano music. From the North Star, which sat just west of the jailhouse and which Haskell was walking up to now, Bear could hear a woman singing along with the piano.

The smile faded from the lawman's lips. The woman's singing made him think of Suellen. Not just Suellen, but his transgression with Suellen, after she'd become Lou's wife. At the time, Lou had owned a couple of high-stakes gambling parlors in Amarillo, Texas. After Haskell had wrapped up an assignment down that way, he spent half a day and the early evening in one of Lou's parlors, drinking on the house. He'd gotten pie-eyed drunk and lost a pile of money, so Lou told him to go on over to his and Suellen's house—Lou would be along soon.

That's how it had happened.

Lou had trusted Bear alone with his wife, and she'd seduced him when he'd been drunk. At least, that's how he preferred to remember it.

What a crazy damned night that had been.

At first, Bear and Suellen had argued after Haskell had confronted her about her past and what he saw as her fraudulent intentions regarding Haskell's old friend and war buddy. Bear had known Suellen before she'd met Cameron. She'd been the daughter of a wealthy plantation owner in Tennessee. The war had wiped out her family, so she'd come west to gather up some of the gold and silver that was said to be spilling out of the mountains and streams.

When she'd found out there was damned little gold or silver, and how much work it took to retrieve what relatively little there was, she'd taken to singing and dancing and anything else to earn a dime. In her brief, turbulent time on the western frontier, Suellen had acquired the reputation of a charlatan— one who seduced wealthy men and abruptly dumped them after she'd squeezed everything she could out of them.

In response to Haskell's accusations, she'd accused Bear of being jealous of his old friend's pretty wife, and had set out to prove it by seducing him.

Try as he might, Haskell hadn't been able to resist her charms. He'd been too damned drunk, and she'd been too damned charming and alluring. His rage had somehow weirdly turned to lust. Or maybe he'd vaguely thought that, by allowing her to seduce him, he would be proving his point. He'd practically ripped the clothes off her gorgeous olive body and mauled her.

Now as he walked toward her and Lou's house, he could hear her infuriating, mocking laughter as he'd banged her, nearly destroying hers and Lou's bed in the process.

Cameron wouldn't have found out about that night if Haskell hadn't told him. Lou had run into so much trouble at work that he hadn't returned home until dawn, long after Haskell had run out of the place, breathless with shame, Suellen's taunting laughter chasing him into the night. Guilt compelled him to confess his sin to his old friend. Cameron had done the worst thing he could have done in response to Haskell's confession.

He'd forgiven him.

And he'd forgiven his pretty wife.

Lou had said he wasn't going to let one drunken debacle ruin his and Bear's friendship or his marriage to the woman he loved. The war had taught him that friendship and life were far too precious to be discarded so easily. No, that night hadn't ruined Haskell's and Cameron's friendship, but it had crippled it. How could it not have? While they'd gone through the motions of being friendly, an impenetrable self-consciousness and guardedness had hovered over their succeeding meetings, few as there'd been.

"That damn woman," Haskell said under his breath, then stopped walking.

He'd heard something.

There were a few trees and shrubs out here, at the very edge of Diamondback, near Diamondback Creek, which he could smell, though he couldn't see it. He wasn't sure what he'd heard, but he'd heard something.

He pricked his ears, listening.

There it was again—behind him!

He wheeled, sliding his Schofield from its holster and clicking the hammer back. What he'd heard had sounded like a boot kicking a small stone.

Haskell stepped behind a cedar poking up on his left. It didn't offer much cover, but if offered a little. He braced himself for a pistol flash and the crash of a round being hurled toward him. That didn't come, however. What he did hear were more footsteps moving off to his left, as though someone had been moving up behind him but was now slipping wide around him, heading off toward the creek.

Haskell wanted to call out, to ask who was shadowing him, but he didn't want to give away his position.

Gradually, the footsteps dwindled into the distance.

Haskell looked around, listening. Hearing no more sounds and seeing no unnatural-looking shadows, he turned and continued on his way to where Cameron had built a small, neat frame house on a slight rise near the creek.

Haskell remembered that during the day the house offered a sweeping view of the Laramie Mountains to the south and the Wind River Range to the west. It was quiet out here, to boot. Cameron had grown up on a farm in Pennsylvania, as Bear himself had, though they hadn't known each other before the war, and Lou had always preferred the peace and quiet of the country to the hubbub of the city. That's why, after he'd lost his shirt in the drinking and gambling business, he'd decided to come here to Diamondback and serve as town marshal—Diamondback being a quiet town on the high Wyoming desert.

The house appeared, a lamp in the kitchen window. He could see the white front porch now.

Haskell quickened his step. Crunching footsteps moved toward him from ahead and on his left. Someone was heading right for him. Again, he snapped up the Schofield and cocked it.

"Who's there?" he said, not having to raise his voice much to be heard on this quiet, windless night. "Name yourself!"

"I will if you will!" came a familiar voice.

"Big Deal?"

"That you, Bear?"

The footsteps resumed. The kid's silhouette took shape in the darkness. Big Deal stopped six feet away from Haskell. He had both his fancy pistols in his hands.

"What're you doing out here, Big Deal?"

Big Deal kept both his Colt Lightnings aimed at Bear's belly. "I was just checkin' on Mrs. Cameron."

"Oh, you were?"

"Yes, I was. She don't like bein' alone, especially this far out away from town. Sometimes the boys from town, when they get liquored up, sometimes they'll pester her. Even did it when the marshal was alive. I kept a pretty close eye on the Camerons' house at night, made sure none of the cowpunchers from any of the saloons was out here, creepin' around, if you get my drift?"

"Yeah, I understand. Holster those pistols, will you?"

Big Deal looked down at the Lightnings in his hands. He gave a wry snort, twirled both pretty pieces on his fingers, and dropped them into their holsters. "They're so much a part of me, I reckon I forgot they was there!"

Haskell holstered his Schofield and looked around. "Did you hear anyone else out here?"

"Anyone else?" Big Deal shrugged. "No. Why? Did you?"

"I thought I did. Comin' up behind me."

"Hmmm. That's funny. Maybe it was one of the ranch hands all liquored up and headin' for Mrs. Cameron's place."

"Yeah, maybe." Or maybe it was Big Deal coming up behind him, then circling around. Haskell pondered.

"That where you're headed?"

"Yep."

107

"You friends with Mrs. Cameron, are ya?"

"I guess you could say that? Does that matter to you, Big Deal?"

"Matter to me?" The shrug again. "Nah."

Haskell cocked his head to one side, frowning curiously. "Tell me, Big Deal—why is it that most folks in Diamondback don't seem in all that big of a hurry to find Marshal Cameron's killer?"

"Oh, I don't know. Is that how they seem to you?"

"Yeah. Leastways, seems like the Bennett bunch isn't in any hurry. They damn near gave me the bum's rush when I went over there for some cigars and forty-four shells."

"Yeah, well, they're an odd group, them Bennetts. I reckon that's all I have to say about them."

"Is that a fact?"

"Say, are you gonna ride out to Weeping Squaw Springs tomorrow, Bear?"

"That's right."

"Need me to ride with you?"

Haskell shook his head. "I'll find the place from your map. You'd best stay here and watch over the town."

"I reckon I'd better, yeah."

Haskell jerked his chin at the house behind Big Deal. "Well, I'll be headin' on over to Mrs. Cameron's now."

"Yeah, I guess I'd best get back to town, see if anyone's bustin' up the saloons or Miss Yvette's place yet."

"See ya, Big Deal."

"See ya, Bear."

Big Deal nodded as he brushed past Haskell and headed back toward the heart of Diamondback. Haskell watched him go, wondering about the kid. Wondering about the whole damned town.

He continued on up the porch steps. He'd just pulled open the screen door and held his hand up to knock when the inside door opened.

"Hello, Bear," Suellen said, standing just inside the door, looking radiant in a deep-purple, low-cut dress and a pearl choker, her thick hair carefully coifed into two neat piles atop her head. Silver hoops dangled from her ears, along with a couple of strategically placed sausage curls. She smelled like fresh-picked roses. "I've been waiting for you," she said. "I was about to start thinking you'd turned yellow on me."

She stepped back and drew the door open wider.

CHAPTER TWELVE

"I've already eaten," Suellen said. "But I kept a plate warm for you."

She removed a plate from the warming rack of the range in her kitchen, set it on the table, and lifted the pot lid she'd placed over it. Steam rose toward the fancy, red-globed, gold-tasseled gas lamp hanging over the table bedecked with a white silk cloth.

Haskell stood in the doorway between the parlor and the kitchen, which was good-sized and well outfitted. He'd noticed when he'd first entered the house that the parlor was nicely appointed, as well. Cameron must have had *some* money when he'd come to Diamondback. Either that or Suellen's tastes had put him in the debt jug, which was entirely possible.

Bear turned his hat in his hands, trying not to look at Suellen, though her figure attracted the male eye—even the of eye of a male who should have been as sated as Haskell, after his tumble with Marlene—like a drunk to a bottle of good whiskey.

Only Suellen was cheap whiskey. Cheap rotgut who-hit-John that would leave one hell of a mark come morning. He had to remember that and steer clear.

"You didn't have to do that, Suellen."

"I don't mind. I bet you haven't eaten much today, have you? Come on, come on. Don't be shy. Peg your hat and sit down."

Haskell had to admit he was hungry. She was right—he hadn't eaten since a hasty breakfast consisting of a plate of the previous night's beans and two bacon sandwiches. He hadn't realized how hungry he was until he'd seen the food.

He hooked his hat on a wall peg, pulled out the chair before the plate, and sat down. Suellen pulled a bottle out of a cabinet, half-filled a tall water glass, and set the whiskey on the table by his plate.

"Bourbon. That's your drink, isn't it? Did I remember right?"

"That's right."

"Any branch water?"

"No, thanks."

"That's right—you take it as dry as Arizona. I remembered that, too." She smiled.

"Congratulations on the good memory, Suellen," Haskell said, a little annoyed by her fawning and sensing that it came wrapped in more than a little irony, though it was hard to tell with Suellen. Everything was hard to tell with Suellen except the succulent body she came wrapped in. More than one man had learned that the hard way, Haskell suspected. More besides himself and Lou.

He dug into the fried steak and potatoes, cutting the meat and eating hungrily. She sank into a chair across from him, the table pushing up her breasts, and rested her chin in her hands. "Where've you been?"

Haskell swallowed a big bite, sipping his whiskey. "Miss Yvette's."

"Oh? Who was the lucky girl?"

"Miss Marlene."

"Ah. She's pretty."

Haskell looked at her. "How do you know?"

Suellen lifted a shoulder. "Diamondback's a small town. Everybody knows everybody. Besides, a pretty girl can attract the eye of a woman just like she attracts the eye of a man." She tittered a laugh. "Well, maybe not *just* like it, but . . ."

111

She laughed again.

Haskell looked at her across the table as he ate. He wasn't going to give her much. Not if she was going to keep flattering like this while staring at him with a hard kind of challenging coldness. She was crazy. He had to remember that about her, too. Cheap and crazy. She'd also imbibed before he'd come. He could see that in her eyes, too. Such a woman shouldn't drink. Or such a man, for that matter . . .

He continued to eat hungrily, throwing politeness to the wind. He also continued not to look at her breasts being pushed up by the table, though he knew she wanted him to take a good, long look.

"Has Big Deal been by?" he asked her, and took another sip of whiskey, glancing at her pointedly across the table but still not looking at her breasts.

"Big Deal?"

"Yeah."

Suellen's cheeks flushed. "No. Why?"

"I saw him outside as I walked up. He said he was checking on you."

"Oh, that's right—he did come to the door. To see if I was all right. Lordy, ever since Lou died, my mind has been in a fog."

"So much of a fog that you forgot that Big Deal stopped by not a half hour ago?"

"Yes, that's right." Suellen frowned, indignant. "What are you sayin', Bear?"

Haskell shrugged and forked another bite into his mouth. "Pretty lonely, are you, Suellen?"

"Of course, I'm lonely. But, no, not just because Lou is gone, though that makes it worse." Suellen got up, pulled the bottle down out of the cabinet, and poured as much whiskey into a tall water glass as she'd poured into Bear's. "It wasn't my idea to move here. To this tiny little town. To this house outside of this *tiny little* town. And then he goes and dies on me, the bastard!"

She threw back a good shot or so of the whiskey, and plopped back down in the chair. She looked at Haskell but didn't say anything. He stuffed the last bite of steak into his mouth, then the last bite of potatoes, and swallowed. He met her faintly sulking gaze.

"Who killed him?"

"I don't know."

"Who do you think killed him?"

"I have no idea. Take your pick."

"What does that mean?"

Suellen swallowed another healthy belt of the whiskey and leaned forward, pushing up her breasts again. "It means that Lou had a lot of enemies. He wasn't the man you remember. Not at the end. When you knew him, and when I first met him, he was sweet. A poet. A rough-hewn poet. That's what I always called him—my burly poet!

"But over the years his drinking as well as his run of bad luck, I suppose, soured him. He turned mean and nasty, Bear. He wasn't so easy to live with. Most of the townsfolk will probably tell you he wasn't so easy to get along with out on the street, either. He was always butting heads with someone. Pushing his weight around in ways that he never did before. He was moody and temperamental. He would make the saloon owners refuse service to certain customers because of old gripes he might have had with such men. Or even because he didn't like how they looked. He once pistol-whipped a shotgun messenger for the stage line. Lou accused the man of having been a Confederate guerrilla fighter during the war, though the man insisted he'd been no such thing. He'd make up stories about people, Lou would. Bad stories. And he'd believe them. It was his drinking."

"I have trouble believing that. That just doesn't sound like Lou."

"You don't have to believe me, Bear. You always did idealize him. He was like an older brother to you—the one you never had. I understand that. But that's the way it was. He ended up getting crossways with nearly everyone in Diamondback. Anyone could have killed him."

"Your grief is overwhelming, Suellen."

She picked up her glass and slammed it back down on the table, a good bit of whiskey splashing out of it. She narrowed her eyes at Haskell. They crossed slightly, beautifully. "It's hard to grieve for a man you'd come to hate."

Haskell drained his glass and sat back in his chair. "Suellen, I'm going to ask you this one more time."

"Ask away." She tilted the bottle over his glass, but he covered it with his hand. She wrinkled her nose at him and set the bottle back down on the table.

"Do you think one of your . . . uh . . . *admirers,* of which I know you probably have many . . ." He looked down at her chest but only to emphasize his point (he told himself). "Could one of them have killed Lou?"

Suellen glared at him. Her eyes were like two howitzers detonated at the same time, flashing. "You go to hell!" She slapped the table hard. A lock of her hair had come undone from one of the piles atop her head, and hung down against her left cheek.

"All right. Well, sounds like that's about all I'm going to get out of this visit." Haskell slid his chair back and rose.

"No, wait—Bear, please, don't go!"

Suellen stood up a little awkwardly, and strolled slowly around the table, brushing the tips of her left-hand fingers along the tablecloth as she did.

"Stay where you are, Suellen."

She stopped at the end of the table to Haskell's left. "He's dead, Bear. Whatever he was, whatever he became, whoever he will always be in your memory, he is dead and buried on the hill over yonder!"

"Ah, the grieving widow again," Haskell said. "Suellen, you're breaking my heart!"

She crossed her arms on her chest and then reached up and slipped the straps of her dress down over her shoulders. The dress dropped down below her whalebone corset.

Haskell's breath caught in his throat.

Christ, even drunk and mean, she was an incredible looking woman.

"I need you to stay, Bear." Suellen reached behind her to unlace the corset. "I'm lonely."

"Stop it."

She adroitly ripped the laces out of the corset, one by one. They sounded like the cracks of a blacksnake. She narrowed her eyes at him, but her lips were smiling. Sneering.

"You remember that night in Amarillo," she said huskily. "Don't tell me you don't. I'll remember it for the rest of my life. Unless I have something better to replace it with."

"I'm warning you to stop it right there, Suellen."

But she didn't stop there. She ripped the laces through two more eyelets. The corset opened, dropping to the floor. Her breasts sprang free. She started to walk toward him again.

Haskell's knees turned to mud. At the same time, fury exploded behind his eyeballs, and he unsnapped the keeper thong from over his Schofield's hammer, slipped the piece from its holster, and cocked it.

"One more step, and I'm gonna pop a pill between your pretty tits, Suellen!"

"Bear . . ."

"Stop!"

She stopped. "Please, Bear. Just tonight. I don't want to be alone . . . *tonight*!" Her voice cracked, she sobbed.

Haskell grabbed his hat off the peg and walked around her, heading for the parlor, which is where the front door was. "I'll send Big Deal over."

She pivoted, following him with her gaze, her swollen, upturned breasts rising and falling as she breathed. Her voice was deep, quavering. "He's just a boy. I need a *man*."

"I'll send a ranch hand over from the North Star."

Haskell turned, holstered his revolver, and strode quickly through the parlor to the front door.

"Bear!" Suellen screamed.

He went out and slammed the door behind him. She screamed his name once more, from inside the house as he strode off into the night. His heart was a racehorse inside him.

CHAPTER THIRTEEN

The next day, in the late morning, the sun already heating up again, Haskell rode toward the X that Big Deal had drawn on the map and found himself staring into a gap between two low, stone-colored buttes where a burned-out log cabin sat, its charred sod roof partially collapsed.

The brush around the cabin was also charred. The stink of burned timber hung heavy in the air. A large cottonwood towered over the cabin on its right. Roughly half the tree had been burned by the fire. The blackened leaves continued to tumble one by one or two by two from the branches, swirling on the breeze as they sank into the yard.

Haskell stepped down from the buckskin's back and tossed the reins over a cedar branch. He walked toward the cabin, the stench growing more cloying in his nose.

There was no porch on the humble place, only a four-by-four square of boardwalk fronting the door, which sagged inward and sideways, propped on inner rubble including a fallen ceiling beam. Haskell stepped up onto the boardwalk and peered into the cabin, seeing only piles of half-burned rubble and gray ashes around a blackened hearth. There were some pots and pans and airtight tins and the skeleton of a rocking chair, but most everything else had been burned beyond recognition.

The pungent stink was so keen that there was no doubt that the fire had happened recently. Within the past two weeks was Haskell's guess.

Had the fire brought Lou Cameron out here?

Haskell moved off the wooden stoop and walked over to a corner of the cabin to take a gander at the backyard. A small log barn had also been burned, though it was still standing. It was nearly entirely charred black, the weeds growing up along its stone foundation burned to the ground. Near the barn was a lean-to stable with a rail corral. The corral gate was open. Whatever stock had been inside had apparently been run off. There was also a chicken coop, to the left of the barn. It had been constructed of stone and logs with a wire fence around it, though the fence was down.

The coop had been burned. Haskell couldn't see any chickens. They were likely dead—either burned in the fire or taken by fox or coyotes afterwards.

The lawman raked a pensive thumbnail down the hard line of his unshaven jaw. He looked around for signs of the culprits. The fire had been no accident, since it had involved more than one building and the stock had been run out of the corral.

He kicked around, eyes to the ground, but not surprisingly, came up with nothing. Any boot or hoof prints would likely have been rubbed out by the wind, the morning dew, or recent rains. There might be some other form of sign, however— something that would give him some clue as to what had happened here and who the culprit or culprits were. He might also find a body or two.

When he found nothing in the yard, he walked out behind the corral to a fringe of cottonwoods and willows lining the bank of a creek bed. A trickle of water ran down the center of the rocky bed, murmuring softly. The water was probably runoff from the springs—Weeping Squaw Springs—Haskell had spotted just before he'd seen the cabin.

He looked past the creek bed and the trickle of water, and something held his gaze.

Two mounds of dirt, sand, and rock.

Haskell dropped down into the creek bed, stepped across the freshet, and climbed the bed's opposite side. He stared down at the two mounds—two graves fronted by crude wooden crosses fashioned from sun-bleached driftwood and rawhide. The mounds, roughly ten feet from the lip of the creek bed, were covered by stones against predators.

Haskell frowned down at the grave on his left, scrutinizing it. He dropped to a knee beside it. At the very top of the mound, the larger rocks had been pushed back to reveal a bald patch of dirt and gravel. A heart shape had been formed in this bare spot with small polished stones likely gathered from the creek bed. Inside the heart lay a small burlap pouch only a little larger than one of Haskell's thumbs. It had a drawstring on it.

Haskell glanced around sheepishly, rubbing his right hand on the thigh of his canvas trousers. The pouch was obviously a memorial, a token of love for the deceased. He hated to desecrate it, but he had a good hunch that the burning of the small ranch and the possible killing of the two people buried here were related to the murder of Lou Cameron, which was the reason he was here in the first place.

Looking inside the pouch was his job. Besides, he'd return the pouch to its place atop the grave when he was finished with his investigation.

He picked up the pouch, opened it, and spilled its sole contents into his right hand. He held up the filigreed gold ring set with a round amethyst stone. It was very small. The ring would barely fit over the tip of Haskell's right pinkie. Obviously a young woman's ring.

Bear inspected it carefully, looking for any possible inscription or initials. Nothing. He could tell by the tarnished condition of the gold that the ring was old. Possibly very old.

"I'll be damned," Haskell said with a sigh, looking around

again pensively.

He slipped the ring back into the pouch, tightened the drawstring, and dropped it into his shirt pocket. He saw something on the ground near his own boot. The imprint of a heel much smaller than his own. It appeared fresh.

He'd just started to crouch over the print for a better look when something screeched through the air just right of where his head had been a half a second ago. The bullet spanged off a rock behind him.

Haskell threw himself forward, hitting the ground on his chest and rolling to his left. Another bullet plumed dirt where he'd first fallen. It was followed by another angry rifle crack. Haskell crawled behind a cedar, put his back to the tree, and tried to make himself as small as possible.

A bullet hammered the opposite side of the tree, making it quiver, spraying bark.

Bear slipped his Schofield from its holster and cursed himself for not shucking his Henry from its saddle sheath. Whoever had ambushed him obviously had a rifle, and the ambusher was shooting from too far away for Haskell's hogleg to be of much use.

Two more bullets hammered the ground around Bear, followed by screeching rifle reports. Haskell glanced around the tree. Smoke puffed from the crest of a low, sandy ridge maybe fifty yards away from him. The bullet hammered the tree again, just as Haskell pulled his head back behind it.

The witch-like scream of the rifle followed an eyewink later.

When no more reports followed, Haskell threw himself to his left, rolling, quickly scanning the terrain around him, then rose to run ahead and left, crouching low, staying as much as possible between the cover of trees and rocks and low swells of ground.

No more shots came. The shooter must be reloading.

Haskell sprinted hard for the ridge ahead of him, which ran roughly from his left to his right beyond another, shallower wash. He had to get to the shooter—or at least get within his Schofield's range of the shooter—before the son of a bitch reloaded.

He dropped down into the shallow wash, tripped over a rock, nearly fell, then got his boots beneath him once more and ran up the far ridge, glancing to his right, which was where the ambusher had fired from. He'd slip around behind the man and then come up behind him.

When he gained the ridge crest, breathing hard from the run, he stopped suddenly. A horse and rider had just bounded out from a patch of shrubs behind a low bluff ahead and on his right. The horse, a black and white pinto, whinnied. Hooves thudded and dust rose as the rider—the ambusher, Bear assumed—galloped off away through the gently rolling scrub country.

Haskell squinted against the sun, trying to make out the rider, who just then glanced over his left shoulder at the lawman. Turning his head forward again, he crouched low over the pinto's neck and whipped the mount's rear with his bridle reins. Because of the seventy-yard distance and the horse's pitch, the rider was a mere blur.

"Goddamnit, you coward!" Haskell barked, gritting his teeth.

Horse and rider dwindled quickly into the distance, the broad arch of Wyoming sky swallowing them. Heading southwest, toward town, Haskell noted.

He cursed again, wishing like hell he'd been smart enough to grab his Henry off his horse. He followed the ridgeline over to where the shooter had fired from, wanting to make sure there'd only been the one. Also wanting to see if the man had left anything behind that might give some clue as to his identity.

Haskell found the spot on the ridge crest from which the

shooter had fired by the several scattered .44-40 center fire cartridges spilling down the ridge's backside, sprinkled around a prickly pear and glistening in the noon sunshine. He crouched to retrieve one of the shells.

Nothing distinguishing about it. A simple .44.

Every saddle tramp in Wyoming carried a .44 Winchester in his saddle boot. Haskell himself carried nothing but .44s, because no matter where he was, he knew he could always find ammo for the weapons, albeit rimfire as opposed to center fire.

He scouted the area carefully, not coming up with more signs than the cartridges. The man's prints were too scuffed to be revealing. All Haskell could tell was that the bushwhacker had small feet. He made a mental note to check the size of Big Deal's boots, then inspected the horse's prints, as well. The only distinctive mark was a slight, curving hairline fracture in its left rear shoe.

Bear made a mental note of that as well, then cast another frustrated glance into the distance where the ambusher had fled. Nothing out there now but prickly pear and sage and the sun and heat blasting off the plaster-pale hills and haystack buttes. Nothing but one lone jackrabbit, that was, nibbling grass growing under one lone, wind-gnarled cedar thirty yards away and casting the human interloper quick, anxious glances, twitching its mule-like ears.

What had the ambusher been doing out here? Visiting the graves? Why? Inspecting his handiwork?

Haskell walked back up and over the ridge. He crossed the shallow dry wash and then the wash through which the freshet ran. He walked up to the two graves, pondering them once more, wishing he'd asked Big Deal who'd lived out here. Knowing that, he'd likely know who was nestling with the snakes under those two carefully shoveled graves.

Who had left the ring and the stones in the shape of a heart?

Haskell cursed as he studied the graves again, then reached into his shirt pocket for an Indian Kid. He bit off the end and struck a lucifer to life on his shell belt. Touching the flame to the cheroot, he thought, *This mystery is growing way too many questions and not one goddamn answer!*

He let the breeze douse the flame and tossed away the match. Puffing thoughtfully on his cigar, he walked back past the cabin to where he'd tied his horse to the cedar branch. He was just reaching for the reins when a bullet slammed into the tree a foot above his hand, sending chips of whitewashed wood into the air around his head.

The horse whinnied shrilly, reared, ripped its reins off the branch, and bolted.

Haskell swung around to face the direction from which the bullet had come, sliding his Schofield from its holster. Two more bullets plowed into the ground a foot in front of him, one after the other, spraying dirt and sand over his boots.

"Drop the hogleg, lawman!"

Haskell froze.

Five horseback riders were just now riding out of the trees and brush west of the cabin. They were forty yards away and closing but riding slowly, casually except for the fact they were all holding Winchester carbines aimed on Bear. They were dressed like cowpunchers in weather-stained Stetsons, wool shirts, suspenders, neckerchiefs, and brush-scarred chaps.

A wisp of gray smoke curled from one of the riders' carbine barrels. The man holding it wore a clay-colored, weather-stained hat with a leather band trimmed with small, round turquoise stones. He had long, straight, yellow-blond hair and a broad, flat face with a badly scarred upper lip, so that his mouth was set in a perpetual sneer. He was the second rider on Haskell's right, and he rode half of a horse-length ahead of the others.

"I said drop the hogleg, lawman!" He snapped his Winchester

to his shoulder and aimed with menace down the barrel, pumping another cartridge into the breech.

CHAPTER FOURTEEN

Haskell cursed under his breath and tossed away the Schofield. He glanced to his right. The buckskin was already a hundred yards away and still going, trailing its reins along the ground.

"Your horse is long gone," said the yellow-haired gent with the nasty-looking lip, chuckling. Spittle flecked out where his lip curved up. He rested his carbine across his saddle horn. "He didn't want no part of this."

"I don't reckon he did," Haskell said. "Can I help you fellers?"

The lead rider reined up about ten feet away from Haskell. The others stopped their mounts to either side of him. The lead rider leaned forward in his saddle and said, "You could have helped us by not ridin' out here today." He slid his small, washed-out yellow eyes toward the burned-out cabin.

"Why's that? You know somethin' about what happened to this place, do you?"

"I didn't say that."

"Well, what do you say?" Haskell said. "Who's in those two graves back yonder?"

"Lawman, you ask too damn many questions—you know that?" barked the rider on the far left of the group. He appeared the youngest of the bunch, dimple-cheeked but with close-set eyes that flashed with emotion. An ash-smudge mustache mantled his girlishly plump upper lip, and a red pimple protruded from the side of his chin. He wore a pinstriped shirt under a ratty brown suit coat, and a tobacco sack hung from around his skinny neck. Three big pistols bristled on his waist.

"Pipe down, young'un," Scar Lip said, keeping his gaze on Haskell. "I got it all under control."

The kid spat to one side in frustration.

Scar Lip said, "What do you suppose it's gonna take for us to convince you that this ain't none of your business and you should pull your nose out of holes it don't belong in, and go on home?"

"I'm a deputy U.S. marshal," Haskell said. "That makes Lou Cameron's murder my business. That and the fact that he was a good friend of mine. Since he rode out here only a couple of days before he was dry-gulched, I'm thinkin' this burned-out ranch and those two graves are tied into his murder somehow. That makes *this* nasty business out here my business, too."

All five riders stared at him over the twitching ears of their horses.

The kid turned to Scar Lip and said, "Ah, shit, he ain't gonna listen to reason. Can't you see that? We're gonna have to kill him, Krantz."

Scar Lip fired an angry look at the kid. "Yeah, well, now we sure are gonna have to kill him, *Willie*! Since you just called me by name, you damn fool!"

"It don't matter!" Willie retorted. "We was gonna have to kill him anyway. He's stubborn as a post. You can see that. He ain't just gonna go on back to Denver and forget the whole thing because you threaten to kill him if he don't!"

"A smart man would," Krantz said, gazing flatly at Haskell.

"Keep in mind he's a deputy U.S. marshal," said the man to Krantz's left, a little timidly. "We sure we want a federal murder rap hangin' over our heads for the rest of our lives?"

Krantz grinned, though because of his scarred lip it was hard to tell when he wasn't, and said, "Who's gonna know?" He glanced to his right. "Jackson, Libby"—he unhooked the lariat from his saddle and tossed it to the man sitting off his right stirrup—"get down there and let's hang us a lawman."

The man took the lariat and chuckled. "Why not?"

He and the man sitting next to him dismounted. Haskell stepped back, spreading his boots wide. There was no way he was going to let these cow nurses play cat's cradle with his head. At least he wasn't going to hang without a fight.

He considered running, then finding cover from which to buy himself enough time to fish the Hopkins & Allen "Blue Jacket" out of his right boot well, but the odds were stacked against his success. These fellers all had their carbines out and ready. They were mounted, and he was afoot. They'd backshoot him before he could get ten feet.

The two men assigned the task of getting a loop around his neck walked toward him, grinning. The one with the lariat was forming a noose and a slipknot at the end of the rope. He swung the noose tauntingly at his side as he continued toward Haskell. The mounted men surrounded Haskell now, closing on him from all sides, hemming him in.

He was trapped.

The man with the rope chuckled as he tossed the noose toward Haskell. Haskell caught the noose in his right hand and pulled on it hard. The man with the rope stumbled toward him, caught off-guard. Haskell hammered his right fist into the man's face.

"*Ufff!*" the man grunted, staggering backward, blood oozing from his smashed mouth.

"Why you . . . !" barked the other man, running toward Haskell with his own right fist raised.

Haskell deflected the man's punch with his left arm and sank his right fist deep into the man's solar plexus. The man gave a great chuff of expressed air as he doubled over. Haskell buried his fist in the same place once more and then smashed the same fist into the man's left ear. The man staggered backward, groaning and cursing.

He tripped over his own boots and fell.

One of the horseback riders tightening the circle around Haskell chuckled. Another one said tightly, "Get him!"

As Bear turned to dodge another attack, a coiled lariat smashed against the left side of his head, burning his left ear. Another coiled lariat struck the other side of his head. Then a horse's wither smashed into him from behind, and he flew forward to hit the ground on his belly.

He could smell horses and leather and man sweat, hear the near thud of hooves. One of the horses whinnied. Another whickered. The riders were ominously quiet. Dazed, Haskell pushed up onto his hands and knees. As he lifted his head again, he saw the ugly bastard otherwise known as Krantz thrust his rifle toward him, butt-first.

The butt smashed against Haskell's left temple.

Haskell's head snapped back. Cracked bells rang with excruciating loudness in his head, and a massive cloud slid across the sun. His body felt heavy. He felt as though a rock had been tied around his neck, and the rock was pulling him to the bottom of a very deep, dark sea.

Vaguely, he was aware of his arms being jerked back behind him. Too late he realized a rope was being coiled around his wrists behind his back. Terror racked him, and he gasped as he tried to pull his hands free, but they were held fast by the rope.

He felt the rake of hemp against his ears, then around his neck. He could smell the burning-weed scent of the rope. His blood turned cold and his heart hiccupped when he felt the noose pulled taut around his neck. The hemp prickled as it bit into him.

"Get him up! Get him up!"

Rough hands pulled him to his feet. Haskell opened his eyes and through a gauzy fog of semi-consciousness saw the five men surrounding him, their horses flanking them. The man with the smashed mouth sneered behind the others. Haskell head-butted the nearest man, who cursed sharply and stumbled backward. The kid, Willie, laughed shrilly. Another man buried his fist in Haskell's belly.

Haskell jackknifed as the air rushed out of his lungs.

The rope drew even tighter around his neck, and they used the rope to pull him over to a stout cottonwood. He ran, staggering, trying to drop to his knees but a man on either side held him up by his arms. Fear and fury were a hot wash inside him. He thought of the Blue Jacket in his boot.

If only he could get one hand free, but his wrists were tied fast behind him . . .

They stopped him. Willie had the rope now. He tossed it up over a low, stout branch of the cottonwood. Catching it as it fell back toward him, he gave Bear a wolfish grin. "Necktie party in your honor, Marshal, sir!" He gave a mock, two-fingered salute.

"I'm gonna kill you, you little fucker!" Haskell raked out.

"Not in this life, Marshal, sir!" Willie laughed.

Haskell bolted toward him. Willie screamed, dropped the rope, and ran. Krantz stepped in front of Haskell and buried the butt of his Winchester in the lawman's belly.

That felled Bear to his knees again. He gasped, trying in vain to draw air back into lungs that felt the size of raisins.

"You little coward!" Krantz shouted at Willie, who turned back, blushing sheepishly.

The kid pointed at Bear as he walked back toward him. "He's a handful, that feller!" He laughed nervously.

"Pick up the rope and tie it to your saddle horn, Nancy boy!" Krantz ordered the kid.

"No need to call me names, Krantz!"

While Bear continued to fight air back into his lungs with only gradual and moderate success, Willie led his horse to the tree by its reins, picked up the end of the rope, mounted the gelding, and dallied the rope around his saddle horn. The other men swung into their own saddles.

Haskell's head jerked up as Willie began to back his horse away from the tree. The rope cut into his skin, pinching off his wind. He fought it, rolling his shoulders and swinging his neck like the proverbial bear he'd been named for. Fury dropped a red veil over his eyes.

He locked his gaze on Willie, as Krantz backed his own horse away beside the grinning youngster. The rope drew tighter and tighter, pulling Haskell up off the ground. Staggering, he got his boots beneath him, trying to put some slack back into the rope. He managed to do so fleetingly, but Willie, grinning at his quarry, pressing his pink tongue to the bottom of his plump lower lip, continued to back his horse away.

Haskell's head was pulled up farther.

Farther . . .

"Ah, Christ!" he tried to say but it was only a strangling sound in his throat.

He heard the bones in his neck grind and pop as the line grew tighter and tighter and his heels rose from the ground.

Willie kept backing away, backing away, that taunting, delighted grin in place. Beside him, Krantz grinned, too, as he talked with the others. Haskell couldn't hear what they were saying because of the gelded boys' choir screaming in his ears.

He knew they were mocking him. Mocking him as they lynched him . . .

His body turned cold as his boot toes rose up off the ground. His spine was drawn so taut that he was sure it would snap like a dry twig. Now he was hanging, his chin pulled so far up that he was staring at the cottonwood's leaves glinting like gold-minted coins in the sunlight. He felt himself jerk as the sky and the tree and its overhanging branches swung around him, though he knew that it was he himself who was twisting and turning at the end of the rope.

He tried to suck air into his lungs, but he couldn't get anything past the rope pinching his throat. His head felt swollen to twice its normal size. He thought his eyes would explode in their sockets. His tongue was like a shoe in his mouth.

As though from far away, his tormentors laughed.

Gradually, Haskell's head grew light. He became dizzy. The chill released its grip on him, and soothing warmth oozed into his veins. Only vaguely he could feel his body spasming, revolting against the lack of oxygen feeding it. His heart, which had been drumming like thunder in his ears, fell quiet.

That massive cloud again passed over the sky, darker than before.

The world went quiet.

Something large and unyielding slammed into the bottom of his boots, threatening to drive his hips up into his ribs. It was a savage, all-encompassing blow. That big solid, angry thing smacked his back and the back of his head, against his will jolting something awake in him. He'd gone to a peaceful place, a place where his misery had eased, and he didn't want to be taken out of it.

His heart gave one logy rumbling thud against his breastbone. He thought he could smell the earth and the hot grass.

Another voice reached his ears. Not a man's laughing voice this time. Not a voice of one of his tormentors, but a woman's voice.

Gradually, as the woman called to him, Haskell's consciousness rose toward her voice until she more clearly screamed, "Oh, damn you, Bear—if you're dead I'm just going to *kill* you!"

CHAPTER FIFTEEN

A diamondback rattler of enormous strength was wrapping itself around Bear's neck, digging into his skin and choking out his life.

He lifted his head with a horrified grunt, reaching up to pry off the snake with his fingers.

"Bear! Oh, no, honey—you're fine!"

Suellen Cameron smiled down at him, the copper light of a small fire glinting in her hair. The fire was behind her. They were outside. It was dark. Looking up, Haskell saw a velvet sky full of twinkling stars.

"Where . . . the . . . hell . . . are we?" he croaked out, his sore throat sounding froggy to even his own ears. He swallowed, wincing against the pain.

"We're in the same place," Suellen said, glancing around darkly. "Where I found you."

Haskell turned his head, grinding his teeth against the stiffness in his neck. He saw the stout cottonwood reflecting the firelight, and it all came back to him.

"Shit," he said.

"It's all right, Bear. You're okay now, honey. Lie back against my lap. That's it. You need to rest."

He realized that his head, filled with misery, was resting on Suellen's right thigh. A cloth bandage was wrapped around his forehead. Her leg was warm beneath him. A wool blanket covered him. Suellen had a similar blanket draped about her shoulders. She wore a green felt hat and a wool-lined denim jacket over a cream shirtwaist and dark-blue wool skirt. Brown leather riding boots rose nearly to her knees.

"What?" Haskell tried, his voice a mere rasp. "How . . . ?"

He gave an anguished grunt and threw back his blanket. His bladder was ready to explode inside him. He struggled into a sitting position, trying to get his legs to work. His head throbbed, the result of Krantz's Winchester love tap. Bear's back was stiff and sore, his neck even more so. It felt as though someone had punched a broken wheel spoke through it, and the splinters were grinding around between the bones.

"Oh, Bear, you must be still!"

"Can't!"

"What're you doing? You can't go after them now."

"I'm not going after anything just yet," he said, frustrated by his inability to raise his voice much above a cat's purr, "except a good piss!"

"Oh," Suellen said.

Haskell stumbled a few yards away from the camp. Fuck modesty. His bladder seams were unraveling. Besides, his body felt as though he'd been trapped for the past month in some sort of torture contraption from the Dark Ages. He fumbled with his fly buttons, hauled himself out, and cut loose with a long, warbling sigh.

"Ah, shit," he rasped with the luxury of his evacuation. "That feels good!" At least something did.

His piss hit the cold ground and steamed.

Behind him, Suellen chuckled.

Haskell looked around him. A small, red-wheeled, two-seater buggy was parked nearby. Two horses, both picketed to pines, grazed beside it. One of the horses was Haskell's own—the buckskin he'd acquisitioned from Fort Laramie.

"My horse," he rasped in surprise.

133

"I found him at the springs when I went for water," Suellen said.

He glanced over his shoulder at her, frowning. "When you . . . ?"

He shook his head. He'd wait and get the whole story when he was finished with the task at hand and was better able to comprehend it. The lack of oxygen had made him foggy and dull. He felt half-drunk.

When he was finished and feeling better at least in that regard, he tucked himself back into his pants, buttoned up, and walked back to the fire. Suellen was poking a stick into the flames, arranging the burning branches. A coffee pot steamed on a rock.

Massaging his neck, Haskell tried again to clear the frog from his throat, achieving moderate success, and said, "What're you doing out here?"

Suellen tossed the stick into the fire and rubbed her hands on her thighs. "I saw you ride out earlier. I'd gone into town to buy some eggs. I was restless, so . . . I decided to follow you. To see where your trail led. I knew you were investigating Lou's murder, and . . ."

"And you were curious what I'd come up with?"

She hiked a shoulder. "Yes."

"You could have waited and asked me when I got back to town."

Suellen's eyes blazed. "Well, as it turned out, if I hadn't ridden out here, you'd have never got back to town—now, isn't that right, dear heart?"

Haskell's ears warmed with chagrin. He sat down where he'd been sitting before. She'd piled his gear there, including his saddle, right where he must have fallen when she'd cut him down from the tree. "I reckon you're right, Suellen. Don't tell me you were able to scare them brigands off!"

"That's what I did, all right." She seemed right proud of herself. "I saw them all gathered around a man hanging from that cottonwood, and I gigged old Rufus right toward them." She rolled her eyes toward the cream gelding grazing beside Haskell's buckskin. "I yelled and hollered and shouted till my lungs were fit to bust, and, guess what? They turned and hightailed it like Georgia shoats smellin' peach-orchard wine on the evenin' breeze!"

Her accent had thickened as her emotion had climbed, and now she sounded as though she'd never left the South, but was sitting on a padded swing chair on some white-painted promenade overlooking dewy jade hills studded with mossy oaks, a fine spring mist spitting down from a soft, hazy Georgia sky. Her eyes danced as she threw her head back, laughing.

"I guess they didn't want to be seen around a dead man, and, since they didn't seem to have the hide for killing a lady, they fogged the sage, as Lou used to say!"

Her laughter was short-lived. She beetled her dark-brown brows. "Who were they, Bear?"

"I was going to ask you the same question."

"I didn't see any of them up close. Even if I had . . ." Suellen hiked her shoulder again. "I've never got out much, got to know the town. I take my buggy for rides in the country from time to time, but I do try to avoid the lowly sorts that populate these parts. I ride out here to get *away* from the people of Diamond-back, not go looking for *more* out in the county."

"How in the hell did you get me down?"

"Lou always kept traveling gear in the buggy for me. He knew how I liked to take my rides, and he was afraid that if Rufus ever went down or I got lost, I'd be stranded overnight. He packed matches and blankets and whatnot, including an ax for firewood. I used the ax to cut you down. Took me a few whacks, but I cut through that rope, by god!" She smiled with concern. "I'm sorry I couldn't have found some gentler way."

Haskell massaged his neck again, then cleared his throat. "It did the trick, I reckon."

"You're sounding better. How do you feel?"

"Better."

Suellen sank down beside him, stretched one arm across his shoulders, and placed her other hand on his thigh. "You seemed to be regaining consciousness when I first found you, but then you passed right out again. I could feel your heart beating, hear you breathing, so I built a fire as quick as I could to get you warm. Then I unsaddled your horse. You were out quite a while. I was beginning to think you'd never wake up, that you'd just lie there and die with your head in my lap."

"I'm still kickin', Suellen."

"I declare, Bear, I don't think I could have bore it—losin' you both so close together!"

"Like I said, Suellen, I'm still kickin'."

"Can't you at least put your arm around me, Bear? I'm cold, and it's awfully dark out here."

"Let's not go back to where we left off last night—all right, Suellen? I got enough on my plate right now."

"Oh, Bear, why do you have to be such an obstinate son of a bitch?"

"Can I have a cup of that coffee?"

"Sure, sure." Suellen strode around the fire and filled a tin coffee cup, using a swatch of ragged burlap so as not to burn her hand.

"You got any whiskey?"

A guilty flush rose in her pretty, classically sculpted cheeks as she said, "Brandy."

"That'll do."

She walked over to where a leather war bag sat on the ground near the trunk of the cottonwood, and pulled out a small, hide-wrapped flask. She removed the cap from the flask and splashed a goodly portion of brandy into Haskell's coffee. She gave it to him, and as she went back around the fire to pour herself a cup of coffee, he blew on his own and said, "Suellen, you know who lived in that burned-out ranch headquarters behind us there?"

"Yes, I do." Suellen set down her filled cup and cast a frown into the darkness south of the cottonwood. "What happened to that place, Bear?"

"That's what I'd like to know. Who lived there?"

"Bliss Lomax and his daughter, Clara."

Haskell frowned. "I thought you didn't know many folks around here."

"Bliss and Clara Lomax are the exception. I've ridden out this way before, and stopped at the springs for water. That's how I met Bliss and Clara, his daughter. Clara's a bit shy, but Bliss is very friendly. He always offers to check Rufus for me, to make sure his shoes are sound, and Clara often brings me out an apple or a hard-boiled egg. They don't get many visitors out here, and I think they're lonely. Clara is a half-breed girl. Bliss told me that his wife had been Hunkpapa Sioux. She died some years ago, when a horse bucked her off and she hit her head on a rock."

Suellen frowned concernedly toward the cabin again. "I do hope they weren't in that fire!"

"I think they were."

Suellen gasped and slapped a hand to her chest. "Bear, no!"

"There's two graves out back of the place. I don't know if it's them or not, but who else would it be? I don't know if they died in the fire, or if they were shot. I'll probably never find that out. But I am going to find out who killed them, though I probably already know."

"The men who hanged you?"

"Who else?" Haskell sipped his coffee, instantly soothed a

137

little by the brandy. "What I want to know is why."

Suellen was staring toward the cabin hidden in the darkness. Haskell saw a tear dribble down her cheek, turning to liquid gold when the firelight hit it. Haskell found himself surprised by her show of emotion. He'd always thought she was so wrapped up in her own sorry story that the stories of others couldn't touch her.

Maybe she'd changed. He supposed even Suellen could change, though he was still skeptical.

Haskell took another couple of sips of his spiked coffee, then rested the cup on his thigh. "Have you ever heard of a man named Krantz? A kid called Willie?"

Suellen turned to Bear, both eyes bright with emotion. She blinked, brushing a tear from her cheek with her hand. "Is Krantz an ugly man with a scarred lip?"

"Yep."

Suellen nodded darkly. "I've seen him in town a few times when I've gone in to shop. He ogles me in the most lewd way imaginable." She shuddered as though cold, and drew the blanket more tightly around her shoulders.

"Did you tell Lou?"

Suellen shook her head. "He would have made too much of it. He would have turned it into something even uglier than what it was." She shook her head again, then sniffed. "I let it go."

"Do you know where I might be able to find this Krantz feller?"

"I have no idea. I'm sure he rides for one of the ranches, but I don't know which one. There are several around here."

Haskell tried to remember if he'd seen a brand on any of the horses. He was sure he had, because, being both a lawman and naturally curious, he was habitually observant. Under the circumstances of his encounter with the five riders earlier, however, he might have been too distracted to let any of the brands burn itself into his brain.

"Let's get back to Bliss and Clara Lomax," he said. "Do you have any idea why Krantz would want them dead? Or why the man Krantz works for would want them dead?"

"Of course not," Suellen said a little defensively. "Why would I know that?"

Haskell studied her. "I'm just asking, Suellen."

"Well, stop asking so many questions!" She leaned against him, rubbing her forearm against his arm like an affectionate cat. "I'm cold."

"It's my job to ask questions. And I got one more."

"Oh, get it over with, then!"

"Did you ever see Clara Lomax in town?"

Suellen took a moment to answer. Then she nodded her head against his shoulder, and said, "Yes. A few times. But, remember . . ."

"I know—you stay home most of the time."

"I don't like to associate with those people. Leastways, most folks in Diamondback. The unwashed lot of them!"

Haskell gave a wry snort and took another sip of his coffee. "You can take the belle away from the ball, but you can't take the ball away from the belle."

"Oh, shut up, Bear. I'm cold. Why won't you hold me?" She looked up at him with her soft doe eyes, the firelight dancing in them. She pressed her chest against his arm.

Haskell tried to ignore the sensation. "Did you ever see Clara with anyone in town? A boy, maybe? A *certain* boy?"

He was thinking of the kid who'd bushwhacked him just before Krantz and Willie had shown up.

Suellen sighed, disappointed by his response, or lack thereof, to her intimacies. "No, I never saw her with any boy. The only person I ever saw her spending any time with at all was

139

Bernadine Bennett."

"Bernadine Bennett."

"That's right. Her father runs—"

"The mercantile, I know." Haskell frowned as he stared pensively off toward the horses munching grass and, occasionally, idly stomping their hooves.

"They appeared to be pretty good friends," Suellen added. "I've never known either to be much of a talker, but when they were together they chatted up a storm. I guess they found themselves soul mates, of a sort." She looked up at Haskell, hugging his arm. "I've always felt that way about you and me, Bear. Despite our obvious differences, of course. Where we both come from."

"Soul mates," Haskell said, still staring into the darkness. But what he was seeing was the heart traced into the top of one of the two graves behind the burned cabin. And the ring snuggling down inside the small, hide sack, itself nestled inside the heart.

"Oh, Bear, you're so tiresome!" Suellen heaved herself to her feet, and, holding the blanket tight around her shoulders, stomped off into the darkness.

Haskell sipped his coffee, thinking over what he'd learned. Making plans for tomorrow. Suellen returned to the fire. She was carrying her boots and socks and some white garments that Haskell couldn't make out in the fire's dim light. She tossed the boots and the garments down by the fire and then walked barefoot over to Haskell.

She stood over him, the fire flanking her on her left. She stared down at him for a long time, her bare feet planted in the grass beside him. He couldn't see the expression on her face. She lifted her right hand. There was something in it. Something heavy.

The firelight danced along the barrel of his nickel-plated Schofield.

Taking the pistol in both hands, she aimed it at him.

Haskell's pulse quickened. He looked at the gun, which he'd forgotten about with his sundry other distractions. She'd apparently found it where he'd tossed it down some distance from the cottonwood.

"What're you doing, Suellen?"

CHAPTER SIXTEEN

"I could kill you, Bear," Suellen said.

Haskell's mouth had gone dry. He cleared his throat, which was finally opening, and said, "Why's that?"

"For what you do to me, and give me no satisfaction," Suellen said tightly, angrily. "I should kill you for that."

Haskell lifted his right hand. "Give me the gun, Suellen."

"He's dead, Bear."

"I know he's dead, Suellen." Haskell paused, his mind twisting and turning in on itself. "Did you kill him?"

"I told you I didn't."

"Why are you aiming my gun at me?"

"Fuck me."

Haskell studied her eyes, like dark pennies in the shadows. "Say again?"

"Fuck me and I'll give you your gun back."

"Suellen . . ."

"He's dead, goddamnit, Bear!"

Haskell lurched forward and grabbed the gun. She gasped with surprise but did not resist. He jerked it out of her hand, and sagged back down against his saddle. Standing over him, she crossed her arms on her chest and slid her shirtwaist off each shoulder. She wore nothing beneath it. When her breasts stood proudly out from her chest, the fire gilding the outside curve of the left one while relieving the other one in alluring shadow, she crouched down, grabbed the hem of her skirt in both hands, and straightened. The dress rose to expose her long, lean legs and the glove-like tangle of hair at the top.

Suellen didn't say anything. She just stood staring down at Haskell, enticing him, taunting him with her beauty.

His heart knocked against his ribs.

He fought his gaze away from the woman standing over him. His throat seemed to be swelling shut once more. He rolled over, set his pistol down beside him, rested the side of his head against the wool underside of his saddle, and said, "Good night, Suellen."

"Bastard!" she cried, and kicked his back.

It wasn't much of a kick. Even if it had been, he wouldn't have minded. His cock was as hard as oak, and he needed a distraction from the image of her bare breasts and her pussy. He closed his eyes, yawned, and feigned sleep.

Sobbing, Suellen lay down beside him. He could hear her pull her blanket up with a grunt, felt her turn over and ram her round ass against his own. Her butt quivered as she cried.

"I'm so lonely," she said. "I'm so, so lonely! You don't understand how lonely I am!"

Haskell didn't say anything. He tried to sleep. His dong remained painfully hard, pressing against his trousers. Try as he might, he couldn't scour from his thoughts the image of her lying beside him, naked under her shirtwaist and skirt, her body quivering, breasts jostling. He flashed on how her pussy must feel—warm and damp with emotion.

Haskell rolled onto his back and looked at the stars. "Sorry, pard. But a man can only take so much."

Suellen stopped crying. "What?"

Haskell rolled toward her, worked his hand under her blanket, lifted her skirt, and placed his hand against the smooth globe of her ass. "I was just asking Lou's forgiveness."

She started to roll toward him, but he stopped her by tightening his grip on her bare ass. She groaned. He snaked his middle finger down between her legs, into the tangle of hair, and dipped it into the warm, tender flesh of her cunt.

"Ohh!" she said, throatily.

He slid his finger farther inside her. *"Oh!"* she said again, lifting her rump a little to meet his hand. She panted, quivered, as he slid his finger deeper, deeper.

"Oh, yes," she said, swallowing, rolling onto her belly and shoving her butt up closer against him, causing his finger to go in even deeper. "Oh, yes . . . god, that feels good!"

"You like that?" he said tightly, anger mixing with the lust she'd ignited inside him.

"Yes," she said, and swallowed again, breathing hard. She turned her head to one side, glancing at him over her shoulder. "But you know what would feel even better, Bear?"

"What's that, Suellen?"

"Your big cock!"

Haskell heaved himself to his feet. "I got just what the doctor ordered, Suellen!"

He unbuttoned his pants, shoving them down to his ankles. He opened his fly and pulled out his jutting dong. She looked up at him, her mouth forming a perfect dark O in the amber-tinted shadows there by the fire. Her eyes glinted.

Haskell dropped to his knees.

"Oh," she wheezed, looking at him. "Oh, oh, god!"

He wrapped his right arm around her belly, drawing her up taut against him. He brusquely spread her legs with his knees and then drew her back toward his hips. The pink folds of her pussy opened. He slid his cock inside.

Deeper . . .

Deeper . . . her love honey closing around him, the walls of her cunt grabbing him tightly, like a fist clenched in desperation.

"Ohhh!" Suellen said, facing the ground now, propped on her forearms. "Oh, fuck me, Bear. Fuck me!"

Haskell rammed himself against her hard, building to a violent crescendo. Suellen tossed her head like a mare being studded, thrashing wildly against his thrusts.

He spent himself and released her. She dropped forward against the ground, mewling.

Haskell stumbled off to relieve himself, then returned to his blankets. Suellen remained as he'd left her, belly down, back rising and falling as she breathed.

"Thank you, Bear," she said.

"Go to sleep, Suellen."

Haskell rolled over and went to sleep.

Haskell rose early the next morning, pulled on his boots, and built up the fire. He worked quietly, letting Suellen sleep. He brewed a pot of coffee and then squatted by the low flames, watching her in the gray dawn light, sleeping soundly beneath her blanket.

She'd gotten up to clean herself at the springs, but then she'd come back to bed, and he didn't think she'd stirred once all night long. She slept now on her belly, face turned toward him. A faint, almost celestial smile curved her perfect mouth.

"She's a woman who needs to be needed," he told himself.

Last night, that man was him. Who would it be once he was gone? She was alone now. She wasn't a woman who could live alone. Yet, she was too much woman for just one man . . .

A thought pricked at Haskell. He realized that it had been nibbling away at the edges of his consciousness for a while now, ever since he'd had supper at Suellen's place two nights ago.

Had Lou become a sour alcoholic because of Bear and Suellen's betrayal?

Lou might have outwardly forgiven them, because he hadn't

145

had much choice aside from losing his best friend and the only woman he'd ever loved. But had he forgiven them deep down inside himself? Or, even more, had he forgiven himself for not being man enough to keep her happy? Despite the fact that such a task was likely impossible . . .

"Ah, Christ," Haskell said, tossing his coffee grounds on the fire.

They sputtered and popped, steaming.

Suellen lifted her head with a start, slitting her eyes and looking around through the fog of lingering sleep.

"What's . . . what's happening?" she said.

"Time to get up. Gather your gear. I'll be pulling out."

She moaned, shivering inside her blankets. "Come back to me, Bear. I'm cold!"

"I'll be pulling out in ten minutes. Get up, have a cup of coffee, and gather your gear." He hooked a thumb over his shoulder. "I've hitched your horse to your buggy."

"Oh, pooh on you!" She smiled at him through the tangled mess of her hair. But even just waking up, she was sexy as all hell. "How do you feel?"

Haskell filled a coffee cup from his steaming pot. "I fucked my best friend's wife. A second time. And I enjoyed it. How do you suppose I feel?"

He walked over and handed her the smoking cup. She beamed up at him. "You just admitted to me that you enjoyed it."

Haskell wasn't sure why, but he felt tender toward her. Maybe because she was alone now, and seemed more pathetic because of it. Maybe because his feelings for her had grown in some way since last night, despite the rough way he'd taken her. He'd wanted to punish her for attracting him so keenly. He couldn't hold a grudge against her anymore, however, though he wished he could.

He wrapped an arm around her, pressing his lips to her forehead. "How could I not have enjoyed it?" he said.

She smiled, hiked her shoulders like a happy schoolgirl, and, holding her cup in both hands, tilted it to her lips.

Haskell studied her. "What are you going to do, Suellen? Now that he's dead?"

Instantly, her happiness was gone. She pouted over the rim of her cup, staring off into the distance. The chill morning breeze toyed with her hair. "I don't know," she said in a little-girl, faraway voice. "I don't know what's going to become of me. Lou left very little money. All I have is the house, Rufus, and the buggy."

Haskell rose and picked up his saddle. He was stiff and sore, but his throat felt better. Everything would feel better once he caught up to Lou's killer as well as to Krantz, though they might be one and the same. Krantz, Willie, and the others . . .

"I'm gonna saddle my horse," he said. "Then I'm pulling out."

"Where are you going?"

"After Lou's killer," he said over his shoulder as he walked out to where the buckskin grazed near Suellen's cream, both horses' coats coloring now as the sun broke loose from the eastern horizon, chasing shadows while casting a dark-orange glow across the chalky hogbacks.

Fifteen minutes later, he watched her ride away in her buggy, heading southeast, following an old, shaggy, two-track trail back in the direction of Diamondback. Haskell wondered about her again, how she'd end up, deciding that if anyone could take care of herself, that person was the former Suellen Treadwell. She'd catch the eye of a wealthy rancher in the area, if she hadn't already, and set up housekeeping in a house similar to the one she'd been raised in.

Returning his attention to the task at hand, he rode around

the burned-out ranchstead, crossed the wash with its trickle of murmuring water, and swung down from his saddle. He dropped to a knee and studied the boot print he'd seen yesterday, tracing it with his gloved index finger. He turned to the grave and studied the stones tracing the heart. He plucked the hide sack from his shirt pocket, bounced it in his palm, felt the ring inside, then dropped the sack back into his pocket.

Pondering, he stepped back into the saddle, crossed the second, shallower wash, and climbed the opposite ridge behind which the shooter had fired on him.

He looked around carefully until he found the tracks of the shooter's horse, and followed them. As he rode, the sun climbed and the day warmed. Birds darted through the air around him. He'd started out wearing his buckskin jacket, but by midmorning he'd shed the jacket, wrapping it around his bedroll, and rolled up the sleeves of his calico shirt.

The ambusher's trail wasn't hard to follow. This sandy country held a track just fine, and the rider had done nothing to cover them. Haskell followed the prints straight south, up and over the low hills and between haystack buttes, up and over the shoulder of the last ridge. He stopped near the ridge crest, near a crumbling escarpment of eroded limestone, and stared down at Diamondback spread out below him, near the base of the ridge.

The town ran from right to left, east to west. The business buildings with their high façades stood at the heart of it, roughly a hundred yards long. The board-and-batten buildings all needed the fresh paint they'd likely never receive. Miss Yvette's sporting parlor stood out from the shabbiness, like a large, gaudily painted jungle bird.

Haskell could see Lou and Suellen's house on the town's far side, at the southeast corner, beyond some brush and willows and near the wash that angled like a lazy snake along the town's southern edge.

Somewhere in the town, a dog barked. There was the regular, ringing clang of a blacksmith's hammer on an iron anvil. A slow, sporadic stream of traffic made its way along the town's main street—the occasional horsebackers passing by ones and twos, now and then a farm or ranch wagon, maybe with a couple of dusty, bored-looking kids in the back with a dog or a crate of chickens to sell.

The breeze churned up the ash-like dust along the ridge, swirled it, let it drop. The sun beat down out of a near-cloudless sky. Haskell sweated, but the dry air sucked it off him before it could soak his shirt.

He was staring down at a banal scene. From this vantage, you wouldn't have a clue about the secrets being housed down there.

Haskell looked at the tracks trailing away from him. They angled across the slope from left to right.

He clucked to the buckskin, and dropped down off the ridge. The tracks led past an old windmill and stone stock tank, a small cabin—probably one of the original shacks—falling in on itself. The tracks brought him to a small barn and corral flanking Bennett's mercantile.

Haskell reined up in front of the corral.

Three horses milled inside, lifting dust as they clomped around. One was a black and white pinto. The horse stared at Haskell, curiously twitching its ears while munching hay. A cawing sound rose so sharply and suddenly that Haskell jerked with a slight start, beginning to slide his hand to his Schofield.

Then he saw the crow glaring at him through small, muddy eyes from its perch on the corral's far corner. The ragged beast had a small piece of viscera caught on its beak. It lifted its head, trying to eat the stringy gut. The crow got sidetracked again, turned back to Haskell, and gave another loud, ratcheting caw, as though it feared the interloper were after its morsel.

A wooden scrape sounded.

Haskell turned toward the mercantile just as the back door opened and Bernadine Bennett appeared in an apron over a checked gingham dress, a broom in her hand. She swept a pile of dirt out the door, dust rising around her blond head. She glanced toward Haskell, turned back to her work, then snapped her head back toward the lawman with a startled gasp.

She stopped sweeping and stared at him, her mouth slightly open, blue eyes wide.

Haskell held her gaze for nearly thirty seconds before he said, "You're a good shot, Miss Bennett. Too damn good. But then again, not quite good enough."

CHAPTER SEVENTEEN

Bernadine Bennett just stared at Bear, her eyes growing larger, brighter.

Haskell plucked the sack out of his shirt pocket, letting it dangle by its drawstring. "I found this."

Bernadine cupped a hand to her mouth and convulsed with a violent sob.

Boots thumped behind her.

"What is it?" a brusque voice said.

Zach Bennett appeared in the doorway behind her, scowling out above her head, shading his squinting eyes with his hand. His pugnacious gaze found Haskell. He grabbed Bernadine's arm and pulled her back into the hallway behind him.

"Get inside!"

Weeping noisily, Bernadine retreated, her hand still clamped over her mouth.

Bennett stepped down onto a small wooden stoop, scowling.

"Did you do it?" Haskell said.

"Get out of here!" Bennett shouted, face flushed with fury, a thin lock of hair dangling over his left eye.

"Because of this?" Haskell held up the bag again. "Because you didn't think it was right—two girls that close? Maybe falling in love?"

"I told you to get the fuck out of here!" Bennett shouted, lunging forward and shaking his tight fist.

"It happens, Bennett," Haskell said. "It happens all the time.

There's nothing wrong with it. That girl, Clara Lomax—she didn't deserve to die because of it. Neither did her father!"

"If you don't leave, I'll get my boys and my shotgun, and we'll blow you out of that saddle!"

"I'm gonna head over to Lou Cameron's office. I'm gonna wait there until I've found the whole story. I wanna know how Lou's death plays into it. I'm not going anywhere until I've been educated, so you'd best get used to the idea."

Haskell clucked to his horse and started forward, heading for a break between the mercantile and a barber shop beside it. "The sooner I've got that story, and have the killers behind bars, the sooner I'll leave."

He pinched his hat brim to the glaring Bennett, and rode on through the break and out onto the main street. He stopped and looked to his right. Big Deal was walking toward him from about a block away, on the street's north side. Big Deal gave Haskell a slow, curious wave, then swung off the boardwalk to climb the steps of the mercantile's loading dock. The younker kept his gaze on Haskell, then slowly, reluctantly, turned away as he pushed through the mercantile's front door, causing the cowbell to jangle.

Haskell turned the buckskin left to trot eastward along the main, mostly deserted thoroughfare. Again, he felt eyes on him, glimpsed gray faces studying him from behind dusty shop windows. He paid a boy loafing around near the jailhouse a quarter to see to the buckskin's tending, then, as the towhead led the buckskin toward the livery barn, he shouldered his Henry and pushed into the town marshal's office.

He pegged his hat in frustration, set his rifle on Cameron's desk, and slacked into the swivel chair behind it. He leaned forward, placed his elbows on the desk, and raked his hands through his hair.

This had become ugly. Damned ugly. And he still didn't know

who had killed Cameron.

He got up, opened the door, and looked up the street toward the mercantile. Suddenly, the street was deserted. No movement whatever except a single dust devil spinning near the town's opposite side. No sounds except for birds and the breeze. The town could have been abandoned. Haskell could see CLOSED signs hanging in several nearby shop windows.

He looked around carefully, the hair at the back of his neck prickling.

Where was Big Deal? Still inside the mercantile?

Or . . . ?

Haskell grabbed his Henry off the desk. He walked to the rear door, opened it, and stared out.

All was quiet out back. Too quiet. Cameron's blood still shone in a couple of grisly brown patches in the brush along the trail leading to the privy.

The privy.

Haskell followed the path, looking around carefully, then opened the privy door and stepped inside. He pulled the door closed. The bottom of the door raked against the floor's warped boards. He leaned the Henry against the wall, then stood over the hole but did not unbutton his fly.

He stared through the cracks between the wallboards.

Outside, shrub branches fluttered and bobbed in the breeze. He could smell the tang of hot cedar. A cicada buzzed. The heat inside the privy was close and oppressive, compounding the stench wafting up from the hole.

Haskell heard something. He turned to peer through a crack in the wall near the corner to his right. A shadow moved. A gun barked. Haskell jerked with a start. The bullet ripped into the wall before him, the bullet slicing inches past him on his left to thud into the wall behind him.

The Schofield was instantly in his hand. He fired once, twice, three times, the roars deafening in the close quarters.

Three ragged holes appeared in the wall before him, waist-high.

Outside, a groan. The sound of a body hitting the ground.

Haskell shouldered through the door and ran out, looking around for more bushwhackers. There was only one, it appeared. Holding his smoking Schofield up high and ready, the hammer cocked, Bear walked over and looked down at the young man thrashing on the ground.

"Big Deal . . ."

The young man rolled from side to side, yelling. Two of Haskell's bullets had caught him nearly dead center. "Bastard!" he cried. "Oh, you bastard. Look what you done!"

Haskell dropped to a knee beside him. "Why, goddamnit? Why'd you kill Cameron?"

"Had to," Big Deal said. "I had to, ya understand. He woulda hurt somebody . . . somebody I was close to. Besides, he was a mean son of a bitch. He slapped me. Hard! Over and over! He was crazy from drink!"

"Why'd he slap you?"

"He knew I knew who done it."

"Done what?"

Big Deal lay still. He stared straight up at Haskell. His body was relaxing, and his eyes were going flat. "Killed them two folks—Miss Clara and her pa. Burned their ranch."

"Big Deal!"

Running footsteps rose in the west. Haskell looked up to see Bernadine Bennett running toward them. She covered her mouth with her hand, dropped to a knee beside Haskell, and stared down at Big Deal, clutching the young man's arm.

"Big Deal—no!"

Big Deal rolled his eyes to her, then swallowed. "You best leave here, Miss Bernadine. You don't need to see this."

"Oh, Big Deal—I told you not to try it. I told you what he did to my brothers!"

"I . . . I had to try. To give you some peace." Big Deal's eyes rolled back to Haskell. "He's a smart one. Cagey sumbitch. He woulda figured it." Turning back to the sobbing Bernadine, he said, "I'm sorry, Miss Bernadine. So . . . so sorry."

Big Deal gave a long, slow sigh, and then the light left his eyes. They rolled upwards. He lay still.

Bernadine sobbed into her hands.

Haskell rose. "Tell me what happened, Miss Bennett. Did your father and brothers kill Bliss Lomax and his daughter? Did they kill them because . . . because of what you and Miss Clara meant to each other? Is that why Big Deal killed Cameron? To protect your family?"

More running footsteps sounded. Zach Bennett ran out from the far side of the jailhouse, and stopped. He was flanked by his three sons—Cotton, Shane, and the tall, lanky Farrell. They all looked the worse for their encounter with Bear the day before. Especially Shane, who wore a thick, white bandage over his nose. His eyes were badly swollen and discolored.

"Bernadine, come away from there right now!" the elder Bennett shouted, pointing commandingly at his daughter.

Haskell didn't see any weapons on any of the Bennetts, but he aimed the cocked Schofield at them just in case. "Stay there, Bennett." He looked down at Bernadine. "Tell me, Miss Bennett. Did your father and brothers murder Miss Clara and her father to try to hide your relationship? Or did they send Krantz to do it?"

"No!" Bernadine said, gazing up at him in shock. "No, it wasn't like that!"

"Bernadine!" her father barked. "Did you hear me, girl?"

Haskell said, "Shut up, Bennett!" To Bernadine he said, "Tell me what happened."

Slowly, Bernadine rose to stand before Haskell, though she still had to look up at him. She shook her head as she glanced at her father and brothers. "No. They didn't kill Clara. I did."

"*You?*"

"Bernadine!" yelled her father.

She stared at Haskell as though in a daze. A thin sheen of tears closed over her eyes. Her voice grew thin. It quavered with emotion. "She didn't want me anymore. She'd fallen for a drover. She said it so cold. So mean. Like we'd never meant anything to each other, when I thought we'd meant so much to each other. Everything! She demanded her ring back. Her mother's ring. She'd given it to me. I wore it around my neck. We were behind her and her father's cabin. I don't know what came over me. I went into a rage. The next thing I knew, I had a rock in my hand. The rock was bloody. And dear Clara lay at my feet. Dead."

Sobbing, Bernadine dropped to her knees. She cried into her hands.

"Ah, Jesus Christ, Bernadine," Zach Bennett lamented. "You didn't need to tell him all that. You didn't need to tell him a thing!"

Ignoring him, Haskell kept his gaze on the girl. "Who killed her father? Who burned the ranch?"

"Big Deal's pards from out at the Quimberly spread. They wanted everything hushed up, so they killed Lomax, too. Burned him up in his cabin." This from Zach Bennett as he walked slowly toward his daughter, an expression of anguish on his haggard features.

"Krantz," Haskell said, half to himself.

"He's the foreman. They're mostly a rustlin' outfit. Old Man Quimberly's been dead for years. His rawhiders stayed on, took over the place, though they don't know how to run a ranch. They're rustlers and stagecoach thieves." Bennett dropped to a knee beside his daughter, and glanced up at Haskell. "What'll they do to her? The law . . . ?"

"I reckon it's up to a judge," Haskell said. "That she confessed is a good thing. A judge might see the killing as a fit of passion, momentary insanity, maybe leave her at home. Living with what she did is likely punishment enough. I'll put that in my report." Haskell broke open his Schofield, shook the spent shells out of the cylinder, and began replacing them with fresh from his shell belt. "Is Krantz around?"

Farrell Cotton said, "Him and the others are over at the Blind Pig."

Haskell thumbed the sixth shell into the Schofield's cylinder, snapped the piece closed, spun the wheel, and dropped the big popper into its holster. He glanced at Big Deal. His heart twisted. Haskell had liked the kid. His having to kill him grieved him. Big Deal had wanted to be all things to all people. He must have loved Bernadine Bennett.

Because of how Lou Cameron had turned out—drunk and mean—it hadn't been all that hard for Big Deal to ambush him. Especially given how tightly wired Big Deal himself had been.

Haskell looked around. *Crazy damn little town out here in the middle of nowhere . . .*

He retrieved his Henry from the privy, then walked back through the jailhouse office and out onto the main street. He looked around. The street could have been any street in any ghost town. Only five horses stood tied to a hitchrack fronting a saloon on the town's far side. He hadn't noticed the horses before, as they were nearly out of sight around a slight bend.

But he noticed them now.

He could still feel that rope cutting into his neck. He could still hear the mocking laughter of the men who'd hanged him. If Suellen had shown up even a minute later, he'd been snuggling with the diamondbacks about now . . .

His jaw set hard with a growing inner fury, Haskell pumped a live round into the Henry's action, off-cocked the hammer, set the rifle on his shoulder, and began walking west along the eerily quiet street.

Again he saw faces staring out at him from behind dirty windows.

His boots crunched dirt and sand and finely churned horse apples. The breeze picked up sand from the street and blew it against building fronts. The blazing sun pushed through the crown of his hat, causing sweat to dribble down his cheeks before the dry air itself reclaimed it.

He approached the Blind Pig. All five horses standing at the hitchrack turned their heads to regard him curiously. Haskell recognized every one of them. He saw now the brands on their withers—the letter Q inside a circle.

Circle-Q.

Haskell mounted the boardwalk fronting the rundown place and pushed through the batwings. He put his back to the wall on his left and turned to face the saloon's five customers.

They all sat together under a grizzly head mounted atop the far wall, playing poker. A young lady in a red corset sat on the knee of one of the men. She was the only one who'd seen Haskell so far. Her and the gray-headed, gray-bearded apron standing behind the bar at the back of the room, that was.

The girl stared at Haskell while the men around her raised and called and tossed coins onto the table, oblivious. The girl placed her left hand atop the hatless head of the man whose leg she was perched on, and he turned his head toward Haskell.

The man's eyes, at first annoyed, found Haskell, and widened.

The man elbowed Krantz, who sat to his left.

"What is it, Haney? Can't you see—?"

"Look there," Haney said.

Krantz followed Haney's gaze with his own. Krantz said,

"Hey!" and lurched up out of his chair. He kicked the chair, tripping, and nearly fell as he stumbled straight backward against the wall, directly beneath the grizzly head. "Hey, for chrissakes, what the *fuck*? Did she cut you *down*?"

He pointed at Haskell, sort of crouched forward, regarding the lawman with bald horror in his belligerent eyes, upper lip curled bizarrely.

The others looked at Haskell and froze, lower jaws hanging.

The kid, Willie, sat with his back to Haskell, but he was turned around in his chair now, staring in shock. "Fuck, we kilt that big son of a bitch!" To Haskell, he said, "What are you—a damn *ghost*?"

"Close," Bear growled. "Too damn close. You're right. The woman who scared you fellers off cut me down about one minute before you'd have been scot-free."

He strode forward, switching his Henry to his left hand and setting it atop that shoulder. He wanted his right hand free for his Schofield. This would be close-range work here today . . .

He stopped ten feet away from the poker table, all eyes riveted on him.

"You fellers are under arrest for the murder of Bliss Lomax and for the attempted murder of a deputy United States marshal. That'd be me. That should bring you about fifteen years hard labor in the federal pen. If you want to make things simpler for yourself as well as for me, go ahead." Haskell curled his lip into a challenging grin. "I'd advise against it, but you ain't payin' me for advice, now, are ya?"

Willie's eyes grew brighter. His mouth opened wider.

He bolted up out of his chair, screaming and reaching for the Colt hanging down over his crotch.

Haskell's Schofield bucked and roared.

The bullet split Willie's brisket wide, turned to pulp his heart behind it, and threw Willie straight up and then back onto the poker table where he lay shivering as though deeply chilled. The whore scrambled off Haney's knee and ran up the stairs to disappear, sobbing, in the saloon's second story.

The four surviving cutthroats stared down at Willie in horror. Silence settled over the room.

Smoke from Haskell's Schofield drifted in front of his face.

"Anyone else?" he asked.

They stared at him hard, shoulders rising and falling as they breathed, cursing under their breath.

Then, by ones and twos, they emptied their holsters onto the table until a small armory of weapons—guns as well as knives—was piled amongst the playing cards, coins, greenbacks, whiskey bottles, and cigarette stubs smoldering in ashtrays.

Haskell told the Blind Pig's barkeep to fetch the undertaker for Big Deal, then led Krantz and the others away to Lou Cameron's jail and locked them up in the basement cellblock. His life would have been easier if he'd been able to turn them all toe-down. That would just mean paperwork. As it was now, he'd have to haul them all, cuffed and shackled, back to Denver to face a federal judge.

On the other hand, for the next fifteen to twenty years he was going to enjoy thinking about them turning big rocks into small rocks in the quarries at the federal pen . . .

Bear and his charges wouldn't be heading back to Denver real soon, however. He'd be stuck here in Diamondback for several more weeks, maybe a month. He had to seat another lawman and wait for the circuit judge to ride out here and try Bernadine Bennett for the killing of her lover, Clara Lomax.

That was all right, Bear thought, climbing the stone steps to the main office, the keys jangling on the ring in his hand. He could use some quiet time to cool his heels and drink some whiskey.

Maybe with some extra time here in Diamondback, he could

take more care with his report and give Henry Dade all that detail he was always barking for.

Haskell stepped into the office and locked the cellblock door behind him. He turned to the main door, which he'd left half open when he'd herded Krantz's bunch into the building. The pretty dove, Miss Marlene, was just now walking toward the jailhouse from the far side of the street.

She wore very little, and her hair was done up nice. Red rouge colored her cheeks. She cradled a bottle in the crook of her right arm. In her other hand she carried two whiskey glasses.

Halfway across the street, she looked up to see Bear staring out at her. She stopped, held up the bottle and the glasses, cocked her head to one side, and cast him one hell of an enticing grin.

Haskell chuckled.

He had a feeling he was going to enjoy these next couple of weeks in Diamondback, indeed.

He drew the door wide. "Get in here, darlin'. If you're not a sight for these sore eyes, I don't know what is!" He winced, swallowed, and turned his head this way and that. "And this sore neck . . ."

"I got just what the doctor ordered," Marlene said as she flounced through the door and kissed his cheek. She gave a sad frown. "I'm sorry you had to shoot Big Deal. I just knew that was coming, though."

"Yeah, well . . ."

She smiled again, an innocent waif on gossamer wings. "Like I said, I got just what the doctor ordered."

"Yes, you do," Haskell said, looking at her in all her female splendor. "Yes, you surely do!"

★ ★ ★ ★ ★

THE JACKALS OF SUNDOWN

★ ★ ★ ★ ★

CHAPTER ONE

Deputy U.S. Marshal Bear Haskell had experienced nightmares this bizarre and horrifying.

But they'd been nightmares.

And he'd woken up from them.

Now, watching the laughing, bearded outlaw hoist the coffin lid over the box Haskell was laid out in—the *coffin* he was laid out in, though he was still alive—he realized with several violent slams of his heart against his ribs that his nightmares were going to have to get a whole lot more bizarre and horrifying if they were going to live up to his present, cold-hard, real-life predicament.

The lid closed over Haskell's battered, beaten body. It was like a giant cloud passing over the sun.

But then the sun came out again as the grinning, bearded outlaw lifted the lid off the coffin to lower his grinning, bearded face so close to Haskell's that the lawman could smell the whiskey and chewing tobacco on the man's sour breath, see the large pores in his ruddy, fleshy face oozing sweat.

The grinning, bearded outlaw, whose name, if Haskell's memory could be relied upon at such a taxing time, was Scully Crow, a thief, murderer, illegal whiskey peddler, and rapist wanted in nearly every state and territory west of the Mississippi. Crow gave a devious wink and said, "Nighty-night, lawman. Sleep tight and don't let the bedbugs bite, now, ya hear?"

He threw his head back and slitted his eyes, laughing uproariously, as he set the lid down atop the coffin once more.

Haskell's heart lurched again, fear and fury exploding inside him. He shoved his elbows against the bottom of the coffin and lifted his head and shoulders, smashing the lid away, gritting his teeth and snarling like a trapped cougar. He was about to hurl himself out of the wooden overcoat's tight confines when a rifle butt slammed into his right temple.

He fell back in the coffin, hearing above the tolling of cracked bells in his ears the cacophony of mocking laughter all around him. The five outlaws in Scully Crow's group were having themselves a high old time. A couple of the soiled doves from the Bare Naked Lady Saloon in Henry's Ford, high in the Colorado Rockies, were laughing, as well, having stumbled out of the saloon to enjoy the festivities.

All went dark again for Haskell.

Not just because the lid had been slammed on the coffin again, but because he was hurling downward again . . . down . . . down . . . down into the greasy murk of semi-consciousness. At the same time, he felt blood from the fresh wound in his right temple oozing down that side of his face, joining the blood from the several other gouges, cuts, and scrapes that the gang had inflicted on him after they'd jumped him in the Bare Naked Lady.

Five against one was steep odds even for Bear Haskell, who towered around six-feet-six inches above ground and whose body looked like something out of a Norse legend—all bulging muscle and strapping sinew laid across a frame stout as a giant blacksmith anvil.

Little good that frame did him now, beaten as it was, his big body one massive bruise—ribs broken, joints swelling, lips shredded, eyes inflamed. He'd had the shit kicked out of both ends, as the saying went. They'd used their fists first, and when their fists had given out, they'd used ax handles and rifle butts.

Bear was as limp as a frost-burned rose.

Deafening hammer blows filled the inside of the coffin. Haskell rose up out of the murk of unconsciousness again as he realized those blows were hammers. Hammers striking nails through the lid and into the sides of the coffin, each blow causing the coffin to lurch as well as the lawman inside it, each blow a dynamite explosion inside Haskell's aching head . . .

Each blow sealing him into this dark box squeezing against his broad shoulders, pushing up against his back and down against his chest and belly. Sealing him into this dark box that would likely be his home forever more, once they got him in the ground and he'd sucked up all the air . . .

His heart turned a somersault in his chest at the refreshed nightmare realization of what was happening, the horrific direness of his situation.

Buried alive!

"Shit!" Bear rasped, cold sweat oozing out of every pore.

As the loud hammering continued amidst muffled laughter, he lifted his hands. He got them about a foot off the bottom of the coffin, but since the coffin was only a little over a foot deep, he had no room with which to push with any real power against the lid. He slid his hands up to his chest, turned his palms toward the lid, and grunted as he pushed upward. But it was no use.

The lid wasn't going anywhere.

The hammering stopped.

"Let me out of here, you sonso'bitches!" Haskell shouted, pressing his nose taut against the lid.

He wriggled around from left to right—as much as he had room for, which wasn't much—but the wooden overcoat had been solidly nailed together. There was no way he was going to break it apart. All his yelling and cursing got him was more jeering laughter from the men who'd nailed him in here.

Through the cracks between the pine boards comprising the coffin lid, he could catch glimpses of the curly wolves standing around the coffin—at least, he caught glimpses of their brightly colored shirts and neckerchiefs and the duns and blacks of their hats, bright in the late day, high-mountain sunshine.

There was a soft tapping sound on several places on the coffin lid. Almost like someone tapping his fingers.

Haskell stopped yelling. The tapping continued. No, it wasn't a tapping sound so much as a dribbling sound. Then he smelled it: urine.

The sons of bitches were peeing on the coffin!

"I'm gonna kill every one of you hog-wallopin' sonso'bitches!" Haskell shouted shrilly against the underside of the lid. I'm gonna gut you *before* I kill you, and then I'm gonna kill you *hard* and *bloody*!"

A few drops of piss dribbled through a crack between the pine boards of the coffin lid and onto his left cheek. Haskell bellowed raucously, so enraged that he thought his brains were going to boil out his ears.

A girl tittered a laugh and said, "You boys got you a big, old, angry bear in that coffin!"

Another girl screeched a crackling laugh.

"Piss on you, Mister Lawman, sir!" yelled one of the outlaws. Tiny Titterman, it sounded like—a no-account from Oklahoma. (But, then, they didn't raise anything *except* no-accounts in Oklahoma.) "And we mean that sincerely, Bear!"

Tiny and Scully Crow and the other three outlaws roared at that, and so did the girls who were standing around Haskell's wooden overcoat, no doubt grateful for the distraction from the boredom and tedium of earning their livings on their backs in a jerkwater mountain boomtown that had gone bust two or three years ago.

It was Haskell's opinion, based on ten years' experience living and riding for law and order on the frontier after four years fighting for the Union in the War of Southern Rebellion, that a bored whore could be as mean and nasty as any gun-toting scalawag with a pecker.

"You ready for a little ride, Bear?" asked Curly, leaning down to stare at Haskell through a crack between the lid boards. His eye was as large and blue as a baby's—albeit, a drunken baby's.

"Ride?" Haskell raked out, still trying to burst the box apart with his shoulders, heart kicking up a frantic rhythm in his chest.

"Come on, fellers!" Curly said. "Let's get this sailor to the sea!"

"Sea?" Haskell bellowed.

They all laughed again as they lifted the coffin by the leather straps built into its sides. Several men grunted, then cursed. Haskell felt the coffin lifted up off the ground, then jerked to each side.

"Christalmighty, this federal badge-toter weighs a ton!" one of the outlaws yelled.

Inside the coffin, Haskell sweated, panicking, rolling his shoulders right to left and back again, trying with every ounce of his remaining strength to break open the consarned box. To no avail. It must have been one of the undertaker's luxury models. Built to weather the ages!

As the outlaws grunted on both sides of the big, angry, and frightened lawman—carrying him only they and God knew where!—the tang of raw pine mixed with the smell of his own sweat and blood, and the leather of his cartridge belt and empty holster.

He could feel his five-shot, "Blue Jacket" .44-caliber pocket revolver, manufactured by Hopkins & Allen, snugged into the small hideout holster he'd personally sewn into the well of his right boot. He hadn't been able to reach for the gun during his beating. There hadn't been time. Little good it did him now. He couldn't bend enough of his body to reach for it.

He continued to fight the box, heart racing, bells of sheer panic clanging in his ears. He thought he could smell the pungent, gamey odor of water. A low roaring lifted. Sure—they were taking him to the river. The Arkansas ran along the east edge of town, in a shallow canyon behind the furniture shop, which was also an undertaking parlor, which is where they must have found his present abode, though this was conjecture, for Haskell had been unconscious at that point.

Haskell stopped fighting the box when he felt the box itself stop moving. The river's roar was louder now. He could smell wet rock and moss.

"Have a good trip to the Gulf of Mexico, Bear!" yelled Scully Crow just before he and the rest of the raggedy heeled brigands broke into another burst of ribald laughter.

"On three, fellers," one of the others shouted above the river's roar.

The box swung backward, then forward.

"One!"

The box swung backward again, then forward again.

"Two!"

The box swung backward.

Forward.

"Oh, fuck!" Haskell shouted inside the coffin, his nose pressed up taut against the lid.

"Three!"

The box continued forward.

Forward . . . and down.

Haskell was falling. If the box hadn't been snug around him, he would have been standing straight up and down in midair. He could see himself plunging boots first toward the Arkansas.

Horror was a coyote wailing in his head.

What was worse than being buried alive? The only thing he could think of on such short notice was being drowned in a box.

The box hit the water with a sudden, violent impact, smashing his feet down against the far end, his head slamming against the underside of the lid. His organs felt like dice shaken in a cup.

Inside, Bear screamed as the wooden overcoat bounced off the water and then, as though shoved up by a giant hand from the river's bottom, the box pitched forward.

"Ahh, *shiiiit!*" he yelled, only to himself and the blackness inside the box.

The coffin hit the water upside down with a splash. The box spun wickedly, rolled, until Haskell found himself belly up again. The coffin wobbled wildly, floating as the current carried him downstream. Bear felt the chill of water beneath him, the wetness bleeding between the boards of the casket to instantly soak his clothes.

His tomb rocked and swayed. The current caught it, and Bear, panting in the tight confines, in the hot, humid darkness, his hands pressed up flat against the coffin lid, felt himself being hurled downstream as though dragged by a hundred frightened horses.

Buried alive in a watery grave.

Ah, hell!

The coffin pitched and plunged. Haskell's belly lurched into his throat as the coffin tipped up. He was suspended for a moment straight up and down before tipping forward and plunging over a short falls. The end housing Haskell's head smashed against a rock with another sound like a gunshot. The end with his feet flew up over his head.

Then he was horizontal again, rocking on along the stream— belly down in the cold, wet sarcophagus.

A back eddy caught him, ground against the box, swallowed one side, lifted the other side, and suddenly he was belly up again.

There was another sound like a gunshot.

Only, this time it *was* a gunshot. Haskell winced at what felt like a bee sting in his right ear. He looked up to see the blue sky showing through a ragged oval hole in the coffin lid.

The outlaws had pissed on him.

Now they were giving him an even grander send-off by shooting at him, as well.

CHAPTER TWO

As the coffin hurtled through the narrow but fast-flowing stream, Bear Haskell, lying facedown in the overturned tomb, pressed his hands against what was now the coffin's bottom and humped his back against the top, trying again to break the thing apart.

Or to at least pry off the lid.

As the coffin spun suddenly, causing the lawman's guts to spin as well, he gave up and merely tried to brace himself, gritting his teeth through which he could hear his own panting breaths raking. He heard the water rushing and gurgling around him. He could smell the piney odor of the green wood. But he knew he wouldn't be smelling anything soon if he continued through Lucifer Falls into Devil's Canyon—a deep gorge about three miles south of Henry's Ford.

Or if ice-cold water kept oozing through the cracks in the lid and through several other cracks between the coffin's pine boards. Haskell was soaked. Soaked and confined in horrifying blackness, brains and guts churning as the angry stream plunged him down its steep-walled canyon, bouncing off rocks, the violent collisions causing the ringing in Bear's ears to grow louder.

The coffin slammed against what he assumed was the stream's stone bank. It must have gotten hung up between rocks, because more water poured into it, and he could feel a fluttering in the end housing his feet.

As suddenly as he'd gotten hung up, the coffin jerked free. It spun wildly. Haskell groaned and gritted his teeth and squeezed his eyes closed against the water oozing around him, threatening to cut off his air.

The foot of the coffin dropped downward. Haskell's head and torso rose, twisted around, and then plunged.

The water in the coffin gurgled as it sloshed this way and that.

Bang!

Another gunshot?

No.

The bottom of the coffin had smashed against the stream's rocky bottom. Haskell heard the crack, then felt wood slivers gouging his left thigh. Now he was face up once more, but the water was coming in fast and furious, filling his nostrils and mouth. He made the mistake of trying to breathe. The water hit his lungs and burned like coals in a blacksmith's forge.

Only a few seconds left now.

His entire body was submerged.

He was vaguely aware of the coffin spinning around him once more.

Then another *bang*!

Both the side and the floor of the coffin gave way. Haskell's feet dropped. His knee smashed against a knobby black rock that he glimpsed amongst a feathery spray of tea-colored water. He rolled sideways, the frenzied current sweeping him along.

Air brushed his face. Instinctively, he drew a breath and got part of it down before the water in his lungs exploded outward. He heard himself choking and gagging. His lungs felt as though they'd burst at the seams. While the current swirled him and pushed him downstream, he tried to gain another breath of the refreshing air washing over him between waves of the rushing rapids.

He managed only a teaspoonful as he continued to cough and choke and vomit the water he'd inhaled when he'd been inside the wooden overcoat.

Ahead, a bird winged out over the frothing stream.

No, not a bird. Bear had caught only a glimpse of the object, but he looked again now, turning his head one way while the river turned him another, and saw a rope.

Yes, a rope!

It extended out from the right bank and was looped over the end of a black log poking up out of the stream.

A pounding sounded from somewhere atop the bank.

A man's voice, high-pitched and womanish, shouted, "Grab the rope, ya big galoot. Grab the *rope!*"

The rope grew in Haskell's eyes until he could see the individual hemp strands twisting and straining as the man took the slack out of it. Haskell threw up his left arm. He hooked it over the rope that cut into his ribs just beneath his armpit.

He groaned. Every rib barked out in pain. But he clung to the rope for all he was worth.

Staring at the rope and only at the rope, praying the log didn't break free, Haskell used his hands to follow the rope toward the right bank. The whitewater beat against his legs and hips. He had little remaining strength. He used every ounce of it to walk his hands along the rope to the bank.

When he'd gained the bank's grassy lip, a gloved hand reached over it. Haskell took it. The man's fingers closed around Haskell's hand, and he pulled Haskell onto the bank with a raspy grunt.

The big lawman collapsed, water gurgling in his throat as he tried to breathe. There was another grunt as two gloved hands rolled him over. A hatted head slid between Bear and the sky. Two watery blue eyes stared down at him from a gray-bearded face as craggy and sunburned as all Nevada.

"Why, ya crazy tomcat—what the fuck you doin' in the river?"

Stumpy Gibbs, government tracker, grinned, showing his oversized false teeth between thin, cracked lips, the lower lip showing a deep blue-black spot where a cheap quirley was always clamped.

Haskell stared up at the far older man for a full thirty seconds before he finally found the strength to push up onto his elbows. He was still trying to catch his breath and hack all of the water out of his lungs.

He looked at Stumpy sitting beside him, staring at him expectantly from under the brim of his badly weathered Boss of the Plains Stetson, which was so big it always made Stumpy's head resemble a brown egg crowned by a stone coffee mug.

"Where in the hell have you been, you son of a bitch?" Haskell raked out, spitting more water to one side.

Stumpy's eyes snapped wide in shock. "Where I been? Where do you think I been, you ungrateful pup? I been gallopin' like a bat out of hell, followin' you downstream so's I could rescue your miserable ass, which I just did, in case you didn't notice!"

Haskell cleared his throat, hacking up sand and other muck from the river, and spitting it to one side. "Why didn't you help me in town when they were beating the living hell out of me? You had to have seen what was happening out on the street. I left you in the livery barn!"

"Oh, I seen what was happenin', all right. Five against one. Them's long odds. But what woulda been the point of my enterin' the fray? I'm ancient and stove up like an arthritic old mutt, and you know my ticker's logy as an eighty-year-old whore." Stumpy pressed both gloved hands to his chest as though to cradle the delicate organ of topic. "I'd have had me a heartstroke before I could have thrown a single punch!"

Haskell looked at the old Colt bristling up from the holster on Stumpy's right hip. "You could have at least pulled that hogleg on 'em!"

"Bear, my eyes!" Stumpy raised his hands to point to the two new compromised organs of topic. "I can hardly see my own hand in front of my face, let alone those five rascals turnin' you inside out and stompin' you clear down to perdition from all the way across the street! If I woulda drawed down on 'em, and had to *shoot* at 'em, I like as not I woulda hit you! Now, you wouldn't have wanted that to happen, would you, ya ungrateful pup?"

"I'd probably be a lot better off, you worthless old coonhound!"

"No, sir—you wouldn't have been!"

"What were you doin' while I was getting beat silly? Watching from the comfort of the livery barn?"

"I don't see why you think it was so gall-danged comfortable, Bear . . ."

Haskell tried to narrow an eye at the old tracker, but, swollen as it was to the size of a pink egg, the eye wouldn't narrow any more than it already had, which was to a very thin slit. "I bet you and that old hog-wallopin' swamper, Vernon Keel, were betting to see how long I'd last, weren't you?"

Stumpy's eyes widened again, and his lower jaw dropped. He appeared to want to say something, but no words came out.

"That's it, ain't it?" Bear said, flaring an enraged nostril. "You two were betting on me."

Stumpy wagged his head slowly, as though deep in shock. "Bear, I can't believe you'd accuse me of such a lowdown dirty stunt such as that. It grieves me. Purely it does—right down to my bones!"

"How much did you win . . . or lose?"

"Huh?"

"You heard me."

Stumpy glanced away. Nervously, he licked his lips, ran his

gloved hands down his thighs, and then gave a sheepish, twitching grin. "Five dollars. Bear, if you could've stood up for just twenty more sec—!"

"Stumpy, you son of a bitch! Do you know the only thing lowlier than you is a horse apple at the bottom of the plop?"

"Ah, come on, Bear! Have a sense of humor, would ya? No harm done. I just decided that since I couldn't help, I might try to earn a little extra cash. Hell, Uncle Sam has cut my wages down to pennies an' piss water. Why, a man can't feed himself on the wages the government pays for my expert services!"

"Expert services, my ass!"

"Expert services!"

"Making bets while I, your partner, is getting his bones ground to a fine salt!"

"They pay me to track, and that's all they pay me for!" Stumpy slapped his knee in anger. "I don't get paid to get into fisticuffs with polecats such as them that turned you to puddin'. I don't get paid for throwin' down on 'em with my hogleg, neither. That there is what I would call hazard pay, and Uncle Sam don't pay for that. I get paid to track and that's it! I bet Marshal Dade won't pay me nothin' extra for running you down and draggin' your sorrowful ass out of that river, neither. Harrumph!"

"Oh, Christ!" Haskell chuckled without mirth and worked his jaw, trying to determine if it was broken.

"You might thank me," Stumpy said, sounding indignant now. Downright pouty.

"What's that?"

"The least you could do is thank me for savin' your bacon. True, it might've come later rather than sooner, but you're still kickin', ain't ya?"

"Just shut up, Stumpy! Why don't you gather some wood and build a fire, for chrissakes. I gotta get dried out."

"I was just gonna do that."

"Well, hop to it, then!" Haskell bellowed. "Or are you afraid Uncle Sam won't pay you for that?"

"You're just one colicky ole cuss, Bear Haskell. One colicky, ungrateful old Yankee cuss! No one could ever mistake you for a Southerner, that's for sure!" Stumpy, who hailed from Alabama and who'd fought for the Confederacy, limped off to where his and Haskell's geldings stood ground-reined.

"Thanks for the compliment," Haskell called to him. "But it's not gonna change my opinion of you, you worthless old Rebel. Before you start gatherin' wood, give me your bottle. I got some pain to kill!"

"Right there's your horse," Stumpy griped, pointing. "Drink from your own damn bottle!"

"I want yours!"

Cursing, Stumpy rummaged around in his saddlebags for a hide-wrapped whiskey bottle, and brought it over to Haskell, who sat back against a rock. Stumpy unwrapped the bottle, gave it to Bear, and said, "What's the plan? Start back to Denver first thing in the mornin'?"

"Not first thing." Haskell popped the cork on the bottle. "First thing, I'm gonna ride back into Henry's Ford and finish the job I started—runnin' Scully Crow and them other stagecoach robbers to ground. I'm gonna hit 'em with the additional charge of assaulting *with the intention of killing* a deputy U.S. marshal . . . while the deputy marshal's tracking buddy lounged around in a livery barn betting on the outcome of the fight!"

"That don't sound like no official charge to me," Stumpy opined. "Don't you think you'd better go on home, Bear? Live to fight another day? Boy, you don't look so good. I got me a feelin' if you face those boys again, the outcome might get even uglier."

"Couldn't get any uglier." Haskell took a deep pull from the bottle, then glared up at the oldster who stood over him, staring skeptically down at him. "If you're waitin' for me to pay you to fetch firewood, Stump, you're gonna get paid in hot lead first!"

"Tarnation, I never seen such a colicky pup!" Stumpy cried, throwing up his arms in defeat as he ambled off in search of deadfall.

"Tracker, my ass!"

"Best one you ever rode with, you ungrateful blue-belly!"

The truth was Stumpy had it right. The graybeard was probably the best tracker Haskell had ever ridden with, which is why he always requested Gibbs whenever there were men to track and damned little obvious sign.

Stumpy had grown up "barefoot-an'-possum poor" in the Alabama hills, where he and his father and brothers had had to track and shoot game to survive. There were no grocery stores out that way. After the war, Stumpy had come west and hired out as a tracker with the southwestern cavalry. Drunk on moonshine, he could track a petal from a flowering peach tree on a windy day, as the saying went, having further cut his teeth on tracking Apaches through that hot, rocky country near the border.

The old man's eyes weren't what they used to be, but they were still better than he let on. It was true that his heart was slowly giving out, and arthritis was gnawing his joints. That was why Haskell wasn't really as mad at him as he'd pretended to be. At least, the anger he'd directed at Stumpy had been more for Scully Crow's bunch than Stumpy, though it did piss-burn the big lawman that while he'd been getting hammered flat and kicked loco on Henry's Ford's main street, Stumpy had been holed up with the drunken livery barn wrangler, exchanging bets.

At least, Stumpy had bet on *him,* Haskell thought now with a wry chuckle, taking another pull from Stumpy's bottle while the oldster scrounged around in the brush along the stream for wood.

And he'd lost five dollars.

Haskell smiled again. He took another long pull from the bottle.

CHAPTER THREE

Haskell had a lousy night's sleep around the fire.

He ached too much to get more than a few winks now and then. He revised his previous assessment of his ribs as badly bruised rather than broken, but badly bruised ribs could bark just as loudly as broken ones.

Add that misery to his battered face and head and swollen eyes and creaky hips, and you had one miserable federal lawman enduring one hell of a long, cold, miserable mountain night under the stars. It didn't help that he had to listen to his trail partner, Stumpy Gibbs, sawing logs loudly enough for three drunken Irish sailors. When the tracker wasn't snoring, he was snickering in his sleep and urging some woman named Marge to "Go a little lower. Go a little lower, will ya, there, Margie?" Then he'd snicker again before the long, raucous snores resumed.

Haskell was awake well before dawn.

He let Stumpy sleep. He was in no hurry to hear the oldster's grunting, yawning, hacking, and ceaseless morning farting. Old age was a bear Haskell was in no hurry to wrestle.

He was also in no hurry to get back into Henry's Ford. He'd wait a couple of hours, giving Scully Crow and the other hardtails time to get good and drunk in the Bare Naked Lady again before he threw down on them. They were celebrating as well as spending the twenty-five-thousand dollars in mine company payroll they'd stolen off the Highland Stage Company out of

Crystal Creek. They likely figured that the lawman who'd been trailing them was halfway to the Gulf of Mexico by now, lolling around in a coffin full of the Arkansas River. Bear didn't want it any other way. In his condition, he needed every advantage he could find.

When he'd built a small fire and set a pot of coffee on the flames to boil, Haskell sat back against a deadfall tree and dug one of his favored Indian Kid cigars out of the watertight tin he carried in the pocket of his red-and-black calico shirt . . . not wanting to risk the precious cigars to rainstorms or near drownings in wooden overcoats.

He'd purchased the Indian Kids, six for twenty-five cents, from a small shop in his hometown of Denver, where he kept a small suite of rooms in the Larimer Hotel. The suite was more expensive than he could afford on a federal lawman's salary, but the tony digs sat just down the street from the federal building on Capitol Hill, which he worked out of, under the supervision of Chief Marshal Henry Dade of Denver's First District Court, serving the states and territories of the Western District.

Prudence would have dictated that a man of Bear's modest means secure a small room in a boarding house on the poor side of Cherry Creek, where his unwashed ilk tended to settle. But Prudence was a haughty bitch whom Bear preferred to ignore. He liked the Larimer just fine; he enjoyed nestling in the lap of luxury between assignments chasing some of the gnarliest bad men on the western frontier. Since he'd fought for the Union in the War Between the States, as a guerrilla-fighting Zouave of the 155th Pennsylvania Volunteers, running dangerous missions behind Confederate lines, he'd become accustomed to the knowledge that life was both fleeting and fragile. Then as now, he could be killed at any time.

And dear Prudence had never promised any man that he'd be able to take the money he'd saved in her honor through those glistening pearly gates everybody talked so much about in glowing terms.

"Hey, you old catamount," he said, lightly kicking the still-snoring Stumpy Gibbs, after he'd enjoyed one cup of coffee and one Indian Kid here alone with just the river's quiet roar and his own thoughts for company. "Time to rise and stretch the knots out of your rancid, hillbilly hide. Time to go bust some heads!"

It took Stumpy a good, long time to get up, get awake, and get dressed, to stop hacking and farting and yawning, and to stop stumbling around and actually get moving. So it was nearly midmorning before he and Bear were riding the trail back up to Henry's Ford.

As they rode stirrup to stirrup, the high-altitude sun burning down through their hats, slowly walking their horses along the steeply pitched wagon trail, Haskell shucked the big Smith & Wesson New Model No. 3 Schofield revolver from the soft holster positioned for the cross-draw on his left hip.

He broke open the top-break piece, which was nickel-finished and boasted a seven-inch barrel, and plucked a fresh cartridge from one of the two shell belts encircling his waist. He shoved the shell into the chamber, closed the gun, spun the cylinder, and returned the Smithy to its holster as his rented sorrel clomped into Henry's Ford—a quiet little hamlet comprised of mostly log buildings scattered along the shoulder of a steep, forested mountain, on the west bank of the Arkansas River.

The town had been a rollicking place at one time. Haskell, who'd ridden through here before, remembered it well. It had once boasted a good seven or eight saloons and nearly that many hurdy-gurdy houses. Now, only three saloons remained, as well as that many sporting parlors, which was still an impressive amount of skull pop and parlor girls for a population that had likely dwindled to well under a hundred, counting whores, feral cats, and mongrel dogs.

Smoke from breakfast fires billowed over the narrow, winding main street from chimney pipes. There weren't many people out and about just yet in Henry's Ford. One stocky young man in a shabby, ill-fitting, mismatched suit was dutifully shoveling horse dung out of the street and into a wheelbarrow. He watched, wide-eyed, as Haskell and Stumpy approached him.

Haskell leaned down and kept his voice low, hooking a finger at the younker, who swallowed anxiously and shuffled forward.

"Boy, are them five jaspers still throwing down in the Bare Naked Lady?" Bear tossed his head toward the saloon just up the street on the left, two stories tall and badly needing paint.

The kid looked at Bear as though he was seeing a ghost. "Y-yessir," he said, his sunburned cheeks splotching white.

"Are they up-an'-at-it yet?"

"Most like. I don't think they never went to bed. They been drinkin' an' gamblin' an' makin' the whores scream upstairs in the Lady all night, but I think they're all back downstairs, gamblin' again now. They . . . they been celebratin' your . . . your . . ."

"Son, the news of my demise has been greatly exaggerated." Haskell winked at the stunned younker, and flipped him a silver dollar. The kid caught it awkwardly against his chest. "For a sarsaparilla later."

The kid thanked Bear and then backed away, still eyeing the beaten and battered lawman as though he were something from another world. Haskell gigged his horse over to the Bare Naked Lady. Stumpy followed him from several feet behind.

As Bear approached the saloon, he heard the loud, raucous, drunken voices of the men who'd turned him inside out and tried to kick him out with a cold shovel. Or a cold river, as the case had been . . .

The big lawman dismounted, tossed his reins over a hitchrack, and turned to Stumpy, who had descended from his own horse and was gazing at the Bare Naked Lady as though it was a giant turd fallen from some massive privy in the sky.

"Stump?"

"What?" said the oldster in a tone of deep dread, staring at the Bare Naked Lady's batwings.

Haskell slid his Henry sixteen-shot repeater from his saddle boot. "Why don't you have a smoke out here while I go inside and get the pleasantries out of the way?"

Stumpy jerked a surprised look at the big lawman. "You, uh . . . you don't think I'd better come in and, uh . . . back your play, Bear? It's five against one. Them's steep odds even fer you."

"True, true. But I think you'd be of more use out here, makin' sure none of them hardtails sneak out around me or skin out a window. I don't want to lose one or two in the imminent foofaraw." Haskell racked a cartridge into the Henry's action, off-cocked the hammer, and rested the rifle on his right shoulder, his hand wrapped around the neck of the stock.

"Oh!" Stumpy said, nodding. "Yeah, I reckon you're right. That's probably what I should do, then. Okay, I'll just stay out here and have me a smoke an' watch the windows."

Stumpy brushed a relieved grin from his bearded face with his fist and then watched as Bear adjusted his hat on his head as well as his two shell belts and the big, holstered, nickel-finished Schofield on his lean hips and climbed the porch's three sun-blistered steps. From over the batwings came the low din of strident conversation as well as the snapping of paste-boards down on a table, and the clinking of coins.

Occasionally, Stumpy heard a bottle clink against a glass, refilling it.

Bear strode across the porch and shoved the batwings wide. He strode through the doors and Stumpy swallowed, wincing, as the saloon's murky morning shadows consumed the big law-man, whose boots thudded loudly on the worn floorboards.

Bear's boots fell silent.

The outlaws' boisterous conversation fell silent as well.

Stumpy winced again and put his back to a stout post sup-porting the porch's ceiling, near his and Bear's horses, and cast his fearful gaze across the street. A man poked his head out a shop door on the street's far side, pointed his face toward the Bare Naked Lady, and then pulled his head inside the shop and slammed the door closed.

The OPEN sign in the window right of the door was turned so that it read CLOSED as it rocked from side to side behind the dirty glass.

Stumpy steeled himself against the coming onslaught.

Silence issuing from inside the saloon weighed heavy on the old graybeard. It felt like an anvil on his brittle shoulders, bow-ing his back. His heart thudded heavily.

Stumpy jerked with a start as a man inside the saloon bel-lowed raucously. Then another man bellowed as well, and there was the loud scrape of a chair being slid across floorboards, the din of coins clattering onto the floor.

A gun blasted.

In the close confines, it sounded like a high-powered Sharps rifle. The sudden thunder nearly caused Stumpy's boots to leave the ground. Both horses lurched as well, and pulled back on their reins. They and Stumpy lurched again as another blast fol-lowed the first one.

And then all hell broke loose, with a gun thundering like a violent mountain storm—BANG! BANG! BANG! BANG-BANG! BANG!

Men screamed and hollered curses.

Boots hammered the floorboards. The hammering grew

louder behind Stumpy. There rose a great screech of breaking glass.

Stumpy turned an anxious look over his left shoulder to see a man flying out a window to land in a shower of breaking glass and shredded window frame onto the porch floor, blood oozing from a hole in his chest as well as from glass shards embedded in his face and hands.

Inside the Bare Naked Lady, the thunder continued. And so did the cacophony of men's screams and stomping boots and the hard thuds of bodies hitting the floor.

All at once, the gun thunder stopped.

Boots clomped heavily behind Stumpy again. The clomping grew louder. Stumpy cast an anxious look over his right shoulder as a man's slack, unshaven face appeared over the batwings. The man blinked once, heavily, and then pushed through the batwings and staggered onto the porch.

He held a smoking pistol down low in his right hand.

Blood oozed from several bullet holes in his upper torso.

He took one more staggering step across the porch, his lower jaw hanging slack. He triggered his pistol. Smoke and flames stabbed nearly straight down from the barrel. The bullet ripped through the top of his right boot. Blood oozed from the deep tear.

The man turned to Stumpy, his face taut with pain, his eyes wide and bright.

"*Ow!*" he cried. It was a plaintive wail directed at the oldster, as though he somehow expected Stumpy to relieve his misery.

His right hand opened. The gun dropped to the floor.

The outlaw's eyes rolled back in their sockets. He fell forward to land face first on the three steps, doing nothing to break his fall. Dead, he tumbled into the street and lay still, dust and finely ground horseshit rising around him.

From inside the saloon came a girl's voice pitched high with concern. Haskell's deep, resonate voice followed.

The girl said, "Oh, Bear, I was so worried about you!"

"You were, were you?"

"I thought those curly wolves had done killed you, you big lug!"

Footsteps rose behind Stumpy. Bear's big face, still roguishly handsome even with his swollen eyes and cut lips and busted nose, appeared over the batwings. So did the face of a pretty whore. The whore had her arms around Haskell's neck. Silver rings dangled from her ears.

As Haskell turned to the girl, he nudged open the batwings far enough for Stumpy to see that while the girl wore a pair of fancily stitched pantalets, that was pretty much all she wore.

Her bare white breasts were pressed up against Haskell's chest.

"All clear in there, Bear?" Stumpy asked, his eyes riveted on the pretty doxie.

"All clear, Stumpy."

"You ready to start back to Denver?"

Haskell chuckled as the girl nuzzled his neck and pressed her hand against his crotch.

Bear turned to Stumpy. "I'm feelin' poorly, Stump. Overtaxed. I think I'm gonna rest up here for a day or two, get started back to Denver by week's end."

"Oh, you are, are you?"

Haskell groaned against the pretty whore's ministrations. To Stumpy, he said, "Why don't you call the undertaker, have him bury these dead coyotes, then buy yourself a bottle? I'll be down when I'm better rested." He turned to the girl, groaned again, then turned back to Stumpy. "Better make it two bottles."

Haskell winked. With one arm wrapped around the dove, he drifted back into the saloon's murky shadows. Stumpy heard the thumps of Haskell's boots as the big lawman and the whore climbed the steps to the saloon's second story.

"Oh, to be that age again," Stumpy said. "Lucky catamount!"

CHAPTER FOUR

Two weeks and some-odd days later—who was counting?—Bear Haskell took the sandstone steps fronting the federal building on Denver's bustling Capitol Hill two at a time, tipping his hat to the pretty young female secretaries busily striding around him but taking the time to blush at the big, darkly handsome man's penetrating, openly admiring gray-blue gaze.

Whistling, Haskell pushed through the heavy oak doors and strode up the building's stately marble steps to the official-looking and –smelling second story corridor. At a door whose pebbled glass upper panel announced CHIEF MARSHAL HENRY DADE, WESTERN DISTRICT in high-handedly neat gold-leaf lettering, Haskell paused and slapped his hand to the breast of the black leather jacket he wore against the mile-high city's early autumn chill.

He'd had a brief moment of panic, wondering if he'd forgotten the report of his last assignment in his suite at the Larimer Hotel, where a succulent young schoolteacher named Evelyn Landusky was likely still sleeping, warm and naked, under the twisted sheets and quilts on his bed. Haskell and the young teacher had nearly destroyed his stout, four-poster bed the night before, making a lie out of the old saw about schoolmarms being as stiff as starched sheets.

There'd been nothing stiff about Miss Landusky, and Haskell still had the aches and pains to prove it. Not to mention tooth marks on his back!

Fortunately, Bear had remembered to snatch the report off his dresser. He could hear the crunch of the folded pages behind his jacket, where the scribblings resided in the breast pocket of his shirt along with a handful of his favored Indian Kid cigars. He'd scrawled the report in pencil on a lined yellow legal pad around campfires as he had made his way out of the mountains.

Bear had taken extra care with the report, trying to give as much detail as he could, for his boss, Chief Marshal Dade, was constantly barking at him for lack of detail as well as the accounting behind his expense reports. Haskell didn't have much time for paperwork. He was afraid of few men, because he'd fought all kinds and lived to tell the tale, but put a pencil in his hand and he'd break out in a cold sweat.

However, he did not want to climb Henry's hump today. Not after the extra time Bear had taken for his "recovery" in Henry's Ford under the "care" of the buxom doxie, Miss Darla Day.

The chief marshal had been a wild old Texas Ranger in his hell-bringin' days, and you didn't want to hand a rawhider like Henry too much ammunition. If you made such a mistake, sure as snow in April in the Rockies, Henry would make you dance!

Blowing out a relieved breath at realizing he was armed with his five pages of detailed scrawl, Haskell opened the door and strode into the chief marshal's outer office, where Henry's secretary, Miss Lucy Kimble, daughter of state senator Luther Kimble, sat behind her desk doing paperwork.

"Good morning, Miss Kimble," Bear said, tossing his bullet-crowned black hat with its braided horsehair thong onto the hat tree by the door. "I do declare what a sight for these sore old eyes you are this morning!"

The young woman looked up from her work with a tolerant sigh and feigned a smile. With her dark-brown hair pulled back into a tight old-woman's bun, with her round, steel-framed, old-lady spectacles hiked up onto her resolute nose, and not a lick of rouge anywhere on her face, her features were prairie plain. Still, Haskell was intrigued by the girl. He had a feeling she'd be a real looker if she chose a less severe style of attire. As it was, she always appeared like she was coming or going from a funeral.

Crisply and officiously, she droned, "Good morning, Marshal Haskell. The chief mar—"

"Oh, I know, ole Henry's probably in his office, still wakin' up, most likely, sluggin' back his first cup of hot mud and smoking one of them stinky stogies of his. Let's give him a minute before I rush in and disturb him, shall we?"

"I don't think—"

"You and I get far too little time to talk, Miss Kimble." Haskell hiked a hip onto the corner of the young woman's desk. "How in the heck are you doing, anyway . . . Lucy? Do you mind if I call you Lucy?"

Miss Kimble opened her mouth to speak but Haskell cut her off with, "You can call me Bear. Enough with this Marshal Haskell business. I am not a formal sorta feller."

"Marshal Haskell, I would prefer—"

"See? There you go again, soundin' so formal. Tell me, Miss Lucy, what do you usually do in your nonbusiness hours?"

Haskell knew via the grapevine that she'd been seeing the son of another senator, with plans to be married somewhere down the road. But these high-society types often prolonged engagements to the point of indefiniteness. That left Miss Lucy, to Haskell's mischievous way of thinking, wide open for a possible minor dalliance or two.

He knew he was being a bit of a rascal for thinking the way he was about the girl, who'd never shown any interest in him whatsoever—in fact, she'd always lifted her nose snootily whenever he entered the chief marshal's outer office—yet, still, deep down he sensed a mutual attraction. And he'd like nothing more than to see how she'd look without her glasses on, lying warm and naked under his bedcovers.

Was the attraction he sensed in his head only, and not one bit in hers?

"What I do in my *nonbusiness* hours, Marshal Haskell, is not one bit *your business.* Now, I must insist that you address me as *Miss Kimble* while I call you *Marshal Haskell.* We are professional associates and nothing more. I have heard more than a goodly portion of rumors about you and your penchant for trophy hunting."

Studying the girl regarding him from over the tops of her glasses, Haskell felt a smile tug at his mouth corners. "So, you been askin' around about me—have you, Miss Lucy?"

A flush rose in the girl's smooth, pale cheeks. The blush even crept up into her ears. Was this the confirmation he'd been fishing for?

Miss Kimble sat up straight in her chair and narrowed her eyes behind her spectacles. "*Marshal Haskell,* I assure you I have not been asking—"

She stopped when the chief marshal's office door opened and Henry Dade poked his gray head out, scowling, thick cigar smoke roiling around him. "Bear, is that you I've been hearing out here? Get your ass in my office—uh, pardon my French, Lucy," he hurried to add with chagrin. Then, scowling at the big lawman once more, he said, "What in the hell is the holdup, anyway?"

Haskell reached inside his jacket and pulled out the folded sheets of legal paper. "I was just giving Miss Kimble my report, Chief. A full, detailed accounting of my last assignment—you know, bringin' down those stagecoach robbers?" Grinning, he waved the pages in the air. "Five pages—imagine that! I was just makin' sure Miss Kimble can read my chicken scratch."

"They better be detailed!"

"How do you think I filled up five pages?"

Dade beckoned. "Stop boring my secretary to death and get in here!"

"Boring *her*?" Haskell exclaimed, phonily indignant. "She was the one doin' all the yammerin', just like always!"

As he strode toward Dade's door, he cast the girl a wink. Again a flush rose in her cheeks, and she looked away quickly. Bear thought he saw her mouth quirk a slight grin just before he stepped into his boss's office and closed the door.

Intriguing, that girl. Damned intriguing. Someday, he was gonna tear down her walls . . . and a few other things.

He imagined her snuggling warm, naked, and well satisfied under his bedcovers . . .

Inside Henry Dade's office, Haskell waved the thick smoke away from his face with both hands, coughing. "Holy Jesus, Henry—when are you going to cut down on them stogies? Hell, I can hardly see you, and you ain't but six feet away!"

He peered through the heavy, roiling cigar smoke at his boss, who was just then making his way around behind his large desk, which filled up most of the small office, and slacked into his high-backed leather swivel chair. He leaned back in the chair and puffed the half-smoked stogie clenched in his beringed right hand. "If you can't see me, how do you know I'm six feet away?"

The chief marshal gave a coyote grin and puffed more smoke into the cloudy room. If the clouds roiling around Bear's head had been vapor clouds, it would have been pouring rain.

"There you go outsmarting me again, Chief," Haskell said sarcastically, kicking the hard wooden Windsor visitor's chair away from his boss's desk and easing into it. The chair was about as uncomfortable as one could find in a federal office building. There was a good reason for that. Chief Marshal Henry Dade didn't like to bullshit overlong with anyone, so he saw no reason to make guests one bit comfortable.

"You leave my secretary alone," Dade ordered.

"I was just—"

"I know what you were doing. That girl hales from Sherman Street, toniest neighborhood in Denver. Her father is a state senator. Some think he's going to be the next governor."

"Are you sayin' she's out of my depth?"

"That's exactly what I'm sayin'. If you try to turn that girl into another notch on your gun butt, the senator will make you disappear. He's been known to do that on occasion. If he doesn't, I will!"

Haskell had pulled the Schofield from its holster and was scrutinizing the grips. "Funny how I'm always being accused of notchin' my pistol butt, but I don't see nary a scratch anywhere on this hogleg!"

"Put that thing away before you shoot your pecker off. And tell me why in the hell it's been two and a half weeks since your last assignment and this is the first I've seen of you. If memory serves, you've done already used up all your vacation time for the year . . ."

Haskell's ears warmed slightly. He'd known this was coming. He'd had plenty of time to prepare for his boss's cross-examination on his way out of the mountains. "It's all in my report, boss. What I didn't write in my wire from Henry's Ford is all in them five detailed pages. I was badly injured. Why, do you know what those rapscallions did to me?"

Obviously humoring his charge, Chief Marshal Dade blew a smoke ring into the cloudy air over his desk. "Pray tell."

"They got the jump on me out back of the Bare Naked Lady. That's the saloon/whorehouse I'd heard they'd been holin' up in in Henry's Ford. Apparently, they knew I was waitin' for 'em. Maybe they were glassin' me an' Stumpy from a ridge above the town or somewhere like that. Anyway, like I said, they got the jump on me, beat holy hell out of me—I'm sayin' they beat the shit out of both ends—and when my life was hangin' by a mere thread—"

"A mere thread, eh?"

"A mere thread, Henry!"

The chief marshal frowned with concern. "I see, I see—go on."

"When my life was hangin' by a mere thread, they dragged me around to the back of the old furniture store there in town. The furniture maker was also Henry's Ford's undertaker, and there was some old coffins layin' around. Well, they plopped my near-lifeless body in one o' them coffins, nailed the lid tight, pissed on me, and threw me in the Arkansas River!"

Haskell sat back in his chair and stared across the massive desk at his little, near tallowless boss with short-cropped iron-gray hair and a mustache two shades lighter than his hair. Haskell was met with a near-blank, unblinking stare, so he continued. "And then you know what they did?"

"No, what'd they do next?"

"They shot at me. While I was lyin' helpless and at death's doorstep in the coffin, they fired at me, notched my right ear." Haskell touched his right ear over which he still wore a small bandage. "Still hurts, in fact, as do my sundry other miseries. I think they broke my nose. My eyes were swollen up like eggs. Ribs turned to powder! If Stumpy hadn't thought fast and sent a rope out into the river, just after the coffin busted apart around me, you'd still be sittin' there in your chair, wondering what in tarnation had become of your prized deputy, Henry. What, oh what has become of Bear Haskell, you'd have been sayin', near tears, no doubt."

"No doubt about it. I'd have been a wreck."

"And I'd have likely been floating around somewhere in the Gulf of Fuckin' Mexico!" Haskell pounded his right fist on his chair arm for emphasis. "So that there is the reason I'm so late gettin' back. I was laid up in a hotel there in Henry's Ford, tryin' to get enough strength into my badly beat-up carcass to make my way back down out of the mountains. Still stiff an' sore but I'm a little better now. Could use another few days off, however . . ."

"Huh, that's funny."

"What's funny?"

"That's not how Mister Gibbs told it."

Haskell felt a burn of dread in his gut. "How'd Stumpy tell it?"

"Well, it wasn't easy. I had to threaten him a good deal about relaying certain information about his checkered past to his wife. It's a shame it took that sort of depravity on my part to get the truth out of him, but when I did get the truth out of that old catamount, he finally confessed that he'd left you in Henry's Ford"—the chief marshal leaned forward, scowling, his sallow cheeks on fire, gray eyes blazing—*"diddlin' whores seven ways from Sunday!"*

CHAPTER FIVE

"There was only one whore," Bear said, when it became clear to him that his self-righteous indignation was getting him nowhere with his boss.

Haskell might have seen it all, but Henry Dade had seen it all and then some, and Dade knew when he was getting it spooned to him.

"There was only one whore, Henry, and she was sort of a sawbones, you might say. I mean, there wasn't no *real* sawbones in Henry's Ford, so she done the best she could patchin' me up. Like I said, I'm still stiff and sore and could use a few—"

"Enough bullshit!" the chief marshal said, blowing another heavy smoke plume across his cluttered desk. "I'm taking a week off your next year's vacation. So you were knocked around a little and given a sailing lesson. Boo-hoo." Henry feigned rubbing tears from an eye. "That was a day off from where I come from—Texas, with the Comanches, not to mention the Comancheros runnin' off their leashes. And without no whores to make me feel better afterwards. So I'm shavin' one week off your next year's vacation allotment."

"But Henry—!"

"But Henry, nothin'! Now shut up so I can give you your next assignment. Your train is due to pull out of here in ninety minutes, so you're gonna have to haul your tender ass back to the Larimer pronto, kick out whatever tart you got loungin' around in there like an oversized cat . . ."

"You been spyin' on me, Henry?" Haskell scowled, suspicious.

"And pack a bag and hustle your mangy hide down to Union Station. If you miss that train, I'm gonna cancel your vacation for the next five years, and send you up to Dakota instead—in January—to chase illegal whiskey peddlers on the reservations up thataway!"

"Christalmighty—that's nasty even for you, Chief!"

"Under the circumstances, it's a gift."

"All right, all right," Haskell said, waving again at the toxic fumes billowing around his head and causing his eyes to water. "Give me the next assignment before I suffocate in here."

Dade plucked a thin manila folder from a two-foot-high stack of other similar folders to his left, and tossed it over to Haskell's side of the desk. "You ever hear of a regulator named Jack Hyde?"

"Of course, I have, Henry," Haskell said, opening the folder and giving the first page a cursory skim. "Every man wearin' a badge has heard of Jack Hyde, otherwise known as 'the Jackal.' " Bear chuckled. "I've heard tell that crazy killer has been on the run so long that there are some mothers out there who tell their kids the Jackal's gonna come get 'em if they don't clean their plates or say their prayers."

"That's the one, all right," Dade said. "Never mind that that's one of the cruelest things you could threaten a child with, considering how vile and crazy ole Jack Hyde is. Poison mean. Surlier than a Brahma bull tossed five Texas miles in a cyclone. They say he was born that way. Bad apple from the get-go. As the file says—and it don't say much, because not much is known about Hyde—he's supposedly responsible for the killings of nearly fifty men all across the west. Responsible for the *cold-blooded* killings of all fifty of those men, though no one's been able to put Hyde away for any one of those murders. No prosecutor has been able to build a case against him. Hyde is sneaky. And he moves fast. Sneaky, fast, and deadly."

"Thus 'the Jackal' handle," Haskell said, flipping through the file. "How come there don't appear to be no sketch of him here, Chief?"

"No one seems to know what he looks like. Leastways, if they do, they're not tellin' the authorities."

Haskell closed the file and tossed it back down on Dade's desk. "Don't tell me someone finally knows where he is. Lawmen and bounty hunters across the west have been on his trail for years. I've never heard of anyone even getting close. If anyone had, we would have heard about it. You know what braggarts bounty hunters are."

"The Texas Rangers think they have him pinned down in west Texas."

"You know what braggarts the Texas Rangers are." Haskell grinned.

Dade merely puffed away on his stogie, regarding the big deputy flatly through the billowing smoke.

"Bad joke, Chief," Bear said, sheepishly clearing his throat. "Well, if these rangers have him pinned down, why don't they go ahead and slap the cuffs on him?"

"Three tried to do that last week. Those three men ended up dead and tossed into a shallow wash. Some cowpuncher found their half-eaten bodies strewn by mountain lions."

Haskell whistled. "Three rangers, you say. My, my, my. How do they, whoever *they* is, know these rangers were throwin' down on the Jackal?"

"*They* is Captain Homer Redfield, out of the field office in Sundown, Texas. He and his men were doing some investigative work, and they seem to think they'd identified the Jackal. Redfield sent those men after him, where the Jackal had last been seen, and next thing Redfield knew, those three rangers had become panther bait."

"Damn."

"Yeah."

"Well, anyway, Chief, what does this have to do with us? We're federal. Neither the Jackal nor Texas is in our jurisdiction. Besides, you know better than anybody how nasty the rangers can get when some other lawman goes sniffin' around in their territory. I've stepped into their bailiwick before, and it got nearly as bad as what I went through up in Henry's Ford."

"Homer Redfield is a friend of mine. He has unofficially asked me for help. He's too proud to go through official channels, so he sent me a personal wire. He needs help because those three dead rangers left only two other rangers, including Homer himself, in Homer's remote field office in Sundown. He's badly undermanned, and none of his men are especially good detectives.

"The town has no marshal. The rangers are the only law in Sundown. There is, of course, a county sheriff in the area, but he has somehow disappeared. It seems there's a shootin' war down that way between one large rancher and a handful of smaller ranchers. Homer suspects that one of those two factions, either the large rancher or the smaller ranchers who have formed a pool, has hired Jack Hyde. Apparently, punchers on both sides of the dustup have been dropping like flies, and Homer believes some of those killings, including the sheriff's disappearance, can likely be attributed to Hyde."

"How so?"

"Hyde is known for shooting men from ambush, in the back, from long range."

"Yeah, with a high-powered sporting rifle, I've heard. A Sharps hybrid with a German scope thing."

"A hybrid with a German scope thing, right. You're smarter than you look."

"Thanks, Chief. They're always appreciated—whatever crumbs you'll toss my way."

"Normally I wouldn't send one of my deputies on a personal errand, and I am not doing that now. Not *officially*, anyway. I've done some digging. Two months ago, in Kansas, a stagecoach driver hauling federal mail was shot in the back. Shot right out of the Concord's driver's boot in the middle of nowhere. A county sheriff out that way believes a saloon owner named Angus Fuller hired Hyde to kill the driver, as Fuller believed the driver was having carnal knowledge of Fuller's wife. Unfortunately, the sheriff couldn't prove his case enough to issue any arrest warrants. But the case is still open. And since that coach was hauling mail . . ."

"We can call this a professional mission, and you can sleep tight at night in the knowledge you're not overstepping your bounds enough that you might get called on the carpet by the congressional committee tasked with overseeing the marshals service." Again, Haskell grinned.

Dade blew another heavy smoke plume at him.

"Your contact in Sundown is Homer Redfield. Whatever else you need to know about this case is in the file. You'll have a few traveling days to study it. Now, get your ass out of here. My secretary has your traveling papers all typed and ready to go. You are not to talk to her, understand?"

"Ah, hell, Henry!"

"Do you understand?"

Haskell heaved himself up out of his chair, hanging his head like a chastised dog. "I understand."

The file in hand, he headed for the door.

"Bear?"

Haskell turned back to the chief marshal. "I know—I'm not to undress her with my eyes, either."

Dade drew another lungful of toxic cigar smoke, leaned back

in his chair, and blew the smoke at the ceiling. "Good work up at Henry's Ford. Nice to know those five tomcats will no longer be tormenting the stagecoaches and trains down that way."

Haskell threw his shoulders back, his blue-gray eyes flashing surprise. "Thanks, Chief!"

"Now get out of here. You miss that train you'll be spending the winter in northern Dakota!"

Bear hurried out.

"Don't kill me! Oh, please don't kill me! I don't wanna die! I'm scared! Oh please, oh please, oh please don't kill meeeeee!" cried a young man due to be hanged three days later in the little jerkwater town of San Saba, Texas. "Where's your Christian *mer-ceeeee*?" the young man screamed.

Haskell had started up the broad wooden steps of the Rio Grande Hotel, but now, hearing the young man's pleading cries, the federal lawman stopped and turned toward the gallows sitting in the dusty, sun-blasted street on his left. Two men stood atop the small wooden platform that looked as though it had been hammered together out of shipping crates and a handful of two-by-fours.

A good dozen townsmen as well as towns*women* and even a handful of boys and dogs stood in a ragged semicircle along the base of the platform. Three half-dressed soiled doves stood on a second-floor balcony across the street from the contraption, leaning against the balcony and smoking, enjoying the festivities. A beefy man closest to the platform and wearing a badge held a double-barrel shotgun high across his chest. His expression was businesslike. A tall man in a black suit stood near the wooden lever—a former brake handle from a wagon, it appeared—that would spring the trapdoors beneath the doomed men's boots.

That gent would be the executioner. He had a sweeping gray

mustache. He was checking the time, as though he had a schedule to keep. Or maybe he was waiting for hell's hinges to squawk at the customary hour . . . ?

Both doomed men standing atop the platform, nooses around their necks, wore flour sack hoods. Both had their hands tied or cuffed behind their backs.

The one doing the screaming was the smaller of the two.

He sobbed and begged for mercy. The crowd laughed and heckled him. One man shouted, "Burn in hell, Kirby Pine. Burn in hell. Both you and your old man!"

The man standing next to Kirby Pine bellowed from behind his hood, "I'm gonna come back as a ghost and murder you in your bed, Ben Malcolm!" He laughed. "Yeah, I recognized your voice. I'm gonna come back and kill you with a hatchet—nice and slow! And then I'm gonna rape your wife and both your purty daughters!"

The women in the crowd all gasped and slapped hands to their mouths.

The man with the shotgun turned and gestured angrily to the executioner. The hangman snarled as he jerked the brake handle to one side. The trapdoors beneath both doomed men opened. They dropped down beneath the gallows floor, the double pops of their breaking necks silencing the kid's wails.

The crowd roared its pleasure.

The dogs barked and chased each other.

One of the doves tossed a pink garter belt from the balcony. It landed in the street beneath the feet of the dead men, who were dancing, twisting, and turning, five feet above the ground.

Haskell gave a wry snort—nothing like a public execution to amuse the local populace—then, shifting the weight of his saddlebags, war bag, bedroll, and rifle atop his overburdened shoulders, continued on up the porch steps. He crossed the wide wooden veranda and then stopped to cast his gaze westward down the wide main street of San Saba, back in the direction from which he'd walked.

The spur line that had carried him here from Amarillo aboard a Kansas Pacific freight and passenger combination from Denver ran along the western edge of the little town. The twin silver rails were all that separated the town from the vast, open west Texas desert spiked sporadically with prickly pear, mesquites, catclaw, and sotol cactus, and haunted by little more than rattlesnakes and brush wolves. What few humans and cattle roamed in that nowhere land were scrawny, pathetic, sunken-eyed beasts, barely recognizable as members of their given species.

There was damned little else out there between San Saba and Las Cruces, New Mexico, but a few craggy, bald mountain ranges and some sandy bluffs and mesas.

The four-car combination that had deposited Haskell here, thirty miles from his destination of Sundown farther south, still sat atop those rails, on the far side of the little train depot that resembled nothing more than a two-hole privy. One badly in need of paint as well as a new roof. Apparently, the locomotive's boiler had belched out of its bowels some necessary piece of equipment and couldn't continue until the part was replaced or fixed. The conductor had told Haskell and the other half-dozen impatient passengers that the repairs would likely be made by dawn the next morning.

Haskell hoped the surly gent wasn't blowing smoke up his ass. It was still summer in west Texas. That meant it was as hot as hell with the fires burning. Bear had a job to do even farther south and west of here. He wanted to get that job done as quickly as possible and get the hell back to the cool mountain breezes wafting over Denver from the Rockies before he melted or dried up and blew away.

He pushed into the relative coolness of the hotel's dim lobby and tramped past a couple of wilted potted palms to the impressively long and elaborately scrolled and varnished front desk. He secured a room from the elderly gent clad in a sweaty cotton shirt, green visor, and armbands. The man's right eye twitched uncontrollably beneath the visor.

Ignoring the malfunctioning nerve, Bear paid for a night's slumber with a government voucher supplied by the enigmatic Miss Kimble and left his gear in the care of the eye-twitching desk clerk, whose name was Galvin Dunstable and who was also apparently the bellboy.

Dunstable assured Haskell that once he'd dined, he would find his gear in his room on the second floor, and directed the federal lawman to the hotel's saloon/restaurant opening off a broad open doorway in the wall opposite the desk.

Haskell tossed Dunstable a fifty-cent tip, then made his way to the open doorway, wanting nothing so much as a few shots of bourbon, a beer, and a steak to fill the empty cavern inside him that long train travel always seemed to carve. He stopped in the doorway and was happy to see that there was only one other customer in the dining room—a pretty, honey-haired gal whom Haskell had spied aboard the train. A veritable princess in a white silk blouse and green tweed traveling skirt.

Haskell had checked her out well enough to know that she was traveling alone.

Bear brushed dust and soot from his calico shirt, adjusted his grizzly claw necklace over his chest, and strode into the dining room like a man who knew his business.

CHAPTER SIX

Haskell headed for a table near the golden-haired princess, who sat near the far side of the room and against the front wall. But when he'd gone halfway into the room, a door opened behind the bar running along the room's right wall, and a burly man in gaudy waiter's garb and a waxed mustache came out holding a large tray high above his head.

The waiter walked over to the woman's table and set a smoking platter down in front of her.

"More wine?" he asked.

She'd been staring out the window, watching the festivities over at the gallows. She had an open book on the table before her, and a near-empty glass of wine. She turned to the waiter now, hesitating for a moment when she saw Haskell, then glanced up at the waiter and said, "Please."

She had a pretty voice—not too high, not too deep. Sort of in the midrange of wooden wind chimes. Her eyes were hazel. Her hair was rich and thick, like spun honey, and some of it was gathered atop her head while some of it hung straight down her shoulders and curled lovingly around her breasts, which pushed against her silk blouse. The first two buttons of the blouse were undone, offering an inviting glimpse of the girl's deep cleavage.

As the waiter refilled the princess's wine glass, she looked at Haskell, tilting her head slightly to one side, frowning skeptically. She'd caught the direction of his gaze. He smiled a little sheepishly, pinched his hat brim, and, deciding to let the princess dine in peace, sank into a table three tables from hers, also against the front wall.

When the waiter came over to Haskell's table, the lawman ordered a beer and a shot of bourbon as well as a steak with all the trimmings. The waiter brought the bourbon and a frothy, dark ale from behind the bar, then headed into the kitchen to prepare the lawman's main course.

Haskell sipped the bourbon, enjoying the burn as it rolled down his throat, cutting through the dust and smoke from the locomotive's stack. Since leaving Denver, he'd had a few pulls from his own traveling flask, but there was nothing like a drink in a relatively cool bar—especially in a relatively cool bar in which a pretty girl was dining.

Haskell saw that the young woman had ordered a steak, lightly charred. She was no dainty eater, this girl. She was busily cutting into the meat, charred on the outside but blood-red rare on the inside, and taking hungry bites complemented with generous forkfuls of her fried potatoes and green string beans.

Between bites, she turned her head to stare out the window and into the street where an undertaker's wagon had been drawn up in front of the gallows. Several men were lowering the two hanging dead men to the ground while dogs and boys ran around, barking and yelping.

It was a grisly scene. The girl was riveted. The dead men appeared not to have dampened her hunger one iota. While she watched the corpses get carted over to the wagons, their arms and legs sagging, hooded heads lolling, she continued to shovel food into her mouth and wash it down with quick, deep sips from her wine glass.

While the girl was immersed in the scene outside, Haskell was immersed in the girl. Even when his own steak came and he ate hungrily, he kept one eye on the lovely vixen fifteen feet away from him.

He found her as fascinating as she was beautiful. Something told him that she was a midwesterner. A young, fresh-faced eastern gal traveling alone in the unheeled west, and she didn't seem one bit frightened or repelled by the gallows scene. In fact, she appeared engrossed, even enthralled by it.

Who was she?

What was she doing out here alone?

Haskell decided to get to the bottom of her story. What else did he have to do? The sun was just now starting to slip down in the west, casting long shadows and salmon smudges into the street. There was a lot of night ahead.

When the doomed men had been hauled away and the crowd had disbursed, the young woman turned her attention from the street to her plate. She finished her steak ahead of Haskell, and slid the empty plate aside. She'd eaten every morsel, leaving only a couple of fashionable bites. Picking up her nearly empty wine glass, she turned her attention to the book lying open before her.

When the waiter returned from the kitchen, he refilled the woman's wine glass and took away her plate. He brought Haskell another ale and then hustled Bear's empty plate away, as well.

When the waiter had disappeared into the kitchen, Bear sat back in his chair, stifling a belch and drawing the waistband of his trousers and his two cartridge belts away from his belly with his thumbs. His hunger had been sated by the large steak and healthy portion of potatoes and beans, not to mention the fist-sized baking powder biscuits.

Fortified, he felt ready to make his move. He needed to move fast, he thought. Three townsmen in business suits who'd likely been enjoying the festivities out in the street had sat down at a table between Haskell and the girl, and they were casting furtive stares her way, muttering conspiratorially amongst themselves.

One of them wasn't wearing a wedding ring, and the two others seemed to be encouraging him, with slight elbow jabs, chuckles, and heated murmurs, to make a play for the blond vixen. Not to be beaten at the game he knew so well, Haskell picked up his ale, slid his chair back, rose, adjusted the big Schofield on his hip, and walked past the three businessmen staring up at him incredulously. He stopped at the young woman's table, and smiled at her.

She'd just turned a page of her book. Now she looked up at the big man staring at her, and sipped her wine. She looked him up and down coolly, as though she were inspecting a horse she might be interested in adding to her *remuda,* and gave a faint nod.

Her face was amazing—skin the color of a half-ripe peach and as smooth as a baby's ass. Her hazel eyes were tinted a bronze that matched the stray hues in her hair.

She had a small mole on her neck and another one just above and to the right of her cleavage. Those were the only flaws Haskell could see. He yearned to search for more. Like the slightest defect in the rarest of diamonds, the flaws made her all the more attractive.

Haskell sat down, tossed his hat onto the table, and ran a hand through his thick mop of unruly, dark-brown hair. "Name's—"

"No," the woman said, cutting him off. "Don't talk." Her left hand lay palm down on the table. She slid it toward Bear, lifting her eyes to briefly glance at the three businessmen sitting behind him.

She lifted her hand. Haskell stared down at a room key. The flat brass fob dangling from the key was inscribed with the number 22. "Pick it up, but don't make a show of it," she said tightly under her breath, then smiled and drained her wine glass.

Dazed, Haskell slid the key toward him, picked it up off the table, and lowered his hand to his lap. He stared across the table at the young woman, who leaned forward to say, "Give me fifteen minutes. Make sure you aren't seen."

Haskell tried to respond, but he couldn't work any air past his vocal chords.

The young woman rose from her chair, picked up her book and a reticule, and walked around to Haskell's side of the table. She drew her right hand back and flung it forward, smashing her palm against Haskell's left cheek with a crack like that of a small-caliber pistol being triggered.

"How dare you make such an uncouth advance, you unwashed heathen!" she cried loudly enough for not only the three men in business suits to hear, but for half the town to hear, as well. "What do you take me for—a ten-cent doxie?"

She glanced at the three businessmen staring in silence behind Bear, and said, "Men!"

Chin in the air, she strode angrily across the dining room and out the door.

Haskell sat in stunned silence, his cheek burning, ears ringing.

The three men behind him broke out in delighted laughter.

Haskell glanced over his shoulder at them, shrugged, grinning, then scooped his hat off the table, got up, and walked back over to his original table. He sat and opened his hand in his lap. The room key and the number 22 stared up at him.

"That foxy little bitch," he mused under his breath. He chuckled, shook his head, and slipped the key into his shirt pocket.

Out of that same pocket he withdrew an Indian Kid and a lucifer. He bit the end off the cheroot, spat it onto the floor, and scraped the match to life on his thumbnail. He leisurely smoked the Indian Kid and sipped his beer, feeling both miffed at and intrigued by the golden-haired princess with the wicked right cross.

Miffed, intrigued, and aroused . . .

He drained his beer while the three businessmen ate fried chicken at the table beyond his, then withdrew his tarnished silver railroad watch from his pants pocket, and checked the time. Snapping the lid closed, he tossed the stub of his cheroot into his empty beer glass, rose from his chair, slipped the old turnip back into its pocket, and donned his hat.

As he walked toward the lobby, a man called behind him, "Say, friend?"

Haskell stopped, then looked back. The three businessmen regarded him with brightly jeering eyes, cloth napkins hanging from their collars for bibs.

"You can find a ten-cent doxie over at Ma French's place just up the street a block," one of them said. He winked and jerked his head to indicate east.

He and the others laughed.

"Much obliged," Haskell said with a wooden smile.

The businessmen's laughter followed him out into the lobby, which he crossed with a nod at the desk clerk, who was also chuckling. The clerk had obviously overheard the commotion in the dining room. Haskell mounted the steps.

"I hope you'll find the room to your liking," the clerk called behind him. "Your gear's all there—safe and sound!"

"Oh, I'm sure I'll like it just fine," Haskell returned with a wave, smiling to himself, feeling a hard pull in his trousers toward room 22.

He walked down the hall lit by a couple of fluttering lanterns, and stopped at the room whose number matched the number on the key fob. He poked the key into the lock, the metaphorical implications of the act causing a greater stirring in his loins, and turned the key until he heard the bolt click open. He gave the door a gentle shove.

Hinges creaked.

She was sitting in a chair at the end of the bed. She wore only a chemise that dropped to the middle of her belly. The chemise was thin. Her pronounced nipples pushed against it, atop the two full, round mounds of her breasts. She had one long, fine, pale leg crossed atop the other. Her arms rested on the arms of the chair.

Her chin was dipped toward her chest. Her lips were pooched out speculatively. She looked at him from beneath her brows, her hazel eyes raking him up and down. She reached up to twist a white arm strap of her chemise.

"Come in and close the door," she ordered.

Haskell came in and closed the door. He scrutinized her in much the same way she was scrutinizing him, and, feeling a throbbing in his chest and a tightness in his throat as well as in his pants, said, "What's your . . . ?"

"No names."

"No names?"

She shook her head and rose from her chair. "None whatsoever. I don't care who you are. You can't care who I am. We just are, that's all. We are here for one reason only. One task—the merging of our bodies. When that merging has been accomplished, I want you to leave. If we should ever see each other again, which I doubt"—she gave a faint, ironic snort at that—"you are to act as though you've never seen me before."

Haskell canted his head slightly to one side. "Are you married?"

"No."

"Then, why . . . ?"

"That is none of your business."

"That slap you gave me back in the dining room wasn't called for."

"Oh?" She arched a foxy brow. "Would you like to hit me back?"

Haskell frowned, his eyes probing her faintly amused ones. "I got a feelin' you'd like that, wouldn't you?"

"Maybe," she said. "Why don't you try me?"

Haskell shook his head and turned back to the door.

"Where are you going?" she said, surprise in her voice.

Haskell turned to her, one hand on the knob. "Lady, you're pretty as all hell, but I don't think I like you. I've paid for women with a lot more heart and conversation."

"Heart and conversation?" She laughed, her eyes dancing in the dusky light streaming in through the window flanking her. "Is that what you came up here for—heart and conversation?"

"That'd be nice, for starters. I guess I didn't really realize it before, but, yeah, I guess heart and conversation means as much to me as the rest of it. Now, I see no reason to waste any more of your time. You might find what you're looking for down in the dining room. He's eating fried chicken."

"Damn you!"

Haskell had started to turn the doorknob. He turned back to her again. She frowned at him angrily, jaws hard, a pink flush rising into her perfect cheeks. She reached up and slipped the straps of her chemise down her arms. The flimsy garment fell silently to the floor at her pretty, bare feet.

Haskell's heart began thudding again.

Silently, he cursed.

She smiled with self-satisfaction. "If you're leaving, leave. If you're staying, *stay.*"

Three hours later, Bear lifted his head from the pillow. A sound out on the street had awakened him. Nothing to be alarmed about. Only a couple of horseback riders passing the hotel, conversing drunkenly.

He relaxed once more. The dark wing of sleep had nearly ensconced him once more when someone moaned.

Haskell looked down. His mysterious, gorgeous lover lay curled up between his spread legs. She lay with her head on his belly. His manhood was nestling in the deep cleavage between her breasts.

He grunted a chuckle, remembering their three-hour romp that had started on the dresser and had moved to the bed and then onto the floor before moving back to the bed for the grand finale. Their near-violent tussle had left him tired in every bone and fiber.

The princess lifted her head and, blinking sleepily, looked up at him. Her face was silhouetted by a lantern still burning from a wall bracket. The light glistened redly in her love-mussed hair.

"Oh, god—you're still here!" she said throatily. "What are you still doing here?"

Haskell laid his head back against his pillow once more. Sleep pulled at him hard. "Fell . . . asleep."

She lifted her head, looking down at his manhood, which she'd been sleeping on. "You have to go."

"Simmer down," Haskell said, sleep continuing to pull him down, down. Thickly, he muttered, "Not mornin' yet. I'll be gone . . . by first light."

"No, you need to leave now," she said, scrambling off the bed.

Haskell only grunted. He started to turn onto his side, but she grabbed his right arm and tugged on it. "You have to leave," she said again, keeping her voice low but pitched with urgency. "You have to leave now!"

"Oh, fer chrissakes," Bear said, grabbing her own arm and drawing her easily onto the bed with him, pulling her over him and onto her back, grabbing one of her breasts with his big right hand, and squeezing. "Quit your caterwauling and go back to sleep, darlin'."

"No!" She grunted as she squirmed out from under him and again scrambled off the bed. Into his ear she said softly but commandingly, "You have to leave. Do you hear? Leave!"

Haskell opened his eyes. She was stumbling around as though drunk, gathering his clothes. He watched her, admiring her beauty accentuated by the shifting shadows cast by the lamp. Her ripe breasts jostled, caressed by the ends of her dancing hair. Her ass was beautifully round. He felt himself getting hard again.

"I don't know what wild hair you got up your ass, lady, but why don't you crawl back in here, and I'll try to settle you down. That's gonna have to be the last time, though. I gotta get up early an'—"

She turned to the bed and threw a ragged ball of his clothes at him. There was one boot in the mix. It smacked him in the forehead.

"Ow!" Bear yipped, slapping a hand to his right temple. "What the hell's gotten into—?"

She stumbled around, grabbing more of his clothes from the floor where she'd tossed them when she'd undressed him, damn near devouring him like a hungry catamount. "I don't sleep with my men. When my men are done pleasing me, they go!"

She tossed his hat, bear claw necklace, and another boot at him. This time he caught the boot before it could brain him. "*My* men? Who in the hell do you think you are, lady?"

She tossed his gun belt at him, which he also caught, though the buckle grazed his cheek. "If you are not out of this room in five seconds, I am going to scream rape at the tops of my lungs!"

"*Rape?*" Haskell laughed dryly. "If anyone was raped in here, Princess, that was *me*!"

She cupped her breasts in her hands, blew a lock of hair away from her eye, and canted her head toward the door. "One . . ."

217

"Now, look, honey . . ."

"Two . . ."

"Jesus Christ—you're serious!" Haskell scrambled off the bed, seeing visions of the princess's room being stormed by half the men in the town and whatever lawman was holding down the fort, throwing a horseshoe into Haskell's assignment. If she accused him of rape, there was likely no man within a thousand square miles who would believe Bear over the buxom blond princess.

"Three . . ."

Haskell grabbed up his clothes, his boots, and his gun belts. He donned his hat and, clutching his clothes against his bare chest, ran to the door.

"Four . . ."

He opened the door and looked both ways along the hall. Thank god it was empty. He turned and curled his upper lip at the princess. "How 'bout a goodbye smooch?"

She stared at him coldly. "On the off chance we should ever see each other again, you are not to acknowledge me, as I will not acknowledge you!"

Haskell whistled and ran his gaze across her succulent nakedness. She was still cupping her breasts in her hands. Her hands were much smaller than her lovely bosoms. "That's gonna be awful hard, honey. After all we meant to each other, an' all!"

She threw her head back and opened her mouth wide, as though about to scream.

"I'm gone! I'm gone!" Haskell fumbled open the door and tripped over his own feet going out. He drew the door closed behind him. He heard her turn the key in the lock. He stood there in front of her door for a moment, pondering the mystery of the mysterious beauty.

"I'll be damned if she don't make me feel like a whore." Shaking his head, deeply indignant, the big lawman padded barefoot down the hall toward his own room. "Yessir, nothin' but a used-up old whore!"

CHAPTER SEVEN

The little town of Sundown was a humble collection of mud-brick dwellings and business establishments strewn across the shoulder of a low, rocky hill.

From a distance, the town had looked like nothing more than the same rocks that formed a spine-like cap on the hill. But as Haskell slid up to the settlement now, standing on the rear vestibule of one of the spur line's two passenger cars, his gear at his feet, his rifle on his shoulder, an Indian Kid smoldering between his lips, he could see that those rocks were the mud-brick dwellings of a town, all right.

Not much of a town. But a town just the same.

He was surprised the spur line had slithered a tentacle this far out into the god-forsaken west Texas desert. Nothing around but sand, rocks, prickly pear, and sotol cactus sending their phallic stalks toward the hot, brassy sky. To the southwest rose the blue crags of the Davis Mountains. Not far south of the Davis Mountains was Old Mexico.

Sundown made San Saba look like a bustling metropolis. But the train station was pretty much a carbon copy of San Saba's. A little larger than a two-hole privy, it had two sashed windows, a shake-shingled roof, and a tin chimney pipe. A wooden luggage cart sat on the cobbled platform encircling the depot. One of the cart's wheels was badly bent, and one of the handles was held together with wire.

The U.S. mail pole drew up beside the train as Haskell

stepped down from the vestibule, his gear on his shoulder now. The conductor poked his head out of the small express car and hung the U.S. mail pouch on the hook. The pouch flapped in the dry breeze. There wasn't enough mail in it to hold it down.

The conductor, a tall Mexican with a formal air, looked at Haskell, touched two fingers to the leather bill of his blue wool hat, then pulled his head back into the express car and closed the door. The train hiccupped to a brief halt and immediately shuddered into motion again, slowly picking up steam as it headed back north.

It seemed to be in a hurry to get the hell out of here. Haskell couldn't blame it. He'd been to some out-of-the-way places before, but the sky out here and the vastness of the desert threatened to suck not only the air out of his lungs but his lungs out of his chest.

He grew dizzy for a moment, looking around, seeing how the vast vault of the brassy sky dwarfed the earth. The land was inconsequential. The sky was everything.

There was no one around him. He'd been the only passenger on the train from San Saba. That, too, gave him a hard, empty feeling. He wondered where his golden-haired princess was heading. When he'd risen early that morning and walked past her room, he'd seen through her open door the maid stripping her bed. The princess, whoever she was, had already left. Bear hadn't seen her in the dining room, either.

Despite his earlier assumption that she was a midwestern gal, the beauty must be the daughter of an area rancher, he now speculated. Probably returning home from a finishing school or teacher's college in the east. Back home to Momma and Poppa, her reputation intact despite her decidedly unladylike hungers.

"Need some help with your bags, amigo?" called a disembodied voice.

Haskell removed the cheroot from his mouth and attempted

to follow the voice to its source. Then he saw the man sitting in the deep purple shade cast by a small ramada extending out from above the little depot building's front door. He was a Mexican in a checked wool shirt and canvas trousers held up with a rope belt. A shabby sombrero sat back off his broad, leathery forehead. He sat in a rickety chair, one sandaled foot hiked on a knee. He was whittling a long stick.

"Gracias, amigo, but I got it," Haskell said. Balancing his gear on his shoulders, he returned the Indian Kid to his mouth and took a few pensive puffs, studying the little man in the shade. "I didn't see you there."

"That is the thing about me," the Mexican said. "I am most often not seen. Even when I am seen, I am not seen." He grinned.

"That's not an altogether bad way to be."

"I'm the station agent," the little man said in a thick Spanish accent. "Who are you, if you will not shoot me for asking?"

"Bear Haskell." He debated whether he should identify himself as a lawman, but everyone was going to know who he was and what he was doing here as soon as he started asking questions, anyway. And he couldn't get much done without asking questions. "Deputy U.S. Marshal out of Denver's First District."

"Whew! Señor, that is a long title." The little Mexican rose from his chair and shuffled, sandals flapping against his brown feet, toward Haskell. He held a bone-handled knife in one hand, the long stick in the other hand. "That is a title long enough for a man in the Mexican government, no?"

He chuckled, grinning up at Haskell, who stood a good foot taller than the stoop-shouldered Mex.

"So, you're the station agent here," Haskell said, glancing at the humble dwelling once more, noting a small kitten drinking from a pie pan just inside the building's open front door.

"The name is Orozco, Señor." The Mexican doffed his sombrero and held it over his heart, giving a courtly bow. "Orozco La Paz at your service, Señor."

"I bet you don't get much business through here, eh, Señor La Paz?"

"Sadly, that is true, Señor. But please, amigo—call me Oro."

"Only if you'll call me Bear."

"Bear?" Oro said, and reached over to finger the bear claw necklace hanging down its wearer's broad chest. *"Oso,* eh? *Oso!"* He chuckled knowingly, showing a mouthful of crooked, tobacco-encrusted teeth.

"Oso, you got it." Bear smiled down at the obviously simple-minded fellow.

"What is your business here, Señor *Oso,* if you don't mind me asking? I am a curious man." Oro La Paz held up his hands and looked around in dismay. "I have little to occupy my time, since visitors like yourself are so few and far between that my mind tends to wander. I find myself curious about things that are none of my business. I will no doubt take a bullet for my curiosity one day. I hope not today." He blinked slowly, glancing down at the big Schofield bristling on the bigger man's left hip, and smiled.

"At the moment, let's just say I'm here to see Captain Homer Redfield of the Texas Rangers. If you could direct me his way, Oro, I'd be much obliged."

"Not only will I direct you his way, *Oso,*" Oro said, shuffling quickly over to the dilapidated luggage cart, "but I will take you to him."

He dropped the stick he'd been whittling into the cart and then wheeled the contraption over to Bear. It rattled badly and thumped each time its bent steel wheel touched the cobble platform. "Throw your gear in here. That is too much heaviness for even such a large man as you to burden yourself with in this heat. That is what my cart is for!"

Chuckling, Oro shuffled with his stick over to the mail pole, used the stick to remove the mail pouch from the hook, then shuffled back over to set the stick as well as the pouch inside the cart. He gestured at Haskell commandingly, and the lawman set his gear—saddlebags, rifle, war bag, and bedroll—into the cart, though he thought he'd have an easier time hauling the gear on his shoulders than the depot manager would have hauling it in the rickety cart.

"Come, come," Oro said, grabbing the cart's handles. "I will take you to Captain Redfield."

Bear followed the small fellow and the cart around to the far side of the depot and then along a well-worn path through prickly pear and catclaw. The path skirted a small lean-to stable and a corral built of woven ocotillo branches to a wagon trail that crossed the two silver rails via splintered wooden planks and stretched out into the western nothingness, the two tracks converging into one pale line far beyond the depot. The trail stretched eastward to become Sundown's main street sixty yards beyond the railroad tracks.

Haskell followed Oro toward the town hunched, pale and dusty, to either side of the trail, most of the mud-brick or adobe buildings fronted with brush ramadas. The few signs identifying the various rough-hewn buildings were badly faded and sun-blistered.

There were only three or four people on the street—all Mexicans in the ragged garb of peones. A few saddle horses stood tied to hitchracks here and there, switching their tails at blackflies.

Oro angled his cart toward a cracked adobe that announced simply CANTINA on the street's right side, roughly midway through the tiny town. Haskell followed Oro and the thumping cart toward the watering hole crouched beneath a wide brush arbor under which a clay water pot and gourd dipper hung. He saw three men dressed in the colorful garb of the Mexican vaqueros walk out of another adobe marked CANTINA SAN GABRIEL on the street's left side and another half a block farther east.

Two young Mexican women also dressed brightly but skimpily were lounging on a wooden-railed balcony above the vaqueros. Both girls stared at Haskell and Oro. One was smoking a cornhusk cigarette and blowing the smoke casually over the rail.

The three vaqueros leaned against stout adobe columns fronting the Cantina San Gabriel, crossing their arms, dark eyes beneath the broad brims of their steeple-crowned sombreros riveted on the newcomer.

"Here you are, Señor," Oro said, stopping his cart before the cantina on the street's right side. "You will find Captain Redfield in Rosa's Cantina." He winked at Haskell, grinning. "He likes Rosa, as do most men in Puesta del Sol," he added, using Sundown's original Spanish handle. "He likes Rosa's beans, as well. You will find him here at noon every day, enjoying Rosa as well as her, uh, beans."

He winked lasciviously.

"Reckon I'm gonna have to take a look at Rosa and her, uh, beans." Haskell returned Oro's wink and reached for his saddlebags. "Much obliged, Señor."

"If you wish, Señor Oso, I will cart your gear over to the only hotel in town. I am heading that way, anyway, with the mail. The hotel is also the post office." He canted his head to indicate a three-story, copper-brick building with a high, false, wooden façade up the street and on the left.

Faded letters on the façade read HOTEL DE TEJAS, and several men lounged on the broad front porch of the place. "It will be safe there with Señor Shep until you arrive. Señor Shep is a man of great honor. I assume that, for whatever reason you are here, you will be spending the night here in Puesta del Sol . . . ?"

"*Sí,*" Bear said, inspecting the big hotel.

He removed only his rifle from the cart, leaving the saddlebags, bedroll, and war bag. Even if he hadn't instinctively trusted the depot agent, he wouldn't have insulted his honor by removing his gear from the cart. Besides, Haskell wasn't carrying much of any value—aside from his guns, that was. And he had all those on his person.

"Thanks again, Señor." Bear rested his sheathed Henry on his shoulder and rolled the Indian Kid, which had gone out, from one side of his mouth to the other.

"*De nada, Señor Oso!*" Oro lifted the cart by its handles and shuffled off toward the hotel.

Haskell looked once more toward the three vaqueros standing in front of the Cantina San Gabriel. All three were watching him closely with sullen interest.

Haskell turned and strode up the three steps of Rosa's Cantina. He pushed through the batwings and stepped to one side, letting his eyes adjust to the murky shadows while trying not to make too large of a target silhouetted against the outside, midday light.

Rosa's was a small, earthen-floored place that smelled heavily of peppers and tequila. There were many totems to saints on the walls, and several wooden crucifixes. Two old Mexican men sat to Haskell's immediate right, playing poker with matchsticks.

Another man sat with his back to the wall beyond the two oldsters. He was seated in a wheelchair and crouched over a board laid across the arms of his chair, serving as a table, and he was spooning beans from a wooden bowl into his mouth. A bottle of tequila and a tin cup sat on the board near the bowl.

A Mexican woman stood behind the ornate mahogany bar at

the back of the room. She appeared in her early thirties. Haskell couldn't see much of her in the dingy light and from his distance of twenty feet, but she appeared pretty in a severe sort of way, with high, Indian-like cheekbones, a hawkish nose, and black hair pulled back into a chignon behind her head. She wore a red and white calico blouse, which appeared quite well filled out.

Pots steamed and bubbled on a range behind her. She was drying shot glasses and beer mugs with a ragged towel. Her black-eyed gaze was on Haskell, but her face was expressionless to the point of ennui.

A black cat sat sphinx-like on the bar to her left, on a small quilted pad. It, too, had its sleepy scrutiny on Haskell. It blinked those green-copper orbs slowly.

Haskell's neck hairs bristled when he heard the slow click of a heavy gun hammer. The slow click of another gun hammer followed close on the heels of the first. "Come in slow, keepin' your hand away from that pistol on your left hip there, and maybe I won't shred you to bloody bits."

Haskell looked first at the two old card-players. They both had their hands above their table, looking speculatively up at Haskell. The lawman then turned his gaze to the only other gent in the room—the one in the wheelchair.

He appeared a gringo despite the ruddiness of his features. The man's right hand was under his makeshift table, and his clear blue eyes blazed in the shadows beneath the brim of his badly weathered cream Stetson.

Haskell walked slowly toward the man in the wheelchair. As he made his way through the shadows and around two tables that had been impeding his view of the man, he saw that the man's left leg was in a plaster cast. It stuck straight out in front of him. His toes were dark blue, the yellow nails as thick as shells.

He wore a silver beard, which accentuated the sky blue of his eyes.

Two small, leather sheaths were strapped to the sides of his chair, pointed straight down to the floor. The walnut stock of a sawed-off shotgun jutted from the left sheath. The twin, round bores of the other sawed-off shotgun glared ominously out from under the board that served as the man's table.

They were like the eyes of a black cobra staring down the prey that was Haskell.

CHAPTER EIGHT

Haskell stopped before the gray-bearded man in the wheelchair, whose blue eyes were rheumy from drink. Maybe from pain, as well. Haskell eyed the man's purple toes.

"Redfield?"

The ranger flared a nostril. "Who're you?"

"Your old pal Henry Dade sent me. I'm Bear Haskell, deputy U.S. marshal out of Denver."

Redfield frowned, vaguely sheepish. "You don't say."

"I didn't see a badge on your chest."

"That's 'cause there ain't one there."

"You can sheath that cannon, Captain."

Redfield smirked and snaked the shotgun out from under the board table and slid it into the sheath on the right side of the chair. Haskell sat at a small, square, badly scarred table beside Redfield and put his back to the wall. He propped an elbow on the table and half-turned to the surly ranger.

"You expectin' trouble, are you?"

"I'm always expectin' trouble," Redfield said, spooning more beans into his mouth, sucking the juice off his mustache and looking around owlishly. "Ever since a diamondback found its way into my sleepin' quarters an' bit my leg—yeah, I been expectin' trouble. Don't see no reason to put a shiny target on my chest, to boot!"

Haskell was about to probe the ranger further, but he stopped when the woman from behind the bar walked up to his table.

Haskell opined that she was, indeed, nearly his age, early-to-mid thirties, but she'd worn the years well. Bear could see why the middle-aged ranger frequented the woman's cantina.

"Would you like some beans?" she asked Bear. "Tequila?"

"You can't beat Rosa's beans," Redfield told the federal lawman out of the side of his mouth, chewing, looking lustily up at the woman. "You can't beat her tequila, either. Her family makes it down in Mejico. Ever since I pulled into this backwater, I been livin' on Rosa's beans and tequila. Asked her to marry me, but she won't say one way or another. I think she's got her another man. Maybe some border bandit who visits her under cover of darkness. That's the only way I can figure it. A looker like her's gotta have her a man somewhere. She won't give me the time of day."

"I'll give you the time of day, Captain," Rosa said, a beguiling half-smile on her wide mouth as she glanced at a clock on the wall behind the bar. "It is a quarter to one in the afternoon." Her smile widened. "There—are you happy?"

"I'd be a whole lot happier if—"

Rosa cut him off by turning to Bear and saying, "I also have whiskey and javelina stew, Señor . . . ?"

"Bear." Haskell smiled up at her.

"*Oso.*" She leaned across Haskell's table and fingered the bear claw necklace decorating the front of his calico shirt. Her blouse drew away from her chest, offering him a tantalizing glimpse inside a thin chemise. "Hmmm. Did you make this yourself?"

"It wasn't my idea. The owner of them claws knocked on my door. I didn't knock on his."

Rosa released the necklace and straightened. "Is that how you treat everyone who knocks on your door, *Oso*?"

"Why don't you find out for yourself?"

She arched a speculative brow, then gave him a cool, slow

blink. "Have you made up your mind?"

"Redfield makes the beans and tequila sound so good, I think I'll have that."

"Good choice." Rosa turned sharply, skirt swirling, and strode back behind the bar to her steaming range.

Redfield glowered at Haskell, his juice-dripping spoon raised to his chin. "By god, how in the hell did you do that?"

"Do what?"

"Make her blush like that. I been workin' on that pretty Mex for nigh on two years now, and she still looks at me like somethin' the cat dragged in." Redfield looked Bear up and down. "Christ, how tall are you, anyway?"

"Six-six."

"That's it. She likes big men. I'm only five-ten when I'm standing up. Shit! I could lose some weight, at least. Christ— look at me!" The ranger grabbed his considerable paunch in disdain.

Rosa brought a steaming bowl and a bottle and a glass over to Haskell's table. The pinto beans, swimming in juice and speckled with chopped chili peppers and onions, flooded Haskell's nostrils with their succulent aroma. Rosa smiled at him, ignoring the ranger, and then strode back toward the bar.

"Goddamnit!" Redfield cursed again under his breath, ogling the lovely sway of the woman's retreating ass.

Haskell splashed tequila into his glass and threw back half. It cut his tonsils like a rusty knife, but it smoothed out the travel kinks. "Snakebit, eh?"

"Yeah." Redfield had resumed eating. "Someone squirreled that snake into my sleeping quarters. No way it got in there by accident. Around here, you make sure there ain't no holes a snake can slither through. Nests all over the place."

"Are you sure?"

"Sure I'm sure. My last man besides me disappeared last

week. Shot out on the range, I'm bettin'. Rodriguez rode out to investigate two more killin's. Two more small-time, ten-cow ranchers killed. Shot in the back from long range by a big-caliber rifle. I can't ride out there myself for obvious reasons. That snake bit me a day after I sent Rodriguez out to investigate. How fuckin' coincidental!" Redfield chuckled darkly at that.

"You think Jack Hyde's the culprit?"

"Many of the killin's around here have the Jackal's stamp all over 'em. Mainly, shot from long range by a big-caliber rifle. Everybody knows Hyde carries a—"

"Sharps hybrid with a fancy scope thing."

"You know about that?"

"Henry gave me a file on what's been compiled on the Jackal. He's been at play out here in the fields of the devil for a good long time, but nobody seems to know much about him except that he carries a Sharps and he's devilish good with it. There doesn't seem to be any agreement on just what he looks like, exactly."

"It's damn odd!"

"One person will say he's a little tow-headed guy, around five-four, and the next person will say he's dark and my height."

Redfield spooned the last of his beans into his mouth, raked a grimy sleeve across his lips, and shook his head. "I been in this business fer a long time, and I've never run across such a slippery critter as the Jackal."

"Is the main reason you think Hyde is down here killin' folks because of his trademark killin' style?"

"That and rumors. And because whoever is doin' the killin' is so damned hard to catch. He's sneaky, coyote-like! He'll stray off course from time to time and do somethin' odd like throw a snake into my sleepin' quarters. That's just like the Jackal! He likes to terrorize and beguile folks before shootin' 'em in the back from long range.

"Some of the boys out to the Box 6, a little ranch down the road a piece, said that someone was messin' around in their bunkhouse for several days, rearranging their gear, messin' with huntin' trophies on the walls, an' leaving dead mice under pillows an' such before two of them ended up belly down out on the range with bullets in their backs."

Redfield gave another dark snort and reached for his tequila bottle. As he did, both the old-timers who'd been playing poker heaved themselves up from their chairs.

That startled Redfield, who dropped his bottle and reached for both his sawed-off shotguns, filling his hands with both big poppers simultaneously and training the barrels on the old Mexicans.

Both jerked with alarmed grunts. One fell back into his chair.

The ranger barked, "Goddamnit, why in the hell are you two bean-eaters movin' so damn fast for?"

They looked at each other before turning their wary gazes back to the four stout barrels aimed at them.

Haskell cleared his throat. "I think they were just gettin' up to leave, Captain." He looked at the two worried oldsters, both of whom were holding their hands up to their shoulders. "Why don't you sheath them cannons before somebody gets hurt?"

Redfield wagged the guns at the old Mexicans. They hustled away from their table to the door, glancing cautiously over their shoulders.

The ranger peered around, as though suspecting more trouble from any quarter, then slowly sheathed the shotguns. "I can't be too careful. Laid up the way I am, I'm a sittin' duck. I'm an old wolf with a bum leg." Redfield glanced at Haskell, then jerked his chin to indicate the street outside the cantina. "You see them young wolves up the street, over to the Cantina San Gabriel?"

"I saw 'em."

"If the Jackal don't get me first, they're gonna kill me. Sure as I'm sittin' here."

"Why's that?"

"Because they want the run of the town. I'm an old wolf with one good leg. They're young. They got both their legs. That's the way things work out here!"

Redfield turned to Haskell, who was spooning beans into his mouth and sipping his tequila while watching the ranger. Bear wondered if there was anything to what the man was saying or if the snake venom was rotting out his brain. It did that to some men. He looked at the man's toes again. They sure looked black. Maybe his brain was the same color . . .

The ranger turned to Haskell, one brow cocked malevolently. "I said I was the last lawman standin'. Not no more." He gave a wolfish grin. "There's you now, too." He dipped his chin to punctuate the warning.

Holding his filled spoon to his mouth, Bear glanced out the cantina's front windows. He couldn't see the brightly dressed vaqueros outside of the Cantina San Gabriel anymore, but several horses were still tied to the hitchrack fronting the place.

"You think those fellers over there ride for one of the two warring factions in these parts?" he asked the ranger, who sat back in his chair now, one hand wrapped around his freshly filled tequila glass.

Redfield nodded dully, as though deep in thought. "That's right."

"Have you asked them who they ride for?"

Redfield turned to Haskell, frowning, as though he'd suddenly realized he'd been sitting here chinning with a crazy man. "Around here, you don't ask questions like that. Maybe up in Colorado, Kansas, Nebraska Territory. Maybe as far up as the Canadian line." He shook his head slowly. "Down here, this close to the border, you don't ask questions like that. Not if you don't want your throat cut, a bullet in your back, or . . ." He glanced down at his near-black toes. "A snake tossed into your sleepin' quarters."

He gave a shudder as though at the remembered image of the snake, maybe at the remembered burning pain of the two sharp fangs sinking into his flesh and pumping his leg full of poison. He threw back his entire shot of tequila, slammed the glass back onto the table, and clumsily refilled it.

Haskell turned to stare out the window at Cantina San Gabriel again. He tapped his fingers on the table, thinking it through.

"Well," he said at last. "Someone's gotta do the askin'. Might as well be me."

"Here's to ya," Redfield said, lifting his glass in salute. He gave the federal lawman a mocking wink and threw back another entire shot.

"Is that good for the poison?" Haskell asked him skeptically as he gained his feet and scooped the Henry up off the table.

"It may not be good for the poison," said Redfield, "but it sure is good for me." He snickered as he splashed more tequila into his glass.

CHAPTER NINE

Bear set his rifle on his shoulder and walked up to the bar. Rosa was washing pots and pans in a tub of warm water on the range. "What do I owe you?" he asked her.

She'd turned to watch him tramp up to the bar, a vague expression of female interest in her gaze. "How much of the bottle did you drink?"

"Charge me for the whole thing." Haskell winked at her. "I'll be back."

"You think so?" Rosa said with a vaguely malevolent twist of her lips. "Maybe, maybe not."

"What does that mean?"

"What do you think it means?" she said, turning to scrub a cast-iron skillet. "This isn't healthy country for lawmen. The captain told you that."

Haskell tossed several coins onto the bar. "Say, Rosa, you appear to be a woman who keeps an ear to the wind. You got any idea who Jack Hyde rides for?"

She looked at him again over her shoulder, her expression flat. "Who is Jack Hyde?"

Haskell studied her. He couldn't tell if she knew the answer to his question or not. He supposed it was unfair asking her out in the open like this. He gave a wry snort, pinched his hat brim to her, and strode on out through the batwings and into the street.

He stopped and looked around. The street was still nearly

vacant, the sun blinding, the breeze churning dust. A mongrel dog crossed the street to Haskell's left, head and tail drooping, tongue hanging over its lower jaw.

Beyond the dog, Orozco La Paz was making his way back toward the railroad depot, pushing his cart ahead of him, sandals slapping against his heels.

Haskell turned to Cantina San Gabriel just as the same three vaqueros he'd seen before stepped through the batwings. They each leaned against an adobe column, arms crossed on their chests, sombrero-clad heads canted to one side in gestures of silent threat.

Haskell grinned and waved. They just stared at him.

Haskell strode toward them. As he did, their expressions changed from surly boredom to vague interest to faint wariness. When Bear was ten feet away from the cantina's ramada, the man who'd been leaning against the center column slowly straightened, dropped his arms to his sides, turned away, and pushed through the batwings.

"He's coming this way!" Haskell heard the man say inside the cantina, in a thick Spanish accent.

"Well, let him come, then," said another man in fluent English.

Haskell kept his face impassive as he stepped between the other two vaqueros holding up columns, pushed through the batwings, and stopped just inside. Two men stood at the bar at the back of the room. They were both Anglos—one a brown-eyed blond with a boyish face. The other was brown-haired, and he sported a patchy beard, pockmarks, and cobalt eyes. The two other men in the room—besides the rotund Mexican bartender, that was—were Mexicans. The one who'd come in ahead of Haskell was just now easing into a chair near the other one, at a table against the wall to Haskell's right.

All eyes were on the lawman. The brown-eyed blond, who

wore a fringed buckskin tunic and sand-colored Stetson with a *concho*-studded band, as well as two ivory-gripped Colts strapped to his thighs, grinned mockingly. A half-filled beer mug and an empty shot glass stood on the bar before him.

He chuckled and said, "Oh, I'm sorry—you bein' a stranger here an' all probably wouldn't know that this here is a members-only club." He held up his hand and waved his fingers at the door. "You're gonna have to turn around and dance right back out through them doors there, big feller."

"And don't let them hit you in the ass!" said the other Anglo, standing beside the blond.

The two Mexicans laughed.

The Anglos chuckled.

"Well, shit," Haskell said in mock apology. "I didn't realize that. I didn't see no sign or nothin'."

Behind him, the batwings rasped. There was the click of a pistol being cocked. The lawman whirled, grabbing for his Schofield. The revolver roared and bucked, flames lapping from the barrel.

The Mexican who'd been coming into the saloon behind Haskell fired his own pistol into the floor as he crouched over the bloody hole in his belly. His head snapped up and to one side when his own bullet ricocheted off the stone floor and clipped his left temple.

He sat down hard, howling, arms folded across his belly.

The lawman whirled again, cocking the Schofield again. The other two Mexicans had begun lurching out of their chairs, but now they froze, faces twisted in rage. The brown-eyed blond and the cobalt-eyed, pockmarked gent had dropped their hands to their pistols. Like the Mexicans, they froze, hands on their gun handles, their backs stiff, anger glinting in their eyes.

The Mexican bartender had disappeared.

"That seems like a mighty hefty sentence," Bear said to the

brown-eyed blond, who seemed the leader of the pack. "Shooting a man in the back—a *lawman* in the back, no less—just for walking into a club he don't belong to."

The pockmarked man pointed angrily at the man grunting between the batwings. "There's gonna be a reckonin' for that!"

Haskell took two steps back and holstered his Schofield. He dropped his hands to his sides and shuttled a hard, challenging look at the two Mexicans, then at the two men standing stiffly at the bar.

"Let's get that reckonin' out of the way, then, so we can get down to business."

They looked at him uncertainly. The two men at the bar glanced at each other. The two Mexicans glanced at each other and then at the two at the bar.

The Mexicans smiled as they turned again to the big lawman, their brown hands hanging down over their holstered six-shooters.

The pockmarked gent flared a nostril and twitched an eye.

The brown-eyed blond looked at his cohorts nervously, frowning. "Hold on, now. Just hold on!"

"What's the matter, Jordan?" The pockmarked man glanced at the brown-eyed blond. "No stomach for it?"

Jordan looked troubled. "You mean, in here? Right now?"

"You know of a better time?" Haskell asked him, keeping his voice pitched with menace. "Or a better place?" He curled his upper lip. "I don't think your friends do."

One of the Mexicans chuckled through his teeth. The other Mexican grinned confidently, but a single bead of sweat was rolling down his face.

Haskell swept his gaze across them once more. He knew he was taking a chance, but something told him the four men before him were more talk than resolute action.

It was doubtful any of them were faster with a shooting iron

239

than he was. Besides, speed in such a situation wasn't always that important. Experience and calm often carried the day. A man could be fast, but if his nerves caused his hand to shake, or caused him to hesitate however briefly, or made him one bit squeamish about engaging in such a savage, close-quarter dustup, he would likely die.

This wasn't Haskell's first rodeo.

While he couldn't get answers to his questions from dead men, the news of what happened here would likely spread like a wildfire. It would call in the jackals, maybe even *the* Jackal himself. There was no way that any of the five men in this current pack was Jack Hyde. They were lapdogs to Hyde's stalking wolf.

The four men stared at Haskell. He stared back, flicking his gaze across them, trying to figure which one would pull first. Certainly not Jordan. The brown-eyed blond might have been the pack leader, but he obviously had no stomach for what was happening.

Jordan held up his hands, palms out, and said tightly, voice quavering, "Hold on, now. Hold on, hold on!"

"Hold this, rich boy!" The pockmarked gent reached for the .45 thonged on his right thigh.

Haskell's own revolver was in his hand a half-second before the pockmarked man got his own pistol aimed. The Schofield roared. The pockmarked man gave a yowl and jerked violently back against the bar. From the corner of his right eye, Haskell saw both Mexicans snap up their own hoglegs.

Bear pivoted and fired, sending one Mexican flying backward. He dodged the second Mex's bullet, then threw himself to his left, diving over a table. He hit the floor as the Mexican's second bullet plunked into a chair fronting Bear on his right.

Haskell rolled onto his left knee, jerked the Schofield, and fired two shots into the Mexican, who fired another round while bellowing Spanish epithets. As the lawman's bullets ripped through his chest, shredding his heart and lungs, he flew backward against the wall, dislodging a painting of a naked, brown-skinned young woman sprawled on a white divan with a come-hither expression on her heart-shaped face.

The Mexican piled up at the base of the floor, screaming.

Haskell turned toward the bar. Jordan had both of his own fancy Colts in his hands. Crouching forward, pressing his butt against the bar behind him, he screamed as he fired. He flinched with every shot, sending the bullets squealing over and around Bear to hammer the front wall and plunk through the batwing doors.

Crouching, Haskell returned fire.

He'd vaguely decided during the shooting to try to leave at least one of these jackals alive, to get some information out of him. He aimed at Jordan's left shoulder, but because the kid was moving so wildly, jerking his arms with each shot, Bear's bullet raked along the left side of Jordan's head instead.

The blond's left ear turned red.

He screamed, dropped both his guns to the floor, and twisted around to face the bar, placing his elbows on the bar top, leaning forward and clutching his head in his hands.

"Oh—*owww!*" Jordan cried, stomping his feet and clutching his head.

Blood oozed between the fingers of his left hand.

"*Goddamnit!*" he bellowed.

The barman lifted his head above the bar, looking owly. He glanced at Bear, who was still holding his smoking Schofield on the kid. The barman swept his dark-eyed gaze around the room, taking in the two dead Mexicans and then leaning forward to see the pockmarked man slumped at the base of the bar as though he'd sat down on the floor to take a nap.

The barman scowled, reached under the bar for a rag, and

tossed it to the howling blond. "Here you go, Jordan. Don't get blood all over the bar!"

Haskell walked forward and kicked Jordan's two guns over to where the dead Mexicans lay in thickening blood pools. He looked at the bartender, who was pouring himself a shot.

"Who are they?" the lawman asked, canting his head toward the Mexicans and then glancing at Jordan.

The barman opened his mouth to speak but it was another man—behind Haskell—who spoke. Roared, rather: "Leave it to a polecat like Henry Dade to send a catamount like you to blow up my bailiwick!"

Haskell turned to see Homer Redfield sitting in his wheelchair just inside the batwings. Rosa stood behind him, hands on the chair handles. She calmly inspected the carnage.

Redfield looked around, too, then laughed. "I'll be jiggered—look at that! Cal Merritt, Sergio Ramos, Alberto Morata, and Diego Costa—wolf bait."

Haskell said, "Who are they?"

Jordan turned from the bar to glare at Haskell. He was holding the bar towel over his right ear. His shrill voice cracked as he cried, "I am Jordan Tifflin. Ambrose Tifflin is my father, you crazy bastard! Ever heard of him? No? Well, you're about to!"

"Yeah, I reckon you're about to," Redfield said, giving a rueful snort. "Tifflin's the big dog in these parts. Runs the Rancho San Rafael for the big English syndicate that bought out the Spanish land grant some years back. Jordan's Tifflin's only boy."

Haskell scowled at the lawman but gestured at young Tifflin. "Did you know he was here when you sent me over here?"

"Sure!" the ranger laughed. "I figured you'd find out sooner or later. Figured later was good enough, I reckon . . . if you lived." He grinned, then glowered at Tifflin. "I was hopin' maybe you'd kill him, though, damnit. Like you done the others. Jordan might have been shat out with a silver spoon in his mouth, but he's got a heart of coal!"

Haskell slacked into a chair and dug an Indian Kid out of his shirt pocket. He raked a match across his thumbnail and narrowed an eye at Jordan Tifflin. "You ride for your father, do you?"

"Hell, he don't ride for his father." Redfield chuckled. "He's no ranch hand. Him an' these miscreants here ride fer themselves . . . *rode* fer themselves, I should say . . . back and forth across the border. Hell-raisers an' stock thieves is all they are. Were!"

Young Tifflin glared at Redfield. "Shut up, you old fool!"

Redfield glared back at him.

Rosa said, "I'd best fetch a doctor to stitch the little dog's ear so he doesn't bleed to death."

She glanced once more at Haskell, then turned and pushed through the batwings.

"Could you yell for the undertaker, too, Rosa?" Redfield called after her, politely.

Haskell looked at Tifflin. "Would have been a hell of a lot easier for you if you'd just answered a few questions. Now look what's happened. Your pards is dead."

"You're about to be dead, too, when my pa sees what you done to me."

"We'll see about that," Haskell said, nodding speculatively while puffing the cheroot. Time to ask the question that had brought him to the Cantina San Gabriel in the first place. "Does Jack Hyde ride for your old man?"

"Who's Jack Hyde?" the surly younker asked. Either the kid was a good liar or it was an honest answer.

"Who else would the Jackal be ridin' for?" Redfield said with an angry grunt. "The smaller ranchers couldn't afford Hyde's wages."

"You don't know your ass from a sack of hammers, you old

fool!" Tifflin laughed with shrill mockery at the old ranger. "Look at you, Redfield. Your leg's rottin' off. An' you're drunker'n a snake in a vat full of whiskey. If that snake didn't kill ya, the hardtails in these parts will. Soon!"

Redfield glared through his red-rimmed eyes. His cheeks mottled dark with anger. He wheeled himself down the room toward Tifflin standing before the bar. He stopped six feet away from the rancher's son, shucked the shotgun from the sheath on the right side of his chair, and pointed it over his black toes at Tifflin's belly.

The heavy hammers clicked throatily as the ranger rocked them back to full cock.

"Was it you who threw that snake into my sleepin' quarters?" The ranger shook his head. "Nah, you wouldn't have the stomach for handlin' a diamondback. But I reckon you could have dared someone else to do it. Bought it done for tequila . . ."

Tifflin eyed the double bores bearing down on him. "Stop pointin' that cannon at me, you old fool. You . . . you don't know what you're doin'. You're drunk. Point it away, you hear?"

Haskell drew on the Indian Kid and watched the old ranger through the billowing smoke. Bear would like to have seen the old mossyhorn in his heyday, riding hell-for-leather with Henry Dade.

Redfield glowered at young Tifflin. Finally, his face relaxed. He smiled coldly, depressed the shotgun's hammers, and returned the big popper to its sheath.

He turned to Haskell. "What you wanna do with him? Throw him in the icehouse?"

Haskell blew a long plume of smoke at Jordan Tifflin. "Nah. I think I'm gonna take the boy home to his pa."

Redfield tipped his head back a little and to one side, and frowned. "You sure about that?"

"Why not?" Haskell drew another deep lungful of smoke from the Indian Kid. "The man might be worried about his only boy . . . in town all by his lonesome."

Redfield looked around at the dead men, then turned back to Bear, shook his head, and chuckled darkly. "You sure don't mind livin' dangerous—I'll give you that. Henry told me he was sendin' a catamount, an' he wasn't whistlin' 'Dixie'!"

CHAPTER TEN

While the local sawbones sewed up the kid's ear in the Cantina San Gabriel, Haskell walked over to the town's sole livery and feed barn and rented a stout saddle horse—a bright-eyed pinto that looked ready to burn off some of the stable green.

Bear had the liveryman, an Irishman named Cecil Moore, saddle young Tifflin's mount, as well. Jordan had been in town longer than his pards, holing up with doxies, and he'd stabled his gelding in Moore's barn.

The lawman, who'd retrieved his gear from the hotel, had decided to head out to Rancho San Rafael even though the sun was beginning its slow descent in the west. According to Redfield, the ranch was a two-hour ride west of town, but there was roughly that much good light left. Depending on what kind of time they made, night might or might not fall before Haskell and his young charge arrived at the ranch. If it got too dark for safe travel, they'd camp.

The lawman saw no reason to let grass grow under him in Sundown. He was doing nothing in town except providing business for the local undertakers, both of whom, two middle-aged Mexican men, were hauling Cal Merritt's carcass out of the Cantina San Gabriel when Haskell rode up, trailing young Tifflin's blue roan.

"You can send the boy out, Cap!" Bear called as he swung down from the pinto's back.

Boot thuds sounded inside the cantina. Jordan Tifflin's blond head appeared over the batwings. He wore a white pad over his right ear. Two red, ragged-edged dots stained the bandage. The kid glared out from beneath the broad brim of his sand-colored Stetson, the silver *conchos* winking in the golden sunlight.

The rattle of wheels sounded behind the kid, who lurched suddenly out through the batwings, stumbling and cursing and turning his head to glare behind him. "I'm gonna kill you, you old fool!"

Redfield pushed through the batwings, using his left hand. He was holding a sawed-off shotgun in his right hand, aiming the barrel over his discolored toes. His right eye twitched, and he said, "I oughta cut you in half right now. Save me a whole lotta trouble in the future!"

"You don't have a future!" Tifflin bellowed, red-faced, leaning forward at the waist.

"Son, that is no way to talk to your elders," Haskell said.

Redfield stared at Tifflin while he said to Bear, "This here is what happens when you leave all the branches on your willow shrubs 'stead of puttin' any of 'em to good use skinnin' a colicky backside. Let that be a lesson to you, in case you ever have a sprout of your own one day." He gave Haskell a knowing wink.

"Good advice."

Young Tifflin turned to Bear. "You ain't gonna have a chance to sow your seed, you big ugly son of a bitch. I doubt you'll make it as far as the headquarters of the San Rafael. Strangers don't live too long out that way. Not these days they don't. Even if you do make it, my old man will see you don't see another sunrise. Not after what you done to my ear. My old man is partial to the Apache ways of torture. Yessir, he admires the Apaches. He'll bury you so deep in the sand you'll be inhalin' ants!"

"Ambrose Tifflin was one hell of an Apache fighter—I'll give him that," Redfield said. "But that was a long time ago, son. You an' I both know it!"

To Bear, Tifflin said, "It's gonna be dark soon. We'd best wait till tomorrow to ride out to the San Rafael. Better yet, why don't you just send for my pa? Ridin' out there is suicide. Are you a damn fool or something?"

"What's the matter, sonny?" Bear said. "You look fearful."

"My problem is I'm not a damn foo—!"

Tifflin cut himself off. He turned to stare at a half-dozen men just then riding into town from the west. They were a ragged, dusty, mixed-breed lot—some Mexicans, some Anglos (though it was often hard to distinguish Anglos from Mexicans in this country where the sun and wind burned men raw).

One definitely had some Apache blood, if he wasn't full. He had on a sombrero, but he wore his blue-black hair in tight braids wrapped in rawhide. He wore deerskin leggings Apache-style—folded down at the knees. The toes of his moccasins curled upward. He wore two cartridge bandoliers crisscrossed on his broad chest clad in green calico.

"Fuck," Haskell heard Redfield mutter from his chair.

"Friends of yours?" Bear asked.

"Friends, hell."

"Which faction do you suppose they work for?" Haskell asked the local lawman.

Redfield scratched his jaw. "Hard to tell."

Haskell looked at Tifflin, who was staring uncertainly at the half-dozen men riding toward him, Haskell, and Redfield. "Who do they ride for?"

"Hell if I know," the rancher's son said.

As the desperadoes passed, dust lifting from the hooves of their fast-walking horses, they all turned to regard Haskell and then Tifflin and Redfield. One kept his gaze on the younker, then pointed at his own ear and said, "Ouch!"

The others laughed.

They passed, heading for the other side of the little town and, probably, toward a watering hole.

"They'll start at that end of Sundown," Redfield said, his voice darkly speculative. "Then slowly make their way toward this end. Come midnight, the whores'll be screamin', an' I don't mean in a good way. That Apache's name is Hector Valderrama. Half-Mexican, half-Coyotero. His ma is one of Geronimo's daughters. He runs with a rough bunch from both sides of the border. I've seen him along the border but never this far north. Shit!"

The old ranger wagged his head bewilderedly, then turned to young Tifflin. "If your old man hired Hector Valderrama and them others, he don't understand what a pack of broomtails he's bringin' into this country. It's one thing bringin' men like that in to do your shootin' for ya. It's another thing controllin' 'em and then gettin' rid of 'em. You tell him that when you see him again!"

Young Tifflin didn't appear to have been listening to the ranger. He was staring after the lobos. He turned to Haskell, his gaze dark. "We'd best stay in town. Crazy bunch ridin' the range these days. You send someone for my old man. He'll come to fetch me with a bunch of his best shooters."

"If those men ride for your pa, you don't have anything to worry about."

Tifflin just stared at him. Haskell thought he saw a hundred to two hundred half-formed thoughts rolling around in the kid's eyes.

"Don't you know who they ride for?" Haskell asked.

"That's right," Tifflin said, shrugging. "I don't know who they ride for. All I know is that west of town is too dangerous for only two men to be ridin' through. These days you don't ride out there unless you got some firepower."

"We'll be all right."

"Give me my guns, at least."

Haskell chuckled.

"Come on," Tifflin urged, tightening his jaws. "Don't be a fool."

"I don't intend to be." Haskell reached into his saddlebags, then tossed the kid a set of handcuffs. "Put those on. Nice an' tight. I'll be checkin' your work."

"You can't ride me through that country trussed up like a pig headin' to market!"

"I can and I will." Bear lifted the Schofield from its holster, clicking back the hammer. "You want a matching pair of notched ears?"

Looking genuinely scared and frustrated, the younker gave a hard sigh, closed one of the bracelets around one wrist, and then closed the other bracelet around the other wrist. Hands cuffed before him, he just stared at the ground, jaws hard, cheeks flushed, shaking his head. The sun flashing off the silver *conchos* on his hat band cast reflections across the ground near Haskell's boots.

Bear looked at Redfield. "You going to be all right, Cap?"

Redfield didn't look a whole lot happier about the situation than young Tifflin did. "Oh, I don't know." He wrapped his gnarled, brown hands around the necks of the shotgun stocks sticking up from their leather scabbards. "Let's just say tomorrow, if it arrives, will be one hell of a gift likely bought with more than a few wads of ten-gauge buck!"

"Maybe you'd better deputize somebody."

"Deputize who?" The old ranger gave Haskell a hard look. "No man in his right mind would want to side an old, one-legged ranger in a wheelchair against the toughs who been ridin' through Sundown of late." He shook his head. "You go on an' do your job . . . an' I'll do mine."

Haskell looked toward where the half-dozen riders were

dismounting at the far end of town. He didn't like the idea of his leaving Redfield alone, but, then, he wasn't here to establish law and order in Sundown. He was here to find Jack Hyde.

He turned to young Tifflin. "Mount up."

Reluctantly, the kid complied.

Haskell grabbed both sets of reins off the hitchrack and swung up onto his pinto's back. He pinched his hat brim to the old ranger sitting in his wheelchair, looking owly as hell, hands still wrapped around his poppers.

Redfield was staring toward the east end of town, where the six curly wolves were just then entering a low-slung cantina.

"I'll be back in a few days," Haskell said. "Hopefully with the Jackal wearin' the same jewelry the kid is now."

"You think so, do ya?" Redfield growled, not looking at him. "I for one hope so. Then maybe we'll have peace again in the valley, as the sayin' goes. Him an' that Sharps of his sure have caused a lot of trouble. Anyways, go with god, son. Go with god."

Haskell reined the pinto around, and, leading the kid's roan by its bridle reins, booted his mount into a trot, heading west. As he and the kid rode past the little depot building, Orozco La Paz was standing by the silver rails, staring west, a black cheroot clamped between his teeth. A white cat crouched on his shoulders, straddling his head.

The station agent turned toward Haskell and called in a mournful tone, "You just arrived in our fair *pueblito, mi amigo.* What causes you to leave us so soon?"

"Got a lost child here, Oro," Haskell said as he crossed the railroad tracks via the rough pine planks. "We'll see you again in a day or two!"

Orozco gave a courtly bow, the cat arching its back and lifting its tail, balancing on the old Mexican's shoulders.

Haskell threw out an arm, turned forward in the saddle, and

raked his spurs against the pinto's flanks, breaking into a lope.

As he headed along facing a westering sun, he found himself in a sour mood. He hadn't realized how much trouble he'd been riding into here in Sundown. In light of the range war brewing in and around the town, Jack Hyde seemed a relatively small matter.

Old Redfield had his hands full just keeping the peace in Sundown. Maybe what Haskell should be doing instead was lending the old ranger a hand in town until Redfield could call in more rangers, or possibly seat a town marshal and a deputy, to help stem the hemorrhaging of law and order.

On the other hand, maybe by running Jack Hyde to ground he'd be helping stem the hemorrhaging of law and order out on the range. The town might settle down soon after.

Might.

Bear shook his head. Henry Dade had told him about the range war, but still, Haskell hadn't realized the size of the trouble out here, nor about the competing directions he'd feel pulled.

Bear plucked a piece of folded notepaper out of his shirt pocket, and shook it open, inspecting the map of the route to Rancho San Rafael Redfield had penciled for him. He looked toward the northwest, identifying some of the landmarks the ranger had written on the notepaper.

The San Rafael lay to the northwest, fifteen miles out. The country between here and there was a vast expanse of low, rolling hills covered with chalky dirt and sand and pocked with tough, wiry brush, some of which Haskell recognized as dog cactus, sage, and willow.

Here and there a yucca or an agave plant bristled out of the thin soil. Prickly pear was almost everywhere, and the wagon trail Bear and young Tifflin followed meandered around and between the dangerous cactus patches.

To the south, the Davis Mountains hovered just above the lemon-green desert and the far horizon, which was the blue of storm clouds.

The heat was still intense. Haskell could feel the moisture being sucked out of his pores. He was glad he'd had the foresight to pack three filled canteens, which he'd rented along with his horse at the livery barn.

As the pinto climbed the shoulder of a low butte, Haskell glanced behind him. In the far distance, Sundown was dwindling. In the near distance, Jordan Tifflin rode hunched in his saddle, cuffed hands hooked around his saddle horn. The youngster look around warily, blond brows furrowed.

"What's got you so damn worried, kid?" Bear asked him. "You look like you think you got a target on your back."

"Everybody's got a target on his back in this country," the kid said, hipping around in his saddle to stare back toward Sundown.

"Yeah, well, that's what happens when you ignite a range war."

The kid jerked an angry look at him. He opened his mouth to speak, then closed it. He gave a shrug and looked away, smiling ironically.

"I'm gonna ask you again—who do those owlhoots ride for? Valderrama and the others. Your old man?"

Again Tifflin regarded Haskell in his customarily snotty fashion. "My old man don't consult with me about the men he hires. I don't know who Valderrama rides for. Could be my pa. Could be anyone."

"All right," Haskell said, turning to look ahead along the meandering trail, which had him and the kid dropping into a bowl between haystack buttes. "Fair enough."

So the Jackal could be riding for Ambrose Tifflin, and the kid wouldn't know anything about it . . .

Well, Haskell had learned something, anyway.

He and the kid pushed on for another hour, walking and jogging their horses by turn. They were riding through a long valley between sandstone rimrocks turning salmon and orange in the dwindling light, when the ragged patter of gunfire rose in the east, from beyond the ridge on Bear's right.

Haskell stopped both horses and reached for his Henry.

"Ah, shit," the kid said, whipping his head around to peer in the direction of the continuing gunfire. "You hear that? I wasn't just whistlin' 'Dixie,' was I?" He turned his sharp, pleading gaze on Bear. "Give me my guns, for chrissakes. I need a gun!"

CHAPTER ELEVEN

"Shut up," Haskell told Jordan Tifflin.

Dismounting, the lawman slid his Henry from its scabbard.

He walked out ahead of the horses and stared toward the orange-hued rimrock rising in the east. Gunfire continued to crackle sporadically. A small battle was being pitched on the other side of the ridge.

Haskell walked back to where Tifflin sat straight-backed in his saddle, staring anxiously in the direction of the pops and wicked-sounding belches.

"Climb down from there," Bear ordered.

Tifflin quickly swung down from the saddle to stand before Haskell, looking up at the taller man imploringly. "Please! I need a gun! You gotta take these bracelets off!"

"Like hell." Haskell reached into his war bag. He withdrew a five-foot length of hemp and pointed the Henry at a rock at the edge of the trail. "Sit."

Tifflin looked astonished. "What do you mean—*sit?*"

"Look, you little dung beetle. I could be hauling you into federal court for the attempted murder of a deputy United States marshal. You could be sentenced to twenty years' hard labor and used as a love toy by men much bigger than you. I'm doing you a *big* favor by taking your raggedy ass back to your old man for a good, old-fashioned trip to the woodshed. Now, sit down. I'm gonna tie your feet, and I'm gonna cuff your hands behind your back. If you keep complaining, I'm also gonna gag you, to boot!"

That lecture cowed young Tifflin enough that Haskell was able to tie his ankles and cuff his hands behind his back with no more sass from the rancher's spoiled son.

When he was done, he returned the handcuff key to his pants pocket and walked over to where he'd tied the horses to a gnarled cedar off the side of the trail.

"What're you donna do?" Tifflin asked in a frightened but wary tone, sitting on the rock.

"I'm gonna see if I can see who's shootin' who. You sit tight and keep your mouth shut."

As Bear slipped the bits and *latigo* straps of both horses so they could forage and breathe easier, young Tifflin said, "If somethin' happens to you . . ."

"You're gonna be in a bad spot." Haskell gave a wry wink. "Best send up a prayer for me, huh?"

Tifflin only gave him a constipated look, then lifted his fearful gaze to the ridge.

Haskell crossed the trail and dropped into a dry, sandy wash that ran along the base of the ridge. He climbed up the opposite bank, pushed through some thorny brush, stepped between two sotol cacti, and started up the slope, meandering between boulders and more brush clumps. The slope was steep enough to get Haskell's heart thumping quickly and the muscles bunching in his thighs and calves.

More sweat oozed from his pores to soak his already damp shirt. His suspenders pulled against his shoulders with each upward-lunging step. He grunted, holding the Henry in both hands across his shoulders, loosing sand and gravel with each step.

As he climbed steadily, breathing hard and grunting, he kept an eye skinned for rattlesnakes. All he needed was to be in Redfield's miserable situation! Guns continued to pop on the ridge's far side, but the reports seemed to be growing more distant, more infrequent.

Halfway to the top of his climb, Bear paused to catch his breath and give his legs a rest. Leaning against a boulder, he glanced back down the ridge and across the wash.

Jordan Tifflin sat on the low, flat rock on the far side of the trail, both foraging horses flanking him. Tifflin's hands were behind him, his ankles tied straight in front of him. He stared up in miserable defeat and wariness at Bear. He found himself in the improbable position of pulling for his captor, which meant he must believe that the shooters on the other side of the ridge were foes of his, not friends.

Since the war out here was between the Rancho San Rafael and a half-dozen other, smaller spreads, why wouldn't Jordan think that at least one faction of the shooters was on his and his father's side? If his father's men knew he was out here, wouldn't they try to spring Jordan from the lawman? Maybe he did think that. But maybe he also worried there was a chance the men riding for the small ranchers would prevail in their skirmish. If Jordan's father's enemies found young Tifflin out here, bound hand and foot, it likely wouldn't end well for the younker. Bear had to smile at that.

That had to be what had the kid so scared, he thought. *Didn't it?*

Another brief burst of shooting convinced him to cut short his rest. He resumed climbing, angling around boulders the size of small farm wagons, some as large as cabins. He was heading for the scattered chunks of sandstone capping the ridge, hoping that once he gained the ridge crest he'd be able to see the other side and get some sense of who was shooting at whom.

A loud snort rose to Bear's left.

He stopped suddenly and whipped around, pumping a cartridge into the Henry's action. He held fire. He was staring at a claybank gelding standing in a large wedge of shade cast by a slanting, tabletop boulder looming over him. The horse was roughly thirty feet from Haskell. It was saddled. Its bridle reins were tied to a stout, hemp-like root curling out of a boulder crack.

The horse stared at the lawman owlishly, twitching its ears guardedly.

Something hammered a rock to Haskell's right. The bullet screamed shrilly as it ricocheted. The scream was followed a quarter-second later by the distant, ragged crack of a rifle.

The horse gave an angry whinny and pitched.

Haskell threw himself right and rolled behind a boulder. He waited, keeping his head down. The shot had come from near the crest. When another didn't come, he decided to try to draw the shooter's or shooters' fire. He lurched to his feet and, keeping his head down, ran upslope, quartering to his right.

Two bullets plumed dirt and gravel in quick succession just ahead and to his right. He threw himself down behind another rock. Another bullet screamed off the top of the rock, peppering Haskell with stone shards. He doffed his hat and edged a brief look over his covering rock toward the ridge crest.

Smoke wafted nearly straight up the ridge from a spot just beneath the crest and above a small nest of rocks.

Haskell jerked his head back down. Another bullet buzzed through the air where his head had just been and loudly hammered a boulder downslope.

The rifle's belching crack echoed out over the canyon.

Haskell stuffed his hat back on his head. He crabbed over to his covering rock's right side, snaked his rifle up over the top, and hurled quick shots toward the nest of rocks near the top.

The echoes of his own rifle fire were still chasing each other around the canyon when he scrambled to his feet once more and ran upslope, tracing a serpentine course around rocks and boulders and wind-twisted cedars and dangerous patches of prickly pear rearing their small, spiny heads above cream pools of slide rock.

Haskell picked a path with the best cover and continued running despite the bullets slicing the air around him and spanging off rocks and boulders. So far, only one shooter was throwing lead at him. That didn't mean there weren't more men waiting for him at the top of the ridge, but it was a chance Bear was going to have to take.

He knew the shooter wasn't his quarry, Jack Hyde. If the Jackal had been shooting at him, he'd be wolf bait by now. Besides, the shooter wasn't wielding a cannon of the Jackal's Sharp's hybrid variety.

When he could tell he was maybe thirty or forty feet away from the shooter, Haskell dropped and rolled up against the base of a boulder roughly the size of a two-hole privy. He pressed his back against the boulder and drew his knees toward his chest just as two more bullets hammered the gravel inches from his boot toes.

Rocks and gravel flew. One stone clipped Bear's left cheek, evoking a snarled curse.

The reports echoed eerily.

When they finished their long, slow-dwindling deaths, only silence pressed down to replace them.

He's reloading.

Haskell dropped to his belly and hazarded a look around the right side of his covering rock. Several good-sized boulders lay between him and the ridge crest. If Bear stayed low, the shooter couldn't see him from his, the shooter's, position. That thought in mind, Haskell began to crawl on all fours—or all threes, for he carried his Henry in his right hand—straight up the slope and into a narrow gap between two large boulders.

He'd try to sneak up on the ambusher. If the man tried to

sneak up on Haskell, they'd likely meet each other somewhere close by.

Haskell crawled out of the gap and into another one that ran perpendicular to the ridge. He crawled into a hollow carved into the side of a slab of granite, and rose to his feet. He had to bend forward, for the crevice's ceiling angled low to the outside. Haskell removed his hat, dropping it at his feet.

As he stood hunched against the rock, the hollow curved tightly about his shoulders, giving him a fleeting, anxious chill as he remembered the coffin in which he'd been sailing down the Arkansas only a few short weeks ago.

No point in hurrying.

Let the shooter come to him.

Unless the man had pulled foot, that was, and was looking for his horse. Then Haskell would have outsmarted himself . . .

It wouldn't be the first time.

Haskell had just started to wonder if the latter scenario was the case, when a horned lark gave an alarming shriek as it flitted past the gap he was in. A faint crunch of gravel rose. Hard to tell which direction it had come from. The stone gap did funny things to sounds.

Bear dropped to a knee and leaned forward against the Henry, which he held straight up and down in both gloved hands, the stock pressed against the ground. His heart quickened anxiously when he heard another crunch.

The man was moving toward him. From his left, Bear thought. But then the breeze fell, dropping a mare's tail of dust tinted orange by the falling sun, to the ground fronting his crevice, and the crunch came again. More clearly this time.

Definitely from Haskell's right.

Bear drew a deep breath, then let it out slowly, silently.

Two, three seconds passed.

A boot appeared just outside the crevice. A man's expensive

suede leather boot with a square toe and fancy stitching on the upper. Something told Haskell that only a man of the Jackal's distinction would wear such a fancily cut boot.

His heart hiccupped with the raw improbability that, despite his earlier assumption, he'd just run into Jack Hyde himself!

Haskell grinned eagerly as he raised the Henry straight up and thrust the butt out of the gap and down. It connected soundly with the toe of the fancy boot.

The shooter's sudden howl was clipped off by Haskell himself lunging out of the crevice and straight into the man, bulling him over sideways with the sheer bulk of his body. All was shadow where the man had fallen behind a boulder, so Haskell didn't get a clear look at him, seeing only a swiftly moving blur as the man bounded fleetly off the ground and lunged toward him.

Bear had been about to aim his Henry at him, but the man was small and fast, like a bobcat. He snarled like a bobcat, too, ramming his head into Bear's broad chest. Haskell hadn't got his feet set after delivering the body blow, so the much smaller and lighter gent was able to tilt him over backwards, Bear's boots slipping off rocks and odd chunks of ancient wood.

Dropping the Henry, Haskell hit the ground on his back, grunting against the sharp rocks and cacti chewing into him.

"You son of a bitch!" his opponent raked out, clawing at his face.

Haskell grabbed the man by his shirt collar and rolled him over, straddling him. Automatically, Bear shucked his bowie knife from the sheath on his cartridge belt, and laid the blade across the man's neck. His assailant must have felt the razor edge of the cold steel. He instantly fell still.

Haskell frowned. The man's face was covered with a thick spray of thick, light-colored hair. Two hazel eyes stared out through the mussed curtain. They were riveted on Haskell's own eyes. It was then that Haskell realized that the supple body he lay atop of was not the body of a man at all. It belonged to a woman. A young one. Practically a girl.

He pulled the bowie away from her neck, brusquely swept her hair aside with his hand, and stared down in hang-jawed awe at the all-too-familiar, heart-shaped face below his.

The face of the honey-haired, curvy-bodied young lady who'd invited him to her room in San Saba and unceremoniously threw him out—naked—when she'd had her literal and figurative fill of him!

"Well, I'll be a two-headed moon calf," Haskell intoned. "Princess Uppity Pants—what in the hell are *you* doing out here?"

CHAPTER TWELVE

"Princess Uppity Pants, is it?" she snarled, slapping his hand away from her face, then shaking her hair out of her eyes. "What am *I* doing out here? What in the hell are *you* doing out here, you brute? Are you following me?"

Haskell still straddled her, staring at her in shock.

He laughed despite his confusion. "Following *you*? If anyone's followin' anyone, Miss Uppity Pants, that would most likely be *you* followin' *me*, since *I'm* out here on official business!"

She looked at him, incredulous. "Official business?"

Haskell poked a thumb at the badge on his shirt. "I'm a deputy United States marshal."

She looked at the nickel-finished moon-and-star, apparently seeing it for the first time. He hadn't worn it on the train or in San Saba, as it tended to attract unwanted attention, including bullets. She looked up into Bear's face as though having trouble reconciling the badge with the rough-hewn features of the man wearing it.

Haskell rose, wincing against his many aches and abrasions, and looked around cautiously. He couldn't hear any more shooting rising from the other side of the ridge. "You alone out here?"

"Apparently not," she said, pushing herself to her feet, then lifting her left arm to inspect its underside.

She winced as she plucked cactus spines from the sleeve of her white silk blouse. She also wore men's denim trousers, but she looked a whole lot better in them than any man Haskell had ever seen. Around her trim waist was a shell belt studded with .44 cartridges for the Winchester carbine she'd dropped when Bear had knocked her over.

"You know what I mean," Haskell said, eyeing her askance.

"Yes, I was alone . . . until now."

"Who's shooting at who on the other side of the ridge?"

"I might have been able to find that out if you hadn't so rudely interrupted me."

Haskell gave a dry laugh. "I'd say your interrupting me was a whole lot ruder than my interrupting you. You tried to blow my head off, you crazy polecat!"

"A girl can't be too careful in this country. When I spied you on my back trail, I naturally thought the worst. And I wasn't too far off the mark. You still haven't told me what you're doing out here. A lawman? Really? I find that incredibly hard to believe!"

"Why?" Scooping his Henry off the ground, Haskell looked at her again, curling his upper lip. "You don't think lawmen can make women howl the way I made you howl the other night in San Saba?"

A rosy flush blossomed in the nubs of her cheeks. "Stop talking about that!"

Haskell chuckled as he brushed dirt from his Henry's stock. "You still haven't told me what you're doing out here. You'd better do so in a hurry or I'm gonna think, as I already do, that you're followin' me around like a pony after a carrot, lookin' for a repeat of San Saba. Only it ain't a carrot you're after!"

"Hush!" She looked around quickly, as though afraid someone might overhear. Keeping her voice low, she said in a tone of grave conspiracy, "I am an undercover operative for the Pinkerton Agency."

It was Haskell's turn to drop his jaw in astonishment. "You gotta be shittin' me. You?"

She looked offended. "Yes, me! You don't think women can be detectives?"

He favored the twin mounds pushing out her silk blouse with a brazen gaze. "Not women who look like you."

Reflexively, she crossed her arms over her breasts. She wasn't putting much weight on her right foot. "What're *you* doing out here . . . if you're not following me?"

"Oh, Christ—we're talkin' in circles like an old married couple." Haskell glanced to the west, where the sun was threatening to tumble behind ridges it was quickly transforming into dark, saw-blade silhouettes. "Gonna be dark soon." He looked toward the ridge of the slope he was on. The shooting had stopped. The shooters were likely gone. Even if they weren't, it was likely getting too dark down there to see much of anything.

Haskell turned to the girl. "I got a prisoner down yonder, and I'm gonna need to find a place to camp for the night. We'll palaver around a coffee fire."

He glanced at her carbine, which still lay where she'd dropped it when he'd knocked her sideways. Her hat was there, as well—a green felt Stetson. "Best collect your rifle and find your horse."

"What makes you think you can give me orders?"

Haskell had shouldered his rifle and turned to start down the ridge. Now he turned back to her where she stood, sort of balancing on her left foot, arms crossed on her well-filled blouse. She regarded him angrily, her badly mussed hair blowing in the breeze. "Let me *suggest* you pick up your rifle and find your horse unless you wanna be caught on this ridge after nightfall. Gonna be a late moon, damn little light." He paused, looking at her boot. "Your foot hurt?"

"No."

She turned toward her rifle but when she stepped toward it, her right knee buckled. She nearly fell, sucking a sharp breath.

"Goddamn you, anyway!" she intoned throatily, sitting down on a rock. "I think you broke my foot!"

"Oh, for chrissakes!"

"It's my fault that you smashed my foot with your rifle, you unwashed brigand?"

"Oh, you're right," Haskell said. "It's my fault you were trying to ventilate me with your carbine. I should have just let you do it and left you with two good feet!"

"I had no idea a lawman was out here. I thought all the lawmen were dead in this godforsaken neck of Texas!"

"Stop your caterwauling and stay there. I'll fetch your horse."

"I wasn't caterwauling! And how do you know where my horse is?"

"Just stay there and try to keep your mouth shut!"

As Haskell walked away, the princess—whose name he had not yet caught—gave a raking, exasperated yowl through gritted teeth. He shook his head. Normally, seeing a pretty, alluring girl—especially one he'd had a good, old-fashioned romp with— would have been a welcome distraction. But out here, with shooters roaming the range . . . and possibly the nastiest shooter of them all roaming the range with a high-caliber, long-range rifle . . . he needed no such distractions.

Besides, he had a bone to pick with Miss Uppity Pants. She had, after all, profoundly insulted him by throwing him out of her room, naked as the day he was born but a whole lot bigger and hairier.

She'd threatened to have him incarcerated for rape! The little bitch deserved to be behind bars for such a blatantly phony accusation.

A Pinkerton, eh?

Well, Haskell would be damned. He'd been a Pinkerton himself, and he'd run into quite a few operatives after he'd turned his resignation in to the Old Man, Allan Pinkerton himself, to join the U.S. Marshals Service. Bear had even known a few female operatives over the years. But none of them could have held a candle, looks-wise, to Miss Uppity Pants.

Haskell wondered if Allan had any idea what the princess did in her spare time—namely, lure unsuspecting gentlemen to her room and, when she'd damned near mauled the hell out of them while taking her satisfaction, throw them out, nude, under threat of being charged with rape!

Despite his peevishness at the complication of running into Miss Uppity Pants out here, now having to assist her after the indignities he'd suffered at her hands, including the most recent one of damned near getting his head blown off, he found himself chuckling dryly. He was somehow able to see the humor in the complicated tableau of his and the girl's relationship. It helped that she'd been such an enticing and exhilarating wildcat under the sheets, not to mention atop the dresser and on the floor, as well.

Haskell chuckled again, then brushed the humor from his lips with his fist, resolving to get back down to business.

The princess's claybank was jittery after the shooting. It shied nervously when it saw the big stranger walking toward it, so Haskell had to take a minute to soothe the beast before untying its reins. He led the reluctant mount back up toward the crest of the ridge, picking his way more carefully now, as shadows were gathering along the slope, making the footing uncertain. When he came in sight of the princess again, she was an inky shadow flanked by the slope. She was wearing her hat.

The shadow shifted. A vagrant ray cast by the fast-falling sun glinted off steel. There was the loud, raking rasp of a rifle being cocked.

"Who are you really?" she raked out tightly, aiming her carbine at the lawman.

Haskell stopped about ten feet away from her. "Oh, for chrissakes!" He continued forward, jerking the horse along behind him.

"Stop right there!"

"Or you'll what?" Haskell said, tossing the mount's reins to her. They bounced off her carbine's barrel and dropped to the ground. "You'll shoot a deputy U.S. marshal?"

"How do I know you're telling the truth? How do I know you're not one of the men shooting each other out here? You could have killed a deputy marshal and stolen his badge."

"Put the rifle down, Miss Uppity."

"Not until I'm certain you are who you say you are." She frowned at him askance over the Winchester's barrel. "You don't seem very professional. Not one bit."

"Oh, you seemed real professional in San Saba!" Haskell chuckled.

"Stop talking about that!"

He extended his hand to her. "I'll help you up on your horse. When we get down to my horse, I'll show you the file I have on Jack Hyde."

"Jack Hyde?" Her frown deepened. "How do you know about Jack Hyde?"

"That's who I'm lookin' for. He has a federal warrant on his head, and my boss back in Denver think he's working for one of the sides in the land war brewing in these parts." Haskell lowered his hand and scowled. "Isn't he what you're out here for? Or . . . just what are you out here for, Miss Uppity Pants?"

"Stop calling me that!" She lowered her carbine and extended her hand to him. "Of course, he's what I'm out here for. What else? We've been hired by several parties to find Jack Hyde . . . the Jackal."

Haskell took her hand in his, helped her to her feet, and wrapped his hands around her slender waist. She gave a startled

"Oh!" as he lifted her off her feet and set her easily onto her saddle.

"You might have given me a little warning before you did that," she scolded him.

"Sorry." He curled his upper lip again when even in the quickly fading light he saw the wine-red flush rise into her cheeks again. "I hope I didn't make you feel funny."

"Brigand!"

"No need for name-callin'." Haskell pinched his hat brim to her, then grabbed her horse's reins and began leading the mount down the slope. "Bear Haskell's the name. At your service."

"I'll take my reins."

"I don't mind leading your hoss for you."

"You don't need to. Only my foot is injured. My hands are just fine."

Haskell tossed her the reins. She caught them against her chest and reined the claybank away from him. "Good day, Marshal Haskell!"

"What—you're too good to camp with me?"

She walked the horse between two large rocks, glancing at him as she said, "I prefer to camp alone."

"Where's your camp?"

"I don't have one. I'm traveling incognito, *alone.*"

Haskell smiled at that. "Well, you can travel incognito with me. We could compare notes, maybe, since we're both on the trail of the same man. I just have my prisoner down there waiting for me, is all. He's all trussed up, so he's no threat. Not that he was much of a threat even before I cuffed an' tied him."

She'd stopped her horse and looked at Haskell over her shoulder. "Who's your prisoner?"

"Son of the big muckety-muck rancher in these parts—Jordan Tifflin. His father is—"

"Ambrose Tifflin." She'd said the name with a pensive air,

looking at the ground beside her horse.

"You've done your homework."

"Of course, I have," she said, peevish again. She looked at the ground once more, as though seeking counsel from a sprite down there. Then she cast her gaze back to Haskell. "I tell you what, Marshal Haskell . . . if you really are who you say you are . . . I'll take you up on your offer to share your fire this evening."

Haskell continued walking down the slope, carefully picking his way in the thickening shadows. "That'd be wise."

"Why would it be wise," she said, putting her horse into step beside him.

"Because you're a girl alone. And this is contested range. Hell, I'm sure you've heard that several rangers were killed out here some weeks back. One even more recent."

Proudly, she said, "I may be a girl, as you say, Marshal Haskell, but I guarantee you that I can take care of myself as well as you can take of *your*self. Mister Pinkerton gives me assignments the same as he would any man, with no regard to my sex or the danger involved."

"What's your name?"

She rode along in silence for a time, her horse choosing its own footing. Finally, with a little, relenting sigh, she said, "Arliss Posey."

"Arliss Posey." Haskell ran the name through his memory lobes. It sounded familiar but it didn't snag on any recollections.

"One more thing about sharing your fire, Marshal Haskell."

"What's that, Arliss Posey?"

She gave him a direct look, mussed hair jostling across her shoulders as she continued down the slope. "Your fire is *all* I'll be sharing. Nothing more. And I want you to promise you will never again, under any circumstances, mention San Saba."

"Ah, San Saba," Haskell said with a dreamy sigh.

"Marshal!"

"Oh, all right, all right. I won't mention it again." Bear gave an ironic snort. "But you can't keep me from thinkin' about it, Arliss. It was a helluva night!"

CHAPTER THIRTEEN

When Haskell and Agent Posey reached the bottom of the slope, it was almost dark. She followed him across the dry wash and then up the opposite bank.

Haskell stopped suddenly. He could see his horse and Tifflin's horse—two brown smudges in the velvety shadows—on the far side of the trail. But there was no sign of Jordan Tifflin. The rock Bear had left him on shone pale as whitewash in the darkness.

"Aw, shit," Haskell said.

"What is it?" Arliss asked, stopping the clay a few feet behind him.

"Stay here."

"I don't like taking orders from you or anyone else," she muttered behind him.

Haskell walked forward, stopping near the rock. "Tifflin?"

A thrashing sounded in the brush beyond. Both horses started at the noise and switched their tails. Tifflin's roan whickered and shook its head.

Haskell loudly racked a cartridge into his Henry's action, and strode over to the brush and cacti. A deer path led into the bramble. Haskell followed it, calling "Kid?"

Silence.

Then, after Bear had walked a few more feet, a man's low voice said, "Leave me! Leave me be! Hyde, that you? You leave me be, now, ya hear?"

Haskell followed the quavering voice to a cedar. Something lay between the cedar and a low shelf of rock that appeared to have issued a spring at one time. The figure, partly curled, moved a little.

It was Tifflin, though Haskell couldn't see him clearly in the dim light. What he could see was that the kid's feet were still bound and his hands were still cuffed behind his back. His face was turned away from the lawman.

"Leave me alone, damnit!" Tifflin sobbed. "I ain't out here 'cause I wanna be!"

Haskell moved a little farther forward, crouched, and poked his Henry's barrel against young Tifflin's left shoulder.

"No!" the kid cried, turning his face toward Haskell. His eyes flashed umber with fear. "Leave me be, Hyde! I got nothin' to do with . . ."

He stopped, narrowing his eyes in recognition at the lawman.

"Got nothin' to do with what, Jordan?"

"Huh?" Young Tifflin was breathing hard.

"Got nothin' to do with what?"

"I thought you was dead."

"I gathered that. And you thought I was Jack Hyde."

Tifflin gave a little, old-woman cackle. "I reckon I did at that."

"Come on out of there."

"I can't, dammit. You got me trussed up like a pig!"

Bear slid his bowie from its sheath and sliced through the ropes binding young Tifflin's feet together. He gathered up the cut rope in his hand and rose. "Come on out of there," he repeated.

Awkwardly, but probably not as awkwardly as he'd slithered into his hiding place behind the cedar, Tifflin climbed out from behind it. He stood before Haskell, looking sheepish.

"You had a scare," Bear said with mock sympathy.

"I thought you was dead. I figured ole Jack Hyde got you and he'd get me next."

"Why were you so sure it was Hyde?"

Tifflin hiked a shoulder. "I don't know. He's sorta like the bogeyman. Everyone around here thinks the Jackal's gonna come stalking and put one o' them fist-sized rounds through his back."

Haskell wagged his rifle. "Get moving. Back to your rock."

When Haskell had followed Tifflin out of the brush, he saw Arliss Posey standing beside her horse, again not putting much weight on her right foot, and aiming her carbine again.

"Don't you think you've used that enough for one afternoon?" Haskell said.

There was a soft click as she depressed the Winchester's hammer. "That your prisoner?"

"He's not Santa Claus."

"A Tifflin, huh?"

Jordan whistled. "Damn, where'd you find her?"

"Shut up and sit on your rock," Haskell told him.

Arliss Posey walked up to Tifflin. "So, you're the son, huh?"

"That's right." Tifflin whistled as he brashly ogled the young woman. "Damn, you're a sight for sore eyes! Who are you, anyway? Gonna be a long night. We might as well start getting acquainted!"

"Shut up, you limp-peckered little rascal!" Arliss snarled.

Haskell rolled his eyes and gave a low groan as he looked around for a sheltered place for a fire. It was going to be a long night, all right.

Hopefully, a quiet one.

Bear chose a camping spot another thirty yards west of the trail.

When he had a small fire going and had made coffee, he looked over to where Arliss Posey was leaning back against her

274

saddle, legs stretched out before her, ankles crossed. She was nibbling a blueberry muffin she'd plucked from a small burlap pouch on the ground beside her. Her coffee cup sat near the pouch, curling its steam into the darkness.

Arliss was speculatively studying Jordan Tifflin, who was grinning back at her from the other side of the fire.

Tifflin was munching jerky from his cuffed right hand.

"What's your interest in the seedling here?" Haskell asked the young woman.

"I think she likes me," the young man said. "Can't take her eyes off me."

Arliss flared a nostril at him and said to Bear, "I hate spoiled brats."

"So that's your interest?" Bear said, skeptical.

"That's my interest."

"You're sure there's nothin' else?"

"What else would there be?" Arliss said flatly.

"Yeah," Tifflin said, still grinning lustily. "What else would there be?"

Haskell glared at him. "If you don't shut up, I'm gonna shoot your other ear off."

Tifflin turned his mouth corners down.

Haskell returned his gaze to the pretty young Pinkerton. "You're thinkin' what I'm thinkin', aren't you? That Jack Hyde is shooting for the Tifflins."

"They would have the money to pay him, whereas I doubt the small ranchers the Tifflins are trying to squeeze out would."

Haskell looked over at young Tifflin again, who was biting another piece of jerky from the ragged chunk in his cuffed hands and which Haskell had found in the younker's saddlebags when he'd unsaddled his mount. "Why did you think I was the Jackal stalking you a while ago?" he asked Tifflin. "You were so scared, I thought you were gonna piss your pants."

"You told me to shut up," Tifflin said, chewing. "I don't wanna get another ear shot off. I'm a good-lookin' feller. Just ask Miss Posey." He cast a mocking, wet-lipped smile at Arliss, who flared a nostril at him again.

Haskell studied them both. He had far more questions than he was getting answers from either of them. He had a feeling Arliss knew far more than she was telling. Why? Or was she just the sort of Pinkerton operative who had a habit of playing it close to her vest?

Haskell leaned his rifle against the log he sat on, and dropped to his knees beside her. "Let me have a look at that foot."

"What? No. Get away from me!"

Tifflin laughed.

Haskell grabbed her right foot and set it on his thigh. "Let me take a look at it. I'm a right good sawbones of sorts."

With a painful grunt, she pulled her foot off his lap and dropped it to the ground. "The foot's fine, Marshal Haskell!"

Haskell gave her a sincere, direct look. "I can tell you're in pain. If any bones are broken, that foot should be wrapped. Otherwise it's just gonna swell until you're never gonna get that boot off without cutting it."

"No one is cutting that boot off! It cost me a pretty penny on Michigan Avenue in Chicago, and"—she cast an accusatory look at young Tifflin again—"money doesn't grow on trees. At least, not for me."

Haskell said, "His old man runs the San Rafael for a big English syndicate. He can't be all that rich." He looked at Tifflin. "Can he?"

"Ah, hell," Tifflin said. "She just has her pantaloons in a twist."

Arliss opened her mouth to give a curt response, but Haskell cut her off with, "Let me slide this boot off while I still can, and set that foot if it needs setting."

"All right," said the pretty Pinkerton. "But leave my sock on."

Haskell pulled off the boot. Her sock came with it. Her bare foot was copper colored in the light of the fire's dancing flames.

Young Tifflin whistled. "Now, that there's a foot!"

"Goddamnit!" Arliss regaled Haskell.

"Don't pay attention to him," Bear said, setting her bare foot in his lap and trying not to get excited at the feel of her bare flesh against his thigh. Hell, only a few nights ago he'd had a look at, and feel of, more than her foot!

Still, Tifflin was right. It was a damned pretty foot.

Haskell inspected it closely. It was a little swollen just behind her toes, in the middle of her upper foot. The second toe was a trifle ashen up to the first knuckle. He pressed his thumb gently against the swelling.

"Ow, you behemoth!"

Again Tifflin laughed.

Haskell gave Arliss a look that reminded her she hadn't protested against his manipulations the night before last. She must have got the message. Her cheeks darkened and she looked down quickly.

"Take it easy there—it's sore."

"He's nothin' but a big clumsy idiot," Tifflin said, staring at the girl's bare foot. "Maybe I'd better take over. You got any other injuries, do you? How 'bout your titties? They sore at all?"

He laughed.

Arliss grabbed her Winchester from where it leaned against her saddle, cocked it, and took aim at the younker. He screamed as he dropped his jerky and raised his hands to his face as though to shield himself from a bullet.

Tifflin cried, "Christ—put that long gun down, girl!"

Haskell looked at Arliss. She stared down the Winchester's barrel at young Tifflin. Her right index finger was drawn back taut against the Winchester's trigger.

Was she really going to shoot him?

"Uh . . ." Bear said.

"Take it away from her," Tifflin cried, glancing around his raised hands at the lawman. "Take the rifle away from her! Take it away! She's crazy!"

"I may be crazy . . ." Arliss depressed the carbine's hammer, and raised the barrel. Her eyes flashed fire at Haskell. "But no man—even one your size—takes my carbine away from me, Marshal. At least, not if there's a breath remaining inside me."

"Right poetic," Haskell said.

"Jesus!" Tifflin said, lowering his head. "As crazy as she is purty!"

Arliss smiled across the fire at him. "Thank you."

Haskell set her foot on the ground, pulled an old shirt out of his saddlebags, and used his bowie knife to tear it into two wide strips. Wrapping one strip around her foot, he said, "What's your interest in young Tifflin there? Your *real* interest?"

She looked at Tifflin, who had resumed munching jerky and was eyeing her now as though she'd turned into a moon-crazed she-cat ready to spring on him at any second. "Like I said— nothing. Nothing at all. It's his father I want to talk to. About the Jackal."

"Well, then, we got that in common," Haskell said, wrapping the second cloth strip around her ankle and foot. "I reckon we'll be riding together to the San Rafael tomorrow."

"Isn't that sweet?" she said with a falsely sugary smile. Turning to Jordan, she said, "Why is he cuffed?"

"He's been a bad boy. Got four of his pards pushin' up daisies. I could charge him, but I decided to turn him over to his old man instead."

"As leverage to ride out to the San Rafael and ask Ambrose Tifflin about the Jackal," she said, arching a knowing brow.

"There you have it."

"You're smarter than you appear, Marshal Haskell."

Tifflin gave a wry snort. "Ain't she a caution?"

Haskell only smiled at the pretty, sharp-tongued young Pinkerton, and shrugged a self-deprecating shoulder.

He tied the second strip around her foot and ankle, then wrapped his hand around her foot, very gently. Despite the sourness of her personality, he liked the way her foot felt in his hand. He couldn't help taking a moment to enjoy the feeling. There'd been so much of her to concentrate on the other night that he hadn't paid any attention to her feet, but they were as sexy as the rest of her.

At least, the right one was.

Holding her foot in his hand, he stared into her eyes. She wasn't telling him everything she knew about the case they'd both found themselves on.

What was it?

What wasn't she telling him?

She was as cunning as she was pretty. No wonder Pinkerton had hired her . . .

Arliss looked down at his hand, then up into his eyes, her expression oblique. Her bosoms appeared to rise and fall sharply just once.

Was she remembering what he himself couldn't help flashing back to—the other night when he'd toiled naked between her spread knees and she'd raked her fingernails painfully across his shoulder blades, howling? Tucking her lower lip under her upper front teeth, she lifted her foot from his lap, then leaned forward to pull on her sock.

"Thanks," she said. "That feels better."

"Should give you a little support. I don't think it'll swell too much."

"I'm sure it will feel much better in the morning."

"Arliss?"

Lifting her coffee cup to her lips, she looked at Bear over its steaming rim.

"You realize that my business trumps your business out here, right? When I . . . or we . . . run down the Jackal, I'll be taking him back to Denver to stand trial on a laundry list of charges. Just so we're clear . . ."

"Oh, of course, Marshal," she said with an innocent shrug and a winning smile. "We couldn't be clearer on that!"

CHAPTER FOURTEEN

Haskell turned in early and woke up early, well before dawn.

Quietly, while Tifflin and Arliss slept, rolled in their blankets on separate sides of the fire ring, Haskell got a new fire going with dry brush he'd scrounged the previous night. He filled his coffee pot from one of his canteens and set the pot on a rock in the flames to boil.

He sat on the log near the fire, lit an Indian Kid, and pulled the file Henry Dade had given him, detailing what little was known about the Jackal's life and times, out of his saddlebags. Smoking, listening to the coffee pot begin to hiss as the flames snapped and sputtered, Bear reviewed the thin file.

Tucked in the back of the folder was an age-yellowed clipping from a Dallas newspaper detailing a holdup many years ago in northern New Mexico. Jack Hyde had been one of the members of a small bunch of west Texas hoorawers who'd robbed a stagecoach carrying over a hundred thousand dollars in gold bullion from one bank to another. The money was being delivered for the American purchase of an old Spanish land grant.

All but two hoorawers had been run down and killed in central New Mexico, south of Albuquerque. Hyde and a Mexican named Oscar Alvear had been the two survivors. They'd got away from two posses and a contingent of U.S. Cavalry, but a month later they were both taken down in Wichita Falls by a local marshal and his deputies. Hyde and Miller were both sentenced to twenty years in the federal pen.

Another clipping, folded with the first, was a brief notice of Jack Hyde's escape from the pen, when a group of prisoners he was part of were being transported from a spur rail line they'd been laying track for to the prison. Hyde was the only escapee of the bunch.

Haskell had read both clippings on the long, slow train ride down from Denver. He read them both again now, hoping to stumble on some important piece of information he'd overlooked before. But nothing rattled his cage. The first clipping was of only passing interest; it offered nothing to help Haskell run the man down now, nearly twenty years later. The second clipping, about Hyde's prison break, was common knowledge. No lawmen had ever been able to lasso him since, though many had tried.

The Jackal was still on the run. And now he was here in western Texas, working for one party of a land war. Haskell just had to find out which party had hired him, try to get a description and cut a warm trail, and bring the slippery bastard to justice once and for all.

Then he could haul his sorry ass out of this west Texas furnace and return to the cool breezes of the high country. It was still hot during the day in Denver, but the nights were wonderfully cool—just right for drying his sweat after a sweet, energetic tussle with a beautiful lady in his suite at the Larimer Hotel . . .

Haskell poked the Indian Kid into his mouth and stuffed the file back into its saddlebag pouch with a frustrated chuff. He wasn't sure why he was frustrated, but he was. He had the vague feeling he was missing something important, but he couldn't put his finger on what it was.

As he reached for the coffee pot, intending to pour himself a second cup of mud, Arliss whined in her sleep.

Haskell looked at her. She rolled onto her back. Gray smoke from the fire was billowing over her.

"Smoke," she mumbled, moving her arms and legs under her blankets.

"Easy," Haskell said.

"Smoke," she said again, shaking her head. "Oh, god . . . smoke!"

Haskell set down the coffee pot and placed his hand over one of her ankles, over her blankets. "Arliss . . . easy."

"Oh, god, *smoke!*" she fairly screamed, and sat bolt upright, reaching for her rifle.

Haskell grabbed the rifle and pulled it out of her hands as she was about to cock it. She stared at him, wide-eyed. For several seconds, she stared right through him. Then she blinked and slowly closed her mouth. Chagrin rose into her pale, sleep-drawn, frightened features.

"Christ!" This from young Tifflin, who was also sitting up now, having been awakened by the girl's outcry. "What in hell got into her?"

"Nothing," Arliss said, blinking, slow to shake off the dream. Nightmare, rather.

"Nothing." Arliss held her hand out toward Bear. "I'll take my Winchester back now," she said crisply.

Haskell extended it to her, stock first.

"Christalmighty!" young Tifflin laughed. "I never seen the like of a girl as crazy as her."

Arliss loudly cocked the Winchester and aimed it at his head. She didn't say anything. She just aimed the barrel at the firebrand's head.

Tifflin shrank back against his saddle. "Ah, shit—here we go again!" He looked at Haskell. "Call her off! Call her off!"

Haskell looked at the young firebrand and shook his head. "You don't learn, do you?"

"I learn! I learn! I've learned my lesson now!"

Arliss pursed her lips until they became a dull pink line across the bottom half of her face. "One more insult out of you, you limp-peckered moron, I'm gonna give you a new belly button."

"I'm done! I'm done!" Tifflin howled, raising his cuffed hands to his face again. "I promise I'm done!"

Arliss depressed her carbine's hammer and set the rifle aside.

"Whew!" Tifflin said, slowly lowering his hands. He looked at Haskell. "I gotta drain the dragon."

"What you just shot down your leg didn't do it, huh?" Haskell chuckled. "Stand up and shuffle over here, and I'll free your feet. But just your feet."

Tifflin cursed and gave a grunt as he leaned forward and heaved himself to his feet. He sort of hop-shuffled over to Bear's side of the fire.

He looked at Arliss and said, "This ain't no insult, Miss Posey, so don't get your neck in a hump. But my pa's gonna get an earful about how you and the big lummox here—I can insult *him,* can't I?—have been treating me. Ambrose Tifflin is gonna get an earful, all right, and he ain't gonna be one bit happy about how his only son has been so poorly treated."

"Let me look around for my fiddle," Arliss said, kneeling to pour herself a cup of coffee, "and I'll play you a sad song."

"Hurry up and cut them ropes, lawdog," Tifflin said. "I gotta pee like a Prussian plow hor—!"

He cut himself off just as Haskell slid his bowie knife from its sheath. Bear felt something wet on his cheek and right shoulder. Rain? He looked up at Tifflin, who stood just ahead of him and slightly right.

Tifflin's chest had opened up. What appeared to be part of the young idiot's shredded heart was hanging from the splintered, pale ends of two or three shattered ribs. Thick blood bubbled out around the gore to slither down the front of the kid's shirt.

Just as Haskell heard the thunderous, although distance-muffled, roar of the big-caliber rifle, he realized the kid was not giving birth to some revolting red beast inside him. He'd been shot!

As the kid stumbled forward, looking down in shock at his shredded heart, Haskell yelled, *"Down!"* and threw himself off the log he'd been sitting on. He grabbed Arliss around her waist and rolled off his left shoulder, tossing her like a bundle of laundry over his right hip and over the log.

As another large-caliber bullet hammered the front of the log, Haskell threw himself over the log to land beside Arliss, who was glaring at him, furious by the way he'd manhandled her and trying to wrap her mind around the reason for it.

Again, the thundering report of the big gun blasted the early-morning quiet to smithereens, sending deep-throated echoes vaulting around the canyon.

"My rifle!" Arliss cried and lurched toward the carbine.

Haskell grabbed her and shoved her back down behind the log. "Forget it!"

"I need it—*obviously!*"

"That cannon blasting away at us is a Sharps Big Fifty, accurate to up to five hundred yards depending on the accuracy of the man shooting it. Judging by the gap between the hits and the reports, he's at least two hundred yards away, maybe farther. You might as well throw rocks at him as try to peg him with your little Winchester from that distance. Now, keep your head down, because you look a whole lot better with it on your shoulders!"

"A Sharps, you think?" Keeping her head down, Arliss cast Haskell an anxious, hazel-eyed glance, her hair in her eyes. "That's what the Jackal uses."

"I know that much about him!" Haskell said a quarter-second before another large slug thudded loudly, angrily into the log, causing it to lurch. Bark and wood slivers flew.

The big rifle belched hellfire.

"He's here," Arliss said, chin to the ground, eyes raised. "He's that close."

"The bastard's got the upper hand." Knowing the Jackal was probably injecting another long, brass cartridge into the single-shot cannon's open breech, Bear jerked a quick look up over the log. Through the gray dawn light, he could see a rock outcropping roughly two hundred yards away, toward the canyon's east ridge.

Aside from the distant eastern ridge, it was the highest ground around. The shooter had to be on it.

The lawman's suspicion was confirmed when smoke puffed and orange flames lanced from the top of the outcropping.

Haskell jerked his head back down behind the log, pressing his chin to the ground, as another large round—probably a .50-caliber—hammered the log. The log quivered. There was a cracking sound. Haskell lifted his eyes to see a long crack running roughly vertically through the log.

"Jesus," he wheezed. "He's gonna try to blast right through the log until he has us in his sites!"

Quickly, he raised his head again and looked around. All they had for cover besides the log was brush and a few rocks, which meant no cover at all. A clump of cedars stippled a low rise that separated their position from the trail, but the cedars wouldn't offer much more cover than the brush.

Not from the size of a weapon the Jackal was wielding.

The killer had the higher ground, and he could keep Haskell and Arliss pinned down behind the log until he'd pulverized it and had an open view of his quarry.

Bear had staked out their horses roughly fifty yards behind

the camp and in a copse of wind-twisted post oaks and sycamores. No real cover there, either. If Haskell and Arliss tried to run to the horses, the Jackal would likely open up on the mounts, and then his quarry would be in an even worse fix.

Haskell looked at Jordan Tifflin, who lay belly down in a pool of thick blood welling beneath his chest, and winced. Tifflin's face was turned toward Haskell, his lips pooched out. His half-open eyes were staring at the blood leaking from his half-open mouth.

"What are we going to do?" Arliss said just after another blast had hammered the log, widening the crack.

Haskell considered. Meanwhile, two more rocketing blasts punched the log, spraying him and Arliss with bark and slivers.

Silence yawned.

Haskell lifted his head, casting his gaze toward the rise.

"What's he doing?" Arliss said, edging a glance of her own over the log.

"Big-caliber guns like that run hot and get jammed easy." Haskell rose and leaped the log, grabbing his Henry and cocking a round into the action. "You stay here. I'm gonna storm the son of a bitch!"

"Bear, wait!"

"No waitin', honey!" Haskell cast a glance over his right shoulder. Arliss was sitting up, staring at him worriedly. "When he starts shooting again, you run back to the horses, mount up, and ride the hell away from here!"

Haskell turned his head forward and ran as hard and as fast as he could, holding the Henry by its neck in his right hand. He bounded up and over the low knoll and through the cedars. Leaving the cedars, he began tracing a serpentine course.

The Jackal's cannon was likely jammed, but he'd get it unjammed before Haskell could run the two hundred yards to the rise. All the lawman could do was run as fast as he could in a zigzag pattern and hope Jack Hyde didn't set a steady bead on him. If Bear could make a hundred yards, he could start throwing lead back at the Jackal—lead that would actually reach the son of a bitch atop the rise!

Haskell's left arm sawed back and forth as he ran. His knees rose high. He stepped on a rock, nearly fell, but then got his boots beneath him once more and continued running. Air raked in and out of his lungs. A sharp pain grew in his right side.

When he'd run what he thought was a good seventy yards, something moved atop the outcropping directly ahead of him. He threw himself to his right as smoke puffed from the rise and orange flames lanced the lightening dawn air. Haskell hit the ground, rolled onto his belly, and heard a crackling thud behind him. He glanced over his left shoulder to see a branch fall from one of the cedars.

"Shit," he said, breathing hard.

He drew another chestful of air, heaved himself to his feet with a grunt, and continued running, first right and then quickly swinging left and then back again. Up on the rise, more smoke plumed. Flames lapped toward Haskell.

This time he threw himself to his left. When he rolled off his left shoulder onto his belly, he saw a tuft of dry grass and sand fly up about eight feet to his right. It was followed by the snarling crack of the big-caliber rifle.

Hair pricked across the back of Haskell's neck.

He threw a glance toward the outcropping. The son of a bitch was trying to lead his quarry the way he'd lead a running deer or a buffalo. Hyde had wrongly assumed that Haskell, seeing the rifle's smoke and flames, would throw himself right. If the Jackal had been correct, Bear's shaggy head would likely still be rolling along the ground about now, back in the direction from which he'd come.

Fortunately, Hyde had got it wrong.

Next time, however, he might get it right.

CHAPTER FIFTEEN

Haskell leaped to his feet and continued running, trying to ignore the growing pain in his side. When smoke and flames shone again from the outcropping, Bear straightened out his course and ran directly toward the rise, hearing a resolute thud and seeing out of the corner of his left eye several pulverized prickly pear ears fly.

Haskell smiled as he ran.

"Fooled you again, you son of a bitch!" he wheezed.

He stopped.

He could see the outline of the shooter atop the outcropping now, in a niche between the sand-colored rocks capping the mound. He could see the slender barrel of the long rifle move as Hyde reloaded.

Haskell raised his Henry to his shoulder, clicked back the hammer, aimed quickly, and fired.

Dust plumed in front of one of the rocks capping the rise, a few feet from the silhouette of the Jackal's head. The Jackal pulled his head back with a jerk. Haskell snarled, "There you go—how do you like it?" as he pumped another cartridge into the Henry's breech and sent three more .44-caliber rounds whistling toward the escarpment.

The echo of the third shot hadn't died before Haskell rose and continued running hard, pumping his left arm.

He was closing on the escarpment—within fifty yards now . . . forty . . . thirty . . .

He stared at the ridge. The rocks up there grew larger and larger. He waited to see Hyde's head again, the barrel of his cannon. When he did, Bear would stop and throw more lead. But neither the head of his mysterious assailant nor the rifle appeared.

Haskell gained the base of the ridge. He was winded, but he started climbing anyway, zigzagging between large rocks. Occasionally he stopped, crouched, and aimed the Henry toward the crest above him.

Still no sign of the shooter.

Haskell stormed the rest of the way to the ridge crest, stopped, and aimed his rifle into the niche in the rocks.

Hyde was gone.

Empty brass shell casings winked in the light from the sun now poking up above the eastern ridge.

Haskell pivoted, swinging his Henry around, raking his gaze along the crest of the ridge. Nothing.

Breathless, his legs and chest aching, he dropped to a knee, lowering the barrel of the Henry. While he caught his breath, he continued to look around. Footprints scored the sand anywhere from three to five feet down the sandy backside of the ridge, near the spent shell casings. The prints were small. Little larger than the sign left by your average woman. There were several fresh, brown, tobacco-flecked plops of chaw juice, as well. The Jackal had spat on one of his empty shell casings, which had rolled up against a jagged-edged rock.

Haskell felt more hair prick across the back of his neck.

Studying the Jackal's sign was like studying the tracks of a reclusive rogue beast of the wild or a ghost. Few people but those who'd hired Jack Hyde to kill for them had ever seen him since he'd broken out of prison nearly twenty years ago. Those who'd hired him had rarely spoken of him. Naturally they hadn't wanted to admit they'd hired him. Many had hired him long-distance—through the mail or by telegram.

So what Bear was staring at now were the leavings of what was, for all intents and purposes, a ghost, albeit a human one.

Or maybe the Jackal wasn't human. No one knew enough about him to know for sure. There were times when Haskell had wondered if the man actually existed anywhere outside of legend.

But now he himself had encountered him.

He'd been shot at by the man's legendary Sharps.

His fingers tingled as he looked around carefully, searching for the Jackal. He couldn't be that far away. Only a few minutes had passed since Bear had last seen him.

Then he saw a thin sliver of dust rising along the base of the eastern ridge. The man was following the wash north along that ridge. He was maybe a quarter-mile away and moving fast.

Another horseman was galloping toward Haskell, this one from the northwest. Horsewoman, rather. Honey-blond hair danced across Arliss Posey's shoulders as she swung her clay in a slow arc toward the backside of the escarpment. She rode the clay bareback, with only a bridle, and she held her carbine across the horse's buffeting mane.

Haskell hurried down the escarpment. He reached the bottom just as Arliss pulled up, looking harried. "Where is he?"

Haskell jerked his chin in the direction the Jackal was headed. "Over there, but you can't see him from here." He strode over to the claybank. "We have to get back to camp fast. I gotta get my horse and go after him!" He leaped off a rock, swinging his right leg over the clay's back, plopping himself down behind Arliss.

"What do you think you're doing?" she said, peevish as usual.

"You don't expect me to walk after him, do you?" Haskell pecked her cheek.

"You do that again, and I'll—"

"I know—you'll gut-shoot me. Come on, darlin'!" He batted his heels against the clay's flanks, causing the mount to lunge into an instant lope. "We got the Jackal on the run!"

While Arliss broke camp, limping on her bad foot, Haskell rolled Jordan Tifflin in his saddle blanket and tied him belly down over his saddled horse. Then Haskell saddled both his own and Arliss's horses. They mounted and galloped around the escarpment from which the Jackal had fired at them.

It didn't take long for Haskell to pick up the man's tracks, his heart beating anxiously, relieved and thrilled to finally be on the trail of one of the most wanted federal criminals in the history of the frontier west.

His relief and thrill were literally doused with cold water when, forty minutes north of the escarpment, mountain-sized clouds rolled in and piled up, dropped fast, and hurled raindrops the size of silver dollars sideways on a chill wind. Haskell and Arliss had been following the wash, but now they had to leave it in a hurry, for it was beginning to flood. The Jackal's tracks were quickly, thoroughly obliterated. Haskell and the Pinkerton rode up the side of the eastern ridge and took cover from the deluge under a rock overhang.

"Shit!" Haskell barked, standing at the overhang's edge and glaring out at the tempest.

He looked at the muddy, roiling, tea-colored water now sweeping driftwood and cow bones down the wash that had been bone dry only half an hour earlier. "That bastard has some higher power looking out for him, I swear!"

Arliss, too, was frustrated. Seated on the ground beneath the overhang, knees raised, she worked her own exasperation out on a mesquite stick with her pocketknife.

"He was headed north," she said. "The San Rafael is north."

"Working for Tifflin," Bear said as he plucked an Indian Kid out of his shirt pocket and snapped a match to life on his thumbnail.

Puffing the cheroot, he walked over to where the horses stood ground-tied ten feet to his left, and rummaged around in one of his saddlebag pouches. He pulled out a hide-wrapped bottle, left the hide in the pouch, and took the bottle over to where Arliss sat. He sat down beside her and popped the cork on the bottle.

"What are you going to do?" she asked, scowling at him with her customary reproof.

"I'm gonna have a drink." Haskell took a couple of deep pulls, then wiped the bottle's lip with his hand and offered the bourbon to his comely partner. "Join me?"

Her scowl deepened. She opened her mouth to give him a harsh rebuke. But then she closed her mouth, looked at the bottle, sighed, and grabbed it. "Why the hell not?"

She tipped back the bottle. Her lovely throat moved twice, and then she jerked the bottle back down, gagging. "Oh, god— that's terrible!" She gave Haskell another incriminating look.

"Yeah, well, that's about all a feller can find this far out in the high and rocky." Bear chuckled as she continued to gag, leaning forward with her head between her knees. "You gonna be all right?"

Arliss dry-retched a few more times, then lifted her head, swallowed, drew a deep breath, and ran the back of her hand across her mouth. In a pinched, raspy voice, she said, "No thanks to you!"

"Ah, hell, it's not that bad." Haskell took another swallow, then one more. "Sorta grows on a feller."

She looked at him, frowning. "It does?"

"Yeah." Bear offered the bottle. "Try again?"

"Maybe I just took too big a sip." Arliss took the bottle and lifted it slowly, tentatively to her lips. She closed her lips over the lip of the bottle. Her mouth was still wet from her previous swig. Staring at her lips, Haskell felt a stirring in his pants.

Arliss lifted the bottle gently. Haskell saw the liquid slosh up through the brown neck. When it started to run into the young woman's mouth, she lowered the bottle almost immediately, and swallowed, pursing her lips and making a face.

She held the whiskey down this time. After a few seconds, she turned to Haskell with a vaguely pleased look in her pretty hazel eyes.

"You're right. It does sort of grow on you."

"See?"

"Good grief," she said with a snort. "You're gonna make a drunk out of me." She lifted the bottle again and took another very small swig, swallowed, and handled the bottle back to Haskell. "I've never been much of a whiskey drinker," she said. "But it feels good . . . on such a day as this."

She stared out at the rain and the churning wash.

Haskell leaned back on his elbows and studied her as the cool wind blew in under the overhang, sliding her hair behind her.

Since there wasn't anything else to do, he finally asked the question that had been nibbling at the edges of his mind since he'd first encountered her on this same ridge, only a couple of miles south of here. "How in the heck did a pretty girl like you get into this business, anyway? Chasin' after scalawags like Jack Hyde . . ."

She turned her head to study him skeptically for a time, her scrutiny dancing between his eyes. She appeared somehow leery of the question, as though she suspected he might have some ulterior motive for asking it.

Haskell hiked a shoulder and took another pull from the bottle. "All right, never mind. I didn't mean to crawl your hump. We'll just sit here and watch the rain."

"That would be preferable," she said, turning her head again.

After a time, without looking at him, she reached out her hand for the bottle. Haskell gave it to her.

From the side, he watched her lift the bottle to her pink mouth and take another tentative sip. She took one more small sip. A little of the whiskey dribbled from her bottom lip and ran down her chin. Haskell felt another stirring in his loins. He remembered how sweet her lips had tasted the other night in San Saba. He yearned to taste them again now, to lick the whiskey off of them. But as she handed the bottle back to Bear, she brushed the trickle of whiskey from her chin with her hand.

Staring at the rain, which was coming down with slightly less vigor than before, she said quietly, "I'm from Illinois. Farm family. My great-grandfather and his wife came through the Cumberland Gap during the Revolutionary War. He wanted to make a fresh start, free of King George. Instead, he ended up fighting the Shawnees who had sworn allegiance to the Tories. Anyway, he was killed in a duel just after my grandfather was born."

"Tough stock," Haskell said. He didn't mention that he shared a similar, frontier-fighting history.

Arliss said, "My father was a farmer and a blacksmith. He also owned a saloon. He got into a feud with a rival saloon owner. One morning I woke to smoke filling my bedroom." She turned to Haskell, her gaze tinged with remembered grief. "I still dream about that night. I was only twelve. I tried to get my mam and pap out of their rooms, but I couldn't wake them. I grabbed my baby brother from his crib and ran outside, but he was already dead."

She stopped as she turned back at stare at the rain. A tear dribbled from the corner of her left eye. She shook her head as though to clear the emotion and continued, "I was taken in by mother's brother. A bad man. He mistreated me . . . in vile ways. One night he came to my room and I cut him with a butcher knife. Cut him in a way that made sure he'd never treat another girl the way he'd treated me again."

She gave Haskell a quick, foxy, self-satisfied grin.

Haskell winced. "Don't doubt it a bit."

"Then I ran north to Chicago. I was eighteen. Penniless. I found work in restaurants and bawdy houses. I never did any work on my back, though the bawdy house owners wanted me to. I would only swamp the place out, wash the linens and empty cuspidors and slop buckets. Disgusting work.

"But it was in one of those bawdy houses I was befriended by a kind man—a man who had lost his wife recently and frequented the bawdy houses to relieve his loneliness. The gentleman was an associate of Mister Allan Pinkerton. It just so happened that Mister Pinkerton needed an operative on the crime-ridden streets of Chicago. There was a spate of kidnappings at the time—outlaw gangs from the riverfronts preying on the silver-spoon folks from the wealthy neighbors. Mister Pinkerton figured that a young woman prowling those riverfront bordellos and eateries could get more information about criminal transactions, including kidnapping plots, than any of his male operatives. And he was right." Arliss gave Haskell a saucy wink over her left shoulder.

"It must've been right dangerous work," Haskell said.

"It was." Arliss nodded. "But I took to it like a pig to mud." She snorted. "That was one of Pap's expressions. Anyway, after a year or so, I'd sort of worn out my welcome on the streets of Chicago. The gangs were onto me. So Mister Pinkerton sent me out here to the frontier. It's here I work now, busting up rustling gangs and fraudulent confidence schemes, tracking killers and kidnappers and illegal whiskey peddlers. You name it, I do it."

She stopped. She was silent for a time and then, scowling, turned to look over her shoulder at Haskell again. "That must be your whiskey talking. I've never said that much to any one man in my entire life."

She looked a little terrified. "You can't tell anyone about any of that!"

Haskell chuckled. "Darlin', if you can't trust a deputy U.S. marshal, who can you trust?"

She squinted an eye at him. "I'm still not sure about you."

"You seemed to be sure enough the other night."

She bunched her lips in anger, drew her hand back, and flung it forward. Haskell grabbed her wrist before it could crack against his face, and held it between them. He doffed his hat, then hers, tossed them aside, and leaned toward her.

He expected her to pull back away from him, but she didn't.

He closed his mouth over hers, amazed to find her lips opening for him and pliant, her tongue pressing against his own. He kissed her harder. She groaned and wrapped her arms around his neck, opening her mouth still farther and kissing him with every bit as much fervor as he was kissing her.

He drew his head away from hers, jerked off his leather gloves, and began unbuttoning her blouse. While he did, she reached down and pressed her right hand against his crotch. He was already hard, but the feel of her warm hand against him made his manhood throb crazily.

He opened her blouse, then pulled her chemise up to her neck. Her breasts swelled from her chest, the pink nipples immediately pebbling as the cool, moist air touched them. Haskell cupped each firm orb in his hands and drove his nose and mouth into the deep valley between them, sniffing, reveling in the warm female scent of her.

"Get out of your pants," she urged, breathless.

Haskell unbuckled his cartridge belts, quickly coiled them together, and set them aside. He cast a cautious glance outside the overhang. What he and Arliss were about to do was damned dangerous, but he figured the Jackal was a good ways ahead of them and likely holed up out of the weather, the same as Bear and Arliss were.

He pulled his pants down to his ankles and then turned to the pretty, flushed Pinkerton, who'd pulled her own pants down to her boots. She grabbed Bear's hard-on and pumped it, nibbling his chin.

Her small, sharp teeth and warm breath enflamed his desire. Groaning, Arliss lay back against the hard stone floor and spread her legs wide, the tangled hair between her legs opening to reveal the red flesh of her womanhood.

Haskell mounted her.

Arliss gave another, louder, deep-throated groan as he slid inside her moist, fleshy portal, and she thrust her hips up to meet his.

CHAPTER SIXTEEN

Haskell rolled off of Arliss sometime later, his breath rasping in and out, and lay against the slope's stone floor. Arliss lay beside him, breathing just as heavily as he was. He rolled toward her, kissed each of her breasts in turn, then lay back once more.

"That, darlin'," Bear said, chuckling, "was one hell of a way to wait out a rainstorm!"

"Indeed," Arliss wheezed.

"You know what's even better about it?"

"What's that?" she said, leaning over to plant a kiss on his dwindling manhood.

"We're not in no hotel room you can throw me out of, and there's no one around to hear you scream rape!"

Arliss laughed as she lay with her cheek resting against his crotch, staring up over his belly and chest at his face. "I do apologize for that, Bear," she said with genuine chagrin. "I know it was rather nasty of me. But a girl on her own on the wide-open frontier can't be too careful—especially one who is also a Pinkerton agent."

Reaching up to give one of his suspenders a playful tug, she said with even more chagrin, "And one with such insatiable desires as I get from time to time."

"There's no shame in it."

"Not ladylike."

"That's silly to look at it that way. We men and women were given different parts for a reason. Sometimes those feelings make us want to use those different parts for reasons other than procreation."

"Oh, you're a philosopher, now, as well as a lawman—eh, Bear Haskell?"

Bear grinned sheepishly and shrugged. "Works for me."

Arliss raked her fingers slowly down his broad chest toward his belly as she frowned up at him, pensive. "I really ran into one when I ran into you—didn't I?"

"If that means you like me, you can go ahead and say so, Miss Arliss. I like you, and there ain't no ifs, ands, or buts about it."

Her mouth corners quirked a beguiling half-smile. "I like you, Bear."

Haskell basked in the beauty of her heart-shaped face, her eyes gazing into his, unblinking. Her breasts sloped toward his curled manhood that swelled a little each time she lowered her head to plant a warm, wet kiss on it.

He said, "If you're worried I'm gonna mooncalf around after you, though, don't waste your time. I may not go throwin' women out of my room under threat of my screamin' rape, but I know when it's time to pull my picket pin."

"I kind of like my way," Arliss said. "I've always had a flare for the dramatic." She smiled, blinking slowly. "Maybe that's why I became a Pinkerton in the first place . . . and why I gave you my room key. I don't do that very often, I hasten to add. Only on the rare occasion when I see a man I think can really grease my wheels, make me feel what it's like to be a woman and not just an operative."

Haskell chuckled and smoothed a lock of hair from her cheek with his thumb. He looked outside. "Well, now that your wheels are lubed, as are my own, I think we'd best get back on the trail. The rain's stopped. We might be able to make it to the San Rafael without drowning."

"I hope so," Arliss said, arching her butt up off the ground to pull up her pants. She stood and turned to Bear, who'd pulled up his own pants and now stood beside her, tucking in his shirt. "What happens if we run up against that damn Big Fifty again?"

"It's just a risk we're gonna have to take. That long gun has kept the Jackal from being run down for years now. I for one am not going to let it allow him to *keep* running. I want to catch that killer, slap the cuffs on him, break that cannon over my knee, and head the hell back to Denver."

He finished buckling his cartridge belt around his waist, grabbed his Henry, and headed over to where their horses waited patiently, occasionally stomping and flicking their ears. "Come on, Miss Arliss. Let's see if we can't close the file on ole Jack Hyde!"

The big lawman stepped into his saddle.

A half hour later, Haskell and Arliss splashed across another wash that had likely been dry before the storm had hit, and leaned forward in their saddles as their mounts as well as the mount carrying the body of Jordan Tifflin lunged up the opposite bank. Haskell's pinto stopped to shake water from its coat, and Arliss's horse followed suit.

Bear held his mount's reins taut as he stared through scattered mesquites toward the yard of the Rancho San Rafael. The two-story mud-brick house sat back against more desert trees scattered along a rise. A long, low, L-shaped bunkhouse sat off to the left, fronting a tall adobe barn and several corrals and stables. A windmill with a mortared stone stock tank sat in the middle of the yard. What appeared to be a blacksmith shed sat off to the right under a sprawling oak. The shed's large doors were closed.

The only sounds were occasional songbirds, the breeze in the brush, and the trees still dripping after the rain. The fresh air hung heavy and warm with humidity.

Arliss glanced skeptically at Haskell. "Do you think he's here?"

The rain had washed out any sign the Jackal might have left for them to follow. They'd come to the ranch because they had nowhere else to look for their quarry. Also Haskell wanted to talk with Tifflin—not to mention deliver to the man his son's body. As always, it was hard to say where Hyde was.

"Doubtful he'd lead us here . . . to his employer . . . unless he's waitin' for us here . . . to ambush us. Again." Haskell slid the Henry from its sheath, cocked it one-handed, off-cocked the hammer, and rested the barrel across his saddlebows. "Keep your eyes skinned and prepare to move fast."

"Oh, you're giving orders again." Arliss gave him another of her hard, castigating glances. She might have softened up some during their tussle under the overhang, but she'd grown that hard, saucy crust back again quickly.

Haskell gave a soft snort. "Just habit, I reckon."

Riding side by side, they followed the trail under the wooden portal straddling the trail and into the crossbar of which the San Rafael's Circle-R brand had been burned. A gray cat of apprehension got up and padded around in the lawman's belly. No one was out and about in the yard. True, it had rained, but the rain was over. A few dripping trees didn't keep ranch hands from their work.

The only movement in the ranch yard was the dozen-plus horses milling in the interconnected corrals behind the bunkhouse. The fresh air was touched with the stench of horse-shit and privies and the perfume of freshly cut hay.

Haskell swept his gaze around, probing every nook and cranny and roofline. If the Jackal was here, he'd likely make his presence felt soon. Haskell wanted to feel it *before* he heard the blast of that big rifle. If he wasn't here, maybe Ambrose Tifflin knew where he was—if Tifflin had hired him, that was.

If not Tifflin, who?

Silently, Haskell cursed his misfortune at having been so close to Hyde only to have the man slip away as the storm hammered down.

Bear and Arliss walked their horses up to the stock tank and then split up, Bear riding around the tank's left side while Arliss rode around the right side. The bunkhouse was on Haskell's left. The long, low, shake-shingled building with a narrow front gallery shaded by a brush awning was silent.

But then a door latch clicked.

Haskell pulled firmly back on his horse's reins.

The bunkhouse door opened. A big man stepped into the doorway. He cocked a carbine one-handed as he poked his head out the half-open door. He wasn't wearing a shirt. He had a large, hard, rounded belly. His right arm was in a bandage sling, and a bloody bandage was pasted against his right shoulder.

He looked miserable. His dark-brown eyes were shiny from drink.

He scowled at Haskell and at Arliss coming around the far side of the stock tank. He looked at Bear's badge, then returned his curious, wary gaze to the big man sitting the roan.

"Lawman?" asked the man in the doorway.

"What happened?" Haskell asked, glancing again at the bandage. Then, when no response appeared imminent, he tried another question. "Is Hyde here?"

This question warranted a response. The heavy brow of the mustached man in the doorway furled dramatically as he said, "Was here. Ain't here now. If he was here, you'd know about it by now!"

"What about Ambrose Tifflin?"

The big man looked at the packhorse and the body it was

obviously carrying, wrapped in a saddle blanket. "What you got there?"

"His son."

That didn't seem to surprise the man in the doorway in the least. He nodded slowly, then jerked his head toward the main house, pulled his head back into the bunkhouse, and closed the door.

Haskell and Arliss shared a glance.

Haskell booted his horse forward, and Arliss followed suit. They reined up in front of the main mud-brick house. It, too, had a brush arbor—a very large one wrapped around at least three sides. A clay *olla* hung beneath the arbor, and a monarch butterfly was winging along the rim as though looking for water. A small chicken hawk perched on the rail at the porch's left end. As Haskell studied the house carefully, raking his gaze across every sashed front window, the hawk gave a ratcheting screech, and flew away.

Haskell dismounted, as did Arliss. They tossed their reins over one of the two worn hitchracks fronting the steps leading up to the porch, and then started up the porch steps. They'd just gained the step when the latch of the big timbered door in front of them clicked. The door had two long loop holes carved through it—likely for holding off rampaging Indians in bygone times—and the hinges squawked as the door drew open.

A woman in a plain calico housedress and cream apron stood in the doorway, raising a long, double-barreled shotgun to her slender shoulder and drawing both hammers back. She was a strange visage—dark-skinned but with long, slanted green eyes and black, silver-streaked hair gathered into two tight buns atop her head.

Haskell judged her age to be around sixty. The skin of her severely carved face was not overly wrinkled, but it was drawn taut across her cheekbones, which were nearly as sharp as arrowheads. The skin at the nubs of those cheeks was a shade lighter than the rest of her face—a dark-yellow color.

The hands on the shotgun looked considerably older than the rest of her. They reminded Haskell of the talons of the hawk that had just taken flight from the rail.

Those long, green, witchlike eyes blinked once, slowly. She didn't say anything but appeared to be waiting for her visitors to speak.

"No need for that . . . Mrs. Tifflin, I assume," Haskell said, holding his Henry straight down at his side and trying to stand as still as possible, sensing that the woman holding the shotgun knew how to use the gut-shredder and probably had on more than one occasion.

"Who is it?" thundered a raspy male voice behind her. "Who's there, Hillary?"

"Your guess is as good as mine," Hillary said, staring at Haskell and Arliss. Her voice was nearly as deep as that of the man behind her. "One of 'em is a split-tail. The other's wearin' a badge."

Haskell thought it odd that one woman would call another woman a "split-tail," but, then, western Texas grew its denizens like their cacti—stout and thorny. The woman standing before him seemed more man than woman, anyway, despite the dress and apron.

"I'm Deputy U.S. Marshal Bear Haskell."

"The split-tail is a Pinkerton agent," Arliss said, her voice pitched with disdain at the woman's terminology. "Arliss Posey."

"Who are they?" the man behind Hillary wanted to know. "The pool? Are they in the *pool*?"

The woman lowered the shotgun and glanced over her shoulder. "The big drink of water is a lawman. The girl says she's a Pinkerton."

"I *am* a Pinkerton," Arliss said tightly, with unconcealed contempt.

"*Who?*" the man's voice boomed behind Hillary.

Ignoring him, Hillary glanced beyond her visitors, squinting her hawkish green eyes. "Who's that ridin' belly down yonder?"

Haskell glanced behind him and removed his hat. "That . . . that's your son, ma'am. I'm sorry."

"Jordan Tifflin is no son of mine," Hillary snapped, turning away and yelling into the darkness behind her. "They got your boy, Ambrose. He's dead!" She'd yelled it like an accusation.

She stomped away, the removal of her body from the doorway revealing a man in a checked bathrobe standing on a broad stairway about twenty feet back in the house, between what appeared to be a kitchen area on the right and a parlor on the left.

Ambrose Tifflin was tall, willowy, stooped, and bald-headed, with an unkempt, ginger and gray mustache that drooped to his chest. The beard was as long and thin and tangled as the hair falling from the sides of his head. He wasn't wearing a stitch under the robe, and his equipment was right out in the open with most of the rest of him, though thank goodness Haskell couldn't see details because of the dense shadows cloaking the stairs.

The rancher, in his seventies, wore a bandage around his belly, which bulged out like that of a woman nine-months' pregnant. The bandage was splotched with blood over the man's left side.

Coming down the stairs, Tifflin closed his robe with one hand over his crotch. In his other hand he held an old-model Colt conversion .44. He hobbled down the stairs, barefoot—a mere ghost of a man, formidable at one time, but used up and breathing hard, eyes set deep in doughy sockets. His face was long and bony and startlingly pale.

His chest worked like a bellows. "What the fuck did that old bitch say?" He might have been old and broken down, but suddenly his voice was loud and resonant, abrasively nasal. "My son is dead?" He took a step through the doorway and looked out. "Jordan's dead?"

"That's right, Mister Tifflin," Arliss said.

Tifflin looked at the Pinkerton, but instead of his eyes showing shock or sadness, they drifted over the girl favorably, vaguely amorously. His son might have been dead, but Ambrose Tifflin wasn't a man to overlook a nicely set-up young filly.

He turned to Haskell and said not with accusation but genuine curiosity, "Who killed him? Did you kill him?" He dropped his chin, widened his eyes, and deepened his voice with anger. "Or did the *pool* kill him?"

"Jack Hyde killed him."

CHAPTER SEVENTEEN

"Oh," Tifflin said, as though the Jackal was the third option he just as easily could have mentioned. "So . . . the pool killed my son, too."

Haskell said, "Are you saying Hyde kills for the smaller ranchers?"

"Of course, that's what I'm saying."

Haskell and Arliss shared a glance.

"What the hell happened to you, Mister Tifflin?" Haskell inquired. "What happened to the man in the bunkhouse? Where are your other men?"

As though annoyed, the rancher beckoned to his visitors with a large hand with long, gnarled, age-spotted fingers and yellow nails as long as claws. "Come in, come in. Damp air out there. If I stand here, I'll be coughin' soon. Coughin' all fuckin' night!"

Haskell let Arliss enter first. He walked in behind her and closed the door. Tifflin swung around and tramped barefoot toward the stairs, again beckoning. "Let's go upstairs. I don't want that crotchety old bitch listening to our conversation. She's been thinkin' for years she's the one runnin' this outfit, but I will tell you the only one runnin' this outfit is me, *sabe*? I'm the one the limeys hired, and they hired me for a reason."

He turned to Haskell and fairly bellowed, "Because I can fucking run a ranch!" He rammed his thumb against his chest, then continued up the stairs.

Somewhere in the house, a door closed loudly.

Tifflin laughed and turned around again. "Hillary's my fourth wife. Scandinavian and Lakota Sioux." He rolled his eyes. "Oh, lordy—for years now I been sleepin' in a separate room and lockin' the door!"

He raked out another laugh and continued climbing.

Haskell and Arliss fell into step behind him, Arliss waving her hand in front of her face. The man's breath was sour, and, mixing with the death stench of the rest of him, it was nearly suffocating.

"I met her up in Wyoming," Tifflin continued about his wife as he led his guests up the stairs and then down a dim hall. "I needed a housekeeper after my third wife died. I could see Hillary wasn't going anywhere. She's the type to make no bones about sinking a taproot. Couldn't get rid of her so I married her. Been ruing that bit of foolishness ever since!"

He pushed through a half-open door and led his guests into a small office with a large oak desk and oak cabinets, a few bookshelves, and a liquor cabinet. A fireplace flanked the desk. There was a leather sofa against the wall to the right of the desk, and two leather chairs by the windows to the left.

The air was sour with the smell of the wounded, aged, and likely diseased old rancher and cigar smoke.

Tifflin ambled around behind the desk, muttering, "The only time I ever get any peace and quiet around here is when my cock's in her mouth." He wheezed a laugh then, leaning forward and planting his fists on the top of his desk, looking at Arliss. "You don't mind talk of farm matters, do you, little girl?"

Arliss canted her head to one side, studying the obviously stewed old rancher dubiously. "Mister Tifflin, you don't look very distraught about your son lying dead across that horse out there."

"Yeah, well, he wasn't much of a man *or* a son."

Tifflin sagged into the padded Windsor chair behind the desk.

"I loved him dearly at one time, but he never took to work. After his ma died, he grew up spoiled and surly. I could never handle him, though I'll guaran-damn-tee you I did not spare the rod on that boy! Broke several of 'em over his skinny ass! He left here when he was fifteen to go make a name for himself. He only came back for money, which I gave him, thinking I could keep him out of trouble, keep my name out of the dirt.

"Didn't work. He was a drunk and a small-time criminal, Jordan was. A rustler and stagecoach thief. Even held up cantinas down south of the border. Ah, hell, I reckon I'm sorry he's dead . . . mostly for his ma, god rest her soul. But it's better this way. But goddamnit"—he pounded a gnarled fist on his desk—"I got bigger troubles than Jordan!"

He narrowed a curious eye at Haskell. "You said Hyde killed him . . . ?"

"Hyde ambushed us on our way out here," Bear said. "What I want to know is what happened to you and your men, Mister Tifflin."

"Hyde was here two nights ago. Shot three of my men out in the yard yonder from that rise north of the house." Tifflin jerked his chin to indicate the direction, then fumbled a cheroot out of a wooden box on his desk. His hands shook with palsy as he struck a match and held the flame and the cigar up to his mouth. "My men and I tracked him the next day to Lloyd Silver's place."

"One of the smaller ranches in the area, I take it," Haskell said.

Tifflin nodded as he inhaled and exhaled blue smoke and tossed his spent match into a brass sandbox beside his desk. There was an open bottle on his desk. He took a deep pull from it. "We didn't know he was leading us into a trap. Silver was waiting for us. He and his men and the whole damn pool was waiting for us—with their entire payrolls. Must have been near thirty of 'em."

"And . . . ?" Arliss prompted the oldster.

"And what, little girl? What do you think happened? A small war. Only it wasn't so small. We gave as good as we got, I'll tell you that. We didn't leave one pool rider standing. Wiped 'em all out 'ceptin' those few that turned tail and ran. Ha!" Tifflin slapped his desk. "Them yellow dogs that ran are prob'ly in Mexico by now."

The rancher paused. He narrowed his eyes pensively as he drew on the cheroot. "Only problem is . . . only me and my *segundo*, Roy Snyder, made it back to the San Rafael alive. I'm a mite short-handed." Tifflin chuffed with wry amusement at the notion that all of his men were dead.

"Is the Snyder place east of that high ridge just south of here?" Haskell asked.

"Lucifer's Anvil, it's called. *Yunque de Lucifer*. And yes, it is."

Haskell looked at Arliss. "That's the shooting we heard yesterday afternoon." He turned to Tifflin, studying the man in silent exasperation. "All dead, you say? All of your men? All of the pool men?"

"That's right." Tifflin gave a wolfish, half-mad grin, his blue lips parting to reveal black gums and rotten teeth. "You got good hearing for a lawman. I reckon I'm hirin'. You're a big, sound feller. How 'bout turnin' in your badge and ridin' for me? I bet I pay better than Uncle Sam. I'll make you foreman. I need a big son of a bitch to keep my crew in line!"

He slapped the table and grinned across his desk and through his billowing cigar smoke at Haskell. The old man's eyes were glazed with drink and dementia.

Bear felt Arliss's gaze on him. He turned to her, and she arched a skeptical brow.

Bear turned back to Tifflin and said, "What about Hyde?"

"What about him?"

"You didn't see him at the Silver place, I'll bet."

"Hell, no. He does his work from a distance with that big Sharps of his, and disappears. What he can't do without the cannon, he don't do!"

"In town, Homer Redfield told me that several pool men had been shot with that Sharps, as well."

"That's what the pool says." Tifflin hooded his eyes and curled another devious grin. "They just wanted the rangers to think that Hyde was workin' for me, so they had an excuse to ride against me . . . to kill my men. Eventually, they'd be swarmin' around this place, takin' over the San Rafael. Silver would likely be movin' into my house, probably fuckin' my wife, if he could stand ole Hillary."

Tifflin rolled a bright, vaguely mocking gaze to Arliss, who regarded him blandly. He was the type of fellow who liked to get a rise out of women by talking dirty in front of them. He didn't realize there was no getting a rise out of Arliss Posey. Haskell half-wanted to inform him he was wasting his time, but he had more important things to think about.

"Why do you suppose Hyde ambushed us this morning?" he asked Tifflin. "That's when he shot your son."

Tifflin only shrugged. "Who knows? Maybe he seen that badge on your shirt, figured the law was on his trail. Maybe he wanted to fuck the little girl." He slid his challenging gaze back to Arliss, who still gave him nothing.

"Maybe," Haskell allowed, nodding. "But maybe Hyde wasn't riding for the pool."

"He sure as hell wasn't riding for me!"

"Maybe he wasn't riding for either one of you, Mister Tifflin," Haskell said. "Ever think of that?"

Arliss jerked a vaguely startled look at Bear.

"Why else would the Jackal be hauntin' this range?" Tifflin asked, poking his cheroot into a corner of his mouth and taking a long drag. Suddenly, he frowned. "Unless . . ."

He shook his head, releasing the thought. "The pool's been after me for years, after I started fencin' in all of the old grant," he said. "So they brought in the fucking Jackal!"

Haskell pondered the question. He could feel Arliss studying him again, but he didn't look at her.

Finally, he asked Tifflin, "How far is it to the Silver Ranch?"

"A good twenty, twenty-five miles from here." The rancher scowled. "Why?"

Now Bear looked at Arliss. "I'm thinkin' we might ride over there."

"I'll ask it again—why?" Tifflin repeated, genuinely befuddled.

"Not sure yet." Haskell rose from his chair. "Good talkin' with you, Mister Tifflin. My apologies about your boy."

Tifflin stood and the two men shook hands.

"Gonna be dark soon," the rancher said. He glanced out a window. "Might even rain again. You won't make it as far as the Silver Ranch before dark. Best hole up in a line shack at the edge of the San Rafael. It's on Jackrabbit Wash. When you leave here, take the trail to the southeast, keep Lucifer's Anvil ahead and on your right."

As Haskell followed Arliss to the door, Tifflin said behind him, "You're gonna find dead men at the Silver Ranch. A bunch. Mine an' Silver's. Me an' Jake were in no shape to bury our own."

"I've seen dead men before," Haskell grumbled.

"And don't go thinkin' about makin' a criminal case out o' none of this, lawman!" Tifflin yelled as Haskell followed Arliss down the stairs. "They're the ones who started the whole thing!"

Haskell stopped on the porch. He stared toward a low rise to the west. Grave markers angled here and there about the rise. A cemetery. Likely an old one, predating the Alamo. Many Mexicans who'd populated the Rancho San Rafael over the years, before the British syndicate bought out the land grant, were buried there. Now Jordan Tifflin was about to be planted there, as well.

Jordan's roan stood under an oak atop the rise, grazing and idly tossing its tail. The body was still tied across the saddle. A bulky female figure wearing an apron, which buffeted in the wind, was slowly, methodically digging a hole.

Hillary.

Arliss had followed Bear's gaze to the graveyard. Now she turned to him, one brow arched speculatively.

Bear gave an ironic chuff, then grabbed his reins off the hitchrack and mounted up.

CHAPTER EIGHTEEN

The next day, midmorning, Haskell and Arliss halted their mounts at the west edge of Sundown, just beyond the old depot hut.

"Something's wrong," Arliss said, staring straight ahead along the deserted main street.

Haskell nodded. "You ever ridden through a mountain valley, far from anywhere, and not seen a single critter? No deer, elk, or coyotes? No songbirds? Even the squirrels layin' low?"

"Yes. I've ridden through such a valley."

"Kinda looks an' sounds like that here, don't it?"

"When that happens, it usually means there's a particularly nasty breed of predator about." Arliss reached forward and slid her Winchester carbine from its saddle boot. "A rogue grizzly or a stalking wildcat."

"Or a jackal."

Haskell's nerves had been on edge since they'd arrived at the line shack on Jackrabbit Wash just before sundown the previous evening. There'd been no telling for sure, but Haskell had suspected that Jack Hyde had holed up in the shack while he'd been orchestrating his dirty work in the area.

Hyde hadn't left behind any identifying markers, but someone had obviously been living in the shack, for the stove had recently been used and there'd been fresh trash—mostly empty airtight tins—tossed onto the rubble pile in the draw behind the cabin.

And the cot that Haskell and Arliss had taken turns sleeping on when the other was keeping watch for the Jackal's possible return had smelled like fresh sweat.

Jackal sweat.

Odd how sweet the sweat had smelled, he'd thought. A vaguely feminine smell.

Cigarette butts lying about had been of the cheap wheat-paper variety. But they'd been deftly, tightly rolled. There had been no liquor bottles. At least none that had appeared recently discarded. Not a one.

Was the Jackal a teetotaler?

Also plucking the lawman's already strained nerves was the sense that he and Arliss had been followed when they'd left the shack and ridden over to the Silver Ranch. And then it was as though the ghost haunting their back trail had suddenly disappeared.

But the ghost had returned.

Haskell could sense it again now in Sundown.

Had the Jackal swung around and ridden ahead of him and Arliss and beaten them back to town?

As Arliss quietly racked a cartridge into her Winchester's action, Haskell shucked his own rifle and cocked it. He stared ahead along the dusty, sunny street. Nothing moved. Not a horse. Not a dog. Not even a tumbleweed.

Despite the heat that had returned after the storm, a bead of cold sweat rolled down the lawman's back.

"All right," he muttered, half to himself, and touched spurs to his mount's flanks.

They rode slowly into town, hooves thudding softly, dust rising.

None of the shops around them had "Closed" signs in the windows, but the shops looked closed just the same. Closed and abandoned.

Soft laughter sounded just ahead. It was coming from Rosa's

Cantina on the right side of the street. A man's voice rose, buoyant with humor. A familiar voice. Another man spoke with a Spanish accent, and that voice was also familiar to the lawman's ears. They were the only sounds in the entire town.

Haskell glanced at Arliss, then gestured to the little watering hole with his eyes.

They turned in. As they did, Haskell spied movement up the street on his left. Three men stepped out of the Cantina San Gabriel and took up positions against the stout adobe columns fronting the place. One was the Mexican-Apache, Hector Valderrama, who'd ridden into Sundown with five other lobos just as Bear and Jordan Tifflin had been riding out.

The mestizo crossed his arms on his chest and grinned beneath his sweeping black mustache.

"Ah, shit," Haskell grumbled.

"What is it?"

"I been to this dance once before."

Arliss dismounted and turned toward Valderrama and the three others. The other two were Anglos, but all three looked as savage as they came, clad in buckskin and deerskin, pistols and knives bristling on their hips. A silver-capped bowie knife was sheathed on Valderrama's right calf, over his knee-high moccasin with the pointed toe that made it look like an elf shoe.

That was the only thing one bit elfish about Hector Valderrama.

"Nice looking bunch," Arliss said. "Who do you suppose they ride for?"

"I have a feelin' we're gonna find out."

Haskell tossed his reins over the hitchrack and walked slowly under the arbor fronting Rosa's Cantina, keeping a cautious eye skinned on the Cantina San Gabriel and the three, hard-eyed men standing in front of it.

Flanked by Arliss, Bear pushed through the batwings. Rosa

looked at him from behind the bar. A smile began to tug at her mouth corners, but then she saw Arliss walk into the cantina behind Haskell, and she arched a skeptical, faintly accusing brow.

Haskell smiled and pinched his hat brim to the pretty Mexican woman. Then he turned to where Redfield sat in his wheelchair, in his usual place, his back customarily against the wall. He was playing checkers with Orozco La Paz, who sat at a table beside the ranger captain. La Paz was just then chuckling enthusiastically through his teeth as he jumped several of the ranger's checkers, cleaning the board.

"Goddamn you, Oro, you bean-eatin' son of a bitch!"

La Paz lifted his head, laughing girlishly. "No disrespect intended, *el Capitan*, but I was setting you up for that move since the very start of the game!"

"Well, you were setting *someone* up for *somethin'*, anyway!" Haskell said, planting his fists on his hips and chuckling.

Both checker players snapped their heads toward the big man standing just inside the doorway, as though they'd been jerked by the same string.

"Well, look what the coyotes dragged down the wash and into our humble abode!" bellowed Redfield. As appeared to be the custom, his blue eyes were glazed from drink. A nearly empty tequila bottle stood on the table to his left, with two shot glasses. "I see you're still kickin', ya big catamount!"

He might have acted delighted, but there was a vague disappointment in his eyes.

Redfield turned to Oro La Paz and said, "Henry Dade said he was sendin' me a catamount, and ole Henry wasn't whistlin' 'Dixie'! We used to ride together—Henry an' me." The ranger's gaze flicked to Arliss and held on her with goatish male interest. "Sayyy, what you brought home with ya, son?"

"*Sí,*" said Oro La Paz, grinning, showing all his large,

crooked, tobacco-stained teeth, his chocolate eyes fairly devouring Bear's comely partner. "What you bring home with you, Señor *Oso*? A *girl*? Where did you find a girl out there in those rocks? And one so pretty . . . ?"

Haskell glanced at Arliss, who rolled her eyes at the seedy checkers players as she turned to stare out over the batwings. She held her Winchester carbine high across her chest, ready for action.

"This here, gentlemen . . . and Señora Rosa . . . is Miss Arliss Posey of the famed Pinkerton Agency. Arliss is a whole lot smarter than me."

"If looks make us smart, she is smarter than us all," intoned La Paz, then glancing quickly at Rosa he added, "Except for Señora Rosa, I mean!"

Rosa beetled her brows at him.

"What do you mean Miss Posey is smarter than you, Bear?" asked Redfield. "Did she help you run down the Jackal? Boy, I hope so." He frowned. "An' . . . what did you mean by your remark about Oro settin' someone up?"

"Oh, don't worry about it, Cap," Haskell said, walking over and slacking into a chair near the two checkers players. "He set us all up. You, me, likely the whole town and both shooting factions out there in the rocks. He's probably gonna kill you—don't you realize that, or are you too damn drunk? Him an' the Jackal."

Oro frowned, curious. "I do not *comprendo, Oso*. What are you saying? Speak English!"

Bear said, "You see, we were sitting around talking last night at the old line shack on Jackrabbit Wash, Miss Posey an' me, and I told her I was wondering if all the killing out here was *really* about a land war. I told her that in the entire file my boss gave me on Jack Hyde, otherwise known as the Jackal, I didn't see any mention of the gold bullion that Hyde and his partner,

Oscar Alvear, stole nearly twenty years ago ever being recovered. I told her I was wondering if all the shooting out here wasn't really about that loot and not about a land war at all!"

Redfield and Oro shared a dubious look.

Oro smiled uncertainly as he turned back to Haskell and said, "And what did she say, the *bonita* Pinkerton?"

Haskell glanced at Arliss still standing by the door, staring cautiously at the Cantina San Gabriel. "I had to prod her a little. She's a good agent, Arliss is. She plays her hand close to the vest. I reckon she was startin' to trust ole Bear, though, so she finally explained how the loot hadn't been found.

"She also explained how this wasn't the first time the Pinkertons had been poking around about it. They had a pretty good-sized, *open* file on that loot, because the government had hired them to recover it way back when it was first stolen. Miss Arliss also explained about how that loot had become somewhat of a poorly kept secret in these parts, and that occasionally men of many stripes, from both sides of the border, passed through here looking for the 'Jackal's Bullion,' as it was called."

Bear shook his head. "As far as anyone knew, no one had found it. It remained where a much younger Jack Hyde and Oscar Alvear had buried it when they'd passed through this neck of western Texas with the frontier cavalry hot on their heels."

Arliss kept staring over the batwings as she said, "Hyde had been wounded during the holdup. After a couple of days' hard riding with just himself and Alvear, as the others in their gang had been run down by the cavalry and killed, Hyde started to lapse into unconsciousness. So he was never sure where Alvear had buried the loot before both men had ridden on to Kansas, where Hyde sought medical help. Alvear had hidden the money because he was afraid the cavalry would catch up to them, which they eventually did, but only after a town marshal—one Homer

Redfield—took him into custody."

Redfield stared, hang-jawed at the pretty Pinkerton.

So did Oro La Paz.

"She's a keeper, that one," Redfield said, splashing more whiskey into his glass. His right hand shook slightly.

Haskell dug an Indian Kid out of his shirt pocket and turned to Rosa. "Miss Rosa, I'd have a glass of your delicious tequila, if you wouldn't mind . . ."

Rosa had been staring as though in a trance, absorbing the information she was hearing. Bear's request snapped her out of it. She grabbed a bottle from a shelf beneath the bar, then walked over and set the bottle and the glass down on Haskell's table.

She looked at Redfield. "So . . . you arrested the Jackal and Alvear?" she asked. "All those years ago?"

"I reckon that's right," Redfield drawled guiltily, his weathered cheek twitching nervously.

"How come you never said anything?" she asked the aged ranger. "You brag about everything, but not about arresting the Jackal?"

Redfield just stared down at his shot glass, a faint smile tugging at his silver-bearded face.

"Because Alvear was due to be released from prison soon," Arliss said from the batwings. "The captain knew that. That's why he had himself transferred here to Sundown, so he'd be in the area when Oscar Alvear was released from prison . . . and he and Jack Hyde and Alvear threw in together to retrieve the loot."

"A conspiracy of old men who needed each other," Haskell said.

"Why you old *diablo*!" Rosa said, scowling at Redfield in shock. Redfield winced, raised his glass in a sheepish salute, and threw back the entire shot.

Rosa looked from Haskell to Arliss and then back to Arliss again. "When is Alvear getting out of prison?"

"Oh, he's done his twenty years," Arliss said. "His sentence was up nearly a year ago."

Haskell looked at Oro La Paz. "Right, Alvear?"

Oro La Paz, aka Oscar Alvear, grinned. He let a little air out through the gaps between his teeth.

At the same time, Haskell heard the heavy, ratcheting click of a shotgun hammer being eared back. He turned to see Redfield aiming both his sawed-off shotguns at him, all four bores yawning wide.

Redfield cocked another hammer and smiled icily.

CHAPTER NINETEEN

"Bear," Arliss said, glancing at him from the doorway.

"What is it?" Haskell turned from the two cocked shotguns Redfield was aiming at him.

Arliss canted her head to indicate the street outside the cantina. "Company."

"Oh." Haskell glanced at Redfield, still aiming the shotguns at him. "That just makes it a little more cozy in here, that's all."

Haskell rose from his table and walked over to the bar. He set his shot glass atop the bar and asked Rosa to refill it. As she did, Bear looked out the cantina's dusty front windows to see the six border bandits file down the street toward Rosa's place. They were led by the big mestizo, Hector Valderrama.

"*Mierda,*" Rosa said softly.

"You can say that again." Haskell sipped his tequila, then said quietly to the pretty cantina owner, "Best be ready to duck down behind the bar."

"When that bunch is in town," Rosa said, "I always am."

Footsteps rose in the street. Arliss glanced at Haskell, then backed away from the batwings. She put her back to the wall opposite the wall against which Redfield and Alvear sat. Redfield was still holding his cocked shotguns. Alvear had set an old Bisley revolver on the table before him. It had a thong hanging from its butt. Obviously, the Mexican had worn it around his neck, inside his baggy shirt.

Redfield sipped his tequila, set his glass down, sighed, and brushed his left forearm across his nose.

Haskell glanced at Arliss. She returned it with an edgy one of her own.

The footsteps got louder, spurs ringing. Hector Valderrama stopped just outside the cantina and peered over the batwings upon which he rested his arms, leaning casually forward as he looked around, grinning. He held a pistol in each hand.

"Shit," Redfield muttered.

"What's the matter, Captain?" Valderrama said, pushing through the batwings and sauntering into the cantina. He held his pistols straight down against his sides. "Aren't you happy to see me?"

"I'm happy to see you," Haskell said. "Hell, the more the merrier!" He held his drink up in salute, then threw it back.

Arliss gave him a beetle-browed, skeptical look.

Five others filed in behind the half-breed Mexican, forming a ragged semicircle in the middle of the room, facing Redfield and Alvear, but twisting around to regard Haskell standing at the bar to their left and Arliss, who stood behind them. She held her Winchester high, right finger curled against the trigger, thumb on the hammer.

The newcomers sized up the pretty Pinkerton slowly, feasting their eyes, lusty smiles etched on their sunburned lips.

"Nice," said Valderrama. "Who does she belong to?"

"Me," Haskell said without hesitation before Arliss could say anything.

She scowled at him.

"She's mine," Haskell said. "And she's not for sale."

"Everything is for sale, amigo," Valderrama said. "Given the right amount of money." He turned to Redfield and Alvear and said, "Which brings us to why we are here."

"Why's that?" the old ranger snarled.

"We saw the powwow over here," said Valderrama. "And we

suspected that something of great significance had occurred."

"Señor Alvear just beat Redfield at checkers," Haskell said. "Is that what you mean?"

Valderrama glanced at him, unsmiling. So did the five other dirty, bearded, or mustached jackals in his bunch. As a group, they smelled as bad as some dead thing a mongrel dog might drag around, well-seasoned by the hot sun in some desert *arroyo*.

"Oh," Haskell said. "That ain't what you meant, was it? I bet you meant the gold."

He thought he heard Redfield groan.

"*Sí*," Valderrama said, nodding slowly and smiling with one side of his mouth, showing where he'd broken a tooth in half. "I meant the gold."

"We were just getting to that," Arliss said.

Valderrama raked his goatish eyes up and down her sweet form again and said, "Señorita, when we're done here and that big lawman is howling with a bullet in his guts, I'm gonna throw you down on a table right here in this room, and I'm gonna fuck you so good you'll get my name tattooed in both your pretty ass cheeks!"

His other men all laughed at that. Even Alvear allowed himself a smile.

Redfield's cheek twitched and he almost smiled, too, but then he remembered what they were all here for, and the trace of humor leeched from his eyes. He caressed his shotgun's cocked hammers with his thumbs, aiming both poppers over his black toes at the border jackals.

"What I'd like to know, just to satisfy my own curiosity," Bear said, splashing more tequila into his glass, "is how many folks are after that loot?"

"A few, amigo," said Valderrama. "Here and there . . . a few. Most who remember the story of the holdup. And those who, remembering, were waiting for Alvear to be released from prison."

Bear puffed his Indian Kid as he said, "So a lot of them shootings out there were one faction or another out looking for the loot shooting another faction out looking for the loot. And the Jackal was out there, shooting both Tifflin's men and the pool's men to keep them going after each other, so they'd finally wipe each other out."

"And the Silver ranch house would be empty," Arliss said, "so that Hyde could go in and retrieve the gold from where Señor Alvear originally hid it—under the Silver house, which got stoned in when Mister Silver and his family built over his original cabin, turning it into a large, sprawling ranch house."

"We saw the house," Bear said, adding grimly, "and all the dead men in the yard, including the Silver family. And we saw where someone had busted in the foundation with a sledgehammer . . . and like as not squirreled out the loot that had been just lying there amongst those beams for over twenty years."

"*Sí,*" said Alvear, nodding slowly. "Jack and I holed up in the Silver barn when we passed through that country over twenty years ago now. No one knew we were there. There was only Silver and his wife and a few kids at the time. Late at night, while Jack slept, I hid the money in some beams under the house, which was propped up on stone pylons."

"You intended to retrieve it soon after," Haskell said. "You weren't counting on having to spend the next twenty years in prison. You didn't tell Hyde where it was, though, because you didn't trust him. He broke out of prison on a whim, when he saw a fleeting chance. He probably tried to find the loot right away, but couldn't."

"So he waited," Arliss added. "With the rest of those who remembered and were hungry to have it—over a hundred thousand dollars in gold coins that has climbed in value over the years."

Haskell looked at Alvear. "You and Hyde fell in together after you got out of prison. You knew that after all these years, you still needed each other. You were both older, maybe a little infirm, not able to fight all the other men who might be after the loot . . . and after you, if they found out you had it. So you fell in together with a new understanding. And Ranger Redfield, the man who'd originally arrested you and had been waiting for the loot all these years, as well, cut himself in.

"He probably recognized you right off, Alvear, when you moved in to the depot yonder as the new station agent. So you *had* to cut him in."

"*Sí*," Alvear said, nodding. "I was fortunate that when I got back to Sundown the spur line was needing an agent. Out here, the job was almost impossible to fill. I was heaven-sent, I guess you could say." He spread his hands and grinned broadly.

"A great cover," Haskell said. "While Hyde and his Sharps waged their war out west of town."

Alvear nudged Redfield with his elbow, "Say, Señor *Oso* is smarter than he looks, *el Capitan*!"

"I get that a lot," Bear said. "But I got a question for you, Captain. How did you help? And why did you have your old friend, Henry Dade, send me down here?"

Redfield stared at Haskell, nostrils flared. He seemed to be considering what he should say or not say.

Then he shrugged and said slowly, keeping his shotguns aimed at Valderrama's men, "From here, I could spread rumors to both ranching factions. Turn 'em against each other. Too bad Hyde felt the need to kill four of my men, but they themselves, having heard about the treasure, had started looking for it, suspecting Hyde might be after it. They were young, sassy. Wouldn't follow my orders. They had to die, I reckon. I waited a lot of years for that gold. Even a one-third cut will be worth a fortune by now . . . down south of the border."

"But why send for me?" Haskell asked, genuinely perplexed.

"I was afraid I might be suspected. After my rangers were killed and the loot was found. After I retired and headed to Mexico. I wanted you to come down here and clear me. I expected we'd have the loot and have split it up before you got here, and you'd just think the whole thing was a shootin' war. So . . . you'd clear me in your report, go back home to Denver, and I'd take my cut of the loot, retire, and head south. No one would be after me. I wouldn't have to spend my last years lookin' over my shoulder."

The ranger sighed. "But, like my friend here said, you're smarter than you look, gallblastit!"

"Who threw the snake in your sleeping quarters?"

"Maybe one of these scalawags standin' before me," snarled Redfield. "Maybe one of young Tifflin's pards."

"Why?"

"A few folks around here knew I was the Kansas lawman who arrested Hyde and Alvear. Someone must have suspected we might have thrown in together. That rumor sorta spread, put a target on my back. More an' more as the years passed and Alvear was due to be released."

Arliss said, "So, as I suspected, Jordan Tifflin was looking for the loot, as well."

"Oh, sure he was," Redfield said. "Along with all the other no-accounts in this country. He didn't mention none of that to his old man, I 'spect, because he didn't want his old man gettin' in his way. He hated his old man so much that he was probably just fine with the idea of the old bastard bein' at the center of a shootin' war. Ambrose Tifflin was so wrapped up in his own problems, I doubt he gave one thought to the possibility the loot might be at the real center of his trouble. And the smaller ranchers was just plain fools!"

Redfield wheezed a sarcastic laugh.

"All that is very interesting, amigos," interrupted Valderrama. "But let's cut to the chase, shall we?"

"Yeah," Haskell said, slamming his empty shot glass down on the counter by his Henry. "Where's the galldarned loot?"

There was a tinkling sound, like a breeze-nudged wind chime or breaking window glass.

One of Valderrama's men hiccupped and stepped forward, nodding his head as though heartily agreeing with what had just been said.

But he hadn't hiccupped.

That was made plain when an open hand–sized gob of blood and brain and skull bone plopped onto the floor in front of Redfield's wheelchair and what sounded like the roar of an angry god rose from outside.

Chapter Twenty

The man who'd just had the top of his head blown off, part of it on the floor, part of it splashed over Redfield's cocked shotguns, dropped to his knees, hitting the floor with a resolute thud.

Redfield stared down at him. He looked at his bloody hands and shotguns, and then, as though he thought the mess had been made by one of the dead fellow's own pards, he loosed a bellowing cry and triggered both shotguns in turn.

The twin blasts were like a single keg of black powder being detonated in the cantina's close confines. Two of Valderrama's men, almost literally cut in half, were lifted three feet straight up in the air and hurled back toward where Arliss stood against the far wall.

Arliss screamed as the bloody bodies hammered into her, taking her to the floor.

Which was a good place for her, as it turned out.

For just then all hell broke loose as Valderrama and his other three men began opening up on Redfield and Alvear as well as on Haskell, who grabbed his Henry off the bar and clicked the hammer back, crouching, aiming, and adding his own rifle blasts to the deafening din.

All Bear could see before him was a lurching cascade of men and gun smoke, flames lancing the smoke and evoking shrill screams and cries. As Valderrama fired two rounds into Redfield, sending the ranger jerking back in his chair and sending another volley of ten-gauge buck into the ceiling above his head, the mestizo twisted around toward Bear, snarling, as he leveled his twin Remingtons.

Bear was falling back against the bar as a bullet clipped his left side. Valderrama fired his twin pistols, and one bullet clipped Bear's right side while the other sailed past Bear's head, within a hair's breadth of the ear that had been clipped in the coffin when Haskell had been sent to sail down the Arkansas.

Haskell dropped the Henry and whipped up his Schofield, the big revolver leaping and roaring in his right hand.

Valderrama screamed as Bear's two slugs plowed through the man's red shirt, sending him stumbling backward where two of his other men were also stumbling, having been shot by both Bear and Alvear.

Alvear screamed and flew back against the wall behind him as one of Valderrama's men drilled a bullet through his belly. Haskell bolted forward, continuing to fire his Schofield into Valderrama, who tripped over a chair and hit the floor, screaming.

A man rose to a knee to Valderrama's right. Wounded, Bear was slow to swing his Schofield toward the man, who snapped off a shot. The bullet was like a branding iron sweeping across Bear's right cheek. Stumbling backward, Bear drilled the man who'd just shot him, then got his boots tangled up in an overturned, blood-washed chair and hit the floor, unable to break his fall.

His head struck the floor. A shrill ringing rose in his ears. The room grew gray and fuzzy around him.

He could smell blood and the rotten-egg odor of gun smoke.

And then he couldn't smell anything for a time, though in the back of his brain a menacing voice said over and over again, "The Jackal! The Jackal!"

He had to get up.

He swam up out of the soup of semi-consciousness, lifted his head off the floor, and opened his eyes. Thickly wafting smoke burned his eyes and nose. One of his legs was propped atop the chair he'd fallen over.

Dead men lay strewn around him, some in pieces. One was moaning softly. Haskell turned his head to see Redfield's overturned wheelchair and the ranger captain's black toes propped on the side of it, aimed at the ceiling.

Two of those painful-looking black toes twitched as, apparently, the old captain gave up the ghost.

Aside from the low, muffled moaning, an eerie silence had descended on the cantina.

Haskell started to lift his leg off the overturned chair, intending to rise, but then he heard the faint ring of a spur out on the street.

Bear froze. He stared at his boot.

His heart thumped anxiously.

The Jackal!

The spur chings grew gradually louder.

A mother's voice at bedtime: *Say your prayers or the Jackal will get you!*

Haskell fought the instinct to heave himself to his feet and prepare to do battle. He wouldn't make it from his position, in his condition. The Jackal would have him before he could get to his feet or raise the Schofield, which he'd dropped when he'd fallen.

Play dead . . .

Bear closed his eyes as boots thumped on the boardwalk fronting Rosa's.

His heart thudded heavily. He wondered if the harried organ could be seen thumping against his shirt. He tried to make his breathing shallow, but it was damned hard.

Outside, a breeze rose. It made a *whooshing* sound against the cantina, briefly pelting the window with dust.

Bear sensed the Jackal peering into the cantina.

He thought that even amidst the copper stench of blood and the fetor of gun smoke he could smell the man. A cloying sweetness . . .

Alvear continued to moan on the floor beyond Redfield.

Hinges creaked as the batwings opened. Boots thudded slowly, softly. Spurs chinged.

Haskell drew a slow, deep breath through his nose, trying to calm himself.

He's here.

Lie still, you stupid bastard, or he'll blow your head off.

That Sharps is likely loaded and cocked and ready to fly!

The Jackal moved slowly, stealthily into the room. Haskell kept his eyes lightly shut, but in his mind's eye he saw the Jackal aiming that big Sharps hybrid with the German scope straight out from his right shoulder, swinging it around the room, looking for any indication that someone here was still alive.

Meanwhile, the breeze rose again. Alvear moaned. The Mexican must have nudged a chair, for there was a slight wooden scraping noise.

The Jackal moved slowly, quietly around the room.

The footsteps grew louder. Haskell could feel a floorboard sag beneath him. The Jackal was near.

The foot thuds stopped.

A smell of sweat and leather and cheap tobacco touched Bear's nostrils.

The Jackal was standing over him, likely staring down at him, aiming that big Sharps at his head!

Hold still, Bear told himself. *Don't breathe . . .*

"Jack?" said a Spanish-accented voice. "J-Jack?"

Haskell felt the floorboard rise beneath him as the foot thuds resumed. The Jackal was moving away from him.

"Jack?" Alvear said in a pain-pinched voice. "H-help me to my feet, amigo."

The boot thuds stopped.

Silence. Outside the breeze moaned around in the street.

A gurgling sound. Then Alvear's voice pitched with terror: "Jack, no!"

BOOM!

The entire room lurched as the Big Fifty thundered.

Haskell opened his eyes, lifting his head.

He looked around for his Schofield. It was under a table to his left. He grabbed it, lowered his leg from the chair, and heaved himself onto his knees.

He aimed the Schofield. "Hold it!"

A man stood facing the wall to Haskell's left, about twenty feet away. The man's back faced Bear. The man held a long rifle in front of him. Bear could see the barrel protruding from the man's left side. The stock poked out from his right side.

There was a metallic click. The Jackal was trying to reload.

"Drop it now or take a bullet in the back, you son of a bitch!"

The man froze.

"Drop it now!" Bear bellowed.

"All right, all right, don't shoot!" said a high, nasal voice, not the voice that Haskell was expecting. Not even close. "Take it easy." The man leaned to his right and set the big rifle on a table. "Take it easy," he said. "Don't shoot me!"

He raised his hands to his shoulders, palms out. He still had his back to Haskell.

"Turn around slow," Bear ordered.

The man turned around slowly until he was facing Haskell.

"You're the Jackal!" sounded a Spanish-accented woman's voice behind Bear.

Haskell glanced over his shoulder to see Rosa standing up behind the bar, staring in wide-eyed shock at the man facing

Bear. She'd taken the words right out of the lawman's mouth. He returned his own disbelieving gaze to the man before him.

Jack Hyde—if that's who Haskell was actually staring at it, that was—couldn't have been much over five-foot-four, if that. Mid-fifties, pushing sixty. A mousy, little, craggy-faced, potbellied man with a thin gray mustache and patchy side whiskers. Round, steel-framed spectacles perched on his nose. His baby blue eyes were bizarrely magnified by the thick spectacles, giving him a fishy, walleyed look.

His face was peppered with liver spots.

He wore a grimy three-piece suit with a ratty, cream-colored duster hanging to his knees, threadbare, pinstriped, broadcloth trousers that sagged on him, and a weather-stained cream Stetson. A string tie was knotted at his throat.

Jack Hyde gave a sheepish grin, revealing one silver upper front tooth. He didn't say anything, just returned Haskell's and Rosa's stares with his own sheepish, vaguely cunning smile.

Haskell groaned against his sundry wounds—none of them overly serious, he didn't think—as he stepped slowly forward, keeping his Schofield aimed at the little man who couldn't possibly be the most wanted criminal in the frontier west.

Such a nondescript little man . . .

Could he really be the Jackal?

Haskell stopped in front of Jack Hyde, who was almost a foot and a half shorter than the lawman towering over him. Hyde's raised hands came up only to the tops of Haskell's shoulders.

Bear looked at the rifle on the table.

A Big Fifty, all right. With a long, narrow, brass scope mounted over the breech. The brass, scroll-leaf initials JH had been embedded in the oiled walnut stock.

Haskell looked at the fish-eyed little man staring up at him. "It is you, isn't it? You're the Jackal."

"Who'd you think I was, you big son of a bitch?" the little

man snarled. "St. Fuckin' Pete?"

Someone groaned to Haskell's right. One of the dead men who'd nearly been cut in two by Redfield's shotguns moved where he lay on the floor, against the base of the far wall. The body rocked to one side, and Arliss lifted her head to stare up over the top of the dead man's shoulder.

"Arliss, you still kickin'?" Haskell asked, grinning with relief, then quickly returning his attention to the Jackal.

"Not sure yet," Arliss said as she moved another bloody carcass away from her, and heaved herself to her feet. "My head hit the floor, and . . ." She retrieved her hat and her rifle and, blinking as though to clear her fuzzy vision, stumbled toward Bear and the little man.

"Who's that?" she said.

"Miss Posey," Bear said, "I'd like to introduce you to Jack Hyde, otherwise known as the Jackal."

Arliss blinked again, scowling. *"What?"*

The Jackal wheezed out an effeminate chuckle, then doffed his hat and favored Arliss with an oily grin.

"Where's the gold?" Haskell asked the fish-eyed little man.

"Over to the hotel," Hyde said. "Where do you think it is? It sure ain't in my back pocket!"

Haskell gave a wry laugh. "You mean you been stayin' over at the hotel this whole time?"

"Sure as beans," the Jackal said. "What—you expected me to sleep out with the rattlesnakes? I had me a rough enough time with the one I tossed in old Redfield's sleepin' quarters!"

He let out a high-pitched, girlish laugh.

"So you had no intention of sharing any of that loot with Alvear or the ranger," Haskell said. It wasn't a question.

The Jackal rose up on the balls of his little boots. "Do I look like a man who'd trifle with the likes o' them mangy curs?" He gave a wry snort, then looked at Arliss again and swept his fishy gaze across her chest. "Now, you'd I trifle with, little girl!"

"You're *the Jackal*?" Arliss kept staring at the little man as though she couldn't believe what she was seeing.

"How 'bout you shoot this big son of a bitch," the Jackal said, glancing up at Haskell, "an' you an' me'll mosey on down Mexico-way and have us a fine, ole time!"

"Let's mosey over to the hotel instead," Haskell said, stepping back, wincing again as his bullet wounds grieved him. He didn't know how much longer he'd be able to stay on his feet. He had to get both the Jackal and the loot over to Redfield's jail for safe-keeping, so he could pass out in peace.

As he and Arliss ushered the Jackal toward the door, Haskell glanced at Rosa, still standing where she'd been standing before, behind the bar, staring incredulously toward the Jackal.

"You all right, Rosa?"

Her eyes swept his tall, bloody frame. "I'm doing better than you, Bear. I'd best get you a doctor."

"Ah, hell," Haskell said, following Arliss and Jack Hyde out the saloon doors. "I been hurt worse than this crawlin' out of bed in the mornin'."

The loot was where the Jackal had said it would be—in his room in Sundown's only hotel, where he'd registered under the name of Scrum Dawson.

The hotelier, Shep Hanson, was as surprised as anyone to learn that the shabby little trinket peddler, Scrum Dawson, was in fact one of the deadliest killers the west had ever known.

One month later, after the Jackal and the loot had been shipped to Denver via train car guarded by twenty soldiers from Fort Davis, and Haskell had made his way back in the same direction after healing from his wounds, Bear suckled Miss Arliss Posey's left nipple in his suite at the Larimer Hotel and said, "I reckon that's how he was able to stay ahead of the law so damn long."

"I reckon it is," Arliss said with a lusty groan, tipping her head back on the pillow. "Who'd have ever thought Scrum Dawson was Jack Hyde? It even took you a while to convince Marshal Dade!"

"Yeah," Bear chuckled. "He thought I was pullin' his leg, ole Henry did. I'm not sure he still quite believes it!"

They laughed.

"What I'd like to know," Bear said, moving his head down from Arliss's swollen breasts to poke his tongue into her belly button, causing her to arch her back and moan, "is how come he didn't go ahead and ambush us again on our way back to Sundown that last day? I know he was behind us—for a time, anyway."

"I reckon we should have asked him," Arliss said, then chuckled. "Oh, Bear—that tickles!"

"I didn't think of it. Too many other questions, I reckon. I got me a suspicion, though."

"Mmmm?" Arliss reached down between them to wrap her hand around his jutting shaft. "What's that?"

Haskell groaned as she fondled him. "I think he might have figured that since his ploy out on the range worked so well, it might work that good in town, too."

"What do you mean? Pitting us against Alvear and the captain?"

"Why not? He'd been following us so he knew we knew he had taken the loot from the Silver house. I'm sure he was well aware of them twin cannons on Redfield's chair, too. He probably figured that if Redfield didn't clean our clocks, Alvear would. And then he'd only have Alvear to finish off himself."

"Bear?"

"Then he could leave Sundown with a packhorse or two under cover of darkness, when Valderrama's own jackals were still makin' the whores scream, and scuttle across the border by dawn. The Jackal likely never woulda been heard from again."

"Bear?"

Haskell looked at her. "What is it, darlin'?"

Arliss smiled up at him as she spread her raised knees and drew his jutting shaft inside her. "Let's be quiet now."

"Good idea," Bear grunted. "Just one more thing."

"What's that?"

"I like working with you, Miss Arliss." He grinned down at her.

Arliss laughed. "I like working with you, too, Bear!"

ABOUT THE AUTHOR

Peter Brandvold has written over a hundred westerns under his own name and his pen name, Frank Leslie. Author of the long-running Sheriff Ben Stillman and Lou Prophet series, he lives with his dog in western Minnesota.

The employees of Five Star Publishing hope you have enjoyed this book.

Our Five Star novels explore little-known chapters from America's history, stories told from unique perspectives that will entertain a broad range of readers.

Other Five Star books are available at your local library, bookstore, all major book distributors, and directly from Five Star/Gale.

Connect with Five Star Publishing

Visit us on Facebook:
https://www.facebook.com/FiveStarCengage

Email:
FiveStar@cengage.com

For information about titles and placing orders:
(800) 223-1244
gale.orders@cengage.com

To share your comments, write to us:
Five Star Publishing
Attn: Publisher
10 Water St., Suite 310
Waterville, ME 04901